2

TO

LISA THE SHOP KEEPER

Patrick Callaghan

AKA

Shaun P Shanahan.

Just Another Gulliver and His Travels

Just Another Gulliver and His Travels

Patrick Callaghan

Rev. date: 09/30/2013

To order additional copies of this book, contact:
Xlibris LLC
1-888-795-4274
www.Xlibris.com
Orders@Xlibris.com
135122

Acknowledgment

As a young lad, I would like to thank all the families in England that allowed me into their lives and homes. As a teenager, all the young people that I had so much fun with in my home town. You know who you are! Your parents embraced me and treated me with respect. They showed compassion and I loved them all. So many people throughout my life have welcomed me into their world. I cannot express my gratitude for all the fun we shared. All my friends in Denmark did so much for me. I love and miss you all. I am so grateful to have loving and caring children, I could not be prouder. How grateful I am to be at my present state. A loving wife that has taken a wild one and slowed him down to appreciate what love is all about.

INTRODUCTION

This book tells the story of a young Englishman's voyage through life. He never experienced love from his mother. As he grew up, he discovered so many lies and deceit. He was denied the opportunity to hold his paternal father. A hug would have fulfilled a dream. He was also cheated from the dream by his aunt. He discovered a half sister in America when he was thirty-three and never connected with his brother; they drifted apart. He was hit by an angry uncle who was his mentor. He was cheated and lost a business that had the makings of a huge success. Foolishly, he allowed good times to override the serious side of life. Thus, he lost his wife, his children, and his beautiful home. A caravan on a farm became his sanctuary, stealing vegetables to survive. He rose from the wilderness and ran with the wind, breaking hearts as he traveled over and through other countries. Later, he married for a bet in a foreign country and soon divorced, only to marry again to an American Christian who emptied his bank account. She left him homeless and penniless. His family and friends discovered he would rise from the ashes and run again. He enjoyed many women; they enjoyed him. Working hard all his life gave him some lovely rewards. He endeavored to enjoy life to the fullest and make friends wherever he went. Finally, at age fifty-eight, he settled down, having found happiness in the Midwest of America. This is the story of how I transformed from a wild young lad to a very content older man.

CHAPTER 1

MY TOWN IS OLD, snuggled in rolling Somerset Hills, and has over five hundred listed buildings and three that are heritage grade 1 listed. The town has expanded a lot in my lifetime, so much industry has disappeared. Changes have been made, old housing areas demolished. Many green fields have become housing areas. The town is situated to the east of the beautiful Mendip Hills and has many hills of its own. At 213 feet above sea level, its higher points go from 295 to 443 feet. I recall from the age of about five, in 1958, we lived in a red-and-white house, which was half a mile above the town centre at the top of a hill. Just up the road was a pub (one of sixty-five in the town at that time). I remember several nights sitting on a bench with a glass of lemonade and bag of crisps, and seeing my mother interacting with people enjoying a beer and the piano going. From our front room window, you could see a large church, which was behind the brewery wall. To the right of that stood my first school. This must have been the place for my first wanton desire of a female because I fell in love with one of the teachers. She had a little 3 wheeled "bubble" car. The only door was at the front. She looked so sexy getting in and out showing some leg and beaming a smile. She always dressed nice, and I would do anything I could to please her. We had a motorcycle shop, a grocery shop, and, just up from that, a building merchant. Beyond that, there was a tool factory with an arch that led out to some nice cottage houses and a corrugated building. To the right of us were some adjoining houses, which were just brick facades, but ours stood out from them all. A short walk from our house would bring you to another junior school, which would have been my next school. But that changed, as we were to be moved. Behind the school stands a church, which was built between 12th and early 15th centuries. It replaced a Saxon building from 685. The church had an almost complete rebuild in 1860. Unusual features are the carved roundels above the nave arcades depicting parables (short stories) and miracles. To the right of the school was a pub, which was a well-to-do house in the eighteenth century. Quaint cottage houses led all the way to the old woollen factory site. The opposite side had a rising pavement with more terraced houses. Alongside it from the top rooms must have been a good view to see the rooftops of the town centre.

The house was owned by Uncle Harry and Aunt Bess. He was a short man with a balding head and enjoyed a cigarette. Most of the time, he wore a white sleeveless vest. Aunt Bess was about the same height. She always dressed nice and enjoyed a laugh. Her blue uniform would always be covered by an apron when kitchen duty called. Across the road was a brewery with a pub next to it. I also had an elder brother who I really was not close to. I hardly recall doing anything with Ralph as a young lad. I think much of the problem was that he was over two years older and could bully me if he wanted. As we grew, I never got his sense of humour. He had his own bunch of friends, and we did our own thing. Our bedroom was at the back of the house. My guardian was a single mother, and there was just one bedroom for us. We slept in the same bed, Mother and me. One night, I got up and wanted to turn on the light. The switch was situated on the wall (about eight inches higher than I could reach) close to the window, which overlooked a backyard. It was a six-foot wall all around and a washing line with a concrete floor. I had to climb onto the window ledge for balance. I reached out, and unknown to me, the window was open. In the dark, out I went heading for the concrete floor only to have my fall broken by the washing line. I was out cold, and when I came around, my uncle Harry was there with his helping hands. I was dizzy, hurting like hell but OK. Several days passed, and the pain had passed. Life continued for this young person. I never had a father, but my lovely uncle was like a dad. He was there for me, and I never knew any different. Dad, I was told, left for America; and we were supposed to follow, which never happened.

Mother was slightly taller than her sister, blondish hair and curled with tongs every morning, and a bit overweight, which never appeared to be a problem when she was working. She was a cleaner, and I recall going with her to a house down close to a church that overlooked the graveyard. We would walk alongside the brewery wall, under a high arch, which was part of the brewery barrel and bottle storage area. That led to a cobbled walkway of a maybe six-hundred-year-old street with delightful quaint cottage homes standing side by side that had seen so many faces passing by. Behind a wall on my left was another stately looking house and had become a club for war veterans. Further down on the right was a social club that held several functions. Most popular were bingo and dance nights. The house in the lower part of the street used to be owned by the rich people back in the sixteenth and seventeenth centuries. Those people were probably landowners or social landlords having many properties to rent. She also cleaned in a corner building at the bottom of a hill that led away from the town centre. This club, with its snooker table, was a bar for the working man to relax. This building was about ten feet wide at the front then widened as its sides rested on two roads. Sometimes, she had the two places to clean on the same day; and with the school holidays, I had to go with her. After leaving the large house, we would cross the forecourt of the church and then go down the steps that lead to a flagstone street where a stream, fed from the spring, runs down the middle of it. The buildings date from the sixteenth century, and a major fire in 1923 did a lot of damage to the street. The buildings are basically unchanged apart from the shop frontages. At the bottom of the street stands a stone cross, which in later years would be a meeting place before enjoying an evening with a girlfriend because back then, it wasn't the thing for a single girl to go into a pub on her own. That idea changed as we approached the 80's. We would walk through the town towards the club; the cars and Lorries would bump around on the rough road surface. This must have been when my interest in powered equipment started, as I loved such things from a young age. The town was also vibrant with people scurrying from hardware store to the chemist or any other store they had in mind.

The town centre is about eight hundred feet or so in length, and just before you cross the bridge, on the right was a building, which is now a splendid home for elderly people. In its day, this was the Blue Coat School, named due to the colour of the uniforms. It was rebuilt in 1726 as the older one was falling apart, which was built in 1461. There are two well-carved male and female statues and are known as Billy Ball and Nancy Guy, which in the sixteenth and seventeenth centuries indicated the building's dual purpose. Nestled alongside the river and adjacent to the fourteenth-century bridge, which was also rebuilt and widened in the sixteenth century, you could marvel at the history as you approached your destination. At the top of the long hill that led towards Bath, my auntie's workplace as a dental assistant was in a lovely house that stood on the right. The dentist was, I guess, well to do. His working room was at the side of the house, which overlooked a beautiful, well-manicured lawn and garden. On a couple of occasions, as the last patient, we would get a ride into the town in his Rolls-Royce. I felt like a millionaire riding in his white chariot and being fascinated by all the gauges and switches.

In olden days, the town was growing in size from its first Norman origins of AD 950, but there is evidence of Roman times—a bustling market town with cloth and woollen products being the town's principal industry around the 1500s and was the only Somerset town that maintained and improved its stranglehold on the business. Also, the forces of the Duke of Monmouth camped in the town after their defeat in a small skirmish not far away in a small village after losing another battle against the king's forces, for that twelve men were hanged in the town for all to see. There was a decline in the wool industry in the eighteenth century, and poverty began to rule, which led to some unrest and some riots before the century's end, which was a sad demise after a Daniel Defoe remarked in 1720 that the town had grown enough that a new Church was built, new streets of houses and they are so full of inhabitants that the town is probably bigger than the city of Bath and should the trade growth continue, it will likely be one of the richest towns in England. Scattered all around the town are buildings from the early days, which are two or three stories high accommodating people with shops below. With the town centre being at the bottom of several hills, getting horses and carts up and down the main hills must have been a problem when snow and ice were on the ground. There are also some tunnels that have been uncovered beneath the older streets of the town—possibly more than one system exists—and are under investigation. Investigators are entering them through house cellars and an opening at the top of a small street.

From my house, within minutes, you would be passing another arched building that looks like an old coach house. You can imagine stables at the back and accommodation rooms in the old building. Further along the road, I would go left into a tight area at the top of a street. There on the left, in these four lovely little cottage houses, was Gertrude. She was my grandmother. Greying hair was taking over her natural colour, which was the same as Aunt Bess's. She would open her arms to share some love, never shy to give a penny for pocket money. If I was lucky to see the man next door, I might get a threepenny bit. I would sit in her little room, which had two armchairs, a table and chairs, a couple of small drawer sets, a fireplace. I always got some coal in the scuttle and logs, placing them at the side of the hearth, ready for loading on the fire on a winter's night. Back in those days, there was no heating system; many larger houses had a fireplace in almost every room, but Grandma's, never. She would boil some water for her hot water bottle and wrap herself around it in bed. She was not alone, because we had to do the same. There was no central heating, and every room in a house would be cold in winter. It was so good to wrap a T-shirt or cloth around your bottle and curl up before falling asleep. She had no television but did have a large brown radio that was always croaking out the BBC news and music. My grandmother would sit me on her knee, give me cuddles, and tell a small story. The friendship and respect that all children should have were given by this lovely lady who had retired from her working life. Most visits we would have a cup of tea and a biscuit. I would dunk it in my cup while she complained that is was not the thing to do. She would waggle off her old index finger, and I would smile. These little places had two bedrooms, and getting to the top one, you would pass through the lower. Before going up the stairs, a wooden door with a metal latch had to be opened, and they were not designed for small children to easily open. The kitchen was through the wooden door at the back of the room. The other side of it was a cobbled common walkway that was arched with old stones that had been chipped to size by labourers two hundred or more years before. The passageway led to the other cottages' back doors. The kitchen was set in a hole in the wall. A gas cooker, sink, and a couple of cabinets were all there was. She would wash her hair from the rainwater captured in a large barrel. It was filled from the drainpipe from the guttering and in the corner of a small backyard. In the opposite corner behind a wooden door was a shared toilet for her and the other tenants. The old cistern that towered above your head had a long chain to pull for flushing. There was also a shared bathroom. She would boil water before taking it and pouring in a tin bath tub. That process took a long time, so bathing was not a regular thing.

Further along the main road, Uncle Harry worked for an asphalt company and was based not far away from the railway station. He was the van driver, and a gang would be anything from four to ten men. He would pick them up and drop them off at their front doors and might travel up to an hour or more to get to the work site. The men would get out and start getting things ready for the arrival of loads of asphalt while he put the kettle on for a morning cup of tea. He was a good working man, and he naturally was my mentor. When he and his Bess moved up to a new home with a large garden, I was like his little helper. I went to his house as much as possible to find out what excitement would happen, what my challenge for the day was. My time there would be most likely on a Saturday, and then after Sunday school, I would help again. Our Sunday school was attached to a splendid chapel, which was built and opened in 1707. Along the side of the graveyard, a black wrought iron fence would hold you back, saving you from falling fifteen feet down onto the road. Across the other side were the old steam powerhouse and the swimming baths. We would have our swimming lessons there when I was at my senior school and travel there on a coach. It was hired from a local bus company. They were the largest coach company around in those days, collecting kids from neighbouring villages and bringing them to the town's schools. One day, a new Chinese Six coach turned up for us. I was so blown away with its four front steering wheels and longer length. (This was probably the start of my desire to work with large mechanical things.) The chapel looks something like a stately home, very pretty and stands almost at the top of steep hill going down into the town centre. I remember a friend sitting on a small bench at the Sunday school photo shoot looking so tough in a thick white woollen sweater; as he went through life, he was tough. I saw him put a lot of guys on their butts. He would never shy away from a fight, but as time took over, he was still trying to be king but was getting some whopping from young men just like we were. What must be admired is that he is a man with values and would stand by his conviction, which is what it was back in the day. Respecting people for what they are, whether older or younger, is a thing of the past; and like time, it's gone forever. I would always help someone in trouble no matter what it might be. But we as people don't anymore. How many times have we seen someone broke down and we drive on by? When I hear stories of people stopping only to discover they will get robbed has changed my way of thinking. How sad the world has become.

Chapter 2

We moved to newly constructed block of flats in a dead-end road. We were situated off a main road, which led out of town to green pastures and herds of cows doing their thing. On a couple of occasions, Uncle Harry had given us a ride in his work van to see the construction area, and I was getting excited about moving. I would be in the back of his van with the smell of asphalt all around. We also walked there several times, going along a main street where the small fire station was tucked into the corner of a church graveyard, another quaint pub opposite. Various shops and small businesses stood side by side as we progressed into an area that had six roads leading from it, and passing yet another three pubs before our new living area came into view. This whole area had houses that were in such a poor condition, the area was demolished. The local council rebuilt three blocks of flats and the rest houses, which we would be able to rent. Just before we moved, the brewery across the street closed. The first thing to go was the chimney; a small explosion at the bottom on one side, and down it came crashing down, creating a large plume of dust. When the dust settled, the dozers moved in; the place was torn apart. Along with it, the houses to our right and the businesses to the left, everything would be demolished. This was part of a plan to improve the traffic problems. A new road was created, which allowed the traffic to go one way, creating the first one-way system in the town. Shortly before moving, a hubcap came off of a car and clipped Pete's (our dog) head, which hurt him so much, he had to be put down. He was a black cocker spaniel and had a heart of gold. He would carry mum's small blue bag with his dog food cans in it—lovely character—and he was my mate. When this happened, I cried and cried.

At Uncle's house, I enjoyed doing many things like gardening, learning to paint, and swinging the axe to chop wood. I was always careful when splitting small logs, which would be used to start the coal fire. I made many a fire ready for a winter's night. Removing the old ashes then crumpling old newspaper was the start; then placing the split wood on and adding some coal before lighting with a match. The smell was special, and when the fire was roaring, the effort was worth it. I know every parent and child in those days would stand with their back to the fire, which felt so good on a cold day. It was also the only way to get enough hot water for a bath. So many places had back boilers that were full of water. With a roaring fire, it boiled. Water would transfer heat to a larger boiler, and after an hour, maybe it was hot enough to take a bath. Aunt Bess was always smiling and supplying a steady flow of soda or tea with a biscuit. Across the road from them was a junkyard. We would roam around it, looking for things that my uncle might be interested in. He was a do-it-yourself man and had an uncanny eye for a bargain. Uncle Harry wanted to build a wall alongside a footpath leading to the town park. I was very involved in carrying the blocks and mixing cement. When it was built, he gave it a pitted kind of finish. Then we put the paint (white emulsion) on, and to this day, it is still standing. They had an only daughter, and she was like a sister. I enjoyed playing with Annette, and we had so much fun. With the big garden at the back of the house, there was plenty of room to play around. As with so many houses, vegetable growing was a big thing. I did a lot of digging, which in time proved to be a good learning experience for the way my life evolved. My uncle's best friend, Terry, would come over, and like always, it was hello, how are you, pat on the back, and show interest in whatever task I was involved in. He too worked on the asphalt, as did so many townsfolk. It was and is a big industry with the quarries spread around the Mendip hills and the asphalt companies in the town. One Christmas, I remember being at Uncle Harry's house. Under the mistletoe, Terry gave Aunt Bess a Christmas kiss, which is no problem at that time of the year. Well, it went on much longer than you would expect. Although at the time I never knew much about that stuff, I sat and thought to myself, *Oh my*. This must have been my first visual lesson in deception. These two cheating people trusted by not only a husband and father but also, a daughter whose heart was to be broken. I can recall the tears that fell on that sweet innocent face when everything came to light.

Where we began to live, transportation was getting heavier. Bottlenecks were frustrating lorry drivers. Vehicles were trying to pass through a very narrow road, and mirrors were getting hit. Cars had to mount the pavement to avoid the lorries. People were concerned with the narrowest part of the footpath being only two feet wide. If a lorry was passing, it could hit you if your eyes weren't open. There was also the local post office. One day, I was at the letter box when a neighbour was also mailing a letter. He had a lovely

German shepherd dog, and although it was on its lead, it sprang on me and bit me in the stomach. The dog was known by all the children that lived in the area. I wanted to pat it as I had done before. I screamed with pain and ran home, where Mother took control. She got some warm water and cloth and wiped the small amount of blood away, exposing the bite mark. After a couple of minutes, she left me to go and plead with the owner not to put the dog down. After about twenty minutes, she came in crying, saying, "He won't listen. He's taking the dog to be put down." He drove past our flat window with the dog on the backseat; she was still crying over it. I, on the other hand, was still hurting, but that was my problem. So I sorted myself out and went to my bedroom, curled up in a ball on my bed, and fell to sleep. All of us local kids had a play area, which was behind some garages and located in the garden of a disused house. We had our toy lorries and a pretend quarry, where I would be loading them with my toy loader. The others would take the load and tip it somewhere else. I was in charge and leading my mates as to where to tip. With their ideas and input, our quarry was getting bigger, our minds running wild. There were three abandoned houses we would go in. We were warned to never go in any of them. Rotten floor boards, mice, and rats didn't make them the most desirable place, but we would be left alone from the parents. These old gardens had wire fencing around and some little old people's flats backed onto them. The old men were grumpy and would keep telling us to "bugger off, yur too noisy." The ladies were much nicer about telling us to be quiet. The abandoned houses were also a place where things like kissing were done before running away from her with a grin and back to the boys.

Down the road from us, there was a lot of activity of people going from shop to shop, getting almost anything they needed. There was a bakery that when the wind was right, you could smell it two hundred feet from the front door. There were also two butcher shops, grocery, chemist, and motorbike shop, and of course the pubs. I remember poking my nose into one of the bars, which had sawdust on the floor, the working men cussing at me to get out. They never scared me because I had no reason to worry about the way life was then. One of my favourite places was the cycle shop. It had such a unique smell because of all the spilled oil getting walked on and working its way into the wooden floor—very typical spit-and-sawdust place like a lot of pubs back then. If this is to be a confession time, then I need to confess. I used to get the owner to go upstairs for a lamp or something, and things would disappear from the shop. Most times there would be three of us (which meant I had more courage to do naughty things). He was about five feet three tall, and the counter was almost as tall as him. With his round glasses and flat cap, he was always enthusiastic about helping people. Their bike problems were his problem, and he would scuttle off to find a part. I just about built or at least rebuilt a bike with new (free) stuff, and it was my pride. I started like other children with a tricycle, which I would do a trick with. I would get it going then lay on the saddle with my legs stuck out at the back (kind of hurts when your brake cable breaks and there's a garage door in front of you!). I progressed to two wheels and, with my skilled hand, painted my bike a light blue, which is my favourite colour. Next to the cycle shop was a smaller business selling sweets and various other things. One thing that I enjoyed from there was broken biscuits. If the owner found any damaged packets, she would mix them up in a large container, then you never knew what type you were going to taste when dunking them in your tea.

CHAPTER 3

My second school was where young boys were always looking for used cigarette packets to play flicks. These packets would be flattened and pressed (then called a card), which, with gentle control, would glide through the air when released from your thumb and index finger. Many a times we would haggle men to see if they had a nearly empty packet that we could have. Many times they would tell us to bugger off and leave them in peace. Tops and stickups were the games. Tops, you would be looking to land on or at least be touching another to win, which would allow you to pick every card up that was on the floor. Stickup was you get a large flick (twenty-packet of Senior Service or Players were favourites), lean it against a wall, and keep playing until someone knocked it over and again; this would allow the winner to pick up every card before a new game began. It was tradition to scramble all your cards on the last day of leaving your junior class because the next school was deemed to be tough, and it was a kid's game. This would happen at every school before going to the next. I had two shoe boxes full of my prized cards. On the wall overlooking the school yard, I threw them out. Handful by handful into the breeze they flew. They were picked up by eager, next-generation flick kings. What a waste, watching all my hard work and effort disappearing like that, but I had things to do, places to go. You soon forget. I remember sitting in the play area with "the boys," and we would be talking about whom we fancied and watching the girls do handstands. Stolen kisses were fun, but if you got caught, it was never pleasant. Go to the headmaster and one hundred lines would be yours, which would be done in your free time while you hear the others winning flick games and having fun. With a little sweet shop just across the road, when you could, a little treat was offered to win affection of the young girl you fancied. We boys had minor scuffles that occurred, but no fistfights because we were not ready for that stuff.

From a young age, I was always in someone else's house and being treated like one of their own. That was where love was shown by nice mums, and over the years, there were plenty. Dads would knock me around, knock their kids around. It was part of the simplistic fun and toughen-you-up stuff. Getting disciplined was something I was used to when at home. Being told to be "quiet," "go to your room," "I'm talking," "don't walk on that, I just cleaned it," and so much no-no stuff. A clip around the ear was normal. It was always good to be part of another family. "I know you can be a bugger, but I love you"—words like that were used by mothers to their offspring, never uttered from mine. I would also get a Christmas or birthday card. I would be happy like any other child until it was fully read. On several occasions, my name was spelt the Irish way on the envelope, the English way on the card. I asked, "Why is my name spelt differently from the card and envelope?"—only to get a pathetic excuse: it was a spelling mistake, and any mother could make them. Every time it happened, I challenged her only to get the question fobbed off again. I had a mother who thought she knew so much about life but in reality knew so little. She would sit in her chair looking out the window, watching people going up and down the street, and making comments about what they were wearing or whom they were with. "I wonder where they are going" would often be the uttered words; if she saw them while walking the dog, she would get the answer by asking them. She was the neighbourhood gossip and spent so many hours going to the next-door houses or chatting over a garden fence. What the hell, half of it was about I do not know and was never interested. As I grew older, I would paint and wallpaper to make our house look like a home. She would sit in her chair and point at anything I missed or was incorrect. It was so annoying to be doing your best only to get pushed backwards with no encouragement.

One thing that I was never keen on would be getting sunburnt. We would go to Weymouth down on the south coast. It was here my back would get burnt on the sand. Sometimes it was so much that when it started peeling, Mother would sit me between her legs on the floor and pick all the skin off. She loved doing it day after day, trying to find more to peel somewhere on me. This was an annual event with the Sunday school with a bunch of parents. With so little interaction between us, this was for me a "looking forward to once a year" thing. Arriving at the train station, which was painted white with a black trim, kids would be jumping from a car or bus running to the ticket box. This would be cause enough for a little rap of knuckles on the wooden windowsill. A stern "calm down" warning from the ticket master would work wonders. The station opened in 1850 and is regarded as one of the oldest still in operation in England. With only two lines, we knew where to look. I would be waiting with all the other just as excited children. We wanted to see that Great Western train as it rolled around the bend and slow down to a stop right in front of us. This mighty steam warrior and coal carriage was trailed by six coaches, blasting its whistle with steam coming from somewhere at the front. Mothers and fathers would be holding their children back until the guard stepped out. A little rush started, and we would find a seat by the window and wait for the guard to blow his whistle, indicating everything was OK for the driver to get moving. We would hear it start shunting as it began pulling the heavy carriages with its precious cargo. As I got older, I would get to the door and open the window. Black smoke billowing from the engine would be flying over the top of us. On a windy day, chances were your face would get sooted up while you were watching the countryside pass by. You could also see the engine as it went around a bend. I would marvel at the train's length. This again was a developing part of me for big mobile equipment.

Sometimes I would sneak downtown, which would mean passing the barbershop where a crew cut was the cut of the day. His shop was on a small raised pavement across from a sweet shop and second hand shop. Every time I went in, it was just the same—cigarette smouldering away in the ashtray and a cup of tea going cold. He would start at the front of your head and take a full sweep to the back. The hair was sucked up by the vacuum—that was it; three minutes, and you were done. Nothing fancy, as he was very limited at what hair he could cut. As the younger men matured, a different barber would need to be found. I enjoyed the hustle and bustle of a busy market town, passing butcher shops where the butcher would be leaning on the door frame, wishing every passerby a nice day. Several times I would go from one shop to another just looking at stuff and was once tempted to steal. This was the devilment in me. I wasn't a bad lad, but I was developing a little rebelliousness in me because of the way my life was transforming. I was getting pushed in places I did not really want to go. Sunday school and the church choir stuff were not my idea of fun. Everything I did was to pacify Mother and no consideration for me. Temptation was quashed in my mind because when I was smaller, I was caught stealing four Black Jacks from a sweet shop not far from home. That experience of a large lady standing in front of me, wagging her finger and saying I was a bad boy, put me off ever trying that on my own again.

CHAPTER 4

MY FAVOURITE SWEET SHOP had almost next to it a quaint sewing shop. It smelt so nice with all the wool and textiles. I would go in with Mother on her shopping trip. She was good at knitting and sewing, and it had to be done in those days because of little money. I would have to be patient while she spent ages talking about everything and anything, which drove me bonkers. Like so many of the small businesses, they disappeared over the years. Those individual shops and their unique smell have vanished with bigger shopping stores. Just around the corner, you would be heading down a road full of small terraced houses that had little old-fashioned front doors that were as small as they really could be. There were no gardens and only three feet of footpath to stagger on when you came of age to drink. There were about three hundred houses that are a good example of a planned grid pattern and were built from around 1660 up to the mid-seventeenth century. This was another major demolition project as so many were deemed slums—that one part was flattened. Thankfully, about two hundred were saved and refurbished due to the historical importance. Those that were flattened had new houses and some flats built on the area. A road to the left leads to another beautiful church that was built in 1837 by Henry Goodridge and is deemed a Gothic-type church. What's unusual about it is the fact that the altar is at the west end, when other Gothic churches' were at the east end. Before you got to the church on the right and across from a pub, there was a fish-and-chip shop. That smell would be a big draw for so many people. Friday night would be the once-a-week treat night; running towards it was like a rush of excitement any thriving alcoholic would get when a new bottle was in hand. After the smell of coal fires going down the street then standing in line waiting to be served cod and chips, scallops, and scrumps (bits of the batter that were scooped up by the fryer man) with salt and vinegar was at times hard to take. Seeing someone already served with their prized possession opened and enjoying it was like being tortured for doing nothing wrong. When your turn came and everything was wrapped and paid for, I would begin scurrying back home with everyone's treat staying warm in newspaper. As time went on, you could get pies and peas—mushy were the best—when you had a skinful of beer on board; that was regarded as the sleeping pill that soaks up the beer, helping you in preventing a hangover. There were so many spread around the town, and most people used the closest as the favourite because microwaves were not invented to reheat your treat.

Later on, when I was old enough, if I was on the other side of town enjoying a pint or two, I would get to the closest chip shop and eat my meal while having a little stagger home from side to side. If I was in the town centre, I could get almost halfway home before my meal was gone then toss the paper over a church iron gate at the top of another steep hill. It all worked well in the good old days because the pubs shut before the chip shop. There were hard decisions to make when the pubs were allowed to shut later than the chip shop. Major questions rolled through your head, like *Do I drink or eat?* Then there were times when you had a girl by your side—what would you do? Feed her when all you wanted was a good time? Give her a beer when all you wanted was a good time? Or my favourite, eat, drink, and be merry! While some of the good pubs have been brought into the twenty-first century and proclaimed to be brassieres, the rest are almost still the same as they were when I started getting in them. I guess that's why I love finding places like that in the countries I have been to. The town had so many pubs when I was a young man. It's not hard to understand why so many closed when cars became more available to get around and go further away from town. Drinking and driving was not a hot topic and would go by the way unless you hit something. That would bring out the police. With bars like we had, I always try to find little shanty bars wherever because I think it's enjoyable finding and tasting the local food, beer, and talking to the locals.

The town had such an array of shops, and each was personal and hardly a big store in the area. There was only one that could have been one of the "big" stores in those days. I recall being in town with Mother shopping in the store one Christmas, which was around my sixth birthday. I watched Mother buy a little car transporter and six cars, as my birthday is just after Christmas. I was so surprised when I eagerly opened the present that was obviously the transporter, only to find that the cars were missing. With sadness in my voice, I asked, "Where are the cars?" I was told to wait three days for my birthday to get them. What does a little boy do when that happens—he cries because he is sad, but when you have what I had for a mother, you soon shut up to please her. There was never much around, and without a father, times were hard. She did work, but there was never enough to say we were anywhere near comfortable. Mother was a good cook (always said she was a pastry chef in a hotel in London), but that was it, no name or place, just London. I loved my Sunday roast like anyone else. I would walk about half a mile to get my aunt Bess's gravy because hers was the best. I would carry a cup to her house one handed or in my pocket. When it was full of gravy, gold dust was in my hands. I would have both hands wrapped around my prize and hurry as fast as I could home. Then it would be warmed again on the stove and poured over my meat, potatoes, and Yorkshire puddings. There was a reason I sort of believed Mother about her history because after my first delight, another would come, apple pie and double cream. Man, it would just melt in your mouth. I have never found anything like it anywhere. My gran made good pastry, as did my aunt, and their mince pies were good but nothing compared to my favourite pastry chef's. I guess that is a nice memory and in total contrast about the rest of her.

When I finally got to getting downtown on my own, there were so many pubs to pass (which were going to be a problem within the next eight years) going from my home down the hill into the hub of the metropolis. These days, it saddens me to see so much gone: the changes that have taken place; my favourite pub shut down; the post office turned into flats. A street with as many as fifty various businesses has nothing more than a few left, and some of them are second hand shops.

CHAPTER 5

IT WAS FUN GETTING ready for a day out to a nice nature area. We would walk up the road with rods and reels at the ready and some worms dug from a neighbour's garden. Turning right to go down a steep hill, there was a pretty view to be enjoyed with the green fields rolling up the other side of a large vale. The excitement grew with the river almost in sight. A lovely quiet area. You could ramble along the twisting footpath shadowed by trees. The sound of the river beside you gave it such peace. As you entered the wooded area, on the right, there was a disused quarry, which had an almost 120-foot shear face. There was a way to get up and down it, which also served as a shortcut to get back to a main road. This was also where fun was to be had with friends by sliding down a grassy area on the upturned hood of an old Jaguar. To stop, you would hit the old security fence that ran along the front and side of the quarry. There was a time when some other kids were playing down there. Instead of being on the bottom of the rock face, they chose to mess around on the top. One of them, a school friend, slipped and fell to her death. The shock waves reverberated around the town, and the painful loss kicked in. "How, why did this happen to this poor girl?" They all knew the dangers, and we all had been warned by different parties over time. Back then, there were no counsellors to help you through such a traumatic time. Mothers and fathers were called upon to hug and cuddle their children. Little was on offer from my mother to console me. There was no compassion, no listening to my pain and loss. My pillow was wet that night. In time, everyone healed, and we moved on, but my school friend has never been forgotten.

As you went further along the path, you would break out into another quarry, which was used for making concrete. Lorries and loaders were there for me to gaze at and wish I could get on one. The disused part of the quarry was overgrown, and if you walked into the bushes at the back, you would find two old limekilns, which were a small amount to find. Seven for big industrial work was normal. These kilns would be loaded by the loading gang with crushed stone, which would be smashed by hand. A layer of coal went in first then a layer of limestone, then another layer of coal and more limestone. This continued until the kiln was fully loaded. Under the grated steel bars, a fire was ignited. This would burn layer after layer until the process was complete. Kilns holding a twenty-five- to thirty-ton load would take a day to load, three days to fire, two days to cool, and one day to unload. We would be fascinated about what they were and what went on there. Our heads pried inside to see as we tried work it out. Just back from the kilns was a bridge, and although unused, you could see how the quarrying was done. Unknown to the workers, they had left us a huge playground, where a couple of small caves were our hiding places. We even built a platform in a tree where we would wait for other people to come along and spy on them with our binoculars. The biggest surprise I ever got was seeing two cars pull up about one hundred feet way, and a lady jumped out of a small car. The local police had a couple of them, and I got a ride in them on a couple of occasions. Police cars then were bog standard, with a sign over the top, "police," and a single blue light. These simple cars with an engine in the back would be cramped with four people in it but were cheap to buy and run. The other car was larger, and I knew these two unsuspecting persons; they were teachers at my school. It wasn't long before I was to see my first adult striptease. Off came her blouse then bra, and I was gob smacked by such a pert pair of breasts; I wanted to play, touch, and caress them as he was. I wanted to reap the rewards of having a naked woman at my beck and call and fulfilling my desires. His shirt came off as did his trousers, then her skirt and underwear. I was really enjoying this spectacle. I watched these two go at it like rabbits, watching her rise up and down. Sometimes fast and sometimes slow. I wondered, *Why is she doing that?* But later on in life, I knew just what was happening. It was over in a few short minutes, and after lying briefly together on the backseat, the clothes were going back on. With a final kiss, they began driving off into the wilderness. Again, I had witnessed more deception, two cheating people teaching me about how to upset everybody close to them, without doubt going to break children's hearts; and when discovered, their lives, marriage, and jobs would be in question.

This was a place that we would all come down to and mess around. It was a summer's day for everyone to be wearing just shorts and T-shirts as we headed for our favourite play area. We went down the side of the rock face and into the woods. We came to the open disused quarry and decided to play hide-and-seek. We picked pairs, and my partner was a neighbour's daughter.

She was rather attractive and developing in all the right places. As we had kissed before, we were comfortable with each other. Off we scampered into the designated area to hide. We went into one of the small caves, which had, for some unknown reason, a lead or steel pipe going across the ceiling and into the side of the wall. As we went further in, it was getting darker. We hid behind a rock, watching and waiting. We had always liked each other, and while waiting, we began kissing, but this was different. Our tongues were getting involved, and the cuddles were more intense. Then suddenly, we were pounced on. We all laughed about it then switched to go and find those that caught us. After a couple of hours, we would begin heading home for a bite to eat and bed. As I lay in mine, so many thoughts were flying around in my head about what might have happened if the others never found us. "Could have, should have been" was at the forefront of my mind, and if she was thinking the same, then surely our time would come.

Once we were playing hide-and-seek in a grave yard. I ran into an iron cross and cut my knee. Like any son, I wanted my mum and limped the quarter mile or so home only to be told what an idiot I am, as the hospital was only two hundred feet away. She covered my knee with a wet cloth, complaining it was going to cost money for a taxi to take me to the emergency room. When we got there, it was so nice to be taken care of by a nurse. Mother never came in to the emergency area; she kept talking to strangers in the waiting room. A doctor put some stitches in and said what a brave young man I was before wrapping my leg in a splint. We lived on the second floor of the block of flats. I had a piece of wood at the back of my leg, which was held on by a bandage. Getting around and going downstairs to see my friends would be awkward. The splint was necessary to let the stitched knee heal. Not long after this, an "uncle" (that's what strangers were called back then) came and left. Mother was trying to find a partner. I have no problem with that because it's something we all need. Then along comes this guy, quiet and unassuming and seemed to like mum. I would look up at this six-foot-two-inch man with grey hair and feel safe with him. There was a huge contrast in size between them. He was skinny, and Mother was plump. If they were happy, who was I to complain? After some time, Albert moved in. I remember the simple wedding at the registrar's office. The reception was held in my uncle Gary's house. My stepfather was nice in his way but not a leader—never taught me anything really; maybe that's because of his way of life when living in Tottenham, north London. I never had much, if any, interest in football. We went to meet his family on a few occasions. They were pleasant, and he missed his brother. When they got together, they would never stop talking. I would be outside playing with other family children who lived just a few doors away while everyone caught up on local news. In having him in my life, I certainly got a taste for his music. Country stuff was his liking, and I enjoyed listening to it. He had a nice gramophone record and radio player, which was his pride. We were not allowed to use it for the first few months of knowing him.

For transport, Albert had a little moped, which popped along about twenty to thirty miles an hour. It was good enough to ride the mile or so across town in his long coat and sixpenny hat. It was not law then to wear a helmet, and I think, once you got a motorbike, then you would wear one. I was never a motorbike man, although I did own two scrambler-type road bikes as I got older. Just riding along the main road to work, he would pass at least eleven pubs, which he never went in, but I did when age allowed! One day, I went to the shed and dragged his moped out. I started it and went flying around the housing area, much to the amusement of my friends. They were shouting and cheering as I flew by with my legs stuck out as far as I could, I guess the noise got him to the window. He then came down from the flat to claim his pride back. Mystery always surrounded their meeting. I once asked my brother how they met, and he said, "She got him from a catalogue," but I had guessed she met him while she worked in London (little did I know!). Being the younger son, it always felt like I was a problem but couldn't understand or even know why. Why would I be the one who was always wrong? I think sometimes my brother did things knowing I would get the rollicking and a clip around the ear. Hand-me-down clothes were what I got from him. But for Sunday best, I did have this nice woollen coat, which I always felt good in. Of course it was a hand-me-down, just like my tight-fitting shoes. So many times I was confused as to why I was always being pushed away. In some ways, it may have been for the best. It made me tough on the outer, but I like to think I am soft on the inner. Home life was boring to a point—watch TV, which I had no say in the matter, or sit in my room and stare out the window and wonder about the world. Sometimes home life was fun when a mother and daughter would come over, or we would go over theirs. We would go to the bedroom to play games or go out and play with others if the weather was nice.

One of my neighbours worked as the delivery man for the bakery. Some Saturdays, I would go on his round. Loading up the old brown van with the smell of fresh bread was so beautiful. My treat was a freshly baked one-pound loaf. The end would be cut off; I would pull out the bread bit by bit until all that was left would be the crust. That was then pulled apart, covered in Moonraker butter, and devoured by a hungry lad. In going around the town, I was learning roads and different neighbourhoods. I would also get a little pocket money, which allowed a treat for my favourite girl when we were in the sweet shop across from our school. At Christmas, households would give a little tip, which if it was my regular house, I could keep, and that helped for little goodies for the girls.

There was also a leather factory across the road from where Mother and Albert married. There at the side door, you could get lengths of leather to attach to your trolley or cart as a steering aid—a simplistic piece of engineering, four wheels and a seat. A friend would push you, and off you go. Down a small hill or slope was enough. With no brakes, the soles of your footwear would be the nearest thing to that, and they wear out rapidly. I recall my favourite trolley. It was made with the chassis being a four-by-four fence post—long in length, eight feet, and with two large wheels at the back and two smaller ones at the front. We would race down the small hill of our road toward the garage area, which was our racetrack. Once I lost my steering when my left side leather strap came free from the staple that attached it to the steering axle. I swung to the right and with my "battering ram"—this was about three feet of four-by-four fence post stuck out the front of me—I hit a garage door so plum in the middle, forcing the doors to lock up. Those doors remained stuck until a council worker could come and release the hinges and separate the doors. I recall the irate owner of a car, which he could not get to for almost three days. He was shouting at us lads and telling us to find other games to play. There was such an array of trolleys, some with the biggest pram wheels you could find at the back and front. Old floorboards from the house could be used. Pram wheels were always the favoured because there was an axle you could attach to the wooden frame with staples or bent nails. The brake was your feet, and your seat was just a piece of wood or a homemade box. It didn't matter; we were construction engineers, and many plans were changed as the hammering proceeded.

CHAPTER 6

ONE DAY, OUT OF the blue, my mother said that an auntie who lives in Tipperary wanted to pay for us to go over to see her in Southern Ireland. I had never heard of anyone that was family living over there. When the news flew around the neighbourhood we would be going, it was like we became celebrities. No one had done any flying, and so many kids were envious and wanted to come with my brother and me. How fascinating it was going to be going a different way than the normal road to London. We were going to Bristol Airport and fly to Dublin. As the date approached, I was getting so excited to go the furthest I had ever been. The morning sun rose. With my bag packed, all I did was look out the window. I wanted to see if the car had pulled up. When it did, my heart was in my mouth. As we went down the stairs, a small crowd of well-wishers were waiting for us. Our uncle Gary took me and my brother to the airport. We were handed over to a guardian who would lead us the gate before handing us over to the flight attendant. My brother was not like me. He was not showing much excitement as we boarded the plane. We were seated and given a barley sweet. The stewardess uttered these words, "If you don't suck it, you could go deaf." In an instant, it was making its way to my mouth. Everyone was on board, and the engines were started. We got pushed backwards, ready to taxi out. I was looking out the window and started saying how much fun I was having. Without warning, my sweet flew out of my mouth and disappeared somewhere on the floor. I lost it. Not just the sweet. I lost my calmness. I began screaming that I didn't want to go deaf and to stop the plane. The well-trained lady who was in charge of us brought another to calm me down. The sensation of the plane taking off was exhilarating, and I guess that was when I became hooked on flying and wanted to do it again and again. Looking down at the Bristol Channel was a thrill. Heading across Wales before heading out over the Irish

Sea was the best feeling in the world. When I looked around, other people were reading newspapers, magazines, and all relaxed. I was so fascinated but could not understand their way of being. After asking why, I was told they were seasoned travellers and felt the sensation many times before.

We approached Dublin. As the plane started its descent, my ears started to feel funny. I again began shouting, "I'm going deaf," as they felt like they were going to explode. Again the stewardess came over to explain I was OK and nothing was going to happen. Those minutes coming in felt like hours, and it was so relieving when the wheels touched down. We were lead through the gates and met this lady who was the "unknown auntie" of Ireland. We received a warm welcome and cuddle. I was confused about the situation but raring to go see something new. Her hand holding mine, we were led from the airport into a taxi. Strange roads with buildings that looked like home surrounded me as we weaved across the city. We arrived at the hotel for a one-night stay in Dublin. This was the first time I was to ride on an elevator. When everything settled down and refreshed with cold water splashed on my face, we went down for some food. I was watching how the elevator worked, and when we could, my brother and I hit the buttons to ride up and down. It ended quickly when the lift attendant got hold of us on our return to the floor level.

Dublin had old buildings like my hometown but very different origins. It became established in the ninth century by Vikings with small rebellions being recorded until the Norman invasion that was launched from Wales in 1169. There was also another and larger invasion in 1171 that allowed King Henry II of England to pronounce himself Lord of Dublin. A magnificent castle was built in 1204 and was the powerhouse that was to rule Ireland, and with its troubled path over recent decades, this may be the reason as to why Catholic and protestants argue, because in 1592, Queen Elisabeth of England established a solely Protestant college and ordered that the Catholic St Patrick's and Christ Church Cathedrals be converted to Protestant. The next morning, a breakfast of cereal and bacon and eggs was served, and then in her large Humber car, we left for her home in Tipperary. We drove over roads with fields that appeared to be greener grass than back home. The car rolled over little dips and swells until the almost one hundred miles of countryside were exhausted. We arrived in her town of residency, Scarriff, County Clare. We drove up a drive to a house that was somewhat similar to an old stone manor house back home. We were introduced to her brother, and he was keen to get doing things, like walking downtown. We went into a cinema, and it was so different than the ones we had back home. The seats went all around the sides and nothing in the middle. Ours had rows going across, aisles down two sides, and the same upstairs. We only paid three pence for our Saturday morning shows with cartoons. I loved the scary man series that would have us kids screaming at the screen, telling the bad man to go away. It cost about the same amount of money to go in, and we were treated by this sociable man whom I had taken a liking too.

One day, it was decided we would be going to the Blarney Village, which is about five miles from the city of Cork. When we arrived, there was yet another beautiful castle far different than the wooden one erected in the tenth century at the same spot. In 1210, a stone castle was built. In 1446, another was built, which still stands today. The word "Blarney" is thought to derive from the then Queen of England, Elisabeth I, who commanded the Earl of Leicester to take possession, and when asked for updates, he dithered so much, she used the term "Blarney." Also there is the Blarney Stone, and in kissing it, you are bestowed the gift of eloquence (never worked for me, or did it!), but most think kissing the stone brings you luck. I believe that is true because of all the good things that have happened in my life. They certainly outweigh the bad by a long way. This is where you would lie on your back. By holding two iron bars, you would lower your upper half to kiss the stone. (Back in olden days, there was no one helping you. It was possible to fall through a hole beneath it and head for what be certain death thirty feet below.) We did several other things, and before long, time was up. We were to be heading back home. The goodbyes to this newfound "uncle" were stretched as much as possible until it became desperate for flight time and get in the car. We drove away with this man standing in the drive. Tears were rolling down his cheeks as he waved a last goodbye. I never thought of it then, and what young boy would, but I did for many years as I matured. Why was this stranger with a small tint of a strange dialect crying so much when he only knew us for six days? Then something clicked when I was aged thirty or so. I was convinced. All the evidence was telling me it was *Dad*. I believe he came over from the USA to see his sister, and they decided to bring me and my brother over from England. How could this happen? Mother was getting letters from him. I recall seeing those letters only to be told it was an old friend of hers that moved over there. I never read them, and they were never seen again by anyone other than her. Maybe when I was sent to my room to play with a friend's daughter, she would be talking about this situation to a friend—in a way, getting it off her chest. It also explained the funny talk I would hear her and her sister blabbing out. We returned home to be questioned about our trip, but it never came up again, and the Ireland connection was never heard of again either.

In 1965, we were to move around the corner into a house just around the corner, which meant I still had my friends, and we would have a garden too. Best of all, I would have my own bedroom. A place that hopefully, when I shut the door, everything in there would be mine. All we had at the flat was a storage shed, and one year, we had so much snow, we made a tunnel out in the washing line area. This was also an area where one year, it was Guy Fawkes or Bonfire Night. This is a time of year in England on November 5th, which celebrates a man named Guy Fawkes who tried to blow up the House of Lords but failed. He was caught trying to conceal his gunpowder by the beefeater's (latter-day security guards) in 1605 and was locked up in the tower. Back in those days, you would be mutilated and hanged, but he jumped from the scaffold, breaking his neck to save the pain. I put a rocket in an empty milk bottle and lit it. Never really paying attention to where it was pointing, it went straight into a second-floor apartment's window, scorching the curtains. Thankfully, only a slight amount of damage occurred. It was very scary running up to the neighbour's door and screaming, "Your bedroom might be on fire!" Not only that but I would also be getting another clip around the ear when everything settled down. Those days, you were disciplined by any adult, not a good walloping but a smack across the head and told to "bugger off home" before you get another one.

It was at the flat that our next dog after Pete, Toby, was getting ill, and frequent trips were being made to the vets. Sometimes we would get a ride down, which was also an opportunity to pop across the road and see Gran. I would put the kettle on for a pot of tea. A tin full of biscuits was in my hands moments after. Mother would be talking about how good everything was, but in reality, she was spinning yarns about our life. One day, Mother decided that she would not bother affording any more treatment for the dog; with her bossy voice, she gave me the lead and two shillings. I was to walk the dog to the vets and have it put down, which just blew my mind. With a heavy head, I left with my poor friend and headed down the road. Some friends were playing and asked why I looked so sad. I explained the situation. They patted the dog and went on up to the play area, leaving me to trudge my way to vet. I passed the back of Gran's and went into the office where other dogs and cats were waiting for treatment. Kind people asked what was wrong with Toby. I explained I had brought it in to be put down, as it was sick, and we could not afford it any longer. They spoke with a sadness and compassion but somehow understood the reasoning. My turn came and with tears falling down my cheeks. I hugged him for the last time and left with his collar and lead, heading to Gran's for a cuddle and some comforting words.

CHAPTER 7

MY LAST SCHOOL WAS a short walk from home. Going up the road there was another pub and skittle alley on my right and a builder's yard on my left. Just before I would get there, I might see one of my girlfriends in her house if she had not left for school. We shared some kiss and cuddle times together but never went all the way. When I finally got into the real world, it was someone else rather than the girls I had been flirting with. I would ride my bike most of the time, but now and then, on dry days, I would walk at the back of the old tall houses along a garden route. Gardens on the right might be full of vegetables; on the left, the old rugby field. It was here that I had my first fight—two young men who disagreed about a girl we both fancied and decided to do the man thing. A short tussle ensued, and the victory was taken by the opposition, as I gave up. After slipping free, I walked away, leaving a smiling boy who was and is my lifelong friend. Several times, Nicolas, as we have grown, should the topic come up, his statement now is "That was my best chance, and I will never try that with you again." The disagreement was about who should have sat with a girl when we were on the coach that took us to our swimming lessons. With sisters in the class, the boys would always go for the prettier of the two. I know I did, and that also occurred in my later life when I swapped sisters. In doing so, I would find out who was better at spoiling me. The backseat was the place where open kissing would be going on; sometimes some fondling occurred, but that would just be someone winding all the others up. When done, the others would see two grinning kids who just had some fun. Once, I was dressed and ready for school and noticed our two cats, Fluffy and Smokey, were missing. I went around calling them, and Mother said she had let them out, which meant I would not have cuddles with my babes. I got my bike that leant against the front wall and went down the path with small mown lawns on both sides and flowered borders. As I turned right, it brought Smokey into view. I walked over to him while calling his name and making those noises cats relate to. He seemed transfixed, and I discovered why. His mate and mine, Fluffy, was lying in the road, dead—obvious he had been hit by a car or lorry, and my heart broke. I dropped my bike and ran in, screaming to Mum that Fluffy was dead. She looked out the window and started to cry too. Albert was summoned, he went out with the garden spade. He picked him up and went to the top of the back garden. He dug a hole under the apple tree and buried him while we looked on. When everything was said and done, there was no way I could go to school. I went to my room to lie on my bed, thinking about my friend. Smokey was with me, and I held him in my arms while he was purring, I don't know if he got over losing his friend that quick or whether he knew his purring would comfort me.

School was the place where I really began getting to know the female body. There were times we would be doing sports things like running and football. Girls in our class would do their thing then; to the other end of the gym hall, we would scamper. In the changing room, they would begin to peel off their clothes. We would peek through the keyhole, desperately pulling on each other's shoulders to see. Various pubic hair colours intrigued us. Things would turn bad if a larger one happened to be the one taking her sports clothes off closest to the door—none of us liked large buttocks blocking our view—so we would scurry back to our changing room to get dressed and ready for the next lesson. I hated some of the lessons, drama being the worse; being expected to do things like prancing around on the stage was not for me. I never liked reading about anything and have never read a book in my life. I enjoyed learning things from the drama teacher. He was also our principal teacher and was informative and nice to listen to. We were getting close to leaving school and going out into the working world. The subject books for a particular subject would get tossed up into the attic in the back room, and that would mean a skipped lesson. One of us would stand precociously on a chair, which was balanced on the bench, and then the books would be tossed into the hider's hands. He would toss them through the hole in the ceiling and, when done, place the attic board back and try to look innocent.

We would also go to other teachers for maths, history, woodwork, and metalwork. Maths I did alright with, but history would do my head in. Why teach me the past when I was interested in the future. I would protest and then would be sent to the headmaster for the cane. This was about a quarter of an inch thick and three feet long, and I would be told to put my hand out, and "six of the best" would be administered. Next step would be to go to the changing rooms and run cold water on my hands. That only helped a little. Chances were, from time to time, I would see my favourite janitor with a warm smile, saying, "What have you done this time?" He was one of the reasons I never wanted a motorbike because one day, he gave me a ride on his 650 cc Triumph, which scared me a little as he roared up the road, and that was it—I was cooked. No more of that for me. I became more of a rebel and refused to do the things I was not interested in. That meant more trips to the headmaster's office were coming. It was finally agreed that I could go to the woodwork and metalwork rooms as replacement learning time.

All I wanted was practical things, which were going to be the mainstay of my life and what I enjoyed. That's what I tried to explain until my cry was heard. I had figured I would be a working man and not a clever guy doing academic things that never interested me. We were kids that were learning about girls. One of the good places to go was in the backroom of our classroom where the books were hidden. There were no windows and no other way in. I was with a girl, kissing passionately, and in came the teacher and found us. He demanded that we separate and get out of his backroom. I had to go to the headmaster. I tried to explain myself, but as always, it fell on deaf ears. Out came the cane, and this time, it went across my arse. There was no way to put cold water there. I walked out of school and went home only to see mother sitting there in the chair of wisdom, demanding an explanation as to why I was home early. I did my thing by responding to her request, saying I was sick of the place. She promptly got up from the wisdom chair, gave me a clip around the ear, and sent me back to school. When she discovered what I had done, I was back in the headmaster's office again!

We would also do a cross-country run, which took us down a hill to our nature area. Running in a big circle, we would come back to the main road and back up the hill towards school. Instead of going into it the normal way, we would cross over the river and go up a narrow lane that led to a small village. At the top of the hill, on the left, there was a small track that led to a field. This is where, with my first car, I was having a good time on the backseat with the doors open. We were in full swing when these car lights came up the track, stopped in front of us, then turned its blue light on. I said to my girl, "It's the police."

And she screamed, "I don't care, don't stop." I did as requested, and after thirty seconds or so, the light was turned off. The car reversed away, which was rather nice of the officer. This was also the country lane I had rode with the horse and cart loaded up at harvest time. Further along, we would go right and follow the old rail track that leads to the old limekilns, turn right again, and run along the trail towards the old quarry and homeward. Many times a couple would be waiting for the runners to pass then come from the thick bushes and join the back of the pack. It was a twenty-five-minute window to indulge in frolicking. A girl and I would duck out from the pack and hide in a hedge until everyone was gone. It was fun seeing them disappear before we would be holding hands then run away for some free time.

Being at this school, I made a whole new bunch of friends. Many lived out of town, and they would come in by hired coaches and then return in the afternoon. If I wanted to hang out with them, I would cycle the three miles to their village, meet at an old castle, and hang out in the village centre or go to their houses. There were a lot of good families and, of course, lots of nice mums and dads. Steven's dad had massive arms, and we never could pin him down. His wife, Shirley, had the warmest of smiles, and I became much attached to the whole family. Steven, after losing his dad, had to make a decision as the eldest of the children. His younger brother was badly hurt in an accident; it was his decision as to whether the life support machine was to be turned off. How hard for a person. How hard it was as a brother. How do we get the strength to make such a call, and go on after? He made the call, and his brother slowly slipped from the world, and reality kicked in. Never to be seen again, never to laugh with each other again. That's it; we and everything cease to be. Once in my room, I looked at the world, and in my hand was a razor blade. I looked so hard at it and looked hard at myself. I contemplated what death would be and how much I would miss. I never had the nerve to follow through, and I am glad I didn't. How much would I have missed in this wonderful world? I have tried to understand people that do take their lives. Some say they are cowards; others say they are brave. I think they are brave; the wanton desire to end life cannot be easy. If desperation brings us to the point, that must be terrible. How cruel life can be for so many.

I also did a paper round, and my round was easy enough. I would start in a short road going up to the park and then deliver in three other roads. When done, we always have to go back to the shop in case someone had not turned up. That would mean double money for doing their round, but trouble, as I would be late for school. I changed to another delivery shop. It would be more papers but more money. After four months or so, and getting through a winter, one day, I left the shop, which just above the town centre, cycled as best I could uphill until I got to the start of my delivery road. Most of it you could cycle, but your legs tired, as I had two large and loaded paper bags, one either side of my bike's back wheel; plus, with no gears, it was hard work. When I got to my third house, I attempted to park my bike by placing the pedal on one of the curb stones that separated the footpath from the garden. Well, I screwed it up big time; and in the rain, over we went, me and the bike, falling sideways, heading for the lawn, which was about eighteen inches lower than the footpath, and thump. I was down with newspapers strewn all around me, and as I tried picking them up, trying to sort the mess out, I said to myself, "f—k this." I went back to the shop, told the dispatcher what to do with his job, and went home. Several times on a winter morning, I would come home cold as cold and, to warm up, have a bowl of porridge with my feet in the cooker oven. Of course, there was a lecture from Mother to be had about wrapping up warmer, and I was used to them. Another thing was after being given a front-door key, I was told from the chair of wisdom not to bring any trouble to her door. This allowed me to come and go without her having to get off her arse and let me in if I came home late from riding around in the lorries. Most following mornings when that occurred, she would ask, "Did you bring me anything?" This was the beginning of the "take, take" era in my mind. Something was always expected of me, and it would be something material. Hugs were out of the window—not that there were many anyway. The best hugs came from my aunt Bess and Mother's friends; they always had time for a little tear away that was beginning to understand what he was supposed to be.

CHAPTER 8

THE TOWN CENTRE WAS known to flood quite often after heavy rains, and about one mile from it still does. The last flood recorded was in 1968; so many times the town was cut off and traffic diverted around the back streets. I don't think the town was flooded for days on end, but I'm sure it happened from time to time through many decades. Shops would have a major cleanup to undertake, and with so many shops, the labour costs were high. The final occasion I was down there with my friend, I urged him to go across to the cake shop; and finally, we went wading through it towards the bridge and the shop, which was situated in the middle of several other shops and a pub. The old people's home was close to flooding, as were other shops that were on the same ground level. Adjacent to them was a small but social pub, which when entering, you would step down into the bars, and with everything else flooded by two feet of water that one would be up to the bar top. I got my reward in the cake shop by giving some buns, which would not have sold then; we made our way back through the water, which was not much higher than my boots. Outside of the post office were three red phone boxes, and a local news reporter took a photo, which was on the front page the following week. I recall having a Donkey jacket on; this is a thick winter coat, cheaper than others but fine for working or messing around in. I had a tea cosy on my head and a big smile, as I was anticipating eating my goodies. Also in the photo was an older man with his little milk container, which may have been full or empty, and I have no idea what he was doing there.

They say time will tell. Finally, my uncle Harry discovered that his wife was having an affair with his best friend Terry. Nasty things were going to happen. Like anyone else who has been in that position, there is little or no reconciliation. Nothing is worth listening to. Nothing can be said to pacify a person who has been scorned by their lover, wife, friend, and confidant.

Harry was beat up and hurting so badly. He threw her out of the house and considered the world an enemy. I was sad having lost my "adoptive dad," the person I looked up to; he wanted nothing to do with anyone who was related to his wife. This I learnt one day when I was going through a residential area towards my friend's home. This single-lane road ran into a dead end. The footpath with a large wall was built next to that. As I was about halfway along the road, the man I so enjoyed came from one of the terraced houses. I began to get excited as my uncle emerged from the house that was his brother's. What more could I do than smile and say hello. Like any other thirteen-year-old, I was sure I was safe in his presence. How wrong could I have been? He began a torrent of abuse, calling me and anyone else with my name shithouses and wagging a finger at me. His finger turned into a fist. A short sharp jab with his right hand landed on my cheek. My balance was lost. I went down, and the pain kicked in. I began to cry. I was in shock that such a thing happened to me, from the man I loved. While lying there on the footpath, looking up at this man who was my friend, my mentor, my teacher, a wild thought sped through my head. He began to walk away, still cursing our name and his wife. I got up with a spinning head. A sense of resilience clicked in me. I ran silently as I could to begin my attack. I knew it would be futile, as he was heavier than me. I never got a lot of speed, but it was enough to push him as I sprang and pushed his back. He stumbled a little, then it was time to run the other way. I knew he would never catch me because he smoked too much. I was a little lion that just got his first taste of an ambush. He never ran after me, and at a safe distance, this young lion roared like one. "One day, I will be a man, and I will come and get you, you bastard." A sense of achievement welled through me as tears rolled down my cheeks. That was the day I became a bigger and better young man. Wild thoughts rolled around my head while my hand was wiping blood from my mouth. This was it—never again was I going to allow that to happen to me. Any perpetrator who may think he or she would damage me was going to get a big surprise. At that time, I never really had a game plan; but as things are now, this must have been the point in my life that my ten-second rule would apply. Simply, if I thought for one moment I was going to be challenged, someone thinking they would land one on me, the rule would kick in, and their chin would be the target. I hit some guys with boxing gloves, and they hit me, but the feeling of hitting someone with my knuckles was something I was going to get a liking to.

CHAPTER 9

My "OUT OF TOWN" uncle Gary had two aggregate delivery lorries, and when I could, I would go with him out to the quarries and be so excited seeing all those big diggers and dump trucks. Gary had a bit of a belly, and a cigarette was in his hand almost all of the time. His wife was quite the opposite. Jean had her styled hair curled like Mother's, slim, and always looked elegant. I recall waiting anxiously at the curbside looking for his Albion lorry with a two-tone blue cab and a smiling face driving it. I loved climbing in the cab over his toolbox and looking down on everyone. Sometimes his son would be with him. One of us would sit on the engine cover, which would get hot and overheat your arse. Huge smiles with the smell of oil and tar wafting up my nose as we headed up the road passing my school and out into the countryside. It was a narrow road, but the 1960s were kicking into gear. Roads needed to be built, and material was needed. The local area had major quarrying operations. These materials were needed to improve and expand the roads and towns. More and more lorries were hauling the rock and asphalt. They passed so close, I'm surprised we were never in an accident. After about three miles, we would come into probably my favourite village, where on the right were the old castle ruins. It was built in the late fourteenth century. In the sixteenth century, it was damaged in the English civil war and was left in ruin after being burnt by the Roundheads in 1645. There are traces of a nunnery there. It was built along a small stream that is linked to the river that flows through my town centre. Modern-day warriors have worked hard, and it has been cleaned up—such a nice tourist attraction with its moat surrounding it. After turning right up the hill and left toward the quarry, large loaders were working, and a face loading excavator would also be loading big dump trucks. I recall seeing this big excavator as it was being transported through our town centre en route to the quarry on a low loader with two big Scammell lorries at the front and one at the back. As it started up the hill, one of the lorries broke a drive shaft, and there it was stuck until they could fix the problem. It may have been twenty-four hours before they got it going, so the town centre was completely messed up. Other young boys and I were watching the unfolding drama. We all wanted to get on it and try our hands because of our little quarry.

There was a chance I might see other neighbourhood kids in the quarry riding with their dads, uncles, or friends. This place had so much going on, and the smell of the asphalt being made was so good. When driving was over for the day, he would park the truck, leaving it for a night loading person. These men would load it with asphalt sometime through the night. The lorry would be weighed, sheeted down, and ready to go. It needed to be on a site at 7 am. Driving home in his car, we would pass a farm where I did some milking which backed onto his land. He had a small holding, growing tomatoes, lettuces and other salad ingredients. There two big greenhouses that I helped play a part in building by carrying blocks to their placement spot. At Christmastime, chickens were to be killed and plucked, ready for the oven. I would help out catching them by diving around or, if we were lucky, get them pinned in a corner. He would cut the head off and hold them while the nerves of the chicken were shaking before its inevitable death. I cut the head off one, which I let go. He sat on his small stool, complaining that the chicken will get bruised because it was running into everything; I, of course, was laughing my head off seeing this for the first time. I also would go with another neighbour in his lorry, and he made deliveries of books to various distributors up in London. When the lorry was empty, another distribution place was our destination. There we got loaded with pallets of washing powder, toilet rolls, and various other cleaning items for the return trip home. We would leave at 2:30 a.m., and it would take almost four hours to get to the first drop-off. It was so exciting to sit in a cab high up above the cars and see so much countryside when dawn would break. I helped push and pull the pallets with the loading and unloading operations. Again he was someone I could look up to and learn from. I would watch how to change gears by double declutching and when to use to splitter gearing.

We would stop just outside of another town on the way home, and the back door was opened, and some of the items were given to me. When I got home, I was so proud to show my rewards for helping someone and, of course, happy to present my spoils to Mother. I think this was one of the reasons she would make the effort to give me a waking call so early in the mornings. We would do three runs a week, Monday, Wednesday, and Friday. Tuesdays and Thursdays and Saturdays were for unloading the return load, ready for local distribution, and then going down to the printing works, which was close to my old school, and getting loaded again. I was learning so much in my school holidays. Seeing so much of the English countryside that, as I began to travel, I knew where I was going. One day, another neighbour came home to show his wife his new articulated lorry. He asked, "Do you want to come with me to get loaded?" Boy, oh boy, this was the longest lorry I had ever been in, and I was so fascinated by it. When it came to backing it up, I was watching his every move because it was so different. It wasn't long before I knew how to throw ropes and tie them as a lorry driver would. Of course, I never had the strength then to complete the job, but I was learning something that would be useful in my later life.

From where we would load up the lorry ready for the London run, there were several pubs within close proximity. When you got to liking a drink, there were many problems to be had with them so close because it was so easy to go to the next bar. Although there were many fights to be seen around the town, not many happened in this neck of the woods. There were some, and if it occurred, outside you go and knock each other about. After, you would pick up the loser and have a beer, not like today's problems. That was when so much more discipline was in order; children never spoke out of place. Neighbours would leave the front and back doors open, which allowed us to just walk in looking for our friends. There was respect for elders, as most people knew each other and got along. Down in the town pubs is where most fighting happened. As we became the next generation of fighters, it was up to us to stand and be counted. Outsiders would come in just to rattle our bones or try chat up the girls. We never owned them, but if they were looking uncomfortable or getting manhandled, we would step in to protect. It was not that we were jealous; it was because we were once school friends, and that's something you take pride in. Several times, the girls would look at us while raising their eyebrows, then like knights in shining armour, we would step in, and the brawl would start.

CHAPTER 10

ALBERT WORKED AT A textile factory and was involved in the loading and unloading side of the business, and one day, he overstepped and fell off the lorry he was loading; that messed up income, and what was upbeat started to go down beat. His back never got better, and he even lost his sense of smell. Pocket money was going to dwindle, so I had to start doing another paper round; but this time, it would be a Sunday one. I would go through the town over the bridge, and to the left of the narrow building, there was a house that had maybe one thousand papers delivered. I would pick up at least one hundred or so papers with magazines and push them in a large pram up one of the steep hills and start my deliveries near my home before being empty after about four hours and back to base. That's where I would get my share and the "boss" would get his commission. About three months passed, and one day, in the rain again, I said to myself, "Sod this game," and returned everything with my statement, "You go do it, I quit." I was offered more money, but, no, my mind was made up, and that was it. I also did help doing some milk rounds, which were fun bombing around on an electric milk float, as horses for that job were retired, and I never really noticed. I did do some horse work down on a farm on the outskirts of town. I am not sure how I started to get into that farm, but on winter days, going out with the horse and cart with straw for the cattle in the fields is a fond memory. I never imagined some thirty years later I would be standing in the little cattle stall, which was now a stable, looking at my excited daughter grooming the horse I had brought her; and even more amazing, the owner was still alive and kicking and remembering having two young boys down on the farm helping out. The other lad was my mate who was in the Sunday school photo, and it was where we would continue forging a lifelong friendship. It was where our little muscles would begin developing by handling hay bales and cleaning up the stalls. Cow s—t was never too big a problem working with, but pig s—t had a more pungent smell about it. One day on another farm, I slipped, and into the stuff I went. I finally got myself composed while around me, my friend and the farmer were laughing their heads off. The smell was nauseating, and there was still work to do, so I just let it dry in the day's heat as I continued my tasks. The day ended, and the smell was awful, and I knew another rollicking was going to be heading my way. What it all boiled down to was, I was making an honest living and creating my own little world where I was liked and respected, not only by my elders but also by known and unknown friends. I also went to two other farms, which were owned by new friends I was to make when I got to my final school. One was down near my favourite playing area, and the other not far from the school. Again it was handling cattle, pigs, chickens, and a bull or two. Boy, oh boy, I was never one to mess with those. They stare at you with those big dark eyes, and the horns—stay well away was the rule. It was back in the late '60s when England was riddled with a rabbit disease called myxomatosis, which crippled them. They would lose their sense of smell, their hearing, and go blind. It also crippled them enough that they could hardly move, and we would go out with shotguns and just walk up to them and shoot them. They were no good for eating (and, yes, they taste very nice when done in a billy pot with vegetables over a campfire); such a waste, but it had to be done so the spreading of the disease could be contained, and eventually the battle was won. Another thing I enjoyed about the farm was harvest time; hard work was rewarded with good food and a drink and a happy smile from the farmer and wife.

CHAPTER 11

WE HAD A DOG given to us, and she was a year old, a German shepherd, and I would love walking with her, lovely colours, and her hind end was showman style. We would walk for miles, and many times, it would be down through the woods and follow a twisting road back home. We would pass the old quarry I had enjoyed for so many years, and I would still look up and see my "kind of girlfriend" reflect on that time and move on along the footpath. Cindy was not the bravest of dogs, as one time, I tried to get her to go up the rock face by taking the shortcut; but, no, she never would, and that meant walking about an extra half mile to get to the same point. With no uncle teaching me and a stepfather unable to show me much, my learning handy things had ground to a halt. Having said that, I wasn't really alone. My friend's dads were to be enjoyed, but I had no one to really hang on to and learn from. Again I would ask what happened to Dad. Mother would say, "All I know is he went to New Jersey in America." Like so many other things, the brick wall was in place. With her sister Bess, they would have this strange way of talking, which I or Albert could not understand. Only they did. It went on a lot through a conversation between us all. With knowing so little back then, I am sure they were talking about my dad. Although not confirmed, like other things that I have discovered, this is my assumption. On one particular day, Cindy and I had been for a long walk, and we came across the field at the back of a large plastics factory. On the left side of the street was the youth club, where I spent at least once a week boxing or just hanging out talking and chatting up the girls. It was also a place where my taste in music was developing and where I would learn to dance, which really worked when the *Saturday Night Fever* song came out. Discos then were simple, and the music was great. Slow records were really making things work for me. I loved to smooch with the girls.

As I headed toward home, on my right across from another old people's home, there was an elderly man struggling. He was doing some gardening in a small lot that sat on top of a five-foot wall. There were plenty of flowers he had been planting. Out of the blue, I said, "Hey, mister, do you want a hand?"

He looked down at me as his old body began to straighten itself. A warm smile came from his face, which had not been shaven. His eyes firmly staring at mine, he said, "Yes, that would be nice." Suddenly, a whole new world opened for me. I went up his drive to introduce myself and shake hands. He asked why I had made such a request. I explained what had happened about my uncle Harry. Mr. Smith was sympathetic as he put his semi arthritic hand on my shoulder. He led me from his drive up the garden path toward his lovely house. We went through the six-foot-high gate that led to a nicely mown lawn. More flowers wrapped around the border of it. Everything was shaded by large trees that overlooked the side of the house conservatory.

His wife had a cup of tea poured and a warm smile, a grey-haired lady that stood slightly higher than her husband. I was offered a cup of tea as the dog began to move toward the lady for a pat. With my tea in front of me, the biscuit tin was opened, and I took one and began "dunking it." She smiled and said, "I enjoy that too." Her husband kept smiling at his hopeful new helper. We talked for an hour or so about where I lived, went to school, mother and stepfather, likes and dislikes. It was decided that the following Saturday I would be coming up and help in the vegetable garden part.

I went home excited about the prospect of not only doing some gardening but also having a new mentor whom I had gotten to like. I got home, and Mother was sitting in the chair of wisdom, asking where I had been for so long. I explained I had met a Mr. and Mrs. Smith, and I will be working in his garden starting next week. Without any hesitation, she looked and said, "Well, that's going to be where you must get pocket money because I have none to give. As you have your own key, then you can come and go as you please." Bloody Nora, what the hell was wrong with the woman. Why was I pushed away and verbally beaten by this cold and heartless mother? I retreated to my room. We lived on a hill, and I would kneel on my chair. With folded arms resting on the windowsill, I would rest my chin on them and look across the rooftops out into the countryside. I could also see a large forest about three miles away and a large steep grassed hill, unknown then it would be a place for fun and frolics with a nice girl and some friends on a summer's night. It was times like this when I would just stare out into space and consider what life was for me. Why did my friends have it better? Because I was young, I could not work it out but pondered so many times.

Saturday came, and I went out the door like a whole new person. I walked and sort of skipped to a new world of learning and achieving. I got there as asked, at 9:00 a.m. At the back of the house, a long concrete footpath led to two small greenhouses and his prized vegetable patch. Mr. Smith explained how he liked to dig and place the seeds. From the first row, we would dig the soil out and put it into a wheelbarrow then tip it at the back of the patch. This allowed room for the rotting waste, from old things like potato peelings, cabbages, cauliflowers, and anything else that was a root vegetable. Placing the rotten waste about eight inches deep all along the row, then the next row to be dug would be thrown on top of the rotten stuff and buried, which was a first for me. As the morning continued, we worked closer and closer to the back. With the first soil we dumped used on the final row of rotten waste, it was done. He would put little markers at the end of each open row. Pulling a string from each end, that was his guideline to plant new seeds. They would grow down and be fertilized by the rotten stuff we buried. It was a clever thing and so different from the way my uncle Harry did things. As time passed, I loved cutting the grass and planting flowers. At least three times a week, I would have my plans set for their house. Trimming the trees' lower branches, I made a footpath of stone, which went around the back of the garage and along its side. I knew how to set up the line and put the levels in. I did this before laying the stabilizing rock, placing the broken stones, and grouting to finish. I was proud of my achievement. My newfound adoptive dad and mother were so pleased too. Every time I went there, I would be given some pocket money and a hearty meal. On the well-mown lawn with its stripes going across it, when they had guests over, clock golf would be played. A hole was made in the middle of the lawn. Twelve numbers laid out in a circle around it, each player would try to putt a golf ball in the hole, resulting in the lowest score being the winner.

After about eighteen months or so of going up and working in the garden, again we would wrap everything up for the incoming winter; any outside pots cleaned and put in the greenhouses. My time there would be scaled back to only once a week. Sometimes I would pop in while walking the dog. He might be working on a sermon for Sunday morning church. As a lay preacher, he enjoyed standing up and talking to the congregation about various subjects he found interesting in the Bible; I guess he put his own spin on it, thus it was pleasing to the ear for his listeners. It was winter, and snow had come and gone, but late one afternoon at home, a blizzard had been blowing all around us. I was sitting on the floor because Cindy had the rest of the sofa along with Albert; the TV was still black and white. We had heard colour was on the way or even here, but it was something we could not afford. I loved cowboy films and was glued to the screen. My feet were toasting nicely in front of the coal fire when suddenly I jumped up and fetched my boots, jacket, bobble hat, scarf, and gloves. Mother looked at me and scowled, "What on earth are you doing?"

To which I just looked at her through some cigarette smoke that came from Albert's lungs and said, "I must go up the road to Mr. Smith." Astonished, she looked at me, saying it was absurd, but I was certain I had to go. I grabbed Cindy's lead, and out we went into the blustery snow conditions and started heading toward the house I loved working at. Cindy was doing what all dogs do in the snow, like sticking her nose in it, creating little sneezes. She loved her time outside. That made things easier as we progressed along a snow-bound road. I always knew she was happy because of the way her tongue hung out of her mouth. The walk was about just over a quarter mile. As I turned left to go up the drive, there they were, outside, struggling to lean some wood that would act like a stake to hold the front garden fence up. After a few minutes of putting my shoulder into the fence with the wind still trying to beat us, we succeeded in securing the fence. New concrete would need to be placed at the base of the fence posts in the spring.

With the problem solved, we went inside to warm up and recover from the hard work. Mr. Smith asked, "Why did you, how did you, what made you come out in this weather? And come here."

I replied, "Something kicked me in the butt, and I knew you were in trouble." He and his wife were astounded that such a thing could happen. In his very next breath, he explained, while they were struggling, he prayed to the Lord for help. I, in return, was astounded that such a thing could happen when I had basically given up going to Sunday school. My belief in the Lord was never there because Mother said it was my choice about going. I was sick of being forced (guess I was a rebel then) to do as she thought. He said a prayer and thanked the Lord for the divine intervention before a totally satisfied young man would start heading home and back to the coal fire. Mr. Smith called the Lord "The Boot" in his Sunday morning sermons, explaining his meaning: when we do something spontaneously and we don't know why, it is the Lord that makes you do it.

I would be working on the front garden, and sometimes a pretty young lady would pass by. I would stop and look with a smile then watch them walk on, hoping she liked what she saw. As they were looking at me, maybe they had the same thoughts. I was also getting older, and if trees needed to be trimmed, I would climb the ladder. With a hand saw, I cut the branches that needed to come off as my mentor was looking up, his arthritic finger pointing to the branch that was to be lopped. In doing this, I was able to see over the ten-foot wall that separated his garden from the terraced houses of a narrow street that you could only walk up. These three-story houses are all part of the Old World townhouses. Many generations have lived there, enjoying the secluded back gardens until I was up the ladder. I could see in the kitchens and bedroom windows. I tried not to be looking like a nosey person (that was left to Mother), but one couldn't help it. One day, a woman came out of the bathroom with a towel wrapped around her and began getting herself ready for whatever. After loosening her hair, the towel was opened. I could do nothing but stare, as right in front of me was a nicely shaped body—lovely legs, which after the hips, went in at the sides of her stomach and up to breasts that deserved to be sucked by a greedy baby. I was sawing in slow motion, watching this unexpected treat. Mr. Smith was holding the ladder for my safety. I was so into wanting this wonderful treat to never end when I heard a voice, "Are you all right up there?"

Suddenly, I came back into the world, finished what I started, and began my descent. My neck was stretching as long as it could to keep watching this beauty continue her task. I asked many times after that, "Are there more branches needing to come down?" but the request fell on deaf ears.

I was used to going into the house to get water or a biscuit. That was all part of the trust that had grown. Their friends would also pop in and out, which was good for me. Sometimes they would offer me a small job, which would lead to more pocket money. One day, a good friend of theirs came over. It was just me and Mrs. Smith. I carried on doing my mowing while they were inside having a cup of tea. I finished the lawn and went into the lounge, which startled them as they broke apart. I was fobbed off that they were sharing a prayer, but this young man had seen and knew what was what. I was shocked that two people in their sixties would be doing such a thing, but then again, what's wrong with the old ones enjoying a little bit of tickling one's fancy? The only thing was, they were not partners, and this was another case of "cheating" that I had witnessed. What was wrong with my development, cheating going on around me by people that I looked up to? Was I alone, or were other children going through the same things? What was I learning about cheating on others? Was this going to play a role in my future? As time went on, these questions have been answered. I now know these teachers of my life have played a big role in mine.

CHAPTER 12

I STARTED GOING TO a drill hall enjoying Tuesday and Thursday nights as a young army cadet. I guess the adult instructors were men I could look up to and do my best like a son with his father. It was soon noticed that I could lead, and one stripe came, then another and another. I was so happy having a task to perform, like a job I guess. If you want to succeed, you have to get at it, get noticed, and be diligent performing your duties. That is one of the fundamentals of life. It helps you to be able to climb the ladder. There was a lot of messing around done. On the other hand, serious stuff like marching, handling your rifle, and shooting had to be conducted. I was of course making new friends that came from other parts of town. As we progressed, solid friendships were born, I would get invited to their houses and meet the parents. I began to have so many mothers. They were called *missus* as a young boy. They were called *mother* when I grew up. It was so nice to be treated like one of their own, and as we came from different parts of the expanding town, I would be opening up a whole new episode of life. Rain or shine, cadet night was cadet night, and there were a couple of older cadets that used to boss us about and rough us up. One of them would take a sweet or drink (because he could) from you. One evening, I decided I was going to teach him a lesson, so I drank my drink. I put a little lemon cleaning fluid in the bottle and topped with water. As I pretended to drink some, he swiped it from my hand and began to drink it. A greedy overweight older teenager was humbled. He spat out the drink and was coughing his guts up. I stood and looked at him with nothing more than a stern face, which was reading "That will teach you." This moment in time, I should have been scared or at least nervous; but, no, that was like a thing of the past. I was fully aware of my actions, and although he was capable of beating the living daylights out of me, I knew what to do. That was to stand by my conviction.

The army cadets were also a great learning tool for other things. Independence was a good one. While Mother would do the washing, my uniform was mine, and I would press it, press the shirt, and clean my belt brasses and boots. The uniform fitted me well. I would march from home to the hall wanting everyone passing by to look at me. The walk along the street was about three-quarters of a mile of pure satisfaction. I was so proud in my uniform. When I had learnt enough or was adjudged to be competent to lead, I stood six feet tall. I also encouraged others to come and be part of a good thing. Several of my neighbourhood friends joined. We would go out camping for a weekend, which was going to be a route march about eleven miles. With your backpack and rifle, it was going to be a hard time, but we did it. Our first time out at night, we were in a farm barn. I could hear the rats running around our feet, but we were not on the floor. We slept on makeshift beds that were the farmers' hay trailers. After a couple of successful trips, we would then be put to the test. We would be making our own bivouacs, which would mean tying your ground sheet together with a mate's. With that done, we would stick some branches in the ground. This was supposed to resemble a tent. That was the home from home for two young boys for the night. The biggest thing you prayed for was "please don't rain"; we were unlucky on the two occasions we were out there. Trying to sleep is one thing; trying to eat something warm was a test. We were supplied with a dead rabbit that we would skin, mix it with vegetables, and boiled in a billycan over a wood fire; it tastes rather good. We also had to do a night exercise. We had blank ammunition and were given details about an enemy target, and off we went. Night fell. If a car came along, we had to hide in the hedge, jump over a gate, whatever it took; we were not to be seen. As we approached our enemy target, a couple of blank rounds rang out from it, which startled us. No one expected the sergeant to be there with his rifle, so we opened fire. Along came a car, which saw all these flashes and heard bangs from our rifles. The sounds and flashes sent the driver into panic mode. We took no notice as the car left the area as fast as it could. Within fifteen minutes, there were blue lights coming at us from all angles. It turned out that the police were not informed of the night exercise. If they had known, the startled driver would have had a reassuring explanation from the police when he called them. The ensuing arguments could have resulted in our captain being arrested, but the police officer let him off with a stern warning. Then it was back to base for a night's sleep. We were also given *The Duke of Edinburgh's Award Record Book*, which if you went all the way to gold, then that would have meant four days out in wild country, spending three separate nights in separate camps and doing at least fifty miles of route marching. I never fancied that, but my bronze award record read that

I took part in a successful expedition, comprising of a fifteen-mile march, a camp overnight in barren wilderness, and a return march to home; correct procedures were observed, overnight camp was properly done, and two meals being cooked; distance covered thirty miles. That was my first major award after winning Cadet of the Year in 1968. This was the first time such an award was made, and again I was in the local paper. Two other occasions, I was in the local paper for leading others and winning trophies. As cadets, we would be involved in any military processions, and a march behind a band was such a good feeling. I think my proudest moments were as orderly corporal and then sergeant. I was allowed to lay the Remembrance wreath in the local park at the Veterans Memorial on two occasions. The bugle player would play "The Last Post," then it was my place to lay the wreath along with the senior cadet officer. Again in my beautiful uniform, I stood so proud of myself.

As time progressed with the cadets, we had opportunities to go to proper campsites and shoot live ammunition. We did out on the Mendips and other camps in Dorset and Cornwall. We once went down to a camp at Weymouth (famous for back burning!). It was the two-week summer camp. So much fun when we were allowed to leave camp, going into the arcades and chasing girls around the streets. What was so enjoyable was not having a parent around. We were free to go where we wanted and no questions. Go-karts were a favourite, but no fun when the money ran out. The older cadets had jobs. We would clean their boots and brasses; money was earned. I got extra money and brought a couple of presents to take home, and once, I actually came home with more than I went with when we were marching. Following the band, those drums and bugles were so good to hear. We by then were fifteen-year-olds, and the learning curve of how to make your fists work had kicked in. With so many boys from many other towns, the rivalry had started. Taunting and calling names would happen when camp was a mile away. On one occasion, there were four of us just messing around. Boys from another town started to brag and boast they were good and going to beat us up. Well, what were we to do, stand and be counted or run? We stood and stood good. I was enjoying hitting someone with my fist. Seeing someone hold his nose and the blood coming out "was never a kick"; it was "you asked for it and you got it." To the best of my knowledge, I have never started a fight because I see no reason; but if one came my way, I never backed down. I think seeing those guys in my early days hitting someone outside of the pub or cafe just happened to work for me. It simply felt natural, and my timing was good.

Just at the bottom of the camp was Chisel Beach; to some, it's known as the eighth wonder of the world. Why it's called a beach, I do not know because it is made up of pebbles, about seventeen miles long and fifty feet high. The current will take you down towards Portland Bay. It ends where a road that leads you away from Weymouth. The sea rolls in and out, beating endlessly on this short, flat piece of land. Travelling the road before climbing a hill, you would pass a small naval base, and then it goes up and up, swings left and right a few times, passing houses and a pub or two. At the top, it flattens out before running out of England's soil. It overlooks the busiest shipping route in the world, the English Channel. From our camp to Chisel Beach, a competition set up by our Superior's. We were given these rescue-attack boats, which sat ten of us; the outboard motor was not attached. It was soon discovered that we would have to paddle the boat across from the camp-side water's edge. The beach to the base, I guess it was about two hundred feet. The strong current just wanted to whisk you away towards Portland. Our senior leader steered, and the paddling was as frantic as could be. When the other side was reached, I, by nomination, had to run to the top and collect a tin and return to the boat. While I lay exhausted, the paddlers would return us to base. It was so hard to run up the side on those pebbles. One foot of climbing amounted to three inches gained, it seemed. With both hands and feet going, I guess I looked like an excited dog chasing a piece of wood. We completed the job and were proud of our effort. The next round of boats started battling it out. One team had the same time as us, and we needed a runoff. We went at it, as did the others. As I did some working out, I was confident about my fitness. Across the water, the guys were screaming "Come on" at everyone involved, and with the rowers paddling like crazy, we managed to pip the others to the post for the win. We all danced for joy before marching back into camp. We all had marching to do on a daily basis. On one occasion, everyone did what was expected: stand tall and march with pride. We were ordered to about-turn. On the smooth asphalt, our boot soles covered in metal studs never held up. We began turning by stopping with the left foot and sliding the right one in to be followed by beginning to turn, and all hell broke loose. So many cadets started slipping, which made them hit the next one, and down we were going. After a few seconds, there were at least one hundred cadets crawling over each other. The laughing and smiling soon dried up as the marching orderly screamed at us for being a bunch of girls and made us do more marching until we were hurting.

CHAPTER 13

THE MARKET DAYS WERE held on Wednesdays, and people would come from all around to buy or sell their cows, pigs, sheep, chickens, and rabbits. I enjoyed seeing all the clothed, capped farmers looking at the animals and the bartering of prices. As I was involved with my friend's farms, this also led me to be part of it during school holidays. So enjoyable to go and round up some calves, put them in a trailer, which was attached to a Land Rover or tractor, and haul them off for selling. As I hit my midteens, I also got into the two slaughter houses that operated in town. One was at the top of a narrow lane that was almost impossible to get a lorry down; the other was down next to a fuse-making factory. Animals were brought in, their heads put between some bars, then locked. A gun was at the ready and placed in the middle of its head. Bang, a six-inch spike would fly out and penetrate its brain, instantly dead then unceremoniously dragged backwards and hung up, ready to cut open. The cattle market farmers would also go off into town, have a beer with a ploughman's lunch—that was a big favourite—then get some fresh bread with a good chunk of cheese, pickled onions, and pickles with a slice of lettuce and tomato. That was a treat every now and then for families—go out into the countryside, find a pub, and have a ploughman's while sitting in the garden. It was a nice pastime enjoying the countryside and chatting. I think it's hard to find such a treat on offer these days. Pubs do so much hot food that the simple stuff got left behind. We also had once a year the agricultural show. Farmers would bring their prized animals to be shown and maybe win a prize. There were many other crafts and things to see. The winners would be able to show their prize animals at the Royal Bath and West show, which started back in 1777 in Bath. Edmund Rack, son of a labouring weaver, was dismayed at the poor standard of agricultural practice in the West Country. In 1780, the then affiliated society had a farm in Bath. That shut down after ten years, and for the next 196 years, they had the headquarters in various sites before finally getting a permanent site in 1974. The highlight in my young life about the show was when the Queen of England came through our town on the way back to London. She was riding in her Rolls-Royce towards the station and the royal train, flanked by police bikes and foot policemen everywhere. She came into sight with her wave and smiles. In a strange way, she looked a bit like my mother, or vice versa. The show was held on a Wednesday, and that was also deemed a day off for the school kids. September was a busy month because at the week's end, the carnival would be held on the Saturday evening. It was formed in 1929 by some workers from a local printing company. There was an early afternoon one for the young children, which covers a smaller route, then the big one would start around in the evening.

The floats that won that evening would be able to go to the Bridgewater. There you would see the best of carnivals that had been held all over Somerset. The local town band would be playing a good tune with the floats following behind, each passing one by one. I always felt proud when a couple of old girlfriends have sat in the Queen's chair on her float. As it passed, the competition runners-ups sat around her. I was in two carnivals with the cadets; one we marched, and the other we rode in the back of a three-ton army truck. Everyone that participates always enjoys themselves, and it is a fond memory for all. Some of the floats were tractors and trailers, and some were the company lorries that I rode to London in. As they passed, people would be clapping or throwing a penny at the truck with funny faces with holes in the mouth, and each penny that landed would go to a charity. The evening was always enjoyable, as before the procession and after, there was the fair. It would roll into town and be ready to open on the Tuesday evening. Some people went down there, but with the day off Wednesday, for me, with little money, that was the right time to enjoy it. Everyone would have a good time going. It was held where the market took place, just at the back of town. As the years of age grew on me, there were some good times to be had that week. I could enjoy more because I had my earnings from work, which was a lot more than when I first started going. To get into the fair the back way, you would walk over the Bailey Bridge, which crossed the river (there is a new footbridge now, which is named after our most famous son who, in 2009, became the Formula 1 world racing champion). This also gave the cars access to parking places then a short walk into town. All the bright lights on the attractions. The smell of toffee apples. Seeing candy floss getting wrapped around a stick, biting into it and getting a sticky face. These smells have been long gone from my nose. The music coming from the dodgem cars. Walk over to a darts section, which had different music;

it would sound strange until one type overtook the other. I enjoyed seeing the motorbikes going round and round with thoughts of *I will never try that*. There was another ride that spun so fast, the floor would go down sticking you to the wall. We would try to lean into the middle, but the force was too great. Townspeople and many people from the outlying villages would all be strolling hand in hand, parents being dragged from ride to ride by their kids. It was, for so many, the highlight of the year.

I had begun to develop some good muscles from hard work and boxing nights at the youth club. It was getting close to leaving school for the working world. Many friendships had been formed and my virginity lost. We were in the park on the seat of a little covered rest area that had a wooden bench—an August night enjoyed by two teenage persons doing what everyone has done or were going to do. Maybe I should have practiced with condoms before the main event. I was nervous and fumbling around, trying to get this baby-safe piece of rubber on me. Jane, she almost gave up until I got going again to fulfil our dreams. For all I thought it was going to be, it was all right. I had to accept, as she did, that we were inexperienced with the sex stuff, but one thing I did learn: I was enjoying passion and the idea that with the right words, I could get my way and enjoy a girl if she wanted sex. But I also understood that if the word no is uttered, you back off and wait for another day. At this time, I had "experienced" several girls, kissing and cuddling, but never had sex with them. Masturbation was going to be a thing of the past; my life would begin to run fast, and they would be left behind, but never forgotten. This little rest area was just across from the bandstand. On a summer's afternoon, people would come with a picnic and blankets or deck chairs to listen to the town band play some favourite tunes. Across the park, there was the bowling club, which has been playing there since 1915; older people would be chatting while polishing their wooden balls ready for their turn. Surrounded by a three-foot, well-trimmed hedge, these gentle folks would roll their balanced balls toward a small white ball with the object of getting the closest. Everyone had to be wearing white uniforms, and not a beer was to be seen, but I would suspect a little tipple of brandy was in someone's bowling bag. Some younger people would be there learning how to bowl along the rink, as it is called. Across from that was the hospital where I was born. In the same room, my son would be born in it too. Just up the road was another hospital, but this was for the elderly and the dying; formerly a monastery and was built in 685AD. It is the earliest evidence of Saxon occupation in the town. One of the first English kings, Eadred (son of Edward the Elder), died here in November 955. My town has a very dated history, and in April 2010, the largest find of Roman coins was discovered—52,500 were found and dated from the third century; some are on display at the British museum.

Time has marched on, and friends are bountiful. Hardly a street that I would go on was there not a friend or friends. In later days, bar hopping was the thing; but at this time, house hopping was in—so many lovely mums and dads that liked me for my outgoing character. I was hardly ever at home, as there was no need to be there because nothing was really on offer. By then, we had a colour TV, which needed money to be put in a slot at the back, and four hours of watching would follow. A sixpence every four hours was a lot when little money was coming in. We also had a nice neighbour who was a painter and was always in his white working overalls. He loved to cut between the houses to the left of us, on through the garage area and into his favourite pub, where he would enjoy a pint of scrumpy (very strong cider and cheaper than beer). On many occasions, he would come home drunk, and I would watch him stagger to the door. The small walkway between the old people's flats and a garden wall had a small step. About ten feet away a gate, which, to help him, he would paint them white so he could see each hurdle in the dark. Many times he missed the step and would crash into the corner of the old people's building, resulting in smashing his face and being scabbed up for a week or two. One Saturday night, after drinking for hours, he came home. He went through his front door and tried to get up the stairs to bed. He managed several, only getting about halfway when he fell. Back in those days, floor trim was not rounded at the corner. He hit it. His wife came beating on our door for help. I ran into the house while Mother called for an ambulance. Albert and I did our best to move him; another neighbour came to our aid. We got him into a chair. There was a hole in his head, which was just above his left eye. It was seeping thick blood, which stopped after a couple of minutes. His wife was doing her best to stay calm. Her hands were shaking as she cleaned the wound. Mrs. Hardy, a neat lady with greying hair, kept saying he would be all right while I was holding his hand. The bruising around the hole began to come out. He seemed to dwindle then recover only to dwindle again. It seemed like forever for the ambulance to arrive, and when it did, he was already dead. I watched this simple, nice, caring man die before my very eyes. His body had stopped shaking. It had become lifeless, which started me and everyone else crying. The ambulance left with him after a doctor pronounced him dead. We stayed to console his lovely wife. Mother was very caring at that point by putting the kettle on for a cup of tea—a night where memories were recalled. The older people talked about the good and bad side of the man.

From my little room, I could see some houses to my left and the old people's bedsits next to them. On the other side of the road, those houses were owned. I would go over to the gardens and play with the children, and they would come over on our side. It was always a nervous time when us young ones came from the back of cars to cross a busy road. Hide-and-seek around the flats where I used to live was fun. Sometimes I would look up at the window where my rocket went in, rush past the shed where I took Albert's moped from and swapped a comic for a fondle. I enjoyed the smell of the coal bunkers that were on each level for each of the three blocks of flats. How strong were the men that delivered the sacks of coal? One hundredweight (112 lbs.) were carried from the lorry on their backs. Somehow push a door open and walk up two flights of stairs in every block. If each person wanted two bags, that would be eighteen bags to each block. Complete that and deliver more coal at the back of the houses. Walking about sixty feet at each house was extremely hard work. They did it six days a week all over town. But that's not just it. They would have to shovel the coal from the floor, fill the sacks until they weighed one hundredweight on a scale, then lift them onto the lorry. They stacked them two high with a slight tilt to the front board so they would not fall off. I recall the son of a local coal merchant at ten years old starting to learn the trade for his father's business. That's my idea of a workhorse, not like today.

CHAPTER 14

SEPTEMBER 1969, AND THAT was it; it was over. No more school, no more homework, no more cane, and only fifteen and three-quarters—what was I to do? I had been looking at the jobs available. There was one job that I fancied. It was close to home, so travelling would not be a problem. I went for an interview and was shown my workplace, which would be making folding doors. This was a large plastics factory, which I would pass going to and from the nature trail. It was also along the road from my favourite garden and youth club. I was introduced to several people as I was shown around. With everyone happy, I got the job. I went home with high hopes of a future that would be given me because I was going to be rich by my standards—a regular income that would allow me to have new clothes instead of so many hand-me-downs; independence was mine, and treating girls would be in my favour. I told Mother I got the job, and she uttered, "Don't forget you have to start paying rent now. I have been looking after you, and now you can look after me." What the hell. It was like a vulture had swooped down and taken any happiness I may be entitled to. All too often, it was take, take, and hardly any giving. It was all so confusing when my friends had such caring, loving mothers. Mine was cold and only interested in having something others never had, like a colour TV, phone, twin-tub washer, and freezer. Then I would be expected to foot the bill! One classic I remember: she was gossiping over the back fence with the neighbour, and when she came in, she forgot to say something. She rang her on the other side of a brick wall and talked with the sound like the queen's voice for twenty-five bloody minutes. When the bill came in, it was "You will have to help pay for this." Unbelievable, I exclaimed, as I gave more money to help!

I started on the Monday. I would be fixing the latch system into simple plastic doors. They had stripes of hard wood with a plastic lug on top. Each piece would be slotted into welded sections of two-sided plastic. Each folding door had a metal piece on either end for stability. One end would be attached to a wall. With an overhead rail suspending the door, that would allow the door to fold. I was fitting the locking latches before they were boxed. I also ventured up some stairs, which led into a much larger workplace to accommodate the large folding doors that were being constructed with steel rod frames; these doors would be used in buildings with large rooms that needed dividers. I settled in. Several times, Brian, who was instructed to show me how to assemble the latch system, came over to help. He was elegant in a way with a small beard that pointed under his chin and always wore a tie. I never really noticed, but he would get rather close to me when showing how to do it. I was unsuspecting, as I needed to lean in to see what was what. My first wage of three pounds ten shillings and five pennies was given to me in hard cash. I had never had so much money of my own in my hands. I ran home, so proud of this brown envelope with its little rattle of cash. I went into the house and proudly showed my reward for forty hours of work. My radiating smile soon vanished when a new monster showed its colours and roared, "Great, now give me half," while sitting in the chair of wisdom. Her hair was very reminiscent of the queen's. Her hand opened and said, "Come on, give me some," and so she had half. This was to go on for about a year or so before I learned more about life and became strong and able enough to defy her expectations.

Just around the corner from our house was a pub, and I fancied going in for a beer. I wanted to test the water. I went through the "off license" door. This had a small window, which would be slid to one side. Someone would stick their head out and ask what you want. Back in those days, it was the owner of the pub that worked, and his time off would be normally covered by his wife. I asked for a half bottle of stout. The owner looked at me and said, "Bugger off, you cheeky young sod, and come back when you are old enough." He was a big enough man to make me scurry out into the night and plot another way of getting a beer.

At the other end of the workshop, several ladies were doing jobs that would lead to me playing my part in the making of the product. As I was the young new man on the job, if I walked into that area, the ladies would taunt me and grab my backside. I enjoyed the banter, and for fun, I would play up to them. There was one, a mature married woman who was rather striking. Jackie was a good-figured lady with a lovely smile; I would make a beeline for her and several times squeezed her butt when she squeezed mine. I was always hoping it would lead to something more. She had captured my imagination and would be the oldest lady I had experienced. She was also one of the first-aid ladies, and it wasn't long before she was holding my hand because I was using a very sharp knife cutting some fabric. The knife rode over the straight edge my left hand was holding. It went up the side of my index finger, across my thumb nail, and stopped about one inch and passed it. Oh the panic as blood was pouring from my finger and thumb. The new blade almost severed the whole side of skin, exposing the bone, and I was in shock mode. Cloths were quickly wrapped around my finger. I was led to the first-aid post. An ambulance was beckoned, and while waiting, my dream lady was holding my hand. With her standing in front of me, I wanted to wrap my legs around her waist and draw her in. As she was bent over and looking across her eyebrows at me, I was melting. Those sexy brown eyes, her cheekbone, those lips all beckoned me to seduce them. The ambulance arrived, and my dream came to an end, or did it? I had eight stitches, and when I returned to work the next day, all the ladies would be fussing as to my welfare. As a thank-you, I wanted to kiss the lady that helped me. As my lips were heading for her cheek, she turned, and I was on hers, a split second that sent my pulse racing, and the wanton desire of a sexual encounter raced around within me. She was startled and moved her lips quickly. There was a look in her eyes. Not anger. Not pleasure. More like "Take it easy, young man."

In order to get around the large spread-out factory, there were these small motorized tandem carts called listers. With an engine at the front and a seat, you would steer by turning the whole front end, which pivoted on one wheel. Your load would be on the back bed, and these little three-cylinder diesel engines would fly you around the workplaces. It was not long before I would be riding one of them. I would go and get more latches from the stores. As time passed, I was asked if I would like to work in the large workshop making the steel framed doors, which I was happy to take because another challenge was on offer. It was here that Robert would show me the ropes. As the work was clean, he was another that dressed in shirt and tie. His bushy eyebrows stood out on this man that liked yellow and pink colours. This door making was much more complicated, as some would be thirty or forty feet long. We would have lunch in the canteen and then back to the workplace for more instruction. A good working relationship was being formed with this elder man. He was another mentor in my life, and I would always look up to these people. The time of year I started meant no holiday money would come my way. For the summer break, I was able to stay on and work with some maintenance men. We would be cleaning parts of the calendars; these were the machines that made the plastic from pellets into rolls. We had one part that was lifted out by an overhead crane. It was being lowered into a large plastic tube of cleaning fluid when it suddenly slipped and came crashing down into the tub. It all happened so fast. The splash sent the cleaning fluid straight at me and into my eyes, and the shock was terrifying, as my mouth got some too. I was beginning to vomit. I was so scared and trying to scream. A quick-thinking mechanic grabbed the fire hose, stuck me next to a roof support, and doused me with water until the ambulance arrived. I was rushed to the hospital. My eyes were washed and washed and, with no apparent damage, released and sent home in a taxi. My mother showed some concern about my welfare, and after eating a little, I went to rest. I was on my bed playing soft music and fell asleep. Several hours later, I awoke. My eyelids would not open. They were stuck by the natural puss that our antibodies produce, and I was so scared. I had all these crazy thoughts going on in my head about being blind: I would never see my friends. Never work again. Never be able to build and create. All these wild thoughts flashed through me as I was going back to the hospital. I had warm water on soft pads stroked by this cute nurse. What a pretty sight to see after she had been touching my face and bathing my eyes. After a short while, I finally was able to see the world again. I was scared to go to sleep again and stayed up for over a day until I was exhausted and had to sleep. I finally got back to work when the holidays were over and production had started again.

Being a large factory, it had a social club, and you could save some of your wages for Christmastime. From what was left of my wages, I saved two shillings a week, which when drawn would give enough at year's end for some presents. I never got to save when I first started but was determined as the New Year started. In the summer of 1970, there was an outing arranged for members to go to London. We were to see a football game at Stamford Bridge, home of Chelsea Football Club. Others went just to go shopping, and a full coach was arranged for the day. We travelled the roads I had travelled as a young boy heading towards the Capital of England. We would pass Stonehenge, which is a prehistoric monument in the hills of Wiltshire. It is in the middle of the most dense complex of Neolithic and Bronze Age monuments in England. Archaeologists suggest this was built anywhere from 3000 BC to 2000 BC. Its early days show it was a burial place with several hundred burial mounds. It is said to have had several construction stages that spanned at least 1,500 years and could have been as long as 6,500 years. It has a lone stone adjacent to the road called the Friar's Heel, which leans toward the circle of stones. There is a folk tale about the devil buying the stones from a woman in Ireland, wrapped them up, and brought them to Salisbury Plain. One of the stones fell into the River Avon, and the rest were carried to the plain. The devil cried out, "No one ever will find out how these stones came here."

And the Friar replied, "That's what you think." The devil threw the stone, which struck him on the heel and landed in the ground where it stands today. We got to London and were dropped off outside the houses of parliament that would be the meeting place for the trip home. I went with several guys, including Robert, down onto the London underground, which was exciting because I had seen the signs but never got to ride on it. We travelled to Chelsea on this noisy, clattering train where no one talked but looked at each other. You were lucky to sit down, so holding an overhead rail was your only stability. We got closer to our destination. Noisier men were joining us as you were forced to squeeze closer to the next person. Robert was right behind me, pressing his thigh into my buttocks. I was trapped; I had nowhere to go, and as the train rocked from side to side, I had no choice but to let it pass.

When we finally got to the stadium, there were police everywhere controlling the crowd. I had never seen anything like it. I had heard of yobbos but never seen masses of them close up. What a bunch of badass people they were, spitting and shouting while half drunk and making obscene gestures, and I was in the thick of it. After we went through the turnstiles and found our place, it was amazing to see forty or fifty thousand people hurtling abuse at one another. The footballers, referees, all got screamed at because of the passion for the game. I never really did like football and got fed up of standing in front of all the noise coming from behind me. I went for a hot dog and walked around the stadium simply amazed at the passion of the spectators but wanting to get the whole thing over and get out. When it was all over, we filed slowly out onto the streets, which were just like going in. Some fighting was going on as we hurried past and into the underground. Relief was in us all as the train pulled up and on. When the doors closed, I found myself in the same position as getting there. It was uncomfortable to say the least to have this man with his thigh stuck in my backside. I began to wonder if it was nice for him. As a young innocent man, the only thing that messed with my butt was the hands of a girl. I had no idea what was to come as we travelled under London. We went into Piccadilly Circus and got a bite to eat and a beer, which he brought. I naturally thought this was nice of him before looking at some clothes shops, when he said, "Do you like the jacket in the window?" I said yes, and he got it for me. I was gob smacked at such generosity from a somewhat stranger but workmate. We also went around Soho looking at the strip clubs and other clubs and, although tempted, never went in to sample the local delights.

It was getting time to get back to the coach; we got back on the tube train and headed for the houses of parliament. On arrival, he said it might be an idea to hit the lavatory before boarding, and I agreed. He led me to this underground car park where he knew a bathroom was. I thought nothing of it as he had been on several other trips. In we went. He waited until I had placed my shopping down and went to a stall. He joined me in the next one. I did my thing as he sort of hovered over me. As I washed my hands, he tried to kiss me, which sent everything in me into survival mode; and I lashed out, striking him square on the chin. He reeled back. I legged it up the ramp and into the others that had gathered for the home trip. Shaking, I kept my nerve and mouth shut as I saw him heading towards us. Before the bus had hardly stopped, I was in the door and made sure I stayed away from the man. My trip home was full of nasty thoughts and silence. I felt it was going to be an awkward Monday morning. That day I was dreading. After clocking in, he was there, and it was obvious he was going to make my life hard. I did what I was told until lunchtime. That is when I went down and sat with Brian, who always sat at his workstation for lunch. I started off with awkwardly trying to get my words out about what happened on the trip. He was listening and understood what I tried to explain while sitting on his workbench across from him. He started to show sympathy and understanding then, lo and behold, placed his hand on my inner thigh and began stroking it, saying, "Not to worry, everything will be fine." Bang, I stuck one right across the side of his face, spun around on my butt, and jumped down from his bench, calling him another dirty bastard. It was a very uncomfortable two days before handing in my notice and leaving.

I went home and explained things, and Mother said, "You'll have to get another job very quickly to pay your rent." As I retreated to my bedroom, I listened to those words while asking myself, *What was wrong with this woman, what was wrong with a little compassion from her?* Why do I get all this coldness, when my friends' parents were so warm? I wasn't a bad kid; I did things around the house like cutting the grass and planting plants while she instructed me. I never, no matter what, could please her.

The week went by, and I had gotten my final wage packet. It was hard walking past the windows that I worked in and seeing those lovely ladies waving and blowing kisses. With my wages and the money from the social club, I was going to be OK for a short period. I could still able to pay "the hand." I asked about joining the army, as I was doing well in the cadets, and Mother would have none of it. She sat in the chair of wisdom and blurted out a very loving and caring statement, "I have one son in the army, and I need the other to stay at home to help pay the bills." Wow, that was such a caring statement; I again hung my head and left for my bedroom. My brother Ralph was, in my mind, somewhat boring. I never understood his sense of humour. One day, he came home on leave and looked rather smart in his uniform. After a warm welcome from his mummy, he got changed and went for a beer with his friends. Several hours had passed when he came home. He almost fell through the door into the kitchen, where I was sitting at the table next to the pantry. He made some sort of quip, which was stupid, and I told him so. He was not happy with that and swung his fist towards my face. It landed on my left side and pushed my head against the wall of the pantry. I was hurting and tried to get back at him, but Mother was there to stop anything. I managed to get away and run out the door, feeling some pain. I was scared to go back in until his mummy came out and said he had gone to bed. Here're two aspirins to take and not to antagonize him while he is home. The next day, when he saw my black eye, there was a sarcastic remark as he went off to the pub again. I ducked and dived from his company until, after four days, it was time for him to go back to his barracks.

There was also a dumb thing I did when I came home drunk one night. I saw an envelope in our front-door letter box. It had the two weeks' rent from the house next door. It was not fully in, and I pulled it out, with the intention of showing these adult people how anyone could have walked up the garden path and took it. By the time I woke, the neighbour and Mother realized the envelope had gone and called the police. I was oblivious to what was happening downstairs until a copper came into my bedroom. There he was, our hometown favourite Bobby. He always stood tall at about six feet four, but we were vague in knowing each other. Within the next year or two, we got to know each other because if there was trouble, chances were I was around it or part of it. He had a simple philosophy: go around the back for a wallop or get taken in. Many young men of our town took the fore rather than the latter. I saw him several times come into a dance or bar, and with one or two heads in a headlock, they were taken out the back for a wakeup call. He got respect from just about all of us young studs and fighters wanting to make their mark. He asked me if I had removed the money because it looked like an inside job. I said I saw it, but so could anyone if they saw the neighbour put it there. He asked a few more questions and then left my room. I laid my head down. The biggest shock of all hit me: I had taken the money. As it was more than I had seen before, I hid it up a drain pipe between the garages across from us. What an idiot I felt—how bloody stupid was I. I dressed and went downstairs. There were Mother and Mrs. Hardy going on about it. They asked me, and I blurted out that from the seat three hundred feet away, someone may have seen it getting put in the door. All the time, *Where the hell, what pipe did I put it in?* I was so nervous, as I had never done anything like this. The next morning, I was going to work, and it was raining. I went through many drainpipes until I found this bundle of wet, soggy bank notes. I put them in my pocket, went to work, and laid them out in my locker. The day was done, and almost dry, I took them home. My chin dropped when I saw the police car parked outside of the house. I went in, and another officer asked why I would make a statement about the seat three hundred feet away. I said you could see a silhouette of someone maybe. He said there's no way. That was it; I confessed to taking the money. I said it could have been anyone, and they should be grateful it was me. I handed the money over. I felt so bad but so relieved, as I was told to never do something like that again. I was truly embarrassed and could not apologize enough. Albert had some quiet words with me later, explaining nothing like that is worth it, which, of course, he was right.

CHAPTER 15

I STARTED AT A garden supply centre, which was about half a mile away from home. It backed onto our old house. It was here that I was going to become a very strong person strength-wise and earn more money than my last place. I told Mother I would be earning the same amount of money and she would still get her rent. Truth was, I almost doubled my money. She had no idea, and that was a one up for me. I was sick of being put down only to be expected to pay up. Questions did arise because of the amount of clothes I was buying plus the amount of beer time I was enjoying. I would look at her and say, "Mind your own business," and walk away. My respect was changing because I was learning about life. When other school friends were not charged anything for the first month of earning, why was I so different? I realized what I had for a mother. I was paying up so she could say to the neighbours, "I have something else new." I also had a small investment policy. With a steady input, I would, by the time it matured over five years, have some money for a deposit on my own home. I was earning more money, so I put a little more into the policy. As I was paid cash, this would be handed over with my weekly rent to Mother. When the insurance guy came each and every Friday, chances were I was in a pub and never paid attention to the payments. One day I asked for my card, which aroused her desire to attempt to fob me off. I again asked and after being told it was in the sideboard drawer, I began shuffling everything around, trying to find it. When I finally got it, there was something amiss. I asked why a couple of payments were missing, and the reply was short, sharp, and to the point. "I needed extra money to pay for something."

I asked, "What?"

And the reply came back. "It was a surprise gift for a neighbour."

"A gift for the neighbour!" I exclaimed.

"Yes, I helped pay a bill for her." I understood her reasoning, and nice people deserve a break, but if my money is being used, I should be informed. I was getting to the point where trust was not something that stood out from this woman. This was a take, take person, with very little anything else. I began to look at myself as "the paymaster." I was expected to carry on as if nothing was a problem. When another request came in, simply put more money into the hands of this not-very-nice user.

At my new workplace, we would have ten tons of cleaned soil delivered and tipped in a heap outside the factory. With a tractor, bucket after bucket would come through a hole in the wall. Inside, bags of fertilizer and sand would be emptied on top of three buckets until there was a heap of about six tons. We would then roll a small belt mixer into place at the base of it. This blender was different than a home one. It had a belt with small rubber lumps on it, set at a speed that mixed the material as we shovelled the heap on. As it mixed the stuff up, another held a bag that would weigh one hundredweight when complete. This bulky weight would have a metal tie wrapped around the neck and be placed on a pallet, which would, with twenty bags, weigh one ton and ready for transporting to garden centres. With the heap dwindling, we would continue this all day, or until the outside heap was gone—a three-man job; and a lot of jokes were shared. If one was not in that day, then the two of us would continue the process. We made four different mixes. If we ran out and a special order came in, a different code would be put on and shipped out, which was yet another lesson in deception. After six months, I was so lean and strong. I would lift one of the sacks above my head with little ease. I was also spending a lot more time in the town pub. My strength was perfect for knocking someone down if they asked for it. Some guys just didn't get the message I was sending; they pushed and pushed me verbally, and I would land one. It was hard to do if you knew the guy; I never wanted to hurt a friend. If I did knock them down, the next time we met, they would say sorry for being an asshole, which I would accept and have a beer.

There was a time that weekend work was required to keep up with demand, and that's when we started getting orders from some friends. One workmate had an idea about selling stuff for pocket money. I wasn't too keen on the idea, and it would only be a little bit of stuff would be sold. We started taking orders from our friends and, with enough sales, loaded the trailer attached to the tractor, and off they would go and sell our wares. I stayed back at the workplace continuing to load lorries, ready for Monday distribution. We always worried if the boss would come in to see how the Sunday work was going. He never did, and when the others came back, we would continue to complete the day's task. When the day was done, the money would get split over the road in the pub while enjoying a beer or two.

There was an occasion when I was putting the buckets of soil through the hole in the wall with the tractor. One workmate kept throwing little lumps of soil at me. There was no cab, and I was getting rather fed up with it. Citing, "I will ram the tractor at you," he continued to taunt me. That just made me more and more angry until I levelled the bucket to waist height and warned him. I shouted that I would carry out my threat, but he just continued to throw the lumps at me. That was it; my head blew, and I swung the tractor at him. I turned the tractor hard and fast, resulting with the tractor on three wheels while hammering forward to the left. I was sliding a little out of the seat, and all I saw was my mate in front of me. He dived to one side, and I smashed into the wall, still screaming blue murder at him. He then realized that I was not joking and, with an ashen face, started screaming at me that I could have killed him.

I retorted, "I told you what I would do," as it began to sink into me. If he never dived to one side, I would have cut him in two. We argued about the situation as one of the older workers was approaching. With stern words, he told us both to calm down or we would be fired. That was enough to calm us young men down. With no other word said, we went back to doing what we should do.

I hit seventeen and was able to go for my driving license; I had a good idea about driving because Mr. Smith taught me at a young age how to drive. We would go out to a farm to see his farmer friend. While sitting on his lap, I would be able to steer his car around the field while he controlled the speed. After two or three trial runs, I was allowed to drive on my own, but he would have his hand on the brake just in case. It was a flat field with some thistles growing and no cattle around at the time. All the farms around the area had cattle. I had done some milking at various times if I was out on the land with a friend. My first time was next to Uncle Gary's place. I was sitting on the three-legged stool with a bucket under the cow. After cleaning the udders, I started pulling down and squeezing, which was the correct motion to get the milk to come out. It took a little practice to get the aim right and pulling right, but once I got going, it was easy. It was never pleasant to be sitting on the stool and see the tail go up, as it meant one thing. I would probably be getting splashes of cow poo hitting me as I was milking. Most days spent on the farm would lead to me getting the smell of it in my clothes. I never really noticed until I got home. That would lead to complaints from Mother, and it was just another scenario for her to moan. Just up the road from that farm was another, which was owned by a family related to ours. It was where I would, with others, go out with the horse and cart along a narrow road that led to the start of our playground until we came to the fields they owned. I loved doing the harvest and bringing the bales of hay back. Loading them onto a conveyor belt that went into a barn was hard work. But in those days, everything that was done on the farm was hard work. I also learnt to drive the small tractors that were about in those days. Everything was leading to bigger and better things.

We had to have driving lessons by a proper driving-school instructor. Mine was a good man who would be with me while driving around the hometown. As we got better, the further out into the countryside we went. His car had dual pedals, which allowed him to control speeds by using his brake pedal. Should someone else learning to drive get into a panic or going too fast, he just took over. My first attempt for my license I failed because I never used the rear view mirror enough. I was livid, which scared the old boy who had to accompany me. I drove back from the test so fast, shouting down the man that failed me. I was ready to fight anyone that got in my way. It was bad of me because the old man that travelled with me was close to having a heart attack. Poor old bugger had his cigarette in his mouth and, with both hands, furiously indicating at me to slow down, but I didn't. When we finally got back to the factory, he got out, looked at me, and said, "Young man, I will never ride with you again because you're as mad as a March hare." I simply smiled and apologized for my behaviour. After a couple more lessons and some wise words from my instructor, "See to be seen," a simple statement that I still carry now. I always use my lights if it's dark clouds and always indicate even if no one is following. My way of thinking is, Why not? With that mind-set, I never fail not to signal, which allows others to know what my intentions are. It wasn't long before I was back and passed. This opened a whole new world for me, including a taxi driver for Mother. Many times as I pulled up at home in any car, which was mine or a work van, the chair of wisdom would be vacant with Mother wanting me to take her to the shop or "run me over to your auntie." Whatever it was, I was expected to do it.

The neighbours never had a phone. People and even families would come into the house. They would talk to whomever. That would ruin any film or show I might be watching. It also gave Mother the opportunity to discover anything that was going on in someone's life. Next thing, the hand would be out waiting for payment. Many times she got the expected costs wrong and would ask me for more money to help pay the bill. Many times I did give more just to get some peace. Another neighbour's daughter would come over. We would sit in my room playing music. We would also do the same at hers. On several of occasions, when Mother and Albert had sat down to watch TV, we knew we were not going to hear anything from them 90% of the time. With my bedroom door very slightly open, I would turn the music down and enjoy a sexual encounter. If the living room door opened; it was our alarm bell. It wasn't every time she came over we would get at it, but we both loved living in such a dangerous way. It was fun being against the odds of "will we, won't we" get caught. It was less fun at her home because her parents went out a lot more than mine, and we were free for an hour at least to enjoy the fruits of growing up.

Being my workplace was across from the school. There were always some pretty mums about, and I enjoyed looking at some of them in the morning and afternoons. One or two caught my eye, but in all fairness, they were another man's woman, and there were plenty of single ones around. Temptation was there for this hungry stud. I was really enjoying sex with the young ladies, but I yearned for someone older. My workplace backed onto my old house, and it was here that, on a few occasions, I would lower myself into our old backyard and sneak into the derelict house that was once a home of mine, when they finally decided to demolish it to make way for the old people's home. I watched with a sad face; seeing the first part of my personal history disappearing almost brought me to tears. Everything was demolished. The land where our house and the shops stood, an old people's home was to be built. My days of sneaking in the backyard of our old house were over. The memories would come flooding back as I dropped down the wall that enveloped the backyard then walk under that clothesline and into the house. Seeing the kitchen and rooms bare but remembering lived situations was strange but comforting. Going back so many years and looking at my history was intriguing. Sometimes a workmate would join me in our lunch break, and I could explain the house's history.

The company was outgrowing the workplace and decided to move out and down into an old car auction site. This was a much bigger place, and we would earn some good overtime. We erected a new storage rack system, and we were able to make much more material with a new mixing and bagging system. I enjoyed working at the new site, but other things to do were at the back of my mind. The good wages were paying for me to enjoy nights out in town, a place that you were proud of; and many a time, some troublemakers would roll into town. They would start something going, but the problem was soon sorted. A good night, there may be a hundred young men enjoying a beer in all the pubs. When the word went around, they never stood a chance. So many pubs downtown were almost on top of each other. If someone from another pub came in and said there was going to be a problem, the young lions were going into battle to stand up for our town and mess with anyone who thought different. We would cross the road into the trouble spot. You could smell trouble; the atmosphere could be cut like a knife. Suddenly, a push was followed by punch. Soon you were in it after weighing up your chosen match.

CHAPTER 16

I WAS WITH THE company for less than a year. My friend David informed me of something different. He knew of an opening as a lorry night loader. I went for the job in a quarry. This was going to be next to the quarry I went to with my uncle Gary. The two were separated by a small stream that ran the entire length of them. We were to be working nights, loading lorries with asphalt, ready for the next day's delivery. Back then, there were no heated silos that would hold several hundred tons. They would keep it warm, ready for loading and delivery, which was done by the driver. That meant the nightshift work we did would become a thing of the past. As I had a driver's license and a small car (Mother's taxi), I would be able to take the job. I knew how things worked from all the time spent with my uncle Gary; I just had to make things happen. We also had articulated lorries. I was able to back them up because of all that I had watched when my neighbour did it. I so enjoyed working six nights a week, and money was being saved because I was out of the pubs. We would start at 7:00 p.m. and work until 11:00 p.m. then take our break and continue until every lorry was loaded, ticketed, and sheeted down, ready for the driver to arrive in the early hours. Lorries going the furthest would be loaded first, and the closest last. Many times there was little to do. We would almost load every lorry but leave six or so for when we woke. The idea being when the morning shift foreman arrived, we would still be working; that was a good thing. After eating, we would pull chairs together and, with a blanket, settle down for a few hours' sleep. There was a problem that arose with this setup. The mixer man would be in his mixing house; this is a room with all the controls to mix hot bitumen with the rock, creating the asphalt. It appeared on many occasions that when he finally decided to wake us, he was drunk. Somewhere in the building, where the silos of crushed rock and hot tar were housed, he hid a barrel or bottles of scrumpy. We spent many hours looking, but, alas, he hid it well, and we never did find anything. We had to get the lorry underneath, and he would open the hatch, allowing the material to come out. As the material filled, we would back the lorry up until the correct tonnage was on board then drive to the scale house for weighing. If the batcher man had been drinking, he would open the batcher door before we got a lorry underneath it, and almost two tons would drop on the floor. We would have to get a loader to move it before another batch could be dropped. This messed the system up. One of the crew would have to grab the button to stop him. The two quarries merged, and all operations went over to the larger side. Our asphalt plant was closed down. Major money had been invested. Heated bins had been installed, and the night loading shift ended. It was here that the big excavator I saw broke down in the town operated. Most excavators draw the bucket towards the operator filling the bucket with material. This machine was known as a face loader. Proper operation meant the bucket would go away from you when filling it. The back would open, allowing the rock to fall into the dump trucks, which would then head for the crusher.

My first place of work after the transfer was in the crusher area. The noise was deafening, as forty tons of rock smashed down into the crusher system. Big rocks would pour from the dumper. The rocks were contained by massive chains dangling from huge girders. A large steel conveyor belt would slowly pull the rock into the crusher. The back side of it solid as the front moved to and fro, allowing the rock to fall, crushing it again and again. The rock would go into a smaller crushing system. When down to a specific size, the rock was separated by screening. At times, a large rock would get into the perfect spot and would not budge. A wedge would be lowered on a rope to get the smallest of bites, which would allow it to drop a half inch, which would be enough to complete the crushing. Sometimes nothing would work. Then the winch would lower a large hook, and with luck, it would catch a corner, enough to get things moving again. I spent three weeks doing the night crushing before being offered the job of driving the big dumpers. I jumped at it, anything to get away from the dust and noise. One night, I had a load on board. As I drove along the haul route, a drop of sixty feet to my right, I was tired, and my eyes closed for a second or two, and that was enough. I started to mount the old rock face on my left, and the truck was tilting. I realized what was happening and hit the brakes. I stopped as the truck was at its most critical point before tipping and going over the edge with what would have meant certain death. I was unable to sit as normal and slid to the right. I was holding the steering wheel with the hand brake applied. If it was not an air brake, then that task would have been impossible. Help came, and with lights, I could see my position. I was as scared as any young man could be. The large face loader came trundling over and put its heavy bucket and boom on the left side. This was very comforting to a man who thought his time in the world was over. I managed to get into a position that allowed me to engage reverse and release the brake. I had my foot hard on the foot brake. Trembling nerves from my toes were moving my knee up and down at a frantic pace. The dumper was automatic; as I released a little brake pressure, I edged back until I was upright. I explained to the foreman what happened and, after a quick rest, was back at it and very wide awake.

The face loader operator decided he would give up his job. My chance arrived. I got in the seat of my dream machine. I took to it like a duck takes to water. It was so easy to glide the bucket across the floor and scoop a bucketful ready to load the trucks. When the blasted rock had run out, we would move the machine away from the face; the blasting crew would take over. They would lower down the charges on the charge cords, pour ammonia in with diesel, and fill the rest up with sand. When every hole was complete, set everything into a charger and boom, the rock face would lift a little then blow outwards; afterwards, a large loader would come and clean the floor, allowing the face loader to get into its new working position. After spending a long night at a wild party and getting home late in the morning, I had little sleep before beginning my first night shift of the week. I did not want to work all night, so I broke one of the rules. As we loaded the rock, if we came across a large boulder, it was to be placed to one side, and it would be "plaster" blasted. When many were placed together, the blasting crew would place small explosives called plaster pads on them. When linked together by cables, they would blast them. That made the rocks small enough to go the crusher without causing major blockage problems. This night, I found one that would not go through my bucket, which "if you stood in the bucket, your fingers would not touch the sides or top." I got it into the dumper and hit my horn, which signalled the driver he was loaded and able to go. He left, and the next one backed up. I loaded it and sent him on his way. The third one got loaded, which by then, the first should have been back. It never came, so I shut down my machine, got into the dumper, and rode up to the crusher area. We went into the canteen for a drink. I was so certain that I would be sleeping shortly because we were not allowed to plaster blast at night. Should we, the people of the local village would be disturbed. I decided I would go see the problem I had caused. Over to the crushing house I went and entered through the door. As I walked under the hopper canopy, all hell broke loose. The night foreman plaster blasted the rock, which sent pieces flying through the roof of the building and into the sides. Those that never penetrated fell down on and around me. With ringing ears and dust in the air, I made it back to the door and knew what my fate would be. The night foreman told us to get back at it as soon as we had finished our night time lunch. While we were eating, a little blue light showed up. An irate copper wanting to know what happened was there. We went back to our job and completed the shift before this weary man could go home to bed. The following day, there ensued an investigation from the quarry manager, and its conclusion was someone would get fired. They chose the night foreman, as he sanctioned the blast. The six nights a week were good for saving money, and every week, someone would go into town to get a fish-and-chip treat or chicken omelettes from the Chinese takeaway downtown. After three months, the company decided to cut out the Friday night shift, and I decided that working only five nights wouldn't cut it for me. I was hot headed about the situation and after words with the new foreman, I left there and then. With nowhere to go at the present time, I had a feeling it might be difficult finding a new job.

I had savings and knew I could sustain an amount of time off, but that's not such a good idea when you want to move on. I would still go out having a beer and chasing the girls. I had made a wonderful friend Alan. At six feet tall, he was a happy-go-lucky person, like us all, with long straight hair down to his shoulders. Many of us were growing moustaches and beards, but he stayed clean shaven. He was becoming a good DJ and created great evenings for dancing with the ladies. He, in September 1971, was killed in a motorbike accident. His death affected so many. Many tears rolled down our cheeks. I was extremely proud to carry his coffin. Sadly about six months later, the same young men carried another coffin with Alex inside. We recovered slowly and continued to pursue fun and beer. One night, there was no girl; there was an old lady! I came home drunk, and our house was the second from the road in an attached row of four. I was saying to myself, as I had said before, second hole in the hedge. This time I fell in the third. I went up the path to the front door, and of course, my key would not work. I was making some noise by complaining I can't get in, when the door opened. I staggered in, going straight upstairs, and turned right as I would in my own home. The next morning, I woke and had no idea where I was. This double bed and its furniture had never been seen by me before. I still had my clothes on and had slept on top of the bed, but I was so confused. I jumped to the window to get bearings as to where I was in the town. I looked out and could see the same view I had from my own room. As I gathered my thoughts, the door opened, and this old age pensioner called Mrs. Hardy stood there with a cup of tea. My jaw dropped, with my brain saying, *Oh no, I didn't, did I?* It soon snapped into gear as I realized I still had my clothes on. I began to apologize for my mistake, and as normal, her warm smile assured me there was no problem. We went downstairs to finish the cup of tea while laughing about my outrageous mistake. Just the other side of the concrete block wall, I knew what would be waiting and what was going to be said. I gave a hug and left her there as I stepped out of the wrong door and into the bright sunlight, stepping over a small plant and arriving at the side door of the correct dwelling. I tried hard not to grin as I walked into the house, and same as ever, Mother was sitting in the chair of wisdom, uttering that sentence, "And where have you been, you dirty little stop-out?"

As straight-faced as I could be, I simply said, "I slept in Mrs. Hardy's bed."

She went into shock, exclaiming, "What, what," as I continued to the door that led to the stairs. It was seconds, and she was up and heading out to discover the facts. I went to my room, played some music, and contemplated how I would spin this one to my mates.

CHAPTER 17

I LOOKED THROUGH THE job section of the local paper for several weeks with nothing really taking my fancy; I was also looking at the bank balance, which was dwindling slowly. I had an offer for my car, so I sold it because I was sure I would get a job in town. Beer money was needed, so was rent money for Mother. My time with the army cadets had reduced to nothing because of my night work. I enquired about becoming an adult instructor—alas, no, due to having enough instructors on hand. I was saddened to walk away from something I really enjoyed. A couple of my friends went into the army. I had to stay at home: help pay the bills, go to the pubs, and chase all the girls, which didn't make it all bad. My mate Nicolas and I were lucky to be in a pub when the window cleaner came in. He was looking for a couple of guys, and we jumped at it. Nicolas was on break from college for his electrical education, and the money would help. We did some schools and shops over the next few weeks. The problem was the boss liked a beer. We did too, but work came first. One morning, we were doing pub windows, and a beer was offered. We had one, then did another pub, and another was served. We had more until several hours had passed, and the boss was drunk. We took him home, and as he was trying to thank us, his false teeth flew out. He found them while we watched with big grins and sniggers. He was lying on the floor, trying to put the top set where the bottom set should be. It never worked, and he got very agitated and threw them on his roaring fire. We were laughing as they melted, and he began to fall asleep. It was several weeks before a new set were back in place.

The weeks passed when something caught my eye. A job was being offered at a timber mill just outside of town. I knew how to run a forklift and was willing to work overtime and occasionally weekends. I called the next day, and within minutes, I was on the bus making my way to the mill.

They had an old mill and a new one just built. The company was expanding, and new labour was needed. The boss had four sons that worked there, and I would work alongside three of them, as would other new employees. The fourth son would be working in the office and accounting. I got the job and was so excited. Monday morning, I was up and ready, waiting for the bus to arrive. After the six-mile ride, there was a short walk to the mill. I started assisting on one of the band saws. An experienced man would feed the saw, which had an air pressured wheel that kept the wood tight to the plate, which was set for a certain width. This was the 3rd part of the process. The whole tree would start on a carriage, which glided on rails. The eight-foot length would be cut by a twenty-seven-foot-long band saw. As it cut each slab of wood, it was transferred to the next saw. That saw cut it into a smaller-sized slab, which prepared it for our saw. As each slab was cut, it would be our job on the next cut to make it its final size. When the slab passed through our saw the first time, I would pull it toward me then feed it back to the operator for the next, and so on. When the last piece was cut from the slab, I would feed a chipping machine, which pulped the bark. After several weeks, I was on the fork truck and helping anywhere a pair of hands was needed. With my level head and ability to learn quickly, other tasks were being demanded of me, which was great because the day went so fast. I would be loading the trailers with metal-tied blocks of cut lengths and then locking them down with special chains. The tractor unit would drop an empty trailer, hitch the loaded one, and take it for delivery. One day, while I was doing several tasks, the operator on the first saw I worked on asked me to help him while his new helper went to the office. The end that should be clean cut had a jagged piece, which happens when the tree is felled and it tears the wood and bark. This should not be a problem as the operator hits his pedal, which removes the air-pressured wheel away, which keeps the wood straight on the block. He was distracted for a second, which meant the wheel was not detached from the wood. As it came to the end, the pressurized wheel pushed the jagged end inward, bringing the front end outward. The front corner of the remaining slab hit me plumb in the groin and sent me backwards into a wall. I was down on the floor holding my crown jewels and in pain. I got my wind back and made my way to the bathroom. I looked down and groped around then I felt this slight swelling.

I was to go home and rest, which I did; then the next morning, there was a much larger swelling. I called the doctor's office and was advised to get there. He looked me over, and I was sent for x-rays. They were studied, and I would need to be opened up in the groin area to see what damage was done. I went home and waited for a call to say when and where. Two days later, I went to a hospital in Bath. After settling in, a rather nice nurse turned up with water in a bowl and a razor. She explained what was to happen, and I was more than happy to let her get the job done. Later that day, I was knocked out and opened up. I came around in a room with three other guys who had problems similar to mine. Unfortunately, one of them was waiting to go in when the three of us were done. I came around, as did the other two after their surgery. It hurt like hell, and the worst thing you could do is cough or laugh. The fourth guy was a funny guy, who kept telling jokes. He had each of us at his mercy as he cracked one joke after the other. We tried not to laugh, but he was so funny. We finally went to sleep, and the next morning, it was his turn for the chopping block. Our pain was still there but had eased a little. When the other came around, the poor guy had three of us telling him jokes, which hurt him as much as it hurt us. After two days, Ralph, who had left the army, came to get me in his low car. I got into it with great discomfort and not looking forward to the ride home. I felt every bump, which had him grinning, and that really got up my nose. When I finally got home, like so many times, I went to my bedroom. The pain was so bad, the doctor was called, and I was heavily dosed. With several days of rest, my crown jewels had begun to lose the black-and-blue look, and the pain was easing. It felt so good to finally go out for a beer with my mates and get back to work. This, of course, was an insurance claim, which was handled by people that knew more than I did. When everything was settled, I was offered an amount, which was sponsored by Mother to accept. I thought it was worth more but accepted the offer. It was a small amount compared to the hurting. I was going to add to the insurance money I paid each week with my rent, which, unknown to me, was never going to happen.

It was a bother getting a bus or a lift because I could not work the overtime I wanted to. One day, I arrived, and the boss looked at me and said, "You don't look happy today. Something bothering you?" I replied with my reasons, and he said, "Give me about an hour." I said OK and went to work. The hour passed, and there he was, saying, "Come on with me," as his huge hand went across my shoulder. He was the strongest man I had ever met, yet he had such a caring disposition. We got into his XJ6 Jaguar, and he offered me a cigar and played one of my favourite singers, Jim Reeves. We headed into town, but it was only me that was clueless. We got parked, and he led me to the motorbike shop that behind it, one evening, I had sex with a horny girl. He led me in, looked at me, and simply said, "Pick a bike."

I was speechless and saying, "What, oh my," while he just smiled and said, "Go on." I picked a bike, which was a road scrambler, and a helmet. He wrote the cheque, and it would be mine in two days. We drove back to work, and I continued doing my job without a word to anyone what we had done. Two days later after work, I was the proud owner of a new bike, which I would pay for each week from my wages. I was in heaven—free from asking, begging for lifts, or waiting on buses. I was independent and able to do what I wanted to do in my spare time and also able to work when required. Many times I would be working with the sons in the evening or weekends, and I would be taken down to the house to eat with the family. I was treated like one of them, which only meant I would give them my all in return. The boss once met my mother, and he said, "I have four good sons, and yours is like a fifth." How awesome was that. Made me very proud, and for once, Mother was proud of me too.

I got back to work and carried on where I left off. I enjoyed so much about the people who owned the mill and the way I was respected. I did some work outside, which was unloading the felled trees that came on the pole carriers. Some trees stripped of their branches could be fifty or sixty feet long. We would cut them into eight-foot lengths, ready for the carriage saw. They purchased a new piece of equipment that was used on Swedish frozen lakes and was capable of picking up a whole tree. I was given it to operate, and it was such a good feeling to be trusted with such an expensive piece of equipment. On some weekends, one of the sons would take the small Bedford lorry, and I would take my machine. We would have our long motor saws and head for the back of a large country house. As you ran along the main road, on the left was the stoned wall that surrounded the house, which was set in about four hundred acres. The house was built in 1788 with stables and a formal garden for Thomas Jolliffe. The house was enlarged in 1855 and 1877, with the west front finally finishing everything in 1901. The formal way in was across from the mill, where a pair of lodges, gate piers, and gates welcome you as you ride down a long road leading to the house. One feature I liked was the 150-foot-high column, which was known as the Jolliffe column. It is a near replica of Eddystone Lighthouse with its glass dome that could be illuminated. The Eddystone is down in Cornwall, which overlooks one of the most important naval harbours in the Plymouth Sound. The first lighthouse there was made of wood, and construction started in 1696 and completed in 1698, during which the builder Henry Winstanley was taken prisoner by a French privateer, which caused King Louis XIV to order his release, saying, "France is at war with England, not with humanity." All in all, four lighthouses have been built there, but the first was lost in the great storm of 1703, which erased almost everything, including Winstanley, who was completing additions at the time. No trace was ever found of him or the other five men in the lighthouse. The fourth was lit in 1882 and is still in use today. It was converted in 1982 to be the first automated lighthouse, and a helipad for access sits on top for maintenance crews. The heavily wooded area had what we wanted, and that was oak trees. They would be felled and stripped of branches before we cut our measured sections. With my machine, which had a grab at the front of it, I would load one eight-foot section on the lorry, which was parked on the road. Like pirates in the night, we would take our prize away and ready it for the next journey. It would take a couple of minutes for us to get back to the mill. I would unload the lorry and place our prized section on the steel tracks that would draw it into the mill. Once it was on the carriage, locking teeth forced down by air would stabilize it. After the first cut, it would be turned, and another cut would be made. Adjudging that everything looked good, we would begin cutting pieces one-inch thick. Each cut piece would be placed on the lorry, and when finished, the tree looked almost like it was still intact. This was the first part of it being turned into polished boards for coffins. Craftsmen would allow it to dry before using their unique skills to create a personal casket.

I worked as hard as I could not only loading the trailers and locking the bundles of timber down but also driving the spare truck and moving the trailers when complete. I got to a point where I was burning out. I was losing myself and going out of control. I needed a break, time-out too gather my thoughts and reassess my life as to what I wanted. I searched deep inside me, wanting to leave and wanting to stay. Fond memories. The gallant effort. All the respect would likely be thrown away. How was I to leave such a lovely family? How was I to work, while my notice was being served? I had no answers immediately in my head and did my best to continue doing my jobs. The times when I would drive his Jag from the pub when he had a beer or two were a fond memory. The times I had gone and gotten the oak trees. How he surprised me with my bike. The way he spoke with pride about me. The whole way the mill operated, and I was a part of it. All these events churning around in me. How could I leave? After a week, my decision was made. I would state my case, and no matter what might be offered, I would go. I had an urge to do something different—go somewhere else and not be confined to one place. I said what I had to say with tears in my eyes and turned to leave everything and everyone I cared for. It felt like giving up all my friends in one hit. I got on my bike and rode away for the last time. Tears were still on my face when I arrived home, where Mother was sitting in her chair of wisdom. She questioned my actions and told me how stupid I was to give up such a good job. I tried to explain my meaning and what I wanted. Like everything else, it fell on deaf ears, which simply meant walk away from the heartless, never-understanding woman and live my own life.

CHAPTER 18

I WAS TO BE best man for my good friend Steven. We were in a pub having a pint. I was letting my mate enjoy his last moment of single time when suddenly, the bride's car went past us. It was heading towards the church, which was just up the road. We were out of there like bullets but too late to be in front of her. Her father looked in disgust at us. In we scampered heading towards the altar, where a disgruntled priest was waiting. It was my first time at doing something like that and fumbled through my pockets trying to find the ring. These entire goings-on in front of nicely dressed people were probably embarrassing. But we were too wrapped up trying to get things right, they were not an issue. Maybe that was the start of things to come because about nine months later, they split. I also had a girlfriend, and strange as it seems, we sort of swapped. She fancied him; he fancied her, and I did get a sense of it; so when it finally came to light, I simply said, if that's what she wants, that's what she gets. I was never going to fight over someone who wants to move on because it's not worth it—what does it achieve? Whatever you do, you are not going to get her back because you beat the man she fancies. That may have been true for me (if that's what she wants, that's what she gets). One evening, a Saturday night off from work, I was on my way down a street. This nice young lady approached me in a confused state. I, of course, did my best to understand her predicament and offer a shoulder. This led to her being in my arms. She just threw herself at me, and I responded by grabbing her. She led me to a small alleyway that ran from the chemist, down the back of the bakery, then behind the motorbike shop, we engaged ourselves. She was wearing a loose dress, which in seconds, it was up over her waist, and my jeans were being unbuckled at a fair rate of knots. Within a minute, we were having sex, her back pressed firmly into a wall and my strong legs pumping and pushing her. She was on a high as

I was; I never questioned anything. If this was the way that she really got turned on, then I was happy to assist. I hung on for several minutes before the pleasure trip was slowed down, two bodies panting and sweating and sounding so grateful for the moment. It felt like my finest moment was achieved with this lovely, good-kissing woman that had my best. We parted slowly with groans uttering from her lips. She pulled her dress back into place, and I buckled my belt. I uttered, "How are you?" as I was brushing any remnants of three-hundred-year-old wall off her back and cute buttocks.

She turned, put her arms around me, and presented me with a delicate kiss before saying, "That was great. Thank you. Now I must get home to my husband." What the heck. What was she like? I felt used and abused. What deceit. Gone was my very principle of not messing with another man's woman. I was the happiest man I could be, grateful for a wild moment then walking away with no hang-ups for either party. We began to part as our hands drew to the fingertips, then into the darkness of the alley she went. Out into the street, I began whistling until I got to a pub, sharing a beer with some mates who could not work out why I was grinning like a Cheshire cat. Like most Saturday nights, I would be going to the disco, and that meant more pleasure would probably be mine.

Out on the town, I bumped into Steve's ex-wife. We had a few beers and made arrangements for a date. We did a date and messed around a bit. Another date was fixed. I was going to her parents' home while they would be out working. An afternoon, we were watching the television, and she began turning me on. The passion took over. I had a wild one; any way you wanted it, I could have it. Some of the positions we got in were good enough for entries into the *Karma Sutra*. So much sex was on offer, and she was like a drug. All the time I was learning a trade. This was going to be fun getting other girls like this if they wanted it. Whether it was the age of no condoms, I don't know. So many times I was never asked if I had any. If they did, I never had any anyway. Everyone was on the pill, and that was all part of the then generation. Stuff like that was talked a little about, but that was it. I knew then that we were not made to be together forever, but I was going to enjoy our time, and I know she enjoyed hers. Sometimes, she would walk up to our house, and Mother would be sitting in the chair of wisdom. When she came into view, the cry would go out, "Your cart horse is coming." This was, I thought, unfair. She would be wearing the fashion-of-the-day platform shoes. With her stocky legs and tight jeans, she walked a little funny; but to me, she was sexy and to be enjoyed. She would come in and sit down. The dog hairs from Cindy would get all over her, then it was my job to stroke her butt, getting them off. Most times I did it as we were walking down the garden path as she watched. Her face would turn crimson because we were outside her home. That was another thing that got Mother's back up, and all I was doing was teasing her, but she would bite every time. When she came up to our house, chances were we would walk through the gate my old neighbour painted and enjoy a beer in the little back room of the pub he drank in, a small lounge with a big orange paper lamp hanging and chairs that was modern for that time. I did have a beer now and then in the bar with Albert. I would put money in the Wurlitzer record player and play some country music for us to enjoy. He never was a big drinker, and our visit would never be more than an hour. When I finally got him to get talking, he would speak fast but quietly; and with his London accent, it was hard to understand him. One sad day, I drove him to London when his brother died. He was sitting in the back of my car; his head half turned to the right and just stared at the world. I felt so sorry for him; he loved the man so much. A couple of times he had come down to stay with us. They would get talking, and everyone left them to get on with it. I was not hanging around, and Mother was sitting in the front, complaining I was going too fast. With that, I just put my foot down more and kept going. She was somewhat surprised that I could drive around London and find my destination. Simply, she was so ignorant of all the places I had been because she never listened and was not interested when I spoke of my travels with the neighbour.

I started another job, and this was working on the roads as an asphalter. It was the same company as Uncle Harry's, but as they had so many employees, chances were I would never see him. Slang word for everyone involved is a "wanker." If one mistake is made, then you were never forgotten. Another word for an asphalt guy was "skin," and that's how it was. You were a good skin or a wanker. Those were the most common words known for someone on the job. We would get fifteen tons of the black stuff turn up around seven in the morning, which would be tipped up; tarpaulins would be pulled over the top to try and retain some heat. Your tools were a shovel and a wheelbarrow. Load it up and push it maybe three hundred feet to empty it then walk back and fill it up again. This operation was done after you had done the same with the rock material that shaped the footpath you were covering. When the fifteen-ton had disappeared, a bite of lunch would be had, and another fifteen-ton would turn up. Again the same thing would be done until the entire path was covered, then another part would be started on. The housing estates we worked on would have winding footpaths allowing access to the back of the house; maybe a small play area would be situated in the middle of one hundred houses or more that backed onto each other. Sometimes there would be an unsuspecting woman doing the household chores, hanging the washing out or cleaning the windows, and she would be naked in my eyes. Summer days meant having no shirt on before all the "safety" regulations came into play; shorts were no problem. It was never fun splashing hot asphalt on your legs, but many times a day, it was possible. Bending down and shovelling the material into a wheelbarrow was hard work, and your body mass showed it. Good muscles, no beer gut, and a young spirit intrigued many house ladies.

We would also pave roads. That meant the big rollers and a paving machine had to be transported to the site. I worked with Jack as we moved from site to site. It would take at least three hours to unhook the low trailer, load, and connect again. We would place jacks at the side and, with six-foot levers, jack it up to free the locking pins, pull the tractor away, and lower the tailor. Heavy road sleepers were used to get the equipment on, which was a heavy load for the old Commer lorry. Once in Bristol, we loaded my ten-ton roller. The steel chassis of the trailer was level with the wooden bed. With steel wheels and a slight incline, my roller slid sideways, and off the side I came. I was stopped by a kerb from sliding further away from the trailer. With a sore head from hitting the door window, we finally loaded everything. Many times, Jack would be in the lowest gear going up a long hill, doing half mile an hour. He would smoke two or three cigarettes while I would be walking alongside. The window would be open, and he would shout, "Is there any sparks?"

"No," I would shout back.

"Well, you keep an eye open, and if you see a spark, throw that five gallons of diesel on it, and we can burn this piece of crap," he would shout. I never saw a spark, and he continued driving the lorry. He finally got a new low loader, and with the air "lifting and locking" system, he was the happiest man ever. I recovered enough to be best man again. Tony and Jean had a lot of people at the wedding. In the congregation, I saw another of Jack's workmates, the man whose hand had hurt me. My blood boiled inside while calm showed on the outside. He had another woman by his side who appeared to be a nice person. I wanted to do to him as he did me, but for my friends, I let it pass.

Not far away from the church, changes were to be made, and things, as we knew it, were going too. The road across from us was so dangerous, the decision was made to pull down the old houses we played in and demolish everything below them. A couple of nice houses were saved, and heavy traffic would be nonexistent, as the road would in effect be cut off. Also to go would be the old people's flats. One of them held a fond memory. As a short-term measure, the local council allowed a younger person to stay there until a proper flat was found. She was my girlfriend. A weekend night, my girlfriend went out on the town with her mate; I too went out with my friends. It was decided to meet back at her one-bedroom flat. The night was enjoyed, and I got home before she rolled in. When she came in, a few drinks too many was evident. I was lying on the bed watching TV; her friend was also tipsy, and as it had been a wet rainy night, I said she should stay with us. My drunken girl and her mate agreed, and my pulse began racing. This is it. My first threesome went flashing through my head. I eagerly took my clothes off and hopped into bed, and then the girls followed one on each side. Snuggled down under the blankets, I turned my attention to my girl, but alas, she had fallen straight to sleep. I rolled onto my back, and the next thing I knew, a hand began touching my thigh. She was lying on her back, and her left hand was getting me horny. I started on her with my right; in a few seconds, we had each other's privates. Her legs opened, and she was so sensual as I penetrated as deep as I could in my position. She was stroking me slowly and with definite purpose. It wasn't long before I rolled over and slid on top. With ease, I entered this moist young lady I had never encountered. With the steadiness of a lion going for a nighttime kill, I gently began my motions, thrusting back and forth. We were both trying to stay motionless to avoid waking my girl as her legs wrapped around my back. I positioned myself with arms over her shoulders and knees sinking in the mattress. My girl stirred, and we froze as I was in as far as I could get, hoping she would remain asleep, but no. She woke up, realized what was going on, and went ballistic.

She was screaming blue murder at me and her friend while putting some clothes on. We sat up in the bed. I was trying to explain if we have not had three in the bed, then this problem would not have arose. That pissed her off even more. She grabbed her cigarettes and slammed the door as she stormed out. I looked at her friend, and we grinned and went back at it until the moment arrived and we came together. After that, I stayed in the bed, and the girl got dressed. She kissed me and said, "Goodbye, big boy. I will see you again." With that, she left; and twenty minutes later, my girl came back in. I awoke, and she was really getting at me. Again I tried to explain what happened. She calmed a little before taking her clothes off and snuggling in with me. I caressed her with my arm sliding around her waist before we fell asleep. She was one of the first to move out, and the other folks followed on. In came the bulldozers and levelled the area. We had a pub just below our house, which was demolished along with several other buildings. On the other side of the road, a builder's yard and a few houses. They all went in the demolition process as everything was transforming. Evolution was progressing; history was disappearing before our eyes. When this was done, it meant, with the road closed off, traffic would be passing in front of our house. That meant there was more to see from the "chair of wisdom." In all, the whole area became safer, and traffic flowed a lot better around the new roundabout.

At times, the asphalt work would dry up. It was either go get your dole money or find something different. This is where the textile factory where my stepfather worked came into my life. I worked for Burt, a man who was a contractor that did anything to keep the wheels turning for the factory.

Whether a building was something needed, removing rubbish, whatever, it made no difference—he was the man, one of the best wheelers and dealers I have ever had the pleasure of knowing, and his younger brother Patrick was just the same. I had known them from a young lad, as one lived on the same road as I did. Not only did I like working for them but also the younger was my asphalt foreman. It was wonderful to see how streetwise they were. Back in my younger days, I would watch them outside of a pub or cafe knocking the living daylights out of idiots. Seeing guys like that was such a learning curve, which helped me make my way through this mad world. The younger brother got beat up one evening at a dance we were at. He came in from the toilet room with blood on his face and had taken some good knocks. He was at the age where the younger ones were the stronger. As a street fighter, it was hard for him to take. He wanted to go in for another go; I begged him to give it up. No way; he went back in only to get beaten more. That was his last fight. Although he was my foreman and about fifteen years older than me, we had some good times working for cash on a weekend. He was good at looking after himself on the street but absolutely no good at looking after himself at home. A Saturday morning before work, I went to his home. He offered me some toast and a cup of tea. He poured his and my cup of tea. He then shouted upstairs to his wife, "Do I have sugar in my tea?" He had no idea, and it was best I made my own toast.

One of my greatest achievements for Burt (no, my best achievement at that time) was that a footbridge needed to be built across the river, allowing workers parking in the gravel car parking area better access to the factory. When we were told to do this, another guy very handy at building and drinking but sober enough to get the job done had a look of disbelief on his face as I did. Our fearless leader had no doubt. We were convinced we could do it. He had said the job would be done; we had to do it. So whatever experience we had started to kick into gear. With this major problem, a solution had to be found. I guess I took the reins and started leading as I did with the army cadets and various other things. We formed the shuttering ready for the concrete on one side of the river. With a tape, I would send my colleague over the river (he balanced on an eighteen-inch water supply pipe with the end of a one-hundred-foot tape in his hand). We were then able to set up the second shuttering ready for concrete. When everything was done and levelled, there were the bolts that needed to be placed before the concrete could be poured. This, of course, had to be exact, and when the complete bridge arrived, it was lifted in place by a large crane; and yahoo, we were spot on. When the back slapping and smiles rescinded, we added the nuts, and off we went to the nearest pub to celebrate with the boss, who had just come back from a holiday nicely tanned and saying, "I knew you boys could do it!"

CHAPTER 19

WE HAD AN ARRAY of dance places, and the best one was above a hotel bar located in the town centre. It was the Friday and Saturday spot to get girls and enjoy good music and a beer or two. On many occasions, fights broke out. The bouncers would come barrelling in to sort it out. There were some really good fighters who just wiped assholes away. Some idiots thought they were so tough and would pick on the biggest, only to get hurt with a good left or right hook. To get to the dance, you would climb stairs at a side entrance. Further up the road past the cinema that we enjoyed on Saturday mornings as young boys, there was a major ironworks foundry, founded in 1851 as a brass and bronze casting works. They made brass ornaments for the church, which then grew in popularity. It also developed and gained the expertise to create a bronze statue of Boudica with her daughters in a war chariot. This was commissioned by Prince Albert and cast in 1902. They also cast the statue of Lady Justice that stands on the dome of the old Bailey courthouse. Down where the fair stayed for a fun week in the market parking area was a small hall. The place sold beer, played the music, and flashing lights would draw you in. Girls were everywhere. Many came from far and wide to enjoy a night out. Some would get tipsy and want a man for a good time. Others simply enjoyed a night of dancing and a sociable atmosphere. The good thing was, girls from out of town could have a great time, and it never got back to their village or town. That was good for the guys in the firing line that took their fancy.

Saturday nights at 11 the town centre cinema would show horror films. I would find a girl or have a girlfriend. With a long coat, we would have a bottle of beer and fish and chips tucked in the inner pocket. The films were good. As the girls got scared, they would hold on to you. If a gory bit was showing, they would put their heads on my shoulder or in my neck. This allowed me to kiss their head, and several times while they were holding my hand, I would slide theirs between my legs. Some would say, "No, not now," but others would be far more respondent. That would only lead to another encounter next to a wall or the backseat of a car. My friend David and I would travel out of town on some Friday nights. About twenty miles away, we would get to Devizes. The town hall would have popular pop bands that were climbing the ladder of music success. The place would be packed, and there was always someone's breast in my back or arm. Several fights happened, and you had to be quick at hitting and getting out. There could easily be a pack waiting to spring. I found the easiest way was to hold them by the shirt and, at close range, plant one on the chin. That way, others were not so disturbed to notice as their mate sunk to the floor. Some women there were wild, and fun was to be had by eager young men from all over the place. The town, like many others, has a canal (the Kennet and Avon Canal) that links London and Bristol, which is about fifteen miles west of Bath. The canal would twist and turn through the countryside and was a major transportation route for woollen and coal goods. Back in the old days, barges were pulled by horses that walked along the footpath. When a tunnel was in front, the bargemen would lie on their backs and sidestep. How it must have been, stepping sideways along the length of the tunnel, which could be several hundred feet or more. The canal was built by John Rennie between 1794 and 1810, and it has to rise, at one point, 237 feet. This is achieved by twenty-nine locks, with sixteen in a straight line that were lit by gas lights. This enabled a twenty-four-hour operation. Only one long narrow barge at a time could go up or down, which took several hours to complete. The train started to become the way to travel. Steam engines rolling through the hills led to it becoming into disuse. But now, its restoration has allowed people to hire old barges and travel along it at four miles an hour.

Like home, it has five hundred listed buildings, with many of them being old coach houses, as it was a staging post for travellers. It was enjoyable walking slowly looking at the old buildings that surrounded the town. Market days were introduced in its first charter of 1141, although the first recorded was in 1228. A castle that was built in 1080 was home to Robert Curthose, eldest son of William the Conqueror in 1106. He was there for twenty years before he was moved to Cardiff Castle. The town appears to have expanded in the eleventh century with traders and craftsmen selling goods to the people who lived in the castle. There was fun to be had in the old building that snuggled in with everything else that was old in the town. David and I would be chatting all the way there, discussing about finding some lady to enjoy when the music was over. We scored a few times, but nothing much was going to happen because neither of us was interested in a long-distance relationship. I did meet one girl. She came from another market town and has origins dating back to Roman times. The town was established on the River Avon and appears to have had a hunting lodge there for Alfred the Great. It also has the railway station with its wonderful arches and buildings that were designed by Isambard Kingdom Brunel, who was the greatest rail engineer ever.

I came over and met the lady who had an instant attraction for me, as I did her. We simply talked and talked over a few beers, and then it was time for me to get myself heading home. We began an embrace in my car, and everything went as it should. I began to turn her on. She was willing but said, "It's wrong week." I accepted the statement, and we agreed to just go as far as we can. We simply got carried away with very involved passion. Without thinking, I entered her, with both of us forgetting there was a tampon that should be removed. We both were satisfied, beads of sweat coming from our foreheads and heavy breaths after a wild ten minutes. After dressing ourselves and still oblivious to what was forgotten, we exchanged phone numbers. We disappeared into the darkness of our own worlds. The following day after work, I called with loads of excitement about wanting another date. She was not happy at all when I said what a great night last night. She started a load of abuse, calling me a "bastard" and more choice words. She had spent some time at the local hospital while they found and plucked the tampon out of her. I was, of course, very sorry and begged that we meet again. "No" was the answer and "go away." I put the phone down with a sense of guilt and a lot of pride. I had turned a woman on so much that nothing mattered; everything about anything was forgotten in moments of passion. It would not be long before this experience I was gaining would be used again. I had the patter to seduce woman and make them all mine.

My brother Ralph was asphalting for the same company as me. I never really socialized with him. I was happy to be in a bar as long as he was plenty of feet away. I had no interest in what he did or whom he did it with. Funny thing was, if I saw him in trouble, I would do my thing to help out. We were working together on a large project, and the company gave me a brand-new paving machine, which was something I take pride in, and they knew it. We worked with diesel (cleans shovels and rakes), and splashes can go anywhere. One day, he cleaned his rake and hung it on the safety rail. Drips of dirty black asphalt were running all down the side of my machine, and I was ready to flatten him. He did things that would wind me up, which would lead to problems later on. One evening, he was somewhat drunk and was boasting he had slept with one of my girlfriends. The situation arose because the lady in question had gotten married. She married Steven in Bath, and I was best man for them. Strange as it may seem, I cared for them both and had mentally moved on. Ralph's statement was history, and I had no problem with it and left the bar. Several months passed, and his serious relationship ended. That was my ticket to get back at him. I got to talking to her, and we ended up in bed a few weeks later. It was a nice one-night stand for the both of us. He got wind of that and wanted to give me a hiding but never did. He backed off, and I went on my way to drink with friends. Later that night, after a few more beers, I got to thinking about when he hit me in the kitchen, and it prayed on my mind. The pubs shut, and I made my way home with so many crazy thoughts going through my mind. I entered the house and ran up the stairs into his bedroom. He was lying in his bed as I grabbed him and stuck one on his chin. There was a lot of noise as I called him everything I could and landed another and another. Mother came in and so did Albert to pull me off. I backed out of his room, and that was the end of any relationship we would share for several years.

CHAPTER 20

I WAS WORKING HARD on the asphalt, which would take me to various towns and sites around the West Country. Like many things, the work would dwindle and pick up. Because of my experience in quarrying, I was able to work in a quarry that belonged to the company, a nice area that has a history. A skirmish between Parliamentary forces and Royalist forces happened on June, 19, 1643, in the surrounding villages where some of my early-day girls lived when we were at my last school. I would run the loader and dump truck. I also did some crushing of the limestone rock that was blown up at the face. One thing that we did a lot of was make asphalt chippings; we would cover 14 mm stones with a small amount of tar, drop batches of them in a truck, and smother them in water, which would stop them turning into a massive block. The equipment was not as large as my first quarry job, which made no difference at this small quarry. I also started doing the "pop" blasting. I would have a pneumatic drill with a long bit. I would drill a hole into rocks that were too big for the crusher. The same thing is done at all quarries, but I was not part of it then. When twenty or more rocks were drilled, a small gelatine charge was required. This is a small explosive that needs an electric charge to blow it. Every hole would be filled with charge and wire then filled with sand. When they were all readied, the main charge line would lead five hundred feet away or more, alarm would set off, and everything would get blown. I would then get the loader, clean the floor, and everything would be hauled off to the crusher.

When I had done my week's work, I went home and readied myself for a night on the town. I had a beer in a couple of bars on my way to the centre, with the intention of going to my favourite pub. I walked into the bar, and to my surprise, there she was—Jackie, sipping a beer and looking at me like she did while wrapping my bleeding finger. I grinned at her and offered a drink before sitting next to her. All the words were said about "how are you, why did you leave, are you OK" stuff. I spun a simple little yarn about not much happening. I mentioned I had no girlfriend, which got her attention. I put my hand on hers and said, "Thank you for helping me when I cut my finger," as I showed her the scar. She took my hand and held it, which was close enough to her leg. I lowered my hand to it and gave a small squeeze, which not only got a smile but also made my jeans want to burst. We talked a little more and then parted company. That allowed her to continue with her friend. It was another two hours before I see her again in a disco. Again, another smile, but more beer inside her. She asked for a dance, and my old smooching lessons began to kick in. I held her tight as we simply moved slowly from side to side. My right thigh set between her legs, our hands running over each other's backs. I moved her slightly, which got me between her legs. I gently pulsated myself into her lower half. It wasn't long before we were kissing and wanton desires aroused. She asked if I wanted to go home, which I readily said yes. She explained there were two daughters who might be up and we would have to be quiet. My head was screaming yes; I just wanted the hell out of the dance. We got a taxi back to her home, and within seconds, we were at it. Clothes were coming off, and a stout kitchen table beckoned. We shared a couple of minutes of foreplay, then we calmed down. She gave me a look that was going to take me to bed. Her dishevelled dress was semi tidied. My shirt in hand, I followed a lovely-looking butt into her bedroom. We settled down for a really passionate night that would leave us both exhausted.

The next morning, we woke in each other's arms. She left to put the kettle on. I dressed and tried to make myself human; looking in the mirror, I could do nothing but grin and say, "Yes, yes." I went downstairs, and there were her two teenage daughters, sitting at the table with killer stares as their mother tried to explain things. Her kids were just being protective and were not taking it well. I drank my tea, and as I left, she came outside with her thumb stuck in my belt, asking to meet again. I, of course, said yes and made my way home.

As I approached the footpath that led to the front door, a face looked at me from the chair of wisdom. I simply raised my eyebrows and grinned, knowing what's next. Mother sat there and repeated words that have run through my head so many times: "Where have you been, you dirty little stop-out?" She could never accept that I was out having fun when her life was dull and boring. I would try again and again to say, "It's a whole new world, and I am going to run with it." While all this would be going on, Albert had his head down, expecting another argument. Most of the time, he would be smoking a roll up, with the dog next to him. I got to a point where I just came and went as I pleased, paying my rent and eating a dinner. My room was mine, and I would play the lovely Toshiba music centre I had purchased. I always enjoyed laid-back stuff that was soothing or sexy. There were friends who liked heavier music, but that never took my fancy. With so much good music to get you dancing, I left it at the disco. I never brought any disco music for home. Putting money in a jukebox would get my hips shaking in any bar.

As I knew about asphalt, I was hired by a local quarry that was expanding at a rapid rate. The owner built a new office up on the side of the quarry. A new road needed to be surfaced. He was on the screws (these controlled the depth of material to be laid) while I drove the paving machine, then I went back to do the rolling. I was with him for a several weeks and had a company van, which was filled at his expense. This meant my company lost track of it. I finally got back to the quarry where the boss had been scratching his head. He had no idea where it was and forgot I had it.

We had many other places to enjoy an evening, and I enjoyed a large social club, the very club I passed with Mother on her cleaning days. This was a place where an evening of skittles could be played, a simple game where ten pins were stood up in the same formation as American bowling, but with a different ball and format. A small rubber ball would be rolled down the alley, striking as many as possible. Many bars had this in back rooms. We also had a local league, which meant we played in various bars around the town. On dance nights, you would go up the stairs to pay your entry fee. My first thing was to scout out the girls and decide which one I might go for. As it was an open night, no club membership was required. Girls from out of town would be there, some wearing those miniskirts showing loads of leg, others a little more reserved but just as cute. I wasn't alone about picking a girl, as other young studs had the same intentions. My way of doing things was, get out there and dance on my own then work my way over to a couple of girls. With a big smile and wriggling butt, I would go for separation. The hotter one of a pair or group was my intended target. On several occasions, I was told to go away by girls who wanted just have a good time with each other. That would not deter me. I would get back into the mix later unless another was by my side. I met one lady who was up for a good night out, and during the evening, we left for a kiss and cuddle. We went into the graveyard, which was opposite the house where Mother used to clean. She was the runner in this match up, quickly getting my jeans undone and doing what she wanted. I stood with a grin on my face before laying her on a two-hundred-year-old tomb for a wham-bam-thank-you-ma'am. It was that simple, and with a little tidying up, we went back into the dance to enjoy the rest of the evening. Life was just a roller coaster, and so many times, there was little I had to do for a kiss and cuddle. I just loved to banter, and most things I said had a sexual overtone, which broke any barriers and put a smile on a face.

CHAPTER 21

MY LIFESTYLE HAD ITS repercussions because the phone at home was next to the chair of wisdom. The house queen always got there first and, after a few brief words, would hand it to me, with her listening to every comment. Several calls were about a pat on the back for a fun night and a good time. Because Mother was listening, I would bring it around to the sexual encounter. This would really get her goat, with faces of discern and disgust. The conversation would get to the juicy bit; I would then turn the phone a little bit away from my head, and this ensured she got every detail. When done, with a huge grin, I would put the phone down then retire to my room or sit back down to watch TV. She always moaned that so many girls were always calling, which gave me an idea. I asked some of my ladies to call me at a certain time the next Saturday. What a response. Call after call came, with girls saying what a great lover I was, how they enjoyed themselves. That was the best Saturday morning I ever had, and it raised so many laughs with my friends when we were in the bar. She looked at me in the most disgusting way. When a call ended, she would be almost red in the face, claiming I would get so many diseases and die of something. All the while, I was grinning at this sad case of knowledge; and in a way, it was payback for all the things she never did for me. With little regard for what I was becoming, she gave so little, never bothered about how hard I worked or what was happening in my personal life. She was, of course, bothered about the money she would get. At this point, I had asked many times about my father; with nothing more than an "I don't know," she would utter the same words over and over. All I know is he went to America and left us behind then another letter might arrive from her friend in the USA. I had to believe what was being said, and my aunt Bess said no different either.

We had the Easy Beat disco on a Wednesday night. This was held in a theatre-cum-cinema, which was just along from my first paper round shop. There was never a time that it was not fun for all. The owner would hang curtains from the upper balcony, which meant we could sit in the seats closest to the dance floor and not behind. That never worked, as it was darker right behind it. So many times you would see two heads, then one, and then both would disappear from view. The owner used to go around with a torch trying to find anyone at it. No sooner had he moved than someone else was at it. At times there could be five to seven or more pairs enjoying the evening. The owner also used to beg us to stop fighting. The disco would stop, lights would come up, and there could a dozen or more at it—outsiders trying to flex their muscles, which never worked. Many times I would have a girl in my arm; we would be standing to one side. If I thought the local lads were on the losing end, I would, like others, go in and sort the opposition out. Coppers would come from all angles, many times led by our favourite; his arms would go around some heads and out the side doors to the back for a hiding. One night, the DJ and his stuff were getting knocked about. I sprang onto the stage and knocked a guy off. This is when after the fight was over and a beer was being enjoyed, he offered me a part-time job as a roadie. This would mean going with him to dances and getting in free of charge, enjoying the evening's festivities then packing up before leaving for home.

The first gig was at a girls-only school not far from town. I thought life couldn't get any better—me being allowed in a girls school was tantamount to giving me a free ticket in a brothel. What fun it was to be part of this setup, which also led me to enjoy wild parties at his house with lots of free-spirited ladies. He showed me and David how to set up the disco. The music would start playing, and dancing was being enjoyed. I had no problem joining in and was a welcome participant in this orderly yet to get-wild girls' party. My mate David also had fun, and with nothing to do for a few hours, we could enjoy the show. The evening was being sort of supervised, and the raunchiness was beginning to come through. These wild young ladies were either part drunk or drugged and were not afraid to show their wears to friends who would fire back by pulling their tops up. We worked into the middle of it, and the competition was fun watching as exposure went from one to the other. Without warning, one girl grabbed my head, and I was thrust into her breast. I was more than willing to play the game and moved to another. Breasts were all around me as I was sucking and caressing one breast nipple after another. David got in on the action, and then another girl put her hand on my butt then between my legs. I was having the time of my life with these rampant women until a supervisor was breathing down my neck. I stood to attention as she ripped into me and the girls. She was good looking enough to join in the fun, but it was over for the evening. We had to do a retreat to the disco and were watched until the night was over and we would be homeward bound.

The DJ had a dance to do down in another small town. This was not a heavily populated place, but people came from far and wide to enjoy an evening of dance and a beer or two. There was not that much trouble at this one; everybody mingled in a social way. Girls would ask who I am, and I replied, "The DJ's roadie." Man, some of them thought it was so cool, and that was certainly a winner for the night. I had a couple of rendezvous outside next to the old pub wall. This small town has the biggest car-manual publishing factory in the world there and is situated where the old dairy factory stood in the 1960s. This was also were I had the stupid idea (along with others) to go streaking. This was an English fad in the '70s, and it was going on everywhere. Simple rules: take your clothes off and run past a crowd of half-drunken people. I did my thing, along with others, with only one problem: they streaked with their clothes under the arm or in their hand; I left mine behind a wall. Much to the amusement of the girls, I streaked back for my clothes. I was astounded when one followed me into the darkness, saying, "Hold on, no rush to put your clothes on." I was simply the happiest guy in the land. She cost me nothing, asked for nothing, but had everything she wanted.

One night, we were to do a big gig at a racing course. This is where many of my friends would go for a Saturday of betting on the horses and some beers. Many times they would come home from there with a wad of money, or nothing at all. This one night, we were all set up, and the music was going, guys and girls mingling in a long bar that held at least three hundred or more. This night it was packed, and some guys were getting fed up with others spilling their beer or waiting then having someone shove in front. Just like home, a tussle started, and one guy really stood out. He had a busted leg; he also had a great time. He backed himself into a pillar, and anyone that came his way, his crutch would land somewhere on their head. He must have gotten two down before a fist knocked him flying. The place was so packed because the group with the number-one song in the charts was playing. They stayed out of the way until the fight and place had calmed down. Again, this was a place for me to have a good time; and in the stands, one night, I was having fun on the last but one step in the stand. Around me, others were doing it too. We were not together having an orgy but, in various parts of the stands, all enjoying each other's partner. I have never been a fan of horse racing but enjoyed the nights I was at the course, and that was the only time I ever went to it. The job was great but interfering with other things I wanted to do, and one Saturday night, it was to be my last.

Everything was going smoothly, and a most attractive lady asked for a dance. She had the most beautiful face, a cheek done with makeup that profiled it. As my eyes went from her head to her feet, there was nothing I could do but want more. I wanted to dance my ass all over the place, but she wanted a smooch. I duly obliged, which only led to other things. I pulled her into me. With my grinding action, she was enjoying herself, which meant I was working wonders. As it was a warm summer's night, little was said as she led me out towards the stand. We walked passed it and carried on until we came to the first hurdle. We walked around the other side of it, and then she dragged me to the floor. She wanted to make love on the grass. It wasn't long before my clothes were off and I was on top of her; it was a lovely night of passion. We dressed and headed back, but oddly enough, there were little words spoken. Back into the dance, she gave me a side glance with those eyes of hers, winked, and walked away from me. What the hell happened, where was my next date? Why did she do this? I figured she had used me. It was my turn to have the tables turned. She made me feel rejected as I had done to others. It was a strange feeling and nothing more than I deserved. Was it going to change me? That was a good question.

CHAPTER 22

OUR TOWN IN ITS day was a good place to be and a lot of fun to be had. Dancing and drinking could and were enjoyed by all on the weekend, and there were plenty of places we could go. A good one was next to my old chapel. There were many steps to get to the door. Everywhere the guys and girls would be smoking, which was not such a profiled habit back then, and no one really gave a damn about it. The cinema also showed a film/documentary about Woodstock. I sat at the back with my girl and, with a full house, settled down to watch this huge event. That two-day festival attended by a hundred thousand in 1969 had transformed every young person, which led us to freedom, smoking dope, make love not war, and in total contrast to what our parents had instilled in us. Almost next to the cinema was a great coffee bar that became the hangout for mods and their scooters with twenty mirrors on them. I was one, but my hair was growing longer as I wanted it to be. It was cool to play pool and see the short-skirted girls giggling as you bent over to take your shot. This was also the place where I had seen the generation before me have a guy outside and give him a hiding. What I think was good about it, it was one on one; others my age that watched must also have learnt that lesson. When we were the boys of the town, it was one on one; no one got their heads kicked in by several so-called tough guys. We, now as older people, are scared to say anything about their mannerisms because we will suffer a fate we don't want. On a Saturday or Sunday, so many scooters would be parked outside; it was a sight to behold. Shining mirrors with gleaming chrome fixed on each side, and maybe ten stacked on top of each other. Sundays, when the pubs shut at two o'clock, a ride in the countryside could happen. My friends Jack and Annette decided to have a party at his flat. They were living together and had been lovers since school. Many turned up, and music that he and his girl liked was playing. Although they were as big a fan of laid-back music as I was, they enjoyed heavy rock too. This was my first taste of weed. I smoked the stuff, and so many crazy things went on in my head; I was a complete idiot. Say a word to me, and I lost it, laughing my head off then settling for tranquillity. There were several girls there, and they too smoked some of it. They reacted differently and simply chilled. We had all gone to the same school, with some afternoons spent in one of their houses if the parents were out. We had been drinking, and many fell asleep or did stupid things. I, for one, must have been doing something because I woke up with a bra on. I was disturbed by Julie. She was bending over me, trying to undo the back. My eyes opened to some lovely breasts hanging over them. I went to caress them, and she stopped me, claiming, "I just want my bra." It was returned and enveloped some pair of attractive boobs. Several weeks passed. Another party was held in a bungalow similar to Uncle Gary's, a lot of doors (thirteen in all); we all got high and drunk. The host went to bed with his girl after we had all sat in the hallway, waiting for two others to come out of the bathroom. When they did, we all shouted and laughed because we knew what went on. He was not supposed to have the party, but Mum and Dad had gone away for the weekend. We continued playing music, and then an idea was plotted: let's remove the doors and stack them up was agreed. We found a large screwdriver and began the task; bit by bit, we took a door off its hinges and leant it against the wall, one by one until eight doors were leaning together. We then left him to it and went home to our beds, agreeing to meet on the Sunday morning in the pub. We were gathered and having a laugh like we always did, and then in he came madder than hell, calling us everything under the sun. We laughed at him while he explained he got all the doors back and cleaned up just before his parents returned.

Our pub was also the place where I, as I was liked, would be asked to take care of the bar for a Sunday. The bars then opened at noon and closed at 2:00 p.m. They showed me what was to be done on the Saturday night then left everything for me to just open up and serve beer. I was so excited about being trusted, with the thought that I, the one who made the silly mistake of taking the rent money, was now the one who was noticed by others to be capable of such a task. With pride, I opened the doors, and in they came, one after the other, for their Sunday pint. This was, for me, the best pint of the week. Some Sundays, it was two hours in the pub then home for Sunday roast. Then after that, a snooze was in order, which readied you for the 7:00 p.m. opening time. I did a stellar job in my mind and had every intention of going home and returning for the evening shift. My friends kept saying, "We always play cards on the last Sunday of the month, so come on." I went down to my friend's house, and we began to play cards and drink. It was never heavy betting, and there never was a fight over them. The good thing I liked about this bunch, they would, if you lost your money, buy you beers until the next pay packet. How fair was that. We played and drank for the hours that the pub was shut. I suddenly realized it was 7:00 p.m. and ran like hell to the pub. I had maybe a mile to go, and for the first time, I flew past Gran's house. When I got to the pub, three old boys were cursing me out. I got the doors open and had a beer with my mates who had followed me down, then another and another until I was drunk. What was worse, I collapsed on the floor behind the bar. I was flat out on the floor in the back bar. I recall two friends taking me in my house with my arms over their shoulders; they led me into the front room. Mother was reading a paper, and as they let me go, my head hit the sideboard as I fell in a heap on the floor. I thanked them for bringing me home as Mother was raising her head over the paper, saying, "And what's the matter with him?" They left and I, with a little help from Albert, made my way to bed.

The next day, when I went into the pub after work, I had my hands up. The landlady was pointing her finger, saying I was a waster. "How could you do that?" she shouted. "Why I let you look after our pub, I'll never know." I made my apologies, and she had calmed down enough, to give me a beer. The final compromise was services rendered. In the same pub on my eighteenth birthday, I had a dumb idea. I will drink eighteen pints, as this will the last time I could drink one for each year, I explained. As it was a Saturday, I had from 10:30 a.m. until 2:30 p.m. to do my best. I got to fifteen. My feet were inside the bar stool as I began to down it. My head was going back, my body was going back, and with the bar stool, over I went. I recall nothing more after that, apart from waking up in my bed with a massive hangover.

When I returned for my Sunday pint, David put his hand on my shoulder and said, "I am proud of you," not knowing what he meant. He explained, "You had your glass of beer going down. As you tilted your head back, your whole body started to go back, and over you went, ending up flat on the floor, and you never wasted a drop!" With that, we laughed and enjoyed another beer together. It was not so good on my nineteenth. My beloved grandmother died. We had good times in the pub Sunday nights; other easygoing people would bring a guitar or musical instrument. We would enjoy singing folk songs, and my Wurzel songs came in handy too. The evening became very popular; the pub owners would bring hot snacks out, and singing went on until closing at 10:30 p.m.

It was with this crowd that a good friend died on the back of a motorbike. We were having a beer, and it was discovered he had left his money at home. I gave him some grief about being "a tight old git" and said "go get some." Another friend volunteered to take him the mile or more to his house. Off they went, and we continued to drink and laugh. About ten minutes passed, we could hear an ambulance. Fire engines and police were speeding by but never for one moment thinking it was for our friends. Half an hour passed by, and questions were being asked, "Where are they? They should be back by now." Then the pub phone rang, and the accident was being explained. Ashen faced, the landlord came out, shut us all up, and made the announcement: there has been an accident, and one has been killed. Oh, the shock, the horror that struck such happy people. We began crying and consoling each other, grown men and women in total shock. There was nothing we could do than suffer the evening and head home. I went in my house, and Mother was sitting watching TV. Albert was sitting with the dog on the settee. I was asked what was wrong, so I looked at her and said, "My very good friend Alan had died."

She sat there, spurting out words that were supposed to console me, words of comfort that never seemed like comforting. After several minutes of almost silence, she blurted out, "You have plenty of other friends, and they will help you get over your loss." What the hell was I supposed to think; I told her what an insensitive person she was and went to my room. That was like the longest night of my life, playing my favourite music and trying to fathom the depth of loss. The next few days were hard, and the pub was the centre point for us altogether. We worked it out that we would like to carry his coffin and then took the idea to his parents. They thought it was a good idea, then the hard part came. We had to go to the undertakers and practice. The thoughts going through my head were that in two days, Alan would be in the coffin. They put weights in, and we learnt how to balance the coffin and work together. The day came, and we left for the Bath crematorium. We wanted to be in place when the hearse turned up. We got to the crematorium, and as we parked, a hearse pulled up; we panicked and ran to it, only to discover it was not our coffin. When our hearse turned up, we did everything right without a hitch. It was so hard to see my mate disappear behind the curtains, knowing that was it. Never to be seen again. Never to laugh with again. Never anything for us. It was over for a budding DJ and wonderful personality.

Since Alan died in '71, I have been to his grave many times. I always will have him close to me. My company had a superman who got the safety aspect up together and guided so many of us. He was devoted to the company before retirement. He told all of us, on a conference call one Tuesday morning, a poem that was written by a man, and if he had followed the safety rules, his mate may still have been alive. At that time, our safety director had no idea how he touched me. What follows in my poem was inspired by him, and now I feel at ease so many years later.

Twas I

Two young boys meeting up after school, both excited to learn it all. One, a loving mum, and caring dad the other, the very things he never had.

Time went quick; the days went so fast, they built a friendship one to last. Off they went into the working world, the book of life opened, the plot unfurled.

Dances, music, beer and girls galore, we had money, and we tried it all. Stand back to back await the fight, what the hell, it's Friday night.

Shovel, pick and wheelbarrow was for one, for the other, a budding DJ had he become. Playing such good music and making a night. Twist, boogie and hold that girl tight.

My friend forgot his money that fateful night, and a voice from the crowd rang out, "Go get some money, ya tight old git." Who would imagine a post he would hit.

With a friend and his bike they sped, we wait for their return, there comes the call. Boys girls and grown men cry, our friends dead, why, why, why.

A real true friend, to that I swear, with five others his coffin I did bear. The tears did flow, the choir sings, I never saw his invisible wings.

They say time heals and with nowt I roam, from place to place to find a home. Where would it be, no one could say, who would have thought the USA.

'Tis years since a flower I did lay, I carried a burden some would say. Because of that phrase I could cry, who shouted it from the crowd, "'TWAS I."

September 2nd 2008

Inspired on August 19th 2008

CHAPTER 23

WHILE I ENJOYED DRINKING in my favourite pub, there were many other nice places. About forty feet across the road was another, and it had a bar that when sitting on a bar stool, there was little room to get by. That too had its own bunch of regulars, and we all intermingled; I guess there was a lot of bar hopping. One particular night, a guy was being very abusive in my pub. Andy, who was no more than 140 pounds, wanted to have a go, which I admired, but he would have lasted no more than a second. I simply got him by the scruff of his neck and, as I lifted his jacket, guided him to one side. I said, "You stay there, and I will sort this out." There was a peeved face as I shifted him out of range. I approached him, requesting that he shut up and grow up. He threw all his thunder at me then took a swing; I simply moved my head then landed one on his chin. Down he went, and I was hoping he would come up for more, but he stayed there. I was never a man to drag someone off the floor and then knock him down again. The young men of the town were the same: have your fight; win if you will, lose if you must, and no more. Knives never came out; bottles were never used at this time of the century. Strange as this may seem, fighting was civilized; Respect was, when down, you're done. I was fired up, wanting to remove him from the bar; the landlord said I should leave as he had called the police. Out I went through the side door as the cops came in the front. I crossed the road to the next pub, and there was the landlord, backed against a wall surrounded by four idiots. I never said a word as I approached and let rip. One went flying into the next, and over they went. The third got one right under his chin, and down he went. The fourth looked at me and backed off. His mates were getting off the floor, and I asked if they wanted more. They refused as a couple of friends had begun to stand next to me; they were scowling bad stuff then scurried away into the dark to lick their wounds.

The landlord was a good man, and so was his wife; they were good, too-nice people, and nothing was a problem. Again, another shock reverberated around the bars and town; we lost another friend on a motorbike. He had an accident outside of town after hitting a lorry. Again, another member of a happy group was lost on a bike. We went back to the coffin training and proudly carried Alex on his final journey from the hearse. Again, when others leant on their parents, I had so little coming from mine. Time passed, and another dance started on the outskirts of town in a motel. This was a classy place, with a nice decor and was likely to be a fun place. I enjoyed several dance nights and gathered some phone numbers. There was a lot of out of town girls, and one Friday night, I started dancing with a rather nice one. I worked on her with smooth words when smooching to a slow record, and then my hard work paid off. We went outside for a rumble in the jungle then back in to finish the evening. We arranged to meet again the following week. She came with her sister, who was rather striking. She had lovely legs and the most kissable lips. I was rather smitten by this lady who was a year younger than her sister. I had a dance with my date then led her sister to the floor. We danced to one song, then another and another. All the time we were being watched by the elder. As we were thrusting hips and hands going all over the place, the elder got the idea, called me an asshole, and went to find someone else. The younger one wasn't too bothered and expected their ride home to be an ugly one. We met the following week, and the inevitable happened. We also made arrangements for me to go over to her town. On the Saturday, I got on a bus for the thirteen-mile ride. I took a bus, as my car was out of action and I never had enough money to repair it. If I stopped my way of life, chances were I could get it repaired, but I was into living. When riding on a bus, one begins to appreciate what he has, and drinking then driving would not be a problem, but busting for a pee on the way home could be. We met with a kiss and began holding hands as we went to a local bar. There was a lot of talking done and so much smiling; I was beginning to fall for her. It sucked being so far away and not seeing her during the week, but I had to live with it, and weekends were always around the corner. I was also in my town still going out for beers during the week and chatting up other beauties that caught my eye. We carried on for several months, but eventually, it was time to part company because I did not want to travel so far for a kiss and cuddle. As we lived in two towns, there was never going to be a problem bumping into each other and feeling any guilt if I was with a new girl.

About a year later, we had a road to surface in her hometown. We would, within a couple of days from the start of the project, begin passing her house at one mile an hour with a paving machine. I was the roller driver, and the paving machine would pass once, but I would pass many times. As I went backwards and forwards, compacting the asphalt, I would look at her house, hoping for a glimpse. Alas, it was not to be; that last pipe dream of us enjoying a bit of passion and maybe one more encounter never happened. We completed the job, packed up our equipment, and moved to the next site. It wasn't easy to forget her, and I never have; she was the first one that I really fell for, but the way I was, I soon made up for any sadness. There was a world to enjoy, and I was going to do all I could to have fun in it. One night, David and I decided to go to Bristol. This was about a fifty-minute drive to the centre, with so much more action to be had. We made a decision to go to a dance and ice rink just off the city centre. We would enjoy trying to skate, and some girls would help as they picked me up of my ass. Getting a wet butt was never a pleasant thing, and I tried so hard to stay on the skates even with the ankle supports I wore. Seeing little kids flying by had me cussing at myself, so wanting to improve. Being hapless on the ice was at times embarrassing; being on dry land was my best bet. We met a pair of girls, shared a drink, and hit the ice. I was my usual self, holding on to the hand rail or on my ass. It soon occurred to me that this was a good "break the ice" for conversation and touching. It wasn't long before we left for another club, where dancing was the thing. We entered, and they followed in a little later. With a couple of beers on board, I always got looser with the chat stuff; David was just the same. Heavy petting on and off the floor was happening. The night passed quickly, and we were certain that we had scored. It was half an hour before the place shut down; they made their excuses and left. We sat there questioning ourselves about how did that happen. We were certain that there would be sex in the car that night. Several times I was on the back seat while David was in the front with his girl. The following week, we went back to the disco; there we met two others who were going to a nurses' party. We followed them in our car after only talking for a few minutes. We were led into a large room under a hospital, where music was going and beer was flowing. Impressed with the occasion, we wanted to get to work on them. As they were nurses, they wanted doctors. David said that's what we are. They asked what type. He looked at me for an answer; I explained that we are not really doctors. Bemused, they again asked what we are. I said we were specialists, and before they could ask, I said, "Asphalt specialists!" David lost it and burst out laughing; I too lost it, and we had a damn good laugh. They never saw the funny side of it, and we were blown out of the water.

I continued doing my job and drinking in the pubs. It was one Saturday lunchtime while I was drinking in my favourite when suddenly something hit me. My bemused friends asked what's going on as I rushed to finish my beer. I explained I had to go to the hospital. Confused, they were asking why, which I could not explain, but it involved Mr. Smith. I left them and ran toward the old people's hospital, which basically meant, if you went in breathing, you would not come out the same. I finally got there out of breath after running the mile, which is uphill almost all the way. There in his bed was my adoptive father, the man I had looked up to for so many years, the man that had taught me so much. He was lying in his bed, slowly ebbing away from life, his wife at his bedside. I joined her on the other side and clasped his hand. He was trying to smile, which I know was a thank-you for making it. With a small tweak of my hand, he took his last breath. This was nothing like the neighbour dying; this was a natural death. His wife began crying, which set me going. Their dear friend held the wife as he led her to his car. I stood there watching, with tears rolling down my cheek, but not crying. That was it; I had discovered death again. I had witnessed someone who had done their best in the world, only to die with nothing. He believed he was going to be heading to heaven, and maybe he was. I believed he was going in a grave, and that was it. I know millions believe there is more, and that is their right. After an instance in my life, maybe I should believe it too. I was saddened by my loss and went back to the pub and celebrate a good man's passing.

When the pubs were open, I would begin my descent to the town, going from pub to pub until I was in my favourite. It was another night for idiots to be around, and they needed to be put in order, when it dawned on me, "I am going to hit the bastard that hit me years ago." I calmly drank my beer to begin the long walk up the long hill, heading for his house. I got there and began hitting the door. I was so fired up, I smashed my way in and headed for the stairs. He had remarried, and she was the first person to come down from their bedroom, while he stood so nervous behind her. I shouted again to stand up like a man and try me now. He was shaking while his wife tried to calm me down. He was simply in the safest place that night. Standing behind a woman meant I would do nothing physical to her. It was not her that hit me. She is a woman and will be respected. I finally uttered the last sentence I would ever say to him, "If I ever see you on a street, I will tear you apart, you gutless bastard." I turned and began heading for a bar and hoping for an idiot to get in front of me; someone was going to pay a price for that man. By the time I got back to my friends and enjoyed some beers, I was calmed down, and we went to a disco for a dance. I loved to dance, and a lot of ladies enjoyed dancing with me, which just about meant I would have a girl in my arm before the night's end.

CHAPTER 24

MY JOB TOOK US further and further away from home, which meant we would be spending anything up to two hours in a van just to get to the job site. At times, it was hard to be sitting in a van sideways with thirteen of us, three sat in the front and five in either side. You can imagine what thirteen men were like! Each of us had our own interests in our leisure time, and one was fishing. We were coming home, and the van stopped at a fishing and bait shop. Several small containers of maggots were purchased, which would be used for Saturday fishing. One man was an animal type, this man who was known to have bitten a budgie's head off. He, one day, as I was sitting in my roller with my lunch, came along and spat a mouthful of phlegm on my cab window. I had a mouthful of sandwich as he was looking up, apologizing for upsetting me. He put his fingers on the window and gathered his mess with a huge grin on his face. Without any hesitation, he took his slimy fingers and put them in his mouth while I choked on my sandwich. I called him everything under the sun as he walked away, laughing his head off. This was also the guy that, with his container of maggots, put some in his mouth and spat them at us. This enraged one of the guys, and a fight started. The van was doing forty or more miles an hour, and with ten guys in the back, it became unstable. The driver hit the brakes, which helped us to separate the two, and the fight was done. There was a time when I worked for a different asphalt company, and we dropped a container of maggots. We were just a five-man crew; three of us sat in car seats behind the driver. The maggots fell onto and under the seats and into the wet weather clothes. We got what we could and left it at that. A couple of weeks went by and travelling home one day, a blue bottle fly was buzzing in the front window. The driver questioned how it got in with the windows shut, as he swatted it. Several minutes passed, and there was another and another. The driver was going daft swatting and driving; we had realized what had happened. We shook the wet weather clothes, and more flies arrived. We were in the back, the three of us dying of laughter.

I enjoyed everything about asphalting, and rolling was one of them. I liked being higher up, and it was useful when short-skirted ladies would drive by in their car. One such occasion, we were on a new housing estate, and a car with an attractive lady driver passed by us. She was looking at me, as I was her, with a long summer dress on. After several minutes, the car came back, with some leg showing and eyes fixed on me. She passed us then came back, with the dress even higher up her leg. She lived in the last house of the estate, and when it was lunchtime, I headed for the door. She was waiting in the window, and the door opened, for me to go in. She was not downstairs when I finally walked into the house; she was sitting on the last step of the stairs with her legs open and her index finger beckoning me. I went up to her with wonderful thoughts racing through my head, like lions hungry for another. Within seconds, I was kissing her legs and starting to undo my jeans. There was so little I had to do; she was all mine. After we were finished, I looked at her. She was lying on the floor with a content look and saying thank you. I went back to my work with everyone saying what a lucky bastard I was. We did the same thing the next day, but in her bedroom. She wanted more and asked if I had a friend who would like to join in. The following day, my workmate and I fulfilled her dream; she was so happy for herself, and I was proud to have been able to assist with her request. Next day, we were on the site; and with a few small details to attend to, the job was complete. We wrapped up our tools and left without any goodbye and never to return. This was also the site we left when the van driver decided to do something rather crazy. We were sleeping, and about eight miles from home, were woken by bouncing all over the place. He had taken a detour, and we were flying down tractor tracks in the middle of some woods. Next thing, we ground to a halt because the centre of the track was too high, and the front axle became struck. So there we were lying on our sides, trying to swing a pickaxe to loosen enough rock and dirt to get going. We freed ourselves only to discover that there were a lot of slippery areas and we could get bogged down. "Stand on the back bumper and hold on to the doors" was screamed out. This we did as the van momentum had to be maintained. We were close to getting back to the road, and we came across two old people walking in the woods. Their normal serenity was disturbed by a big van with six guys screaming, "Geronimo," as we hurtled past them. They stood looking at us with jaws almost on the floor, and we were laughing our heads off.

It was a Friday, and that's the one night I enjoyed more than most, as chances were we would not be working on a Saturday unless I was doing some private work. I chatted up a girl who had some good looks, and after a few beers, as we got on well together, it was decided to go to a dance. We were with a group of guys whom I had been drinking with before I met her. On the way, I asked if she would like a bag of chips. I went into the fish shop and left her outside with my friends, whom I trusted to look after her. I came out with two bags of chips only to find one of them was kissing her. I dropped the chips and got hold of the perpetrator and yanked him away. This was spotted by two coppers sitting in a police car. They got out, and another friend decided to take them on. It was very quick, and another police vehicle was on the scene. Out jumped several officers from a Land Rover and overpowered him. He was handcuffed and thrown in the back. The first cop came over to me and said he had to arrest me, as the sergeant saw what I did to start the trouble. I knew the cop because he had picked me up in the police car. One of the hills leading out of town was a narrow street, and I was on my hands and knees, drunk as a skunk, trying to get up. He stopped and put me in his car and gave me a lift home on the way to the station. It was because of this that I never lost control of myself and maybe do something more stupid than I had done.

I woke the next morning in a police cell with a hangover and a pending court appearance. The station was across from my old school, and home would only be a short walk. When I arrived, sitting in the chair of wisdom was Mother and the same paragraph, "And where did you sleep last night, you dirty little stop-out?" I explained the situation, which was met with a barrage of "you stupid boy" things. I was fined fifteen pounds for my stupidity, and my mate sixty for his. I vowed I would never spend another night in a police cell, and thankfully never have, which is pretty surprising because of my life. The night of fighting occurred because I had parted with a girlfriend. The relationship was volatile at times, which led to stupid verbal fights and split-ups.

One day, we bumped into each other, and she said, "Hey, bastard, I'm pregnant. What are you going to do about it?" I paused for a moment and then stated I would do the right thing and support her. We talked more, and then finally we decided to live together. My girlfriend got a flat and moved in. I packed my stuff and, for the first time, left home. All my clothes, music, and stereo were packed, and such a happy man was leaving for good, certain he would never return. I was handy at doing things, so creating a nice home would be a breeze. We moved into a small two-bedroom flat in a block of four. There was an elder lady and her dog above the ground-floor neighbour's flat.

One night, I heard a knock at the door and went to answer, but no one was there, so I assumed it was kids messing around. I sat down to watch TV again, but something never figured right. Who hit the door? I jumped up and ran to it again. I looked up to the right, and there was smoke coming from the kitchen window. I shouted to get the fire brigade as I began to jump over the garden fence. I got to the door and rammed it with my shoulder. Second go I was in, and at the top of the stairs was her barking dog. The smoke was beginning to filter down the steps, which started me coughing. The acidic taste was awful as I got to the dog, and just to the right of him, his owner was struggling to breathe. I picked her up and began the descent to fresh air. The fire brigade was pretty quick to put the burning chip pan out, and only smoke damage was caused.

The neighbour and I had gardens front and back, while those upstairs had nothing. I made a lawn at the front of this simple two-bedroom flat and another at the back, which was smaller, as I wanted a small vegetable garden. I also did the whole inside, and it was comfortable for the three of us.

I was also involved in the squash club. This was the most enjoyable sport I had ever played. When the first glass-back court was installed, I worked hard at smashing the old block out to help save some money for the owner. I trained and worked hard at getting better, but enjoying a couple of beers before playing would not get me to the big leagues.

In 1977, my first was due and was to be born in the Royal City of Bath, a beautiful city, and its main hospital is the Royal United Hospital, founded in 1788. The casualty hospital was founded because of injuries sustained by workers building in the city. In 1864, Queen Victoria awarded the title of "Royal" when a new wing named the Albert Wing was opened after the recent death of Prince Consort. I went to the maternity ward, but nothing was happening, so I went to the nearest pub for a beer. I went back and still nothing, and back to the pub. I was almost three parts to the wind. A little girl was born, blonde hair and blue eyes; I was so proud. It was wonderful to see this little bundle of joy come into a big wide world. I called the club to get the champagne ready.

I drove the thirteen miles home while a little intoxicated, and when I got there, we went into full swing. I was so high when we finally got her home. We were doing all right as we progressed with our young daughter. Occasionally, an argument would start, but we would get over it. We would go out together to enjoy a laugh or two downtown. Her mother or mine would do the babysitting. One night, she wanted to go out with the girls; I was to stay at home and look after our girl. "No problem, you go and I will do my duty." She went off, and I was on the phone with Mother. "Get a taxi and babysit for me, I must go to the club." Sure, she would be babysitting her first grandchild, but she would also get money for it. She had done it before, and it also gave her the opportunity to go through the drawers and look at our personal stuff. She was unknowingly showing me what a selfish, small-minded person she was. I set things a certain way, and when I returned, everything was rearranged in the drawers. I got to the club to enjoy a couple of pints and discuss some upcoming games.

It was past eleven when I got a taxi back home then sent Mother on her way. It was almost one in the morning when a rather tipsy lady came in the door. She was madder than hell, screaming, "You can't look after your daughter for one bloody night." I tried innocence, but to no avail. Someone from the squash club was in the dance and told her I was down there. A wide swing of her fist was coming my way, and I let it land on my chin. It was nothing but enough for the decision to be made; I was to move out. I tried to calm her, but when my squash kit landed in the cabbage patch, I knew that was it. I loaded my car with my stuff and headed home. I hit the front door. The bedroom window opened; Mother looked down and asked what I wanted. I told her I had left and needed my old room back. She looked down at me, saying, "I have been expecting this to happen." My, what a condescending person she was. She came down to open the door and as I got some things from my car. I finished bringing all my possessions in before falling sound asleep with my old purring cat laying on my pillow.

There was a guy in town that resembled me. Several times, idiots thought I was him. I would simply get fed up of stating I was not their man; this led me to take drastic action. I would shut them up with a good right hook then walk away. He had a lovely dog, which did as it was told. Many times I had seen him order it to stay under a bench; if it came out, he gave it a smack across the nose. I was an animal lover and never liked what he did but was helpless to say anything. One day, he was drunk and offered me the dog; I too was drunk and said yes. There I was in a pub with a dog that was looking for his owner, but he was long gone. I took the dog home and introduced it to Mother. I gave her a cock-and-bull story, which was enough for her to keep the dog. Sonny was his name, and it was all right to keep the dog, as our other had died several months before. I would take the dog out for rides in the van, and he would sit on the passenger seat with his head held high. He was not one for sticking his out the window that much but did from time to time. I loved the way he would lean as I went round a bend, and one day, I took a left-hand bend hard, and he was leaning into me with his head on my shoulder. Such a sweet and caring dog that, like me, shared some fun times down in my favourite play area. He loved water and would, when off his lead, run and spring into the river for a swim. One day, while walking through, I had to put him back on the lead because another dog was coming with its owners from the other way. I got him on a short lead and allowed the other people to pass. He must have seen a fish or water rat in the river that got his attention. Without warning, he was going in the river, and I was going with him. With a huge splash, we were in; he was doing his thing as I was cussing him out. At that point, the river was not too deep, so I began some breast strokes and walking at the same time; and next to me, he was paddling with that look of "I am loving this."

We would also go bar hopping, and he knew all my hangouts. From home all the way to town, he had the pubs in his head. I say this because one day, I left him at home and went for some beers. I left my first pub stop then the next, until several pubs behind me; after having one beer in each, I was in the last before heading back through the pubs to go home. Out of the blue came Sonny with that lovely face of his and jumping up at me while I hugged and patted him. It wasn't until I began my homeward walk that I realized just what had happened. We went into the fourth pub, and some friends said, "Found your dog." Then I asked what they meant. They replied, "He came in looking for you, and we told him you were in the across the road." When I got to the next pub again, same story, but they told Sonny to look in another. It was amazing that he managed that, and I knew I had a beautiful dog and wonderful friend. He showed that one day in a coffee bar. A mate grabbed me around the neck as a surprise hello. He got a bigger surprise when, without warning, Sonny was at his arm to protect his master. My mate was not hurt but was shocked (just like I was) that this wonderful dog could be that special.

My work was taking me out of town from time to time, and a hotel would be home for several weeks, and seven days a week was what we were expected to do. We did our duties and then hit the pub before getting a take away. I enjoyed going to various areas up around London or south of it. No matter how long the day was or how early we would start in the morning, it was always good to find a dance on Saturday night. I went to one where again I met a sister whom I liked, and she liked me. It was not hard to get her into bed, and it was enjoyable. We spent a few weeks together, and she decided it was enough, so we parted company. Maybe two weeks passed, and in the bar, she and her sister came in. She was nice enough to share a smile and introduce her sister. Again, like any other time, I had the hots for new fresh skin. She was more businesslike with her way of being and came across like this was going to be a hard nut to crack—how wrong could I have been. We were in the bar sitting at a table when her hand went straight between my legs. She laughed and asked if I was shocked; I said no and stuck mine between hers. That was it; we were made up for passion. That night, I went back to her house and kept going back for the next several weeks. She was fun, independent, wild between the sheets, and classy yet trampish. I enjoyed everything about her, but time was running out. The job would be winding down, and we would be moving on. I broke the news, which was greeted with a simple "OK." I was unsure if that was it, but it was. She explained that she was aware I would be moving on and only wanted to have a good time and then find another. How simple was that mentality. I agreed with myself that this would be the way I would go. I was not going to promise anything other than the fact that I would move on when the job was done. We spent one more week together, sharing and fulfilling each other's desires as a last cuddle before the final goodbye.

CHAPTER 25

EVERYTHING WAS WRAPPED UP, and as we were only contractors, we would go home and wait for another large project to come up. Normally, we would call a company that knew us, and we would be taken back on. There was a slow time for everyone, and little work to be had. It was all right to go down the pubs for the first few days because good money had been earned. As days passed, you begin looking at what you have in the bank then assess your chances of survival. I had nowhere to go for work. Everyone I knew had their work set up and labour sorted. I was talking to a friend in the squash club who offered me a carrot: "Come and fell trees for me out in local forest." I asked what was to be done, and it was so simple. Cut down a row between rows to allow the other to grow. We would fell them, cut them into lengths, load them on the tractor and trailer, then drive them out to a stack of others that would be lifted onto a truck and off to a mill. A lot of the wood would be used for field and house gate posts and gates. I had my car, and it would be great to be able to take my dog too. We would meet at the edge of the forest and then get to the row that was to be felled. These were marked with a spray paint and were not very big in girth. As I had felled larger trees, this was going to be a breeze. I would fell one then trim the branches while my dog would lie down just watching and looking after the day's lunchbox. We were on the edge of the forest, and down below was a farm and farmhouse. They had a cow that had had a bad birth, and she was just lying on the floor. Poor girl was hurting, and the farmer and his wife tried hard to roll her to keep the bones and muscles working. After watching their plight the first day, the following day, I was going to go down and help him. I watched and waited for the farmer, then we made our way to the cow. I offered help as I looked into her big brown eyes. You could almost see she was begging for help, and we did our best to roll her. Poor girl was dead weight as we huffed and puffed to shift her. After four days, he gave up, and I saw the knacker's yard truck pull up and shoot her in the head then get dragged up the ramp into the truck before leaving. It was hard work and not much pay but at least, I wasn't wasting in a bar.

I was involved with the squash club and playing plenty of it. The owner wanted to start a professional player who would be good for the club. He had a property on the town bridge that he wanted decorated. I said I would do the job, and the deal was done. I started and got everything done with only the front room to do. It was a Saturday in 1979, and I was painting the window. Below me was the river, and walking over the bridge was a beauty. She had lovely hair, a pretty face, and a body that needed me. She never noticed me in the window, as she was talking to her friend. I painted the window for the next two hours, but to no avail. She never came back, or if she did, I missed her. I spent that evening and many more thinking about her and where she may be. I would go from pub to pub trying to find her. As I had never seen her before, chances were she was from out of town, and I may never see her again.

One Saturday evening, she walked into my favourite bar. I hit my mate and said to him, "She's here, she's here." I just looked at every inch of her and so wanted to manhandle her body. I went over to start my chat-up rapport, which I thought was funny, but only managed a couple of forced smiles. We carried on talking when my stupidity settled down. After a couple of beers, I had her name and achieved what I set out to do; a date was set. The next week of waiting was tough but so well worth it. We had chemistry between us. Monica was getting my humour and put up with me because she was smitten. We became a courting couple, and one day, I was to go to her home and meet the family. She was always told not to bring a long-haired man to his house; well, I had hair that was long, but above my shoulders and not on them. I held my breath as we walked in the door, and there was Geoff with his wife, Mary. He had a warm smile, and with a handshake, a relationship was born. I got the same treatment from Mary, then a beer was to be drank. He, like I, enjoyed a beer, and it was not long before we were in full swing. We hit it off big time, just us two sitting in the dining room with beer flowing and playing his favourite music. Everything was working out well, and we had a chance of a small bedsit just outside of the town centre, which was a couple of houses away from the club my mother cleaned in. We set it up nice and held a party, which, I later learned, should be no more than six, and we had fourteen. The builder was surprised the floor never caved in. We were doing well, but something was going around in my head about having or doing a complete change. We were strong and engaged, so if there was to be a break with me going out of town, we could handle it.

In the summer of 1980, I wanted to become a barman somewhere away from home. I looked at several things and went to London to find out about a live-in position in a pub near Wembley Stadium in London. We decided I would give it ago, and I packed my bags for a mystery ride. I knew no one, but I was strong enough to look after myself. I got the job. A last night of loving was shared, then a train for my destination.

After unpacking, I was shown around bars also and met some of the locals. Next day, I was finding my way around when another barman came over and shook my hand. I had a funny feeling about this man. Although nice enough, he was gay. This was a subject that was not really open in my town, or in my life. I, like others I know, had reservations, but I am also a "live and let live" person. It was not me to put someone down if they never crossed my path. After a few weeks and getting to know him, some others suggested that we go out for a late-night pizza and beer. Off we went somewhere they knew. After getting into the restaurant, we sat down; and to my surprise, he wanted to sit next to me. I was easy with everything; I sort of knew he would not "try it on" but was prepared if he did with a weapon tucked right at the end of my wrist. I knew what it was capable of and I would survive. After a few beers, some of the others had moved to the bar, and I was left with him and his best friend. She was sweet, interesting, and knew so much of his past. He asked about my life, and I explained it in very plain terms. He explained himself, why he was what he was and how it came about. Then right out of the blue, without warning, he took me totally by surprise. He explained about the night he was raped. My jaw dropped to the floor. He came right out with the story of how five men attacked him on Hampstead Heath some six months before. I was shocked, and I was still in shock for some time after. How could people do such a thing? I realized I was not in the farming community anymore. I was in the thick of things where anything goes—where dog eats dog and where no one really knows you. I was not in a place where everyone knew everyone. If not for the few in the pub, I was anonymous. I could do nothing but put my hand on his shoulder as he cried on mine. It was about ten minutes before he finally got himself back together, and for me, I had a totally new mind-set, a new way of thinking and understanding what others unlike me need.

After everyone got back together, we went to a dance, which was so much more than I had ever been in. I was amazed how everything was illuminated, and the place was hopping. People were dancing, enjoying their night. I sat down to relax with my beer. On the dance floor was my newfound mate. He was dancing with his friend. Blimey, I had never seen two men kissing and groping each other. I was flabbergasted, but more than that, I accepted it. I had turned a corner in my life that I never thought possible, or at least was furthest away from my thoughts. If that happened in my hometown, they would have been beat and thrown out.

I missed Monica, and one day, when I called her, I said, "I have a good job. I am in charge of catering, and you can work here too." She was unsure about a move but eventually packed up her job to move to London. When she got there, I did as was done to me and showed her around the bar and introduced some locals. She was an instant winner, but then how could she not be? The smile, hair, and figure were enough to get any man going. With a beer in hand, she looked somewhat confused, which begged the question, "If you're in charge of the catering, where is the food?"

I smiled and replied, "It's here, my dear," as I pointed out the crisps and peanuts.

"What?" she exclaimed as I tried to calm her obvious boiling blood. I used all my powers of persuasion to make someone happy, and the introduction moment passed off peacefully. We did well there but knew we could do more.

We saw an advert for a couple to learn pub management. A major brewery company was looking for a good couple, and we applied. We were asked to come and have an interview. On our day off, we went to Southgate, which is in the borough of Enfield, North London. We would be in the same area as the house that tea magnet Sir Thomas Lipton lived in. The next borough over is Finchley, which is where the prime minister of England's conservative party headquarters are. We met the manager, which was a success, and he asked us to step out his office. With the door slightly ajar, we heard him call his boss and say, "I want these two." We were doing all the excitement things in silence then tried not to show it when he came out. He took us in his car to central London. After meeting him, the job as assistant managers was ours. We served our notice and, with packed bags, headed to another new home.

We had a small room above the bar, just a room with a bed and shared facilities. It was so nice to get fed for free and eat food prepared by an à la carte chef or his sidekick. It was only on Sundays when we were allowed to eat in the restaurant with proper service. This was part of our training, and I had to try a small drink of any bottle so I would know what I was talking about when serving. I so enjoyed the personal side of that job, fussing over people, rather than just pulling pints. At the back of the banqueting hall was a small room, and outside was a bowling green just like the one at home. This small room with a bar and piano was where I would encounter my most nervous evening.

I was to be in charge of the then prime minister Margaret Thatcher. She was the leader and MP for the Finchley Conservative Party, and their annual dinner was to be held in our hall. She was PM from 1979 to 1990 and known as the Iron Lady, which was given because of her stand against the Miners Union and the Falkland Island conflict. It was my duty to ensure that anything the lady wanted, I was to take care of it. For three days, armed police and officers with dogs patrolled the place. They were looking everywhere for bombs and anything else suspicious. The evening arrived, and people were gathering and enjoying polite conversation while I was as nervous as anyone could be. Margaret Thatcher arrived, and I welcomed her before leading her across the floor and into the small room. Everyone was applauding, and I was thinking to myself, *I was laying asphalt eight months ago and now look at me.* I served her and her son Mark a drink, then after some nice words being said, I led her to her place. That was my time to stand back and let the evening progress. Everything went well, and the boss patted me on the back, saying I had done a great job. For me, I was extremely proud.

Weeks passed, and we did more things and, with that, grew more responsibilities; then out of the blue, I was summoned to my manager's office. As I sat across his large desk that looked like the one in the White House, I was wondering what I had done wrong. This had never happened before, and all the bad stuff was going through my head. I had time to think because he was on the phone while I pondered what my future would be. I never wanted to go back asphalt, and at that time I did not want to go back home as a failure. He finally finished and began a discussion about our future. He described how he liked the way we bother and interact with customers and how we handle the pub business, like stock taking and handling staff. Then right out of the blue, he said, "If you were married, you would have a pub," which took me by surprise; not only that we had never talked about marriage but also we had never considered we were good enough for such a challenge. We had every notion that we were good at our job, but thought more time and education would be required.

CHAPTER 26

I LEFT THE OFFICE and proposed to my fiancée Monica. We agreed to marry and told the family. Arrangements were made for a registry wedding in Enfield. We told the families of our intentions, then with two locals from the bar, we got married. There was a lot of fun to be had the night before, and when we returned to the pub after getting hitched, the manager said, "Here's my car keys. You have one and a half days to go home and return." We were so surprised and grateful. With a quick phone call to get a party ready, we sped off home. Such a great time was had before time was up, and back to the pub we headed. It was about one week before I was pulled again into his office, and this time, it was so different: "There is a pub in Wembley that needs a relief manager, and you have been nominated." Although we both went to see, I was to run it, and Monica would stay put for a short while. It was a large pub that sat on top of a hill, and I could see the Twin Towers of Wembley from the upstairs flat. I started to take on the challenge, and there was much to do. Bit by bit, I sorted out the staff and began to run the place. I made some changes, and we were doing some good business. There was an open bar that was at least sixty feet long and shaped like an L. At one end was an area for food, and we had a four-foot-high glass cabinet displaying various meats. I had five guys come in one night, and they were, in my mind, wanting to cause trouble. One particular man was swearing, and I asked politely for him to cut it out to which he basically told me to screw myself. Well, what was I to do? I grabbed him with my left hand and pulled him into the display cabinet and then let rip with my right hook. I banged him three times on the nose, then as another had come behind the bar, I got one on his chin, and then they took over. I was going down with punches and boots hitting me when the artillery arrived. My dart team came through the door and piled in to help me. I was so grateful as I got off the floor with some cuts and bruises and happy to see the bad guys shoved through the door like it wasn't there. They were rewarded with some late-night drinks from a grateful manager who was hurting a little.

Monica finally, after seven weeks, got to join me, and the whole place changed dimension again. She whipped the waitresses into shape in the upstairs restaurant, and business began booming. We were managers, and we reaped rewards. There was no accommodation, gas, electric, water, or anything else to pay for, and we had a chef, waitress, and dishwasher to look after us. We went home for a break and decided to bring my dog into the pub. It was a tough area, and Sonny would make a good guard dog, plus he would be with his mate. One night, when everything was finished, tills checked out and paperwork done, we sat down with a couple of staff for a glass of wine. It was nice to be able to make that decision, as our boss told us never to fraternize with staff. I agree that's a good call, but I am also a human that enjoys other people to talk about life. Suddenly, the dog went flying downstairs, and we had no idea why. I called and called him, but it was to no avail. I went downstairs, and in the far corner, the window was open; he was gone. We had a burglar, and he had chased him off. Problem was he had not stopped chasing him. He kept going, then when everything was done, he would be lost. I ran to the block of staff flats and hit my chef's door. He was a CB fanatic, and he sent out a message: if anyone sees a black dog with a white chest, call in, and they will get a free night of food and drink on me. We had a couple of calls, and he was at least a mile away on the busy six-lane North Circular Road that wrapped around London. I was so scared for him. He was in the central reservation and obviously scared to death. We scoured the streets most of the night, looking for my friend and treasured possession. I went home exhausted and in tears. I was hurting because I felt I had failed him. I failed to follow immediately downstairs as he would have done for me.

The days passed. On day six, I went for one last option. Could he be at the Battersea Dogs Home? After seven days, if unclaimed, he would be put down. I left and got on a tube train that clacked all the way to Battersea. I went in and explained to the people what had happened, and they said he probably would have been killed on that road. Everything was welling up inside me as I went to see some dogs that resembled Sonny. There were these lovely faces looking for their owners or just wanting one. Then right there in front of me, my black-and-white best friend tried to come through the wire cage. He smelt me; he knew his mate had his back and could not hide his love. I got him out and put his lead on then paid what amount was required plus an extra twenty. (I said earlier I was only human, and as I write this, I have tears in my eyes. This dog was amazing. Simply adorable in every way and would never hurt any child or person. I am proud to have been his friend.)

We got outside and ran so fast. It was a matter of minutes before we were on Battersea Bridge. There was a hot dog stand. I got us one each and a cup of tea. I was sitting on a bench with Sonny looking at me, panting and his tongue hanging to one side, when there was a screech of brakes and horn sounding. Right in front of us was a good friend of mine. He was in his refrigerated lorry doing deliveries. How could anyone expect to see his drinking buddy from home in the middle of London? It was one of the most magical things that had happened to me in one day. Did kissing the Blarney Stone have something to do with it, or was it something else? We went on the underground heading back home. Sonny had no fear of anything and looked to be enjoying himself going down escalators. He was so bemused when sitting in the train and seeing his reflection in the window; he had no idea what to make of it. He was tilting his head from side to side and throwing a little growl at himself from time to time. I got back to the pub, and Sonny lay quiet for two days until he was back to his normal self.

Several weeks went by, and it was time for pipe cleaning. I always did this at night then, in the morning after soaking them in cleaning fluid, clean them out. Sonny always followed me, and as I went up from the cellar, he stayed there. I noticed he was missing and went back down. There he was with his head in a bucket of beer. I said stop, and he looked up. He was licking his jaw then stuck his head back in. I got him and led him upstairs where we would have a good-night drink. Sonny sat upright all the time, but on this occasion, his right-side back leg was flopped to one side; I came to the conclusion he was drunk. I said "come here," which he did. I said "sit," and he did, and then his back leg would flop out. He was hilarious, and you could do no more than love him more. It wasn't many days before my mate pulled his huge lorry into the car park for a stopover. He would be fed and watered for free before leaving in the morning. I had a local family that used the pub, and the father worked as grounds man at the stadium. It was his sixtieth birthday, and his wish was for a piano. I knew of one at my last pub, and arrangements were made, so I went and got it. His birthday night was fantastic. He was knocking out tunes, and his four sons were playing the spoons. They were so in sync with each other, and the whole pub was partying all night long.

Sometimes my wife and I would go for a walk, and at night, I would carry the butt end of a pool cue up my jacket sleeve, about fifteen inches long, and ready for anyone who thought they would mug us. Life there was so different than my hometown, but I had an answer for the bad guys. I was not carrying it when one day when I was going to the bank with the takings. I turned a corner and walked straight into a bank robbery. They were running out to a waiting car but not firing any weapons. With the door right on the corner, I was almost ran into by a guy with a sawn-off shotgun. His menacing eyes stared into mine, and I backed up to give him a clear shot at the car. They sped off as police sirens could be heard in the distance. That moment was the scariest thing I had ever encountered. Not even being chased by a herd of cows while walking across a field with my friend was that scary. We thought it was thunder until Nicolas turned and saw them coming at us. What stuff we dropped was trampled over as we ran toward a barbed wire fence that had the river on the other side. We vaulted over the fence and landed in the river, and the fence stopped the cattle from coming in.

We were to take over another pub in Guilford. This would mean Sonny was going back home to Mother. When I got him there, we walked in, and he was happy to see another dog we had and the cat. Mother sat there in the chair of wisdom. No hug, nothing more than "what's happening, are you earning money?" It was so very different going over to Monica's home and seeing her family. Her father and mother were lovely people and so was Granddad Davis. He was a diamond and knew Albert from the textile factory. We took this pub, which had a larger restaurant and two bars. We did well again, which was a good selling point for us. As some managers were leaving our company and going to another in the Midlands, we were offered the chance through recommendation of a new concept pub in a central town of mid-England, located in central Warwickshire with the River Leam flowing through it. The waters were known for their medicinal qualities, and in 1814, the Royal Pump Rooms and Baths was opened close to the river. The grand structure incorporated the world's first gravity-fed hot-water system, thus becoming a spa town. Queen Victoria came as a princess in 1830 and as queen in 1858. With Birmingham not so far away, it became a place for retired people and middle class. We took the opportunity to view the place and give our assessment of its potential. This place had no eating, just real ale, lager, and fancy new shaker drinks. It was red and green with a great sound system and flashing lights like a disco. The bar seats were old Fordson Major Tractor seats welded to a heavy stand, and the bar had half-cut fifty-five-gallon oil drums along the front. There was a small flat upstairs, and I felt this would be a great challenge, and the wife agreed. We resigned our position, and while there was still a lot of work going on in the pub, we managed to get our stuff through the spread-out materials and into the flat above.

We had time to get around the town and see the other pubs, which were traditional, just like so many other towns. Ours was going to be very different, and assessing all the pitfalls and possibilities, I knew we were on a winner. Not far away, one of the managers who had left our previous company had settled down in Coventry, second largest in the West Midlands after Birmingham. Back in AD 700, the Romans built a settlement that was left in ruins after the then King Canute's Danish army destroyed it in 1016. The nunnery was also lost, but Lady Godiva and the Earl of Mercia built a Benedictine monastery in 1043. Like my hometown, it was a thriving cloth trading centre in the fourteenth century. Coventry is a city because of its cathedral, and that's the same for any city in England—a town must have a cathedral to be deemed a city. This one is rather new, as the older one was all but destroyed by the Luftwaffe in November 1940. He had a pub that blew me away with its size and popularity. I was to see an amazing thing. His cellar had three six-hundred-gallon tanks for beer, and they would be filled three times a week! How much was that! Just pints alone, it was 43,200 pints a week without all the other drinks and food. It blew anything we knew away, but that's my kind of challenge. How can I make what I have better? Nothing is impossible is my way of thinking. I knew I could get to the top if I never decided I was settled and never wanting to go further.

We opened, and within days, a regular crowd was coming in. My real ale was a hit with many, and one guy would come in every day, and it was he that got the first taste of any knew barrel I had tapped. Real ale needs to be racked and left to settle for at least a day or two; this allows the sediment to settle before tapping the barrel. Tapping is with the barrel set with the breathing vent at the top and the tap cork at the bottom, a new breather tap would get hit in the top and the tap at the bottom. When settled (usually after twenty-four hours), the top breather is loosened, and a sample is tried. If it's clear and looking good, then it's ready for the general public. As I enjoyed lager, he was the chief taster; and of course, we were building a friendship. We had what we called the "window bunch"; they were rich kids who would turn up in the parents' Bentley, Rolls-Royce, and Jaguars; they were a great bunch, and on several occasions, we would have a late drink.

After several months, the place was packed every night. It was hard to get to the bar. The small beer garden would be packed as well. We had good staff that put in a great effort, and at closing time, it was hard to get rid of the customers. I still had my lovely Toshiba music centre and decided to do something that would drive them out the door. I had the idea: what if I was to record the songs I knew onto a tape and, with my mike, sing along? (Who knows, I may have been the first to make a karaoke.) I had it ready for a Friday night, and as usual, the place was packed. To get the attention of everyone, I stopped a great song halfway through, which started people saying, "Hey, what you doing?" This was when I played my "harmony" tape. I, like the wife and staff, thought everyone would start piling out the door, but, no, they loved it. It was so popular that during the week, it was a much-requested tape; I duly obliged, and fun was had. It was after ten months that we were asked if we would like to look at a large pub in Birmingham with two restaurants and four bars. We went to see, and without doubt, this was going to be a hard one to crack. The whole place was in shambles—manager had lost it, and the staff did what they liked. One of the waitresses, with her mother, thought they had total control; and to a point, they did. Our question was, do we go in and take on the fight, or wait for something better to come along? We decided on getting stuck in and pulling the place back in shape. We accepted the company offer and broke the news to our friends and staff in Lemington. Then it was of onto a new and exciting challenge. We had left only a few short weeks when we heard one of the lovely young ladies of the window crew had died in a car crash. We went back for the funeral, and although a couple of times, they came over to Birmingham, we would lose all contact with them.

CHAPTER 27

IN ITS EARLY DAYS, it was described as a medium-sized market town, and now it's described as the second-most populous urban area with a population of over 2.3 million, and its metropolitan population is over 3.7 million (that's what I call growth!). It was not until the eighteenth century that international prominence was recognized because of its developments in the science world. The city has a history that shows hominid (humans and relatives of humans closer than chimpanzees) activity dating back some five hundred thousand years ago. The pub was in the hub of the insurance and financial part of the city, and a lot of money walked through the doors. We were in an area where three other pubs were; they had large bars, and two were owned by the same brewery. We were another food outlet, and it would be busy. With the service being sloppy and poor, that would be one of the challenges. Monica got all the staff together and clearly stated, "This is how we will have the tables set."

The old guard would stand there and say, "This is how we do it."

Again, she stated her case and said, "If you don't want to do it this way, then goodbye." Daggers were drawn and eyes glared, but the word had been spoken; we were going to be in charge no matter what. The office was in disarray, as were the kitchen and everything attached to it. The bar staff were also set in their ways and had their favourites that I was certain were getting a free one now and then. This is something hard to detect when your back is turned, and it rang true in the Guilford pub. I would walk around my domain, looking for anyone wanting to complain or start a fight, or trying to steal. A barman was cheating and thought I never knew. I passed the busy bar many times, whether behind it or in front of it. I noticed the small shot glasses were moving from one side of the till to the other. I knew I was onto something and went for a spare till. I did a print out and stated that "if this till is the same amount as those glasses, your fired. Sure enough, he was cheating me and had his ass kicked out the door. I sensed something was going on here and very often did spot checks; this resulted in a couple of staff going. They had this union thing, which is OK, but they thought they would hide behind it. They never stood a chance with stealing. Slowly we were turning the tables. I spent several weeks in the kitchen showing chefs how I wanted things prepared, cooked, and presented. Although the menu was mainly steak and fish, there were many other items that needed attention to detail. The restaurant upstairs was used mainly for the fish plates. The kitchen was a mess, and it was hard to keep an eye on the chef and inspire him to do better. The whole room was old and had great character with arches along the wall and pictures depicting Lord Nelson and his ships. After speaking with my boss, I shut the restaurant down and got rid of the staff. This enabled me to concentrate on getting everything else running smoothly.

There was another thing that was not looking right. Any conversation I had with my boss and how I was going to execute it seemed to come back at me. When I had meetings with my assistant, explaining my next intention to turn the pub around, the union would be on my tail. I had a feeling that something was going on and set out to find out what. I sat my assistant down and fed him a cock-and-bull story. It was not long before the union was breathing down my throat. If I was on the street, he would have gotten a beating. I went ballistic on him and sent him to my office. I let him stew for a while then entered, slamming the door behind me. I gave it my all and chewed his ass out. He was full of apologies, but that did no good. I wanted to fire him, but instead, another idea was executed. He would be given a trouble pub on the outskirts of the city. He went there and quite often got a slap from some rough local who told him he could not shut the bar. He was so miserable, and this dog, when he popped over for a progress update, was having his day. There was a price to pay for betrayal, and he was paying it. I felt like telling his wife what he was up to when she came begging for them to stay in the area, but, no, enough was enough. It wasn't long before the front barman said he would be leaving. I was glad but never showed it. His last night, he was to be working his bar. He asked if I minded some of his friends coming over for a small party. No problem, I said. They started coming in, and he would welcome them, give a drink, and charge them. I knew if I was not there, he would be giving them away. I leaned across the bar and said, "You're finished. I will pay you for tonight, so stay in the bar with your friends, and I will serve." He was there for another ten minutes. He left, and so did his friends. As others came in and with only me there, they turned and walked away. He must have thought I was stupid. Would I let a barman have a party on his last night? Yeah, sure. It was around this time we heard our old pub had closed its doors. Word had it that they could not find a pair like us to run it. All that work, the finance had gone to waste. I am not sure if it was a tribute that it failed. Does its failure mean we were the best? There was enough time for someone to make their mark. Everything was set up; it just needed characters, and I am tempted to say maybe, just maybe, we were the best.

Success was being achieved with everyone sailing the ship in the right direction and profit being made. This meant we could get my idea up and running. The old kitchen was torn out and done up to blend in with the beautiful surroundings already there. I installed three three-quarter-sized snooker tables in the old restaurant area, and with the new carpet, it was just the coolest room ever. Without anyone there, it was alive, and Lord Nelson ready to watch over the proceedings. The bar area was large enough for a pool table and darts board and several lounge chairs. With a membership of over one hundred anxiously waiting members, we opened the doors. A local ex-World Snooker champion hit the first balls and showed a host of trick shots to a gasping crowd. The place was an instant hit. The offices across the road and ones that surrounded us would book a table and enjoy their lunch break. Our customers' flexible hours had some wanting to play as early as nine in the morning, then others would be playing throughout the day. With all the food and drinking, the place paid for itself in a short while, and profit was reflecting in the company bank account.

We had an old car, which was reliable but not that good looking, and we purchased a five-year-old XJ6 Jaguar just like what one of my old bosses had. It was a lovely red with white-walled tyres. We went to see our old manager that started us in London. He was in Leicester. We hit the M69, and I thought about seeing what this car of ours would do. I have never been as fast as I had that day. We got up to 145 miles per hour, and that was it; I was not going to take it any higher than that, and I never did it. It was there that I saw the next step for us. A large hotel would be the next challenge and, as I saw nothing stopping us, assumed that would be the way.

Christmas came, and we shut the pub, and due to being in the financial area, there would be little business, so we were allowed to shut a couple of days. We were driving down the M5 towards home with a bottle of champagne, and the world was ours for the taking. After partying with family into the early hours, I settled down on the sofa, and Monica went to her old bedroom. Next day, we went to Mother's to say hello. Aunt Bess was there; Mother was in the chair of wisdom. We talked, and soon her hand was out and asked, "Any money for your mother?" with a smirky face on.

The conversation was going along, and I twisted it around. Again, I asked, "Where is Dad? What happened to him?" but the same reply came back. Not a word more came from either, which I had to accept.

Everything was good and out of the blue; the wife said she was pregnant. There was a lot of excitement throughout the family. Staff and friends were happy too. In 1985, the day came we went to the hospital; and after settling in, I went back to the pub to eat. I came back in a taxi, which was a good idea because if the little one took a long time, I would be getting a beer. I went in, and nothing was happening, so over the road I went for a pint. I came back, and nothing had happened, so I went back to the pub. This was a repeat performance, and I knew it. I again got back just in time and was asked to help take the bed to the delivery room. I, of course, did and, with the epidural drip trolley, proceeded to lead the way. I was banging into the wall and haphazardly went banging through the door. It wasn't long before another daughter was born. A bundle of joy with fair hair and blue eyes was in my arms. I rang the new grandparents, and in the background, a champagne bottle could be heard opening. I called the pub and made my way back for a party.

We got the baby home, and it was a chore getting the baby buggy up and down three flights of stairs. The grandparents came up to see us. Geoff always enjoyed a Guinness, and to please him, I rushed cleaning the pipes and, by mistake, failed to do it correctly. He drank Guinness and pipe cleaner, which made him pretty sick for a day or two. We got to take our little one home and show her to the rest of the loving and caring family. When she was presented to Mother, there was something that I don't recall. I guess she was good to me for the first few months when Dad left, then the caring stuff wore off. I was pushed to one side. I know I paid a price that I am certain of. Her rejection from the man she loved caused me to be rejected. She had a different way with the little one. There was a different way of being, and it was evident. I saw compassion. I never knew she had it in her. Monica missed the family very much, as they did her. Because of my history, it wasn't hard for me. I had a daughter growing up, and I was missing her doing that. That's a price we all pay when you work away from home.

On our first trip home, I contacted the local newspaper, and a photo was taken. Five generations were recorded—and all girls. A big decision had to be made: can we, could we, would we give up a great job for the sake of family? We had it good, but that means nothing if the heart strings are tugged. I had no problem staying there, as I never hankered for family like the wife. I could have let her go home and I continue on alone. No went through my head. I had one daughter with no dad, and I did not want another. I also loved the missus, and after a couple of phone calls, our minds were made up. We were homeward-bound. I called a couple of asphalt companies, and they were more than happy for me to come back and work for them. I had not gotten lazy; I still worked out in the gym and had the strength needed for the job. I was lucky enough to be in the gym when one of England's favourite boxers came in. He was a huge success with his knockouts in the ring. I was amazed to watch his power training and happy I was not on the end of his arm.

CHAPTER 28

THE STAFF WERE SHOCKED, and so were a lot of the locals. We had a last goodbye party, and the next day, we got in the car, and off we went. I had a different car then because on a trip home, a shop owner saw my Jaguar and fell in love with it. He gave me cash the following day, which meant taking the train back to the pub. We got to Birmingham, and as an exercise, I said to a taxi driver in my best Somerset dialogue to take me to the pub. What should have been a five-minute ride took twenty, and I was watching the meter turning. We arrived at the pub, and he asked for the meter amount. I said to the driver that as I had lived here for the last year, I knew the way home, and he was way off the mark. He demanded his fare, and I took his number, which resulted in him getting what it should be. It made me wonder about how many other people are ripped off in a day, not only in Birmingham but also in every other place on earth. How many rip-offs can occur each hour of the day, and how much money is it worth?

We got back, and as a temporary fix, we lived with the wife's family. With what would be described as "overcrowding," we would soon have a place. We were offered a new house that was built along with about two hundred others. The houses were rental and were situated on a hill where I used to go with my army cadet mate. He had two sisters and two brothers and a very sweet mother. His dad was a great man and would, like other friend's fathers, rough us up when we jumped on him. His wife was a kind and caring mother and treated me like one of her own. Many times I was sitting at the large round table tucking into a Sunday roast and a whole loaf of sliced bread and butter to mop up the gravy. Just down the road, you would go up a couple of steps and enter a small church built in 1863; it was where I was best man for a third time. I was best man for my mates five times, and three times was the same friend. He married five times, and the last time, I said, "If I was best man for the five times you have married, we would have a man from the Guinness Book of Records here!" We fell about laughing before the wedding began. This small church is a very quaint place with its small decorated sanctuary ceiling. After the ceremony photos were taken and then at the reception, the photographer had a problem with the church photos, and we had to go back a week later and do it all over again. It felt strange that when we completed it, we changed clothes and went to a pub.

I was doing my asphalt work, and this was for a guy who lived in the Midlands where my friend married. Things were good, and some of the work meant living away from home, but the money was worth it. We worked seven days a week so we could afford some small luxuries and save too.

The Iron Lady was the prime minister, and she was standing for all of us when Argentina invaded one of our islands in the South Atlantic. We call them "the Falkland Islands," and they call them "the Malvinas." The Argentina government (junta) thought they would regain control of the islands and decided to invade. The driving force for the invasion was their admiral, Jorge Anaya; he was the one who ordered his vice admiral to create a plan for the invasion. He was also the one who planned to sabotage a British warship harboured in Gibraltar, only to be thwarted by a communication interception. In 1985, he was acquitted in the Trial of the Juntas; his charges included kidnapping, torture, enslavement, concealing the truth, and false declarations. He died in 2008 while under house arrest on charges of human rights violations. The war, also known as a conflict, began on April 2, 1982. A naval task force was dispatched from England, with everyone waving goodbye from all over the country. The British atmosphere was full of pride. British bulldog was going to kick ass, and it would kick hard. The pride in every Englishman and woman was so very evident. They were to make an amphibious landing to retake the island. Four thousand miles away from England is a small island. Ascension had, by mid-April, Vulcan bombers refuelling aircraft and phantom fighters also; this is where a small task force was sent to another island that had been taken. South Georgia was to be retaken by marines from 42 Commando. Special Boat Service and Special Air Service members were to do a reconnaissance for the approaching marines. Submarine HMS *Conqueror* arrived, and Victor planes were flying over, mapping the island. With the changing weather and having two helicopters crashing in fog, the invasion was held off. With the submarine being sent to deeper water to avoid detection, a few days were needed to regroup an attack. On April 24, they were ready to go in; and on the twenty-fifth, a submarine that had resupplied the Argentinean soldiers was spotted. HMS *Plymouth* and HMS *Brilliant* launched helicopters that, with their torpedo, had direct hits that were enough to stop it from diving.

The crew abandoned the submarine at the jetty at King Edward Point. With seventy-six men, Major Sheridan decided to make a direct assault; and after a naval bombardment from HMS *Antrim* and *Plymouth*, the soldiers surrendered without resistance. When Her Majesty was informed that the White Ensign and the Union Jack were flying side by side, Margaret Thatcher broke the news to the British public with a quote, "Just rejoice at that news"; we did. A lot of drinking was getting done.

The main task force was sailing south and being shadowed by 707 jets that belonged to the enemy, and two aircraft carriers, *Invincible* and *Hermes*. The ship SS *Canberra* was requisitioned and set sail with the 3 Commando Brigade; the Fifth Infantry Brigade set sail on RMS *Queen Elizabeth*. The whole task force was a total of 127 ships: forty-three royal naval vessels, twenty-two royal fleet auxiliary, and sixty-two merchant ships. The 707s were intercepted by Sea Harrier fighter jets and were not shot down because the UK government had not fully decided to commit itself to armed force. On May 1, the Vulcan bombers began to fly the eight-thousand-mile round trip and began dropping their payload on the runway of Port Stanley. This would stop fighter jets getting off the ground or landing, and in order to perform the task, the mission required multiple times of midair refuelling. The five raids, known as Black Buck, had little effect, and any damage done to radars was quickly repaired. With only three airports, none was really good enough for the fast jets, and Argentina was forced to send their jets from the mainland, which eventually had to fly over the British fleet to bomb anything on the island. Air combat broke out, British Sea Harriers and Mirages engaged, and one was shot down. The other was damaged and was forced to try and land at Port Stanley airfield. With not the best-trained fighters, they began to shoot at their own jet as it approached to land, which resulted in it crashing and exploding. They tried decoying, flying civilian jets, simulating strike aircraft about to attack. One was shot down, which was being flown by a squadron commander who was the highest-ranking Argentine officer to die in the war. With five submarines submerged just outside the territorial limit, they would post incoming planes that would attack, and British fighter jets were ready. Submarine *Conqueror* had moved into the waters off the islands, and that's where the ship ARA *General Belgrano* was sailing. The nuclear sub fired on torpedoes into its side, and down she went; 323 sailors lost their lives, and over 700 were saved. Although this hardened the Argentine resilience, it also had a crucial effect. The entire naval fleet was pulled back to port, ending any threat of a ship-to-ship battle.

Back in England, cries of "good job," "that will teach them a lesson," "hurrah," "blow them off the face of the earth," and many more phrases were said over a celebratory beer. The happiness lasted for just two days when news came in that HMS *Sheffield* was hit. A French Exocet missile fired from an attacking fighter jet. She was hit amidships and burst into flames. She was part of three ships sent forward to provide long-range radar. When hit, it opened up so many questions as to why she burnt so easily. Twenty sailors lost their lives, and twenty-four were severely injured. After seven hours, she was abandoned, gutted and deformed by fire, and finally sank six days later. Back home, we all shared the grief. What a dreadful impact that had on the people. We were hurting like the Argies. It led to an attempt to put SAS men on Argie soil and blow up any more Exocet missiles. A Sea King helicopter was dispatched from HMS *Invincible* on May 17 but was unable to get the job done. Bad weather forced the helicopter to land fifty miles away from the target. When the weather passed, the pilot flew to Chile and dropped the team off before setting fire to his machine and surrendering to the authorities. Four days later, four thousand men were beginning an amphibious landing on beaches around San Carlos Water. This was also known as Bomb Alley because of so many low-flying Argie fighter planes. We suffered more losses. On the twenty-first, HMS *Ardent* went down; on the twenty-fourth, HMS *Antelope* was also lost; and on the twenty-fifth, *Atlantic Conveyor*, which was carrying a vital supply of Chinook helicopters, was lost. The same day, HMS *Coventry* was lost. *Argonaut* and *Brilliant* were badly damaged. While all this was happening, the Argentines were suffering losses also. All in all, twenty-two planes were shot down with several pilots lost also.

The soldiers were having success on the ground. Enemy soldiers were surrendering with little resistance. Some battles raged. British perseverance prevailed, and Argie soldiers were getting rounded up. That allowed our soldiers to begin heading toward Port Stanley. On June 1, another five thousand troops arrived. This was enough manpower to begin an offensive against the enemy in Stanley. Air assaults continued killing another fifty-two; thirty-two were from the Welsh guards on *Sir Galahad* and *Sir Tristram*. It was so sad to see these burning ships and the losses as the news feed broke it. I myself never questioned if this was all worth it—why would I? This was an English-speaking country. The people wanted and still have the government they want to rule them. And while saddened at the losses, I was proud of our servicemen that went so far for their country. One place, Bluff Cove, was where we at home would watch Argie planes bombing ships, then helicopters hovering in thick smoke winching survivors from burning ships. It was harrowing to see; tears ebbed down my cheeks at such a travesty, and I know I was not alone. On June 14, seventy-four days passed, the British flag was again flying in Port Stanley. We lost 255 personnel. The Argentines lost 649 personnel. The island lost three islanders. All in all, Argentine had

1,188 nonfatal casualties, and England had 777. It was not long after that the junta fell and a government was reinstated by the Argentine people. For me, I was sad about all losses. Extremely proud of our servicemen. Happy that the British bulldog spirit was alive and kicking. To have been able to have the opportunity to walk where they fought. To see blue skies not filled with belching smoke from burning ships. To stand next to memorials. To read strangers' names. To be able to listen and shake the hand of the man that lost his daughter and granddaughter—two of the three islanders that were killed. To sit on beaches watching whales spout that may have passed a sunken ship or plane, oblivious of how it got there. To sit at the highest part of the island and ponder the conditions, the dodging of bullets, the missiles flying overhead, and the way troops walked for miles with backpacks weighing up to ninety pounds, and more when wet. To have that chance in life to be close to those we lost. Those moments touched my heart, and I could not have been more proud and sad.

CHAPTER 29

WITH THE WAR OVER, the British government decided to beef up the security on the island. They were looking for thousands of men to build a whole new airfield and radar site. As we were an asphalting town, it was obviously a good place to look. My friend Steven was getting the word out. Job interviews were being held in London, and after talking to the wife, I went, as did many others from the town, for an interview. I had many talents and would be useful in whatever I did. The terms were laid down, and it looked like we would be on a winner, provided I could remain on the island for my duration. The work was the talk of the town. Excitement was growing, and anticipation of the rewards was the focus point. So many families had dreams of buying a house. I may have had one already if my insurance money policy wasn't cashed in by a deceitful mother.

The time came, and after a last goodbye between the sheets and hugs from my girls, it was time to head for Brize Norton airbase. Travel was to be on a 747 jumbo jet. This was going to be the best flight with such a large machine. We walked out onto the airport tarmac, and I was marvelling at the size of it. I had never been so close to one but seen plenty when they flew over our heads while working on a site outside of Heathrow airport. A major airline had a contract to fly down with workers and return with others that had done their time. We took off, and I was just sitting there looking out the window, seeing places where I had laid asphalt. We kept climbing, and soon it all disappeared. After eight hours of sitting still and pondering what I had left behind, thinking about not having a kiss or sex for months, was hard for this one. I had to make this; I knew if I could get through it, then there would be enough for a house of our own. We began our descent, and all I could see was water. I thought something was up until the captain said we would be landing and refuelling on Ascension Island. We had flown over France, Portugal, Morocco, and Africa to hit this little island that played such an important role before. We got off the plane and waited in an area where tea or coffee was available. The plane was refuelled and, with us on board, weighed over three hundred tons. We taxied out and, like before, were expecting it to ratchet up the engines and take off. We were pushed backward to the end of the runway, and with the brakes on, the captain opened the throttle. We were going nowhere until the brakes were released, and the g-force kicked in. What a rush—who needed drugs when this baby was all you needed! The short runway leaves nothing but fly or swim. What a sensation, and we all loved it. With another four thousand miles, the epic trip would be done; we would be where so many brave men fought and died. Nothing but water and sometimes a giant super tanker was down there, which looked the size of a park pond boat. The weather was rough. High winds had the captain increasing the engines then reducing them. The wings were bobbing up and down, trying to hold the plane level for the landing. We finally got onto the runway, which was built by the pioneers.

The pioneers were the ones that went down when the job was first getting together. They built housing that we would be staying in, and before they were ready, they slept in the containers they emptied. My brother was one of them, and we never met on the island; and in fact, I never knew he was there until he told me when I had been home for some time. We got off the plane early in the morning, and after getting a room and work clothes, we started work. Project managers were asking about what talents we had, and one thing they wanted was a hot bitumen lorry driver. I said I could handle the job, and I got it. I fancied the job because it would have me going all the way to Port Stanley. A new road was constructed, and parts needed to be sprayed and chipped. I knew the concept but had no idea about how the system worked on the lorry. Bitumen needs to be hot, which makes it manageable. My problem was, how do I load the stuff and what happens when it needs to be sprayed? My brain is good at solving problems, and it wasn't long before the system was my slave. I suggested we could make the extensions longer, which we did. I also said that as it takes so long to warm the material in the morning, I would need to start early for it to be ready. Everything I suggested was accepted by the project manager, and the best part was, I was getting overtime every day. I was introduced to a stranger who, like me, was clueless about the spraying operation. With practice, we got things going. I was the driver, and he was the spray bar operator. The plane that arrived two days later took off with a load of guys going home, and that's when one guy swore he would never look up again. It was depressing too see guys going home to family and friends, but they had done their job and deserved it. Some men landed, looked at the place, and hit the high road back. They flatly refused to stay and work, and some just came for the ride, got a memento, and went back on the next available flight. The road to Port Stanley was built in places with a material that was a semi concrete type of material. We would spray the bitumen on, and a chipping machine would lay a blanket of small rock chips on top, thus protecting it.

We were constructing the roads because outside of Stanley, there are none, only tracks. Now known as Darwin Road, this was constructed by the pioneers. Grading and adding additional rock until another section was complete. We headed out towards Bluff Cove and Fitzroy Ridge. Day by day, areas that had been constructed would get sprayed and chipped. The finished job looked good and was ten times better than before. We were working in the area that the *Sir Galahad* and the *Sir Tristram* were sitting targets for warplanes. A calm bay, and one day, the tide was coming in. The boss came up to my lorry and asked for help. There are some sheep going to drown because they are stuck out in the rising water. We went to investigate, and then he urged me to go and get them. I couldn't believe my ears—four sheep were going to drown if I did not go and get them. "Let them die," I said. They are not worth it, and I don't want to get them. He insisted I go get them. I gave in and went after them. The water was freezing, and the further I went, the deeper I got. I knew the water would be no deeper than a couple of feet, so I was not that worried. I got about twenty feet away, and lo and behold, they swam towards the bank. I went back to my truck madder than hell that I allowed this to happen while my partner sat in the warm cab grinning away.

Further along the road was a quarry. There were several places that crushed rock to make the road, and with several, hauling the rock would not involve a long haul. We went into one place where there were a couple of men sitting by a fire, enjoying a beer. We shared one with them while they explained why they were there. It was an outpost and was hardly ever visited by a boss. They were almost like forgotten but had supplies and, when needed, would go to the new airport for supplies. Mount Pleasant Airfield, as it was known, was like a Mecca in a dessert, housing two thousand plus men at any one time; and once you were inside, you were undercover. A well-thought-out place, and when the construction was done, the army and navy servicemen visiting the island would have it. The men were part of the quarrying teams, blasting rock and crushing it to make a decent material for the roads. After leaving the area, the road that led to Port Stanley was just rock that twisted and turned as you headed further away from home.

We were on a mystery trip. There was nothing better if it was raining than go sightseeing. We could not spray anything if it was wet. We were not really allowed to go back to camp either, as this would not go down well with boss. If we were getting paid, then it was expected of us to be ready to work.

We came across fenced-off mine fields, places where Argentine soldiers had abandoned artillery guns and old trucks. Food rations scattered everywhere. Did these men surrender or fight to the death? went through my mind. Was I stepping on ground that had caressed a dead man on its heather surface? My mind would run away with me, imagination going crazy with thoughts of screaming men wanting to kill each other. My working partner and I had no answers to the question. Further along, about halfway between MPA and Stanley, I came across a sheep herder. With a long semi grey beard and at least eight dogs, he was moving them over to new ground. Each dog knew what it had to do, as they control some six thousand of them. He paused, and we enjoyed a conversation then, after a couple of photos, went on his way. We passed a lovely area that had a small river running alongside a small rock face cover in yellow flowered bracken. A surreal place in the middle of nowhere, and at the top, a small white fence sat. I thought it was a small holding place for newborn sheep or something; I did not know what it was until about two weeks later. We carried on until we went over Mount Tumbledown and our first glimpse of Port Stanley, the capital and the harbour. Tumbledown along with Wireless Ridge were the last two places of battle. When the Argentine general realized he was surrounded by sea and land, he surrendered himself and the remaining 9,800 Argentine soldiers. This effectively ended the war. We drove around a little, looking at corrugated houses, and even saw a pink Land Rover. Several old Argentine lorries had been commandeered by the islanders. and with important equipment coming in huge crates, the wood was being used to make sheds and other useful things. It was fascinating to have seen such a faraway outpost on the British Empire, and as time was getting on, we then decided to head back home to our living quarters.

We had a couple of bars where cheap beer would flow and cheap cigarettes were in abundance. With so many strangers, you would soon get to know the regular ones. Also by being put in certain teams, if more had come from your partner's home area, chances were new friendships would be borne. Some of the men from my hometown were doing the asphalting. They were good at it and conscious about making a good job. We would work six days a week, and the free day was to go see or enjoy a sport. Several times, I would fish on an inlet, trying to catch sea trout. I was also able to work out in a gym and enjoy my favourite game, squash. I wasn't the best on the island but was pretty damn close. It also gave me the chance to teach others. I enjoyed seeing the fruits of their labour working on the court. There was a small rough-as-hell golf hole, but with the weather down there, I never did much. We were lucky men, although some of them you could never please. Your work clothes were washed for you. You food was cooked for you. Your room was cleaned for you. It was like living with Mother and them paying you. Everything was free except personal things. Not a bad deal, really, and a chance of adventure. The first ship that ever arrived there for the massive construction project was shored up in one of the inlets, and others that arrived would come alongside, and its cargo unloaded by the fixed ship crane. In the empty hold, a wooden squash court was made; so strange to play on a court with wooden walls. I guessed one of the pioneers enjoyed the game and put old grates to good use. Just up the road on Bertha's Beach was a colony of penguins. They would be coming out of the water and getting back to their partner. They would almost be in a single file as they waddled along. As one bunch came in and approached them, they simply started to go around me then head back to the line of direction they were on. On a good day, way off shore, you might see whales spouting in the cold South Atlantic waters.

In the two large bars, on most nights, you see your hometown mates and talk about the day's work. Just like home, eight thousand miles away, if you made a mistake, then the word "wanker" would come into play. It was also a good time when we could talk about home and our families. We were all in the same boat with our girls back there. At Christmastime, cards and presents arrived from home. It was hard to see little pictures drawn or painted by our children. Then there were the gut-wrenching letters from your lady, wishing you were home. Of course, we could phone home, and it was not hard to hear a conversation while waiting in line. One such call was an eye-opener. He was talking dirty to his missus, and he had my imagination going. Everything I tried not to think about was pouring out his mouth just a few feet away. I was not alone, as there were a few more phone lines with men raising their eyebrows. I had no idea what he did and never saw him again. Maybe he was a lucky one going home and wanted to fire up his wife or girlfriend. We headed back towards Stanley to spray another area when another islander stopped for a chat, nice enough man who had come from England thirty-three years before. I asked, "Why on earth would you want to come here?" He explained with a simple story that I could relate to. Back in the day, he had five pounds; fare to Australia would have been that on a merchant ship. He had a going-away party and spent a pound getting drunk with his friends, which screwed that idea up. However, four pounds would get him there, and that's what he did. We were smiling, and I commented about the island being so barren with no trees, but the flower colours like the ones on the cliff face were so pretty. He explained that this was his daughter's and granddaughter's favourite playing area, and as they died, he was the one that built the white fences that surrounded their graves. He shed a small tear before bucking himself up and thanked us for building the road. He was leaving in his Land Rover as he said that it took only an hour to get to Stanley when before it took twenty-four.

CHAPTER 30

IT WAS XMAS DAY 1984, and many of us had been on the island since September. We had endured biting winds that could tear you apart and warm sun that tanned you. The cold was different, much crisper and fresher than anything I had experienced. This day it was warm, and we made our way to the highest point on the island. Mount Pleasant has a silver-looking cross with two brass name plates with four names on it. We were told that underneath was a bottle of Brasso and a rag. Everyone that went to the cross was expected to clean the name plates as a mark of respect. Six of us climbed to the top and did our duty. We were also told that the cross was made from the blades of a helicopter that was shot down by our men, as the identifying bleeper that should identify it as friendly had failed. How sad can that be? It's enough to lose men in battle, but this must cut right into the heart of the brave.

We had also found a fish-and-chip shop in town and enjoyed a few beers in the bars. Once, my partner and I were waiting in line with all our thermal clothes on when the door opened, and we looked down at a young kid about ten years old, and all he had on was a T-shirt. His cheeky little face and dark-blue eyes looked around, then they landed on us. Looking up at us, he simply said, "Are you cold, mister!" Man, I felt like a wimp. I felt like picking him up and standing him outside for an hour. But what would that do—he was an islander and used to the inclement weather. There were a lot of women that did the cleaning and cooking. Some stayed true to themselves, and some were as horny as hell. One friend had two on the go. As he worked nights, when the cleaning girls came round, he would be in bed, and it all went from there. Another met a lady, and they got it going, but I don't think she was ready to settle down. He was a bit jealous, and one night, she was in another room when he tried to kick the door in. He broke his leg, and as sometimes in the passageways you might get mugged, no one opened their doors when he was screaming in agony. Several muggings had taken place while I was there. Two men to a room and maybe thirty rooms per passage, which were set in blocks, it was hard to police. Getting help was never easy, but eventually, it would get there. He was airlifted to Stanley then shipped home. She stayed to work, and when she left for home, they got back together and married was the last I heard. Another man got so drunk that he brought a small horse from an islander in one of the bars and took it back to his room for the night. Rumour has it, the horse had its head right next to his face, and when he woke and saw it, he had a slight heart attack! One problem down there was, when you had been there long enough through working the hours and any overtime earnings, if you went home before your time was up, any bonus would be lost. Most of us signed up for six months, and it was best to hang on.

Some just said, "To hell with it, I want to go home." In doing so, they may have to wait a week or more for an empty seat. Others would take extreme measures that sort of guarantied the next flight. One night, a huge D9 dozer was stolen and moved to the end of the runway. The engine was getting revved up and down while the back ripper was set to rip the runway up. The army with a loud speaker said, "If you move one inch, we will fire." It was never known what would be fired, but he did enough for the man to be on the next flight home. Another went flying around a bar on a scrambler motorbike; he too was on the next flight home. My partner and I had finished with the spraying, and the truck was drained of bitumen and parked. It had been a good job for us apart from when we were spraying around the main construction site. Roads and footpaths needed to be surfaced, and we were playing a part of it. One fateful day, a large dump truck was reversing to a spot to dump its load. The foreman instructed the driver to back up as he turned and began walking. The dump truck was going slightly faster than his pace. It was not long before the truck had caught up with him and caught his ankle. He was semi hard of hearing and never knew it was so close. He was unable to do anything, and the truck kept going and passed completely over his body. The site was shut down for an investigation while a donation fund was set up. Several thousands of pounds were collected for his wife, who would have had him home six weeks later. Several men lost their lives doing what they enjoyed doing. The drive and mentality to earn and better ourselves go before us. To fulfil dreams for a family and have more and do better is a must for every breadwinner. So many factors come into play for the sake of money, and so many have paid a high price for it.

My partner went and did something else while I was given a large excavator. I was to expose a large pipe and had to be very careful, as it was a live one, and any problem would be a major headache. They gave me another machine with a hydraulic hammer, which was needed to break concrete that surrounded it. I had no help, no spotter, and plans were not at hand. I got going. Bit by bit, I broke out what was required. My partner was going home a few weeks after we finished working together. As I watched the plane take off, I raised the arm of my large excavator. The bucket was like a hand, and as the plane lifted, the bucket was high in the air, waving goodbye to a friend I would never see again. I spoke with him once when I followed home six weeks later and never heard from him again. When it was time for me to be going home, I was pondering the men I had met. I would never see the young man that spent so much time burning wood between barrels of bitumen, warming them enough so it could be pumped into the tank on the lorry. He did get relief from all the smoke, sticking a bar in the hole and stirring the stuff. Relief was a decanter; this would have hot bitumen in it, and when the barrels were opened and held upside down, the heat allowed the material to slowly drop. One day, the decanter caught on fire, and the brigade was called. "Let it burn. Let it burn. We need the practice," a fire-fighter said, so we left it!

My time came, and goodbyes were being shared over several beers. One thing that must never happen is getting arrested by the site police, which could cost you all your bonus. A guy tried to hit me with a chair on the final night. He threw another and another. They were spread around the floor of the dance place. I finally got him and piled my fist in his face several times. When I released him, he held a roof support pillar and slid to the floor. I had whopped his ass when others were saying, "Stop, that's enough."

When everything settled down, I proceeded to my room and got to thinking that I should stand up and be counted (which is a part of me, if, and only if, I make the mistake). I knew he had cuts because of the blood on my clothes and knuckles. I washed my hands but never changed my shirt. I went to the first-aid post, where I leaned against a door and heard him say that I had sprung him while trying to steal his money. I walked in with my hands up, looked at the officers, and said, "I'm your man. It was me that did it." They took me to a room and, after explaining what really happened, led them to the dance hall and pillar. They agreed that I was telling the truth and, by the rules set down, had to take me to the station.

For the second time in my life, I was looking at walls and sitting on a very unfriendly bed, only this time there was a difference: the door was left open. It was so obvious what lies they had been told—they knew that I would not be a problem; it was only that they had to follow protocol. There was a shout: "Would you like a cup of tea?"

"Yes, please," I said as I walked out of the cell. They were nice guys, and after ten minutes or so, the cold, hard truth started to hit. It was possible I could lose everything I had worked for. That entire bonus and overtime could be lost. I knew it was about 5,000 pounds of hard-earned money could be gone. Why should I have to lose when I never started anything? Maybe I should have walked away from someone threatening me. Maybe that would have led to more aggression. But why should I, why should I walk away from someone clearly set on trying to do me damage? I must stand and be counted, or the very core of my being would be rendered useless. I got some good advice from the site police. They only had jurisdiction for the site and knew what to do in this case. I got hold of my boss. I told him the problem. He wrote a letter of commendation for the arbitrator. He asked me first what I had I done for the company while on the island to which I explained. He read the letter from my boss that explained how much effort I had put in to get the road built and all the hours I had worked to make it happen. Then he asked the site police what they thought and what they found. It was agreed that I was provoked and protected myself as a last resort. I was told to go and pack my bags as the plane had landed. I ran to my room and threw all my stuff in a case and large carry bag. I had little time to properly wrap the little pictures of my girls, so little time for anything. Sweat was pouring from my head; the beer was coming out. I headed back up the passage and got to thinking, I could be free. If nothing was signed, they could not stop my payment. I was so close to the departure area when a man stopped me. "Yes, it's me you're looking for," I said with my heart in my mouth. "What have I lost, how much did that asshole cost me?" He gave me the board with the paperwork on to sign; £250 was my fine, and I was over the moon. I was ecstatic to know our dream was alive. So happy with the opportunity to fulfil our dream and better ourselves.

I boarded the plane, which was not full as I expected. I was by a window at the back, where I like to be. We taxied out and began to increase speed. I looked at the roads that were built, the buildings that were erected, and the men still there continuing the work that thousands before had played a part in. Briefly, I remembered those that had died as I began to lean back, reaching for the sky. Up we went then banked to the right, where so much more came into view: the splendid runway that I witnessed a Chinook helicopter dance along to clear dust before a plane could land. The pure excellence of the pilot was truly amazing. The noise was loud, but nothing like Concord, the deafening sound when she took off from Heathrow Airport heading to the USA. Every morning, as we laid asphalt, she would roar over our heads. The very first test flight brought the plane over my hometown. That day, eyes were firmly glued on a marvel as it passed over our heads. How easy it was to forget so much of its beginnings when they become an everyday thing. We as humans forget most of a new man-made beginning unless it's a child of our own. I was also looking at the hangar area where a man constructing it went to the top for his cigarettes and a gust of wind sent him to his death. This area is where a 747, after landing with a spare engine, strapped under its wing next to the fuselage for a stricken Tri-Star plane. What a sight and memory. I sat back and shut my eyes after the long night, knowing I was four thousand miles to ascension and halfway home. We landed for refuelling, and as we were going home, beers were allowed to be drank. There were many rousing goodbyes there. We knew when we landed at Brize Norton, we would go our separate ways and, with most guys, never to meet again. It was time to get back on and relax for the best takeoff ever, knowing in about twelve hours, my arms would be full of happiness.

CHAPTER 31

WE LANDED, AND I went by bus to the rail station. The ride took me to Bath and then a bus home. I got the job in a bar and decided to have one before I went home. It was good to have a pint in your local and catch up with the news. But what does that say when I have been gone for over six months? I got home. Monica was angry with me, then it was hugs and kisses and loads of talk about the experience. I got so many hugs from my daughter and was ready for some from my eldest. After a couple of weeks, the phone was going, and it was another manager asking if I wanted to go back to work as the bitumen tanker again. I asked what percentage of bonus, and he said fifteen, as before. I said twenty-five or no deal; alas, there was no deal. There was no going back to such a remote place so far away. There was no work about on the roads. Once again, another lull in the construction industry. I spoke with a friend who had a little enterprise going, and I began hauling waste from the local creamery. This a not very nice-smelling fluid, which was good fertilization for fields. I would load a vacuum tank then haul it to fields then empty the tank by spraying over a specified field. I also would go to a pig farm and suck their waste up and do the same thing. One day, I had the back window open and turned with the wind behind me. A gust blew the fine spray in the cab and covered me, which was not a good idea. Later, I went to the pub for a beer. This was the one day no one wanted to know me. I was playing with them, putting my arms out and begging for a cuddle while they were scurrying away. It was not too good when I got home either. The moment reminded me of another time I had mates scurrying away. I was at the quarry doing the pop blasting, and I came home with gelatine, an explosive that is useless unless wired to a detonator. I was in the bar where I pulled the stuff from my jacket pocket and hit the bar with it. They asked what it was, and I told them as I hit it on the bar again. They called me nuts and moved well away while I was laughing my head off. I also had the idea that would maybe stop tourists from looking at Stonehenge. What if I was to blow it up, would that help us black top boys? Tourists used to slow us up, looking at the place when we wanted to get home for the four o'clock closing on market day. Who knows? England celebrates Guy Fawkes Night, and they may have had a night for me too!

The man I worked for was losing the work, and I could soon be looking for something else. Another man asked if I would work for him doing the same job. This was the farmer whose land I learnt to drive on. He purchased a big road tractor and tank. I was so proud of it and continued to enjoy doing the job. I had to do ten loads a day, and that meant he would be making a profit. I understood that and did my utmost to ensure in whatever weather, he made a profit. I enjoyed rolling around the countryside looking at green fields and farmers getting the fields ploughed ready for planting while my music was turned up and me singing my head off. One day, I was back in the farm yard around midday, washing the tank down, and he asked what I was doing. I said the ten loads were done because I started at first light, and I was going golfing. He was not happy and said, "Go get some more." I explained what we agreed, but he was having none of it. He said, "Go get more loads."

I paused, looked at him, and said, "You go get more loads," and walked off. I packed the job in there, and then and as luck would have it, I went back on the roads. The money had come in from the Falkland work and was just over the £5,000 I had expected. The £250 were taken out, but we were happy with the reward of separation. We decided on looking for a house, as we had a good deposit. I went to London, and work would be seven days a week and long hours. While I was working and living in a big static caravan with three other men on the M25 London Orbital motorway, house hunting was under way. Our job was to close up the last of the 117-mile radius. The road was originally discussed in the early twentieth century and is the second-largest orbital in Europe, with the longest being the Berliner, which is 122 miles. At the London Heathrow interchanges, there were 196,000 vehicles recorded in one day; and with too many users, it is known as the largest car park in the world. So many times if an accident happened, the flow of traffic would almost stop, and a massive backup would begin. One small section is not deemed a motorway because certain types of banned motorway vehicles could not cross the London River and do their local business. When completed, there is a story of a man that drove the whole way round and claimed to be the first to do it to the Guinness Book of Records. He failed to pass where he came on, and the half mile from exit ramp to entry ramp was the reason. That had to have been a really bad feeling day.

Monica was looking for the right house and found one in a nice cul-de-sac on the far side of town, a semidetached three-bedroom house and garage. Everything was sorted out, and we moved into our pride and joy. Decorating began when I could get home; I would do all I could. The motorway work paid good money, and sometimes we would cook in the caravan; but most nights, a take away was the chosen dish. As this was a large project, I met up with a couple of guys I had met in the Falklands. They came from the North, and we came from the South, and we met in the middle to build a road. How strange to first meet them eight thousand miles away. Some days we worked fifteen or sixteen hours, and after a couple of beers, the bed was calling. One morning, I woke up and was heading to the shower block, and there was a head slumped over the steering wheel that belonged to a hung over man. Steven had gotten a takeaway and sat in the van to eat it but fell asleep. It was still in his lap, and he was a hard one to wake up. This was a way of life for us. Work like a dog. Live like a dog, and all for the sake of money. We would almost every night go to a bar to wind down. Steven met a local lady and left his third wife for her.

A local was talking about scrumpy that comes from down our way and asked if I would get some on my next trip home. This is cider at its best, or worst, whichever way you look at it. Never clear like run-of-the-mill cider, this is cloudy and knocks you sideways if you do not respect it. A good Somerset landlord would, when you walked in, maybe allow you a half pint. You might, the next day, get one pint. He would watch to see how you react to it. I know that four pints would send me through the sound barrier. It's very potent and can ruin a good man when drunk on a daily basis. I got drunk on it once, and that was enough because I went to the pub the next day, and two good mates had marks on their faces. I enquired what happened to them. They started to call me everything under the sun because I had lost it and started hitting them. I had no idea what I had done, and I have never drunk it again. I went home and got a gallon from the farm. I took it back, and he paid me, but a lot of questions were being asked about it. "Can you get me some next time you go home?" Several weeks later, I went home and wound up bringing twenty-seven gallons for the boys. I tried to tell one man to treat it with respect, but, no, he had the top off and started guzzling his gallon down. About half an hour passed, and he was pickled. His eyes were popping out of his head while sitting on his bar stool; his head thumped the bar and was left resting peacefully for the rest of the night. He was also the one that had a bet about how long he could go before taking a shower. Twenty-one days! He was dirty and smelt rotten, and the thing was, he was proud. The worst thing was, we were sharing the same caravan.

While there were times when weather would stop everything, I would rush home to work on the house, and that stopped when a loader operator was needed in a temporary railhead. The train would come in and unload stabilizing material into a bunker, which came from the quarries back home. That's when it was flat-out time to get the material moved as quickly as possible to allow the train to empty and get back into the rail system. Many times, if the train was coming in early, I would sleep in the back of my estate car to ensure we were ready to go. It was not a problem, as I could cook a morning meal when we were done, and it saved me money by not going to the bar. This material would be loaded on site lorries and hauled to a waiting paving machine to lay it. One thing that had to be done was pull a string line or fishing line across the new road. Setting pins every ten yards with tape on them would define the road level. The machine operators would measure down, and we then would find out if we were in the tolerances that engineers had set out. It was a boring job, and some innovative thinking was done. A fishing rod was cut off above the second eyelet. With line and reel, a weight was required to make it fly. A box bolt or a large nut would work, and it did. The rod was cast, and over it flew to a waiting man. The line pulled tight, and levels were checked, then wind it back across until the next set of pins. One such time, the receiver was not aware it was on its way, and he was hit on the head. We saw him tip sideways and roll down a bank into some water. We ran over, and as he came into view, he was flopping around, cussing everyone and ready to kill. We stood at the top, laughing our heads off. We also had a game that we would use a piece of wood: lay a shovel on the floor, put the wood on the handle, then run and stamp on the shovel, which would catapult the wood into the air, and whoever got it the furthest won money. One guy did it with a brick. He lost it in the glaring sun and down it came onto his head. The ambulance rushed him to hospital for stitches as we were chuckling away and working.

The work wound down, and we were looking at going home. There would be no more driving big all-terrain four-ton dumpers down semi completed roads with four drunks in the pan and one driving it at night. No more enjoying camaraderie while messing around while waiting for a delivery of material. We were to part company without knowing where we would meet again. I, like so many, was much better to be doing jobs and staying close to the site, as you got lodging money. Long hours meant more money, rather than letting someone drive for two hours, do a day's work, and drive you home again and get no travelling time. I got back and started for a small company that was based out of town. This is a large village with a population of around five thousand. The ride across the Mendip Hills is about eighteen miles and leads you into a gorge that drops down some three hundred feet. The road twists and turns around rocks carved by water millions of years ago. The further you go down, the rock faces engulf you. Goats live on the cliffs, and almost at the bottom of the largest gorge in Britain, there are caves, which are beautiful to walk through and marvel at its huge stalagmites and stalactites. From the face, you can go in about 1,300 feet and see its carvings made by an underground river. Several limestone quarries are there, and this is where cheddar cheese is derived from. One favourite there is the strawberries and cream, or my favourite scones, jam, and cream. It's so rich and such a lovely treat every now and then. This is where Britain's oldest complete human skeleton, Cheddar Man, was found in 1903 and is estimated to be nine thousand years old. A period dating twelve thousand to thirteen thousand years ago, excavations have uncovered remains from that (Palaeolithic) era. Cheddar in the tenth (Saxon) century boasted a royal palace and a chapel, where remains were found in the 1960's. While modern-day folk have heard of the Seven Wonders of the World. The gorge is recognized as the second natural wonder of Britain. Water runs down on side of the road, and evidence shows water mills were there that ground corn and made paper. Not far away is what's deemed as the smallest city in England, Wells, although the City of London is actually smaller; it is not surrounded by a huge metropolitan conurbation and therefore takes the title. The first church on the site was in 705, the present building dates from 1175 to 1490, it became dubbed as "the most poetic of English cathedrals." Also in the precinct is the splendid Bishop's Palace surrounded by a moat and wall.

CHAPTER 32

SO MANY TIMES I, "Where is Dad?" fell on deaf ears from Mother and Aunt Bess. Monica and my brother's wife and children had gotten us brothers to be closer. I still wasn't close, but we lived not far from each other and did our best to make nice homes. I said to myself one day, it's 1987, and with all this technological stuff out there, he must have a phone. Mother's face was a picture when I disclosed my plan to find him to which she just looked at me and said, "Why bother? It's been so long. Just forget it." Well, that was like taking meat from a tiger. It fired me up to rip her apart, and I began my hunt.

I went to the local library and asked about phone numbers for the state of New Jersey, America. That's all I was ever told, but it was enough as a pointer to get me going. They said I would need to go or call the Bristol Library, which was a lot bigger. They said, "No good here. You will need to go the Central Library in London." I went home and said to my brother this is what I need to do and made plans to book into a hotel and spend whatever time was needed to find him. Again, the tiger began to roar; I could see fear in her eyes as she continued to say I was wasting my time.

On the day I was on a train and heading to the library, I had no idea what was a head of me, but that was like a lot of things in my life. I enjoyed adventure and small amounts of danger, and this was going to be something like that. I went to the hotel and then headed to my destination. I was stepping back in history as I walked through the doors of a building with large arched windows. Founded in 1841 on the initiative of Thomas Carlyle, its original site was in Pall Mall and based in this glorious building since 1845. I approached a well-dressed gentleman and gave my reason why I was there. I said, "I would like every phone number for the state of New Jersey in America."

With raised eyebrows, he looked and said, "Will it be commercial or residential?"

"The latter will do," I exclaimed.

He again looked and said, "There are 2,876,563 phone numbers. How many would you like?"

"I will take the lot."

As he handed me drawer after drawer of cards with names and numbers, he said, Good luck." I began looking, and after two hours, I was getting nowhere until something began to make sense. I was looking at names that led to another name and another, then there they were right in front of me. I began to breath heavy as my last name was profiled; my heart was thumping as I looked at every card, and small beads of sweat were appearing on my forehead. Fingers were shuffling, and the others writing. I found 107 in the file drawers.

I took everything back to the gentleman, and he asked how I fared. With joy, I said, "I believe I have found my father," with the biggest grin I could ever produce. When I was done, I was bouncing along the footpath back to the hotel.

I never hung around. After leaving the place, I called Ralph and said, "I have found him. I have a number." All the way home, my heart was in my hand. Dad was all I saw; nothing else mattered. At last, he would be mine. I always said to Mother, "If I find Dad and he shakes my hand, I will shake his. If he decides to ignore me or disown me, I will put him on his ass."

I got to my brother's house, and he called the number, explaining who he was. He also explained that his younger brother was standing next to him. The voice on the other end was totally lost and so out of it. The voice was Brenda, his daughter. She had never heard of us and had five children. What on earth was going on? For thirty-three years, I never imagined I had a half sister. Never in my wildest dreams did I contemplate such a thing. He again asked for Dad, then the most chilling words were uttered by Ralph, "He's dead." That hit harder than the man that hit my front tooth out. I just stared into space. My dad, the one I had wanted for so long, was gone. I had and never will have that hug I had promised myself. I cried to the world. I cried in my heart. I cried for him. How he kept it a secret from them, I do not know. Mother was inquisitive as to the results and seemed relieved that it was in the open. It never occurred to me before, but this was why Mother had a mysterious illness. A couple of years earlier, she was in a hospital bed for six weeks and losing weight with no symptoms. Albert was there constantly, and he was confused as everyone else was. She came home having lost fifty pounds or more, never saying what the cause was, although she and her sister knew (she knew he had died). In saying that, who would have written a letter to say he had died?

She still said nothing but "if you never went looking, then you would not be hurting." Bloody hell. What a cold-blooded creature she was. About an hour later, Ralph's phone rang, and it was our father's brother; he lived in Birmingham. He asked what we were playing at as he had a call from America. My brother explained what we knew, and he suggested we go meet. Two days later, we were on our way to Birmingham. With us were a photo and any other snippets of what we knew. We found his house, and there was a warm reception. We sat down to talk, and looking at my newfound uncle, there was a slight resemblance to my father's photo. Looking at his son was like looking at my brother with glasses. It was uncanny to be in a room with near-perfect twins. After a few hours of talking, he called America and said, "I have no doubt about it, it's your brothers." Brenda, her mother was still alive.

We went out for some food and a beer or two, and during simple conversation, I mentioned I had a pub in the city. I explained where it was, and they knew it. One weekend, they had gone in there for a bite to eat. If I was not in Somerset, I may have noticed something about them and started a conversation. How close was I to having the opportunity to hug him? We left and from that day have never seen them again. Was it, or is it me that lets contact die? Should I fight to keep the strings of contact together? Why should I question myself on that point? Do others bother to contact me? Come and see me? Hardly ever. It's always me to pay for the plane, sit on the thing for hours, and hang around in airports. I was intrigued about America and wanted more information about my dad. I booked a flight for Christmas because the asphalt construction industry shuts down for about a two-week period. I went to Heathrow on a train, then it was my turn to board my bird (an expression used in the Falklands). Memories of the Falkland flight were going through my head, but this end result would be very different.

We landed, and I got to the passenger arrival area and walked past her, but that was only for a brief few seconds. She was much smaller than me and gave the warmest of cuddles. I tried to talk, but it was hard getting a word in. She was so excited, and I had a job to understand the New Jersey dialect. We got to their house, which was very nice with a pool at the back. After meeting her five young kids, a great husband, and a lovely mother, that was enough for the day. The first night was a blur, young children looking at me like I landed from another planet and not England. After a few beers and a bite, I was led to a bed for a good-night's sleep because the next day, I was going to Dad's grave. I stood over his grave in Parsippany, and that was as close as I ever would get unless the man in Ireland was my father. This is something I must live with and will always wonder. My half sister took me shopping, and one day at the checkout, I said, "I fancy a fag."

With a horrified look, she looked at me and said, "You're not, are you?"

"I am not what?"

"You're not, you're not gay?"

"Bloody right I'm not," and then I realized what I had said. I explained that I fancied a cigarette. She was so relieved, but for the fun of it, I should have played on it a bit more.

The way of life in America is very different than my home. I always want to go out and see things and people. Drinking in a bar is one of my pleasures, especially when I am finding out about the area. For me, sitting at home is not an education; I am a people's person and enjoy interacting. Maybe that's why I have so many friends in various places. We went out to a bar one night, and I enjoyed doing what I like doing. Once I had my bearings, I could walk the three miles or so for a pint. My second Christmas, I did such a thing; I took the dog and walked to the bar. I never said I was going to do that because I would probably been told, "No, you don't want to do that." I got there and enjoyed some beers and began walking back home. I guess I was gone a few hours, and walking the road home, I heard scrambler motorbikes up in the woods. I followed the noise, and there were people in bikes enjoying their freedom and passion. I sat and reflected when I rode my scrambler bike that was brought for me. Memories of watching the races I would walk to at Leighton scramble bike circuit. It was always an enjoyable weekend seeing professionals doing their job and thousands watching. I was there for an hour or so then headed back to the road and on to my sister's. I was walking down a road with little traffic on it. Suddenly behind me, a car pulled up and put on his siren for a second. I turned to see a police officer, with lights ablaze, getting out the patrol car. Bemused, I asked if I was at fault. They explained an APB was put out for a lost Englishman.

I grinned and retorted, "Do I look lost?"

He smiled and said, "No, but do you know where you are going?" I told him what direction I was heading, and with that, he said, "Fine," and returned to the car. I continued and was home in the next half hour to a very warm welcome.

The following year, I again came at Christmas, and Brenda wanted me to play Santa Claus. I was to dress up in the suit and come in from the patio with my sack and lay presents under the tree for the little ones to enjoy. She had the video camera ready, and I went outside. It was freezing, and after sorting out a small problem, she beckoned me in. "Stop" was the cry because the battery was flat. She went off to the store for batteries. Her husband and I had another beer on top of those we had already consumed.

She came back and got things ready to go again. I was told to go outside, and I was freezing, waiting for my cue. "Come on in," she shouted. I slid the door back and tripped on the door rail support. With my sack of goodies, I was hurtling towards the tree. I managed to just stop by landing on the floor before taking the tree out. I then proceeded to take the presents out while we were all laughing our heads off. I looked up at the camera and said, "Kids, if you believe this, you'll believe anything," while still laughing like hell. Next morning, the children were gathered to see Father Christmas delivering the presents. I was discovered in a second by the kids, and we all had a good laugh. I got one of the kids a present, which was a simple glider that when thrown would do a loop and come back to you. He could not do it and beckoned me onto the front lawn in the snow to try. I put it together and threw it. It went as programmed in a loop then came back and hit me on the side of my head. Over I went in the snow, much to the amusement of my videoing sister. She sent it to *America's Funniest Videos*, which it aired, and we won $250. I spent time sitting in the annex of the house with my father's wife, a lovely lady who got me thinking when she said, "If your father was alive, he would have done a runner for a few days." Well, who did that remind me of? She explained the night he was drunk and fell in the local lake, and I explained the day I was drunk and fell in the local river. Many things she said about Dad gave me feeling of joy, and when I reflected on them, so much of it was me. I was industrious. I cared about things and never caused trouble, but could finish it. After my first visit, I was so torn up because I missed my chance by only two years. Disgusted as I was, I had to hold it in until I was standing in front of her. I stormed through the door, said sorry to Albert, and let her have it. I blew my top and called her so many things. My pent-up anger triggered so many emotions, and if a gun was to be had, I would have wasted her. How could she keep telling me Dad used to beat her when he was a big ole softie? I walked away vowing I was done with her and her sister and stuck my fingers up.

All in all, I came over six times. As I was almost always on the move, the closeness started to drift away. I never kept in contact, as my personal life was constantly changing, and I took on jobs that would take up my time. I began doing my own thing, and although she was in my thoughts, I never beat myself up for not holding on to the memory or writing.

CHAPTER 33

I KEPT BUSY, AND work was good. I was laying kerb stones, plus I was someone who knew the job. The other employees needed someone to guide them, and as work was picking up for the company, I was able to help. After several months, I was asked if I had ever thought of starting my own business. The company agent said that the possibilities were very encouraging. I am sure if they knew that I was responsible for stealing one of their tractors, it may not have happened. This one particular night, I was drinking in a pub on the outskirts of town. No taxi was available, and it was a long way to go in the drizzle, so I stole a tractor with a compressor on the back. It was being used for some road repairs, and I drove it home. I went a good mile along semi dark roads then parked it not too far of my home. The next morning, it was still there as I walked past and got into a van that picked me up to go to work. Boisterous laughter rang out as my workmates saw it and knew it was me. When I came home, it was gone, and Mother was asking about how it got there; she had her suspicions, but I denied any knowledge about it.

I spoke with two friends I knew who were good at kerbing and asphalt. I offered them a job, and that was it. A new construction company was born. With the correct paperwork in place and having knowledge of basic employee requirements, we were up and running. I paid a deposit for a van, and the three of us would travel into the West Country every day. It was hard work laying kerbs, but it was good honest work; and looking back at your kerb line, you would be satisfied with what you had created. I so enjoyed reading plans and creating a simple masterpiece. Everyone would have to follow it as the roads and footpaths came together. We were asked to lay some asphalt with some other men who worked for the company, which was not a problem. The agent asked if I could put a crew of six together, as there was so much work. I went around tarmac city asking the right men I knew if they fancied joining me. I got the crew together and another van, gave them some tools, and off they went to do what they are good at. I was spending time doing the paperwork and spending little time with my family during the evenings.

One day, I was out having a beer when I was talking to a friend of mine about what was going on. His wife, Jessica, turned and said if I was looking for a secretary, she could do it. As it would be part time, we agreed an hourly rate; and the following day, I showed her what I had done and gave the paperwork to her. When she did invoices and other book stuff, it all looked professional and correct. My name began to go around in the asphalt business fraternity, and another request came in for a gang. I again got the men and a van with tools, and off they went. It was so nice to have guys asking me for work, and as I knew them, I would do my best to find more work and keep them going.

The business was going well, so I, of course, got the Jessica on full time. Tight curly hair and round face were some of her features. Not too bad a figure, at times looked rather inviting. Her house became the office, and that's where the men went for their weekly wages. I got a mechanic who was already established with a garage just down the road from the flat my wife lived in before we got together. He was David's younger brother, and I knew he would be good and useful. I was beginning to step back from working the shovel and more on the lines of overseeing my men and the jobs. One job was down in Weston-super-Mare, which is a seaside town and a quaint place for older people to retire. Here was where many years before, when we never had jackhammers and mini excavators, my mate and I were installing a drainage system in a school play area. He had the shovel and wheelbarrow, and I had the pickaxe. I had my head down and swung again and again, breaking up the old asphalt and rock underneath. I would stand back, and he would clear what he could, and I'd start again. He did his turn and was supposed to step back but never stood back far enough. As I brought the axe down, it never made it to the floor. He was standing to close to me, and the point of the axe went into his hand. I looked up, and there he was shaking and his face turning red. "Look, look, there's a hole in my hand," he was saying. The point went plum between two knuckles and the attached bones. He was lucky that the axe was blunt and the skin was slightly punctured. He hurt for a few weeks and had to change his drinking hand. He lost money because of no work. I felt so guilty, I went to his home and offered half my wages. He told me to bugger off and buy him a pint instead. I was more than happy to buy my friend a beer or two. To this day, he still has a mark on his hand where I hit him.

Things were really looking good with the local work. Men on the motorways were doing fine, and money was being earned by everyone. I hunted for a three-ton pickup truck with a tipper. This would be used to move material, and I would be getting the haulage money for its use. I found one and gave it to my mechanic. He went over it and sprayed it black and the cab red. It was needed in a hurry, as I had so much work ready and needed it to get going. I got it from his workshop early in the morning, and the paint was hardly dry as I hurried and picked up one of my men before heading out.

It was a lovely summer's morning driving across the Mendip Hills, passing the splendid golf course and then down into the gorge. As this was a large-enough truck, it was not advisable to hurry around the tight bends; but unknown to us, a lady was coming our way, hurrying around the bends. I was swinging to the right, and she was swinging to the left, and her back end came out. She hit my right front wheel into the base of the cab. My passenger hit the windscreen and bounced back into the seat. I sat there holding the wheel in disbelief. I climbed down and saw the damage and was going to go off my head. My senses came together when I smelt petrol. I ran to her small MG sports car and got her out. She was shaken but no physical damage and kept saying, "I was in a hurry and lost it." The next car went for the police, and then photos and statements taken. We got towed to a garage, and that was the last my truck would run. It was written off. No more than forty minutes did I have it in service; I missed a great chance of working it. I got a letter from her insurance company, and it stated I had caused the accident. It was so obvious what had happened, but she was adamant. We went to court, and she was blown out the water. Why would anyone blame someone else when they are at fault? The time it cost. What a waste trying to save her insurance going up.

Things began to turn for the better, and I got more men working on motorways. All they needed were the transport and tools. Equipment was supplied by the contractor. With my name known by several national asphalt companies, it was all falling into place. My secretary was on top of everything, and things were going well. So much time going over things and looking at the next step we were to take. With this, I was spending so much time on the business and was leaving my marriage behind. I was ignoring her and our daughter. I saw success, and that would be so good for us further down the road. She became pregnant again, and I was flying all over the place. I had commitments. It all took time when men were spread so far and wide. The day came for my child to be born. It was going to be in the morning. The hospital said I could come up at 9:30 a.m., as there was plenty of time. I went to my sister-in-law's for a cup of tea and then made my way. I got there at 9:30, and I had missed it. Junior was born in the same room as me, which did little to soften the blow that I had missed his birth. My son was wrapped up in a cot. I again was so proud as I caressed him for the first time. I had another fair-haired, blue-eyed darling. I saw visions of him working alongside his dad and learning a business that would take care of him and his sisters. After an hour or more, I gave some last hugs then made some business and family calls before going to a bar to celebrate. I was at it all day and so out of being in charge of my company. I just let the boys and the secretary sort themselves out. My three children have done something they can't remember. At one year old, they were sitting on the bar of the squash club and given a five-pound note. That would buy their dad a pint, then they could keep the change.

The next morning, I had a head beating and a phone ringing. A company wanted information about getting some of my manpower, yet another large company wanted my men. That was it for me; business would come first, and I would be on the ball to glide my firm in the right direction. Monica came home, and with the two kids, we were proud parents. Time was needed for me to be dad. All too often, I would be on a site somewhere, and the family life started to fall on the back burner. Things were so good that I decided to extend the back of the house. We were going to have an open-plan kitchen, and to do this, the back garden had to be ripped apart. I put two men on the job working in the backyard, diverting the sewer pipes and preparing the foundations. One day, one of the men came to the back door and said to Monica, "You better get the fire brigade because your drier is on fire." That statement sent her into another bit of frenzy. With dust everywhere, me hardly ever home, the wheels were beginning to fall off the wagon, but I was never there to see it. There was a lot of pressure on her to be looking after the children and the back of the house pulled apart. Little breaks down on the coast were never enough to make up for all the time I was working and a lot of times playing. I would still find time to drink, then so little time for home. This life I was living was like I was taught: what is close to you simply push it away and don't care about it. It wasn't hard to ignore. It was like second nature to me using any words that sprang to mind to fob off the situation. I was not being a husband and certainly not a father. Hardly any time to do anything but keep the company wheels turning. I knew things would map out in the end, but that was not enough at the time.

One day, I was with a gang of lads driving them home. I had to pull over and let someone else drive. Confused, they were asking what's wrong, and I blurted out, "She's left me with the kids. She's not there at home anymore." They thought I was crazy until the moment arrived. The next hour was agony, and as we turned onto my road, I was right. No lights on. Curtains not drawn. I knew the result, so I never even went in. I asked the boys to drop me at a bar; a couple came in with me. They were a great shoulder to lean on, and I got drunk. I reflected the next day and called her father, who said she did not want to speak. I understood, backed off, and went to a bar to drink myself away again.

I finally spoke with the wife, and she wanted a divorce. I said, "Sure, but it's not about us, it's about the kids." I told her to get some driving lessons, and when she passed her test, we would pick a car. This she did, and she picked a car. I gave her my mechanic's phone number and told her where to get petrol on my account. I could have begged her to come back but knew it would be a waste of time. Monica was a tough one, and I was not prepared to fight. For the first time in my life, I was emotionally beaten. With so much happening in my life, I just gave up. As long as the kids were OK was the main thing. I knew they were in good hands. I continued working on making a success. The business was good, and all the time, I was improving my house. The kitchen came in, and I built a lovely fireplace with a solid oak top. I had so much done, which made the home cosy. I tried to relax more and enjoy it. I still had to get out on the road during the week and so looked forward to the weekends when things slowed down a little.

One weekend night, I was very drunk and drove my car home. At one point, I had two wheels on the road and two on the pavement. As I approached my drive, I had an idea that if I was to reverse onto my drive, I could simply drive off in the morning. My neighbour's drive was flat, and mine dropped about a foot. I backed in, got out, and went inside. The next morning, I saw the neighbour looking around his garden. He was picking up white pieces of plastic. I went out, and there was my car half on his drive and half on mine. With a smile, he said, "You know, I didn't like that plastic fence either." I had shattered it as I backed the length of the drive before parking. Heavy drinking was happening far too much. Although during the day I was on top of everything, by early evening, I was looking forward to a drink. I was getting information from Jessica and would be looking at the paperwork. For some reason, it was all too confusing. She would talk to me about money for this and that, but my mind was elsewhere. I would accept what was told and go to enjoy a beer. Life to me was easy, and anything important I was missing. This went on for some time, then some friends suggested going to Spain for a two-week break. I was ready for it and left the secretary and the gang foremen in charge. After picking up two rental cars, we headed towards our final destination. Four men and a wife were going to have some fun. The bars and beaches were to be our playground, and the world would pass us by. Rules were made, like whoever had the first shower would be the last the next day, and stuff like that. It was decided the couple would get the master bedroom. With only two more beds, I would get the couch, which I had no problem with because when I am drunk, I can sleep anywhere.

We went exploring, and there was a great bar down on the beach. We went in, and the barman was a happy-go-lucky fellow. We got to make acquaintances quite easily. There was a French ski instructor on a working holiday with a friend of hers. How I wished that I had gone to the French lessons at school. I wanted to say something nice, but my actions would break through any barriers. What a beauty. Very athletic with gorgeous eyes and a smile to make you faint. I was like a cat on a hot tin roof. I guess she was too because we had an instant attraction. It was not hard work to get her between the sheets. The single guys in the group were hoping to get the same luck with someone too.

On the second night, I took her to the apartment, and we got at it. We were grunting and groaning doggy fashion. I saw a small light from the corner of my eye. It was the bedroom door that had opened and then closed. The married lady headed for the bathroom. I heard a flush, and it was several minutes before I saw the light again. We were being watched in the darkness. I thought it was a turn-on, so I ramped up my proceedings for these prying eyes to enjoy. With the settee backed on to a window, she could see my half-body silhouette as I was on my knees enjoying this encounter. The following morning, I was getting looks that showed a kind of thank-you for the show last night. I was willing to give another if she wanted it.

The following evening, we were in the bar. As I was single for the night, I was simply being me, having fun and laughing with other holiday makers. Although there were a few free ladies, I was having a night off from fornicating. It was around midnight, and a lot of beer was on board. Someone said, "Let's go skinny-dipping." About ten of us ran the short distance to the non-tidal Mediterranean Sea. With clothes off and a full moon, we began splashing around. After a short while, the event calmed down. One pretty girl was lying on the water without a care in the world. Others had given up and gone back to the bar. She was floating so easily. I could see the outline of her torso in the full moon. I had thoughts racing through my mind. She looked so good in my eyes and very inviting. I never could float on my back and asked, "How do you float like that?" She got a hold of my butt and lifted me in the water. I could hide nothing. She held my butt and upper back for a several seconds then pulled me in and kissed my thigh. She let me go. As I tried to stay up, she went back to floating. As usual, my feet headed for the floor. Again, I was looking at the lovely body. Gently, I touched her ankle and pulled it to the left. This began her feet turning towards me. Her legs were slightly apart. With an ankle on either side of my face, my mind was going daft. I was smiling from ear to ear as I put my fingers at the back of her ankles. I rolled them like a parent beckoning its child to come to them. She began floating into my face inside of the full moon. This female was sailing at half a knot towards me, and pleasure would be ours for a short while. We finally got back to the party, and I carried on drinking until the night was over.

What could I do but smile as my mates knew what I was up to. There was a look of dis-tern from the lady in our party. We all continued to have fun and relax. When our time was up, I said goodbye to my French beauty. We headed home to get down to business again. For the next three days, I was so tempted to return. I had left a sexual drug that I wanted. Work brought me down to earth. I never did.

Motorway gangs were doing well, and I did more local business. I was given a lead for a customer not far from home. This was a lady who wanted some large rocks delivered for her garden. She had a nice four-bedroom house, which was at the back of a pub. When I went to her door the first time to see what was required, there was an attraction. I picked rocks from the quarry face and took them back to her house. She directed me as to where they were to be placed. Every now and then, she wiped the sweat from my forehead and arms. She was about twelve years older than me, and over the days, I made several trips to the quarry then her house. One evening, when I turned up with the last load, she said, "When you're done, would you like a beer in the pub?" We had a few then went to her house to get my pickup truck. The garage was open as she led me to the kitchen door. Suddenly, she pulled me to the wall. She was raring to go, and we had sex against the wall of her garage.

So reminiscent of my encounter many years before, but there would be no end surprises. That one was a shocker when some two and half years later, we passed each other on a street in another town. She looked at me. I looked at her. I looked down, and there was a young child with blue eyes and fair hair. I looked at her and looked down again, then without a word, she began walking away as I stood opened mouthed, wondering, *Could this be a child of mine?* Her expression of pinching her lips and slight tilting of her head with raised eyebrows had my head spinning. I was stuck to the spot. Should I chase her and insist on an answer? Her walking away means it will never be known. It is a moment of my life embedded in a small part of my brain. It pops up when I reflect on my life. Is my eldest the eldest? I and my children will ever know. This lady would not create such thoughts. I did all I could to make her happy and then left for the ride home. I had a cheque in my pocket and a smile on my face and knew we would, like so many others, never see each other again. Why did I have to keep moving on? Were these nice women I had known paying a price for my mother? Did she do me so bad that I had to use others as she did me, or was this part of a larger plan that I had no idea about?

I had to rely on the secretary more and more, and she saw my vulnerability. She took more control and had my head spinning. Money started to disappear, and I never saw it. The kitchen and chasing work all over the Southwest and East was keeping me away from looking at important stuff. She talked me into letting her do the cheques, which were fine, I thought. She would give me a book of them. I would sign every one, while the rest of it was blank. We never knew what hours to pay. There was no consistency, so it made sense at the time. I never saw that she was writing cheques for hundreds of pounds to herself, sometimes two or three a day, we discovered. She was hiding things, and I failed to see them. I looked at the books. She had them sown up and looking good. I had to start chasing around companies to get money. I could not see why, with twenty-seven men working for me, I had little money in the bank. Again and again, more stories came out of her mouth. Everything was getting out of control.

One day, I was reading the local newspaper. There on page 4 was the pickup truck I had used for my sexy rock lady. The photo was very confusing because the van was on its side, and the photo was taken five days before. I could not believe what I was seeing and went looking for the driver. I found him in a bar. When I challenged him, "Sorry, mate" was all he said. I looked at him, and after a few more words were shared, I had a pint with him. I should have kicked his ass, but he was a friend more than an employee, and there was no way I could hurt him. He was stood in the spot where I did someone some damage.

Several years later, I put a man's head between the four-hundred-year-old wall and my forty-year-old fist. I went into the bar and saw a young lady whom I had known since she was almost born. Her elder brother and I were the ones who went shooting the rabbits to rid the disease. It was the first time I had seen her in years. She was wrapped in my arms getting a hug when her jealous boyfriend got all arty farty. He pushed me away, which tore a couple of my shirt buttons off. Rather than let things escalate, I left for another pub. A friend saw my shirt. I explained. He enquired, "Have you gone soft?" How right he was. I put my pint down and went back to the pub to execute revenge. I hit him hard. Within seconds, my two arms were being held by two men; a third had his arm around my neck. I still wanted to take him apart, but after a minute, I calmed down enough and told the boys to release me. Gingerly, they released their pressure.

The one that had my neck said, "Thank god for that, my arm was beginning to ache." I thanked the boys for doing what they did and returned to my pint.

The following day, I saw this man that I had known for thirty years in another pub. With the biggest swollen face and eye I had ever produced, he walked up to me with his hand out and apologized for being an idiot. I smiled, shook his hand, and apologized also. Then we shared a beer and talked about the lovely lady he had in his life.

At least twice a week, I would go to Mother's. "Oh, that's a nice new car. You must be rolling in it." Then as usual, "Any money for me?" she would say with her hand out. She always said it with a semi type of laugh, but deep down, she really expected it. I wanted to just turn and walk away to leave because that's all I was hearing. Never was there a pat on the back for getting on with things and winning in the world. There were times I would go to her house and take Sonny out for some fun. He was getting on but still had some zest in him.

Sundays I would try a get my eldest and go out to Monica's parents' house to get the kids. We all enjoyed going somewhere for primetime fun. These were treasured moments for any parent that has lost their child to separation. My wife's family were very caring and considerate people, and we had shared some real good times together. One day, I returned the eldest to her mother then drove the other two children to their mother. After seeing the woman I had achieved so much with, I was wishing the clock could be turned back. I said goodbye to the children and began the lonely walk away from everything I had had. As I walked to my car with tears in my eyes, my daughter ran after me and said, "Granddad said come and enjoy a barbecue with the family." I was over the moon. Nothing else mattered. I was dragged back by an enthusiastic daughter to a warm welcome. What a great afternoon of laughter on the patio I had built for Geoff and Mary. Laughter was shared when we talked about the time they came to our house one day. I saw them pulling up and quickly got some hand cleaner to remove oil stains from my hands. They were covered in a gel, which had turned black as the doorbell rang. The missus was heading for the door when I jumped her from behind and grabbed her breasts. They were perfect for my hands, and I left two black hand imprints on them. She opened the door, and everyone burst into laughter and happy grins. My favourite great-grandfather Michael was there with his wife. We shared a beer and talked about the good times. Instead of digging the garden, we were up at the legion club, drinking and playing snooker. He always got into trouble, and when he did, I would scurry off and leave him to it. I had enough beer that afternoon, and I needed a taxi home. Another in the morning to go back was a bonus to see the kids and have extra cuddles from them. It was a whole new world to be with a family I enjoyed so very much. I knew I had failed their daughter, but I had not failed them. They supported their daughter, and that is what family is all about.

I had met a lady who was fun and relieved me from some of the business tensions. One day, I was on a motorway. It was raining and early evening, and the work had stopped. I called on my car phone and asked how she was, and she replied, "I'm hot and lying on the bed." My mind went daft as I suggested I should be lying there with her. Without a hint of shyness, she said, "My hand will be told what to do by you." Well, we got into a right frenzy of explicate words. I was far enough away from anyone in the dark. She had talked me into having my jeans open. There I was parked on a motorway project with my seat leant back. My mind was going back to my young-man days when doing such a thing was being practiced. After a while, I hit the panic mode. I was trying to find something to fire into and contain the mess, but, no, too late. It went everywhere. I was covered in the baby-making stuff. I never had any tissues to use. A good sweater went to waste after cleaning up the mess. Two weeks later, I got the phone bill, and there was the cost of the call. It cost over eleven pounds for some good phone sex. And on top of that, VAT (value added tax) was added. The government taxed me for masturbating! We had fun, but I was not going to get tangled up, and she knew it. We eventually called it quits, and both moved on.

About two weeks later, I was out having a beer and bumped into another woman who fancied me. We had been together before. It was years before when four of us thought we were going to get a gang bang. The lady was willing to have and give a good time. We went to a friend's house, and his parents were still up. She had followed on her motorbike. Our car was parked, and I convinced the three of them to go in and try to shove the parents off to bed. We waited for several minutes. She took me by the hand and had sex on the side of the house. She left, and I had a cigarette before going in. They came out before I had finished it saying the coast was clear and "where is she?" I told them what happened and legged it. Thankfully, I outran my three assailants. After the day's work, I was in a pub and pulled another. Again, we enjoyed each other. I said goodbye in the morning. The following night in the disco, I was dancing with another nice lady. We wound up in my bed. The taxi driver was smiling every time he picked me up to take me home. He would pick me up when I was going out for the night. He always shared a joke about my lifestyle. Things were going crazy, and it had to stop. How could I carry on like this? The Sunday morning, I kissed her goodbye. I decided I was done with women for a while. I could take no more of this life I had gotten into. I needed to leave women alone until I had myself back on track.

I went down for a Sunday lunchtime beer, telling friends I was done with any more women. We left the bar and went to another pub. There was an ex-barmaid, Wendy, saying hello to friends and sharing a drink. It was a nice surprise to see her. We had a hug, and I just kept looking at that lovely smile. She had a slim attractive body, which I never looked at. After a short while, we got talking, and she explained she was divorced. I started blurting out I was getting divorced as I was getting the hots. We talked a lot about what was happening in our lives. I was so happy to have this lady next to me. I believe she was happy having me next to her. We went home to continue talking and ended up in bed. The next morning, before saying goodbye, we agreed to see each other again. Her son was grown up; it would be easy for her to come over when the weekend arrived. After several months, we were doing well together. Around me, my business was failing. Wendy asked Jessica many questions. We ran into brick walls and bullshit. Wendy had a job, and I was beginning to fight for mine. I came to a point where I could take no more. Running all over the country asking companies for money, which wasn't due for at least two weeks, was pulling me down. How could this be happening when I am still seeing I am solvent? A couple of paycheques bounced, and that was the final straw that broke the camel's back. If I was unable to pay my hardworking men what they were entitled to, then I was not fit to run a company.

I got all the guys to work with the companies they were with and went to the bank. A heavy heart. All my dreams shattered. Everything that was possible for my children and their future was gone. Anything I thought I could be had sailed down the river, and ultimately, I was to blame. I spent too much time drinking with friends. If I spent more time with my family, could things have been different? Maybe, but what if it all fell apart with them in my life, where would we go, what could be done? As it was, the timing was good. Monica had got a council house. I met the bank manager and said, "You have the deeds, and here's the key. I'm done." I walked out and went over to Wendy's home. I called the wife and told her what I had done. I then said, "Whatever you want, go and get it now before anybody else gets it." She did, and I was glad she did. The one thing I did love in my house was the huge sofa and chairs. I waited a long time to get them. Everything else needed to be done before delivery. A lady used to call me every week and ask if I was ready for delivery from the warehouse. She never came from my area, but I got it out of her where she was. I called her one day and said I would be up that way, and we agreed to meet. Again, after a few beers, we were in her bed, and the hotel room was unused.

It wasn't long before the secretary's world was falling apart. We had begun to go through all the bank statements and chequebooks. We had to get them in order to begin understanding what she had done. As we made progress, I was getting messages from those that knew us. She was getting wind of what was happening. Many friends said she's looking like a worried person. I would grin and think, *D-day is coming, lady*. I wanted her to pay for playing a part in ruining my dreams. I may have been foolish, but her greed did a lot more damage. Everything that success would have given my children was ruined. I dreamed like every father has: to give more than he ever had, and it all looked possible.

CHAPTER 34

WE STARTED LIVING TOGETHER. I went into a semi hiding mode, ashamed to go back into town, and being accused became a fear. I tried to find some work. At the same time, we began to discover what she had done. Different chequebooks on the go at one time showed in different business books. It took us countless hours to sort them and write down every cheque number in an effort to find a pattern. I always wondered why the bank never notified me. Something was amiss with all the transactions and lack of money. I did ask. They should only contact her. How do you make that happen? I went to her house wanting to rip her head off her shoulders. My core was collapsing, as trust was something that was never there, only deceit. Foolishly, so much drink was on the main menu for me, and many times, I would succumb to the desire of need. Going for a beer is my social outlet (never anything hard, only beer). I enjoy banter with others. It was not my only escape but also the easiest. Her husband obviously knew nothing about what was happening. Naturally, he wanted to protect her as I demanded my books. He never had an idea she was cheating me. I left him to it to find out from her. At last, we had loads of evidence and took it to the police. A detective spent time with us, then several days after going through the paperwork, he called us to say that he was going to bring her in, and we jumped for joy. All our hard work was going to pay off. We hope she gets sent to jail was the cry as we chinked glasses. They went to her door and arrested her. With all the evidence, we thought we had gotten her.

Some three weeks later, we were told there was not enough evidence, and they would not prosecute. That knocked us sideways. How? Why? We pleaded, but it fell on deaf ears. How could they not see at least 30,000 pounds missing? What the hell happened to justice? We could only think she had everything so tightly wrapped that it was too confusing or expensive to unravel it. This put a lot of stress on us. We tried hard to get over it and move on. The trouble was, I could not get over it. I looked at someone with trust and got a huge kick in the mouth. Her husband was also disgusted. Eventually, he divorced her. Friends would throw insults at her in the town, and she became a leper. We carried on being us. I was asphalting, and Sundays, we would fetch the kids for some time together. All the time I was fighting with myself.

After a year, I was nothing to what I was. I never went into town and lost a lot of my character. I was and had become a burden for a caring lady. Wendy was getting pulled down too. A decision was made. We would go on holiday to a small island. We talked and talked about us. For the best we decided. When we get home, we should stop being together, and I would move on. My heart was sunk and heavy; Wendy was the same. I was at my lowest ebb. What would I do? Where would I go? This was never supposed to happen to us. Time had turned me into a shadow of myself. Wanting to argue and fight someone was always on my plate. The hurt dug deeper; failure flew its flag. The first van I brought I still had. I purchased a cheap twenty-foot caravan. The time came for me to load up and move on. We never hated each other; we still cared, but enough was enough. I had to stand up and be strong to move on. The next morning, the last hug was shared. That final touch would always be remembered as I walked away with my head hung. Tears were running down my cheeks. In such a short time, I had lost so much. There was another pain; I would be losing my kids as I was heading north. With sore eyes, I tried to concentrate on what was at hand. I had lost everything except what was with me. Wonderful memories flashed in my head. They were never enough to console me.

I drove north heading for where I knew a mate would be. I went about a hundred miles and wound up in village in the Midlands. He knew of a farm. I pulled into the local pub car park to stay for the night before going the last couple of miles and set up in the morning light. We shared some beers and talked for hours. Next day, I was parking on the side of a barn with a fishing lake about ten feet from my front door. I was so tired and worn out from all the drama that I just laid low for a day. What was going to happen to me? I had left my children behind. So many friends would be on the back burner. What future was in store for this stranger with a different dialogue? How would I do in this new area that was going to be home? I struggled for the first few weeks, trying to save what little money I had. The dead of night became a friend. I would sneak out and steal some vegetables to feed myself. I had no meat for two weeks. Times were hard, and I had many talents that could be used somewhere; I just had to find the start. The farm had an outside shower, and it was not that nice. Cold stone walls. A lukewarm shower. This was a long way from what I was used to. I had gone right down on everything except for the luck of the Blarney Stone. On a cold night, when you turned the shower off, you would be freezing in an instant. I was one hundred feet from my humble home and warmth. Rain and cold would make miserable nights. Two or three nights of rain sucked. Why should I be paying this price? *I had not stolen anyone's money* would roll through my mind. One day, I asked the farmer's daughter, "Could I use your shower tonight?"

"No problem, just come on over." She was a nice person who had her own problems. There was plenty for us to talk about. One night, I went over, and her son was in bed, so I had a long hot shower. When I came out, it was so good not to freeze.

She asked how it felt, and I said, "Lovely, the only thing now would be a nice blow job." That was it; my towel was off, and I was treated to a sensual moment. We continued for the next few weeks, looking after each other, but both knew it would not last long. I got some bar work, and then a break came in a phone call. I got some work resurfacing a road near Manchester. What a nice place, and it's what dreams are made of. With the money I earned from that job, it gave me a whole new way of being. I had money for food and beer, and maybe a date.

At the pub, everyone enjoyed a weekend night, a busy packed bar with a lot of beer being drunk. A lady would seem to be where I was and bump into me. On several occasions, when I was collecting glasses, she just seemed to be there, older than me and quite a good-looker. By the night's end, we had exchanged numbers. A couple of days later, we met. She was a classy lady, well dressed and obviously had money in the bank. We met a couple of times, then one night, we were to eat at her place. I went over. She had a very nice three-bedroom detached house. It was decorated nicely, and top of the range furniture could be enjoyed. She said, "Here are your slippers." I asked why I would need them. She explained that for future visits, they would be useful.

I looked at this lady who wanted only the best for the two of us and said, "I don't think so," and left. I was not going to get tied down again. I knew I was hurting her, but if I never did it, then she would feel more pain later on down the road.

Work became better, and decent money was being made. I again was working with my friend Steven. He had met another nice lady, and he was to marry. She had two children and looked very happy. They married, and I was again with his lovely mum, Shirley, and her new man. Steven's dad had died several years before. Steven was so much like his mother. They both had a great smile and blue eyes. A great day was enjoyed, and we worked together a few more months before moving to separate jobs. The last I heard, he had run off with the nanny, and I had never seen him again.

My mate Richard who had his caravan next to mine asked if I fancied going on holiday. Yes was the answer, and we booked a flight to Spain. As before, we landed at Alicante and hired a car. We had the notion we would go see Barcelona and take the Old Coast Road. What beauty there was for us to behold as we followed our noses and got to Valencia, a beautiful city steeped in history and boasts the fifth-largest container port in Europe. Founded as a Roman colony in 138 BC, a beautiful historic centre that spreads out, it covers approximately 169 acres and is one of the largest in Spain. Its ancient monuments and cultural attractions, a delightful encounter.

The day was passing, and a place to stay overnight needed to be found. We went down a road that hugged the seashore and headed towards Barcelona. Another mystery tour was in full swing. We stopped in a town with a sandy beach. Richard decided on getting in the water. I sat on the beach looking at women, and he purchased a blow-up bed. He was exhausted when he took some sun on the water. He was so out of breath when he blew it up; it was not going to be let back down. We moved on the next morning. He lowered the back of his passenger seat, put the bed in, and lay on it. Unable to look out of the windows very well, I explained what I was seeing. Many times I was talking to myself as he fell asleep so easily. We stopped at various beaches until we reached the outskirts of Barcelona.

We drove in early in the morning. Traffic was very light as we found the Olympic Stadium. We looked around the place then saw through the smog some spires (Basilica and Expiatory Church of the Holy Family, or Sagrada Familia). "Let's head for that," Richard said. We had no map or guidance system, but it was not impossible. After an hour somehow, we got near the area. We asked in a hotel. Surprisingly, we were very close. We parked and went to see. The half-built church and its spires were magnificent. It was designed by Antoni Gaudi, who died before it was complete. Started in 1882, he joined the following year and took over the project. It had a complicated design. Estimates then had the completion date around 2026. Building was interrupted by the Spanish Civil War and resumed in the 1950s with intermittent progress as it relied on private donations. We marvelled at the splendour and pomp that this part structure demanded, which was finally proclaimed a minor basilica by Pope Benedict XVI in 2010. We went up one of the spires, and through the pigeon holes, you could see things getting smaller as we went higher. When we came down, I counted 273 steps and was dizzy by the time we were out. After that, it was "Let's find our way out." It was like a racetrack. We had no idea where we were going, but in the end, we left the mayhem behind.

We saw another small church way up on a hill. We stopped to look at it. Richard noticed some clear water. The water came from a mountain spring, and we were probably three hundred feet above the road. It was a small reservoir that the vineyard owner had made, about fifty feet long and twelve feet wide. We enjoyed having a dip in the hot weather. We got back to the old area I had been a few years before, and it was nothing. The bar was closed, and only memories remained. No longer was there a small Spanish waiter putting a gun to his head, saying, "No more, no more." We had one more night's sleep in the car, then it was homeward bound to find more work.

Several weeks later, in the bar, I was wearing my tracksuit top that I brought while in the Falklands. A quaint old lady was drinking her sherry and asked what the emblem meant. I explained about MPA in the Falklands Islands and added that I was the chief penguin picker-upper. Bemused, she asked for me explain. I told her that when a helicopter flew over, one or two penguins might look up. As it passed over, then they would fall over, and I was responsible for picking them up. "How nice of you," she said. With a big smile, I added that I had helpers; and if a whole squadron of helicopters flew over, we would have a lot of work to do to pick them all up. "How splendid," exclaimed this sweet lady. I added another story about how we knew the army had found another minefield. She enquired; I explained that the army would commandeer a herd of sheep and charge them over the suspect area. What blew up was put on our plates. She was horrified and said she would send a complaint to the British Army. I walked away, laughing and ready to tell someone else and give them a laugh.

I met another nice lady, and we enjoyed a fun relationship without any hang-ups. We both had gone through enough, and a sociable partner was all that was required. I took another trip over to America. A week was enjoyed with my half sister and family. I never knew at the time, but this would be the last time I would go to see her. It was not planned that way, and I can't really explain it. On my return trip home, I sat at JFK airport in a coffee lounge and saw a single lady. I approached and asked if she minded me sitting on a vacant chair. She smiled, and we started a conversation where we discovered we would be on the same flight. We also lived about fifty miles apart. In an instant, we had hit it off and, within the hour, had decided to share the flight back together. I had no girl, and she had no man, so what could be the problem? I stated to the hostess that we were apart and wanted to sit together. We took off, and the hostess led her to me. I was sitting in the back of the plane, which had hardly anyone else. I was in the middle section on my own, and she joined me. After hugging, we kissed and held each other like lovers do. We were fed, and blankets were available to sleep the flight away. We had lifted the arms of the seats up and snuggled in. My hands were beginning to stray, and there was no rejection. As I progressed to explore this new body, she was getting into it and pushing herself closer to me. Within minutes, I had my hand stroking her legs beneath her dress, and she was attempting to unzip me. With the lights down and a blanket as cover, I entered her from behind. She was so receptive, and I was so willing. After a short while, we were in the mile-high club, and smiles were all around. When we landed, we exchanged phone numbers, and we were to meet again, which we did. Fun was enjoyed for a few months until it fizzled out. My social network was increasing, and I did not want a long-distance relationship anymore.

I started going to another village and drinking in a local pub where the people were friendly and the food was good. I soon got some new friends, and a barmaid was very nice. After several weeks of getting to know each other, she asked where I live, and I told her. She said, "I have a spare bedroom if you want." *Well, I never*, I thought to myself, *here we go again*. We agreed the rent, and I moved in. I sold my caravan and my work van to get a car.

I was, at times, a bad man for drinking and driving. Way out in the countryside, many locals were of the same mind-set. One morning, I woke in my new home and asked myself a question, "Did I drive home last night?" I jumped up from bed, and there on the drive was my car. My question was answered. I lay down again, but something was odd. I looked again, and the left-side parts of the front and back bumpers were gone. *What the hell, how did I do that?* Later that morning, I walked the long way to the pub. I would use this way to avoid the police on the main road. I found nothing. Having a pint, I pondered, *Did I take another way home?* Maybe I did drive the direct way. Some two weeks later, I was out near another village. As I passed a lamppost, I saw some things that resembled what I had lost. Sure enough, they were my bits of plastic bumper. How on earth did I find this new shortcut? I was four miles from home and will never know.

I loved music and made up some tapes for the pub owner. A local man that had a bar on a holiday island in the Mediterranean asked where she got her music. She pointed at me. We talked, and I was commissioned to make tapes like I had done. No problem, and it opened a door for work. He was away a lot, and I would do the handiwork around his house. I would be fixing things he never had time to do. I could also tend to his greyhound that had pups, eight in all, and they were a handful. I started helping with the feeding and, after a few months, walking them.

A female relation came back from running the pub he had abroad and stayed at the house. Annette had a charming personality and enjoyed a whiskey or two. The dogs needed to walk and be trained for racing. In his large field, I built a trap with a spring and rope on the gate lock. I would ride a mountain bike as fast as I could. A dog was released to catch a piece of meat tied on some string. I never stood a chance getting far from them. They caught me so quickly, and the meat was theirs. After a few times, I was too tired to do more. We got a motorbike, and that was much more fun, but they still caught me. One day, I rode my bike down, and we were going to walk the dogs later in the day. I did some handiwork, then off we went. It was a nice walk along the country lane towards the village. Walking greyhounds is the way to build their muscles. We got to the pub, and she fancied an early drink. I had a feeling this could be trouble, and my, was it! We sank a few pints sitting in the bar with four dogs that should have been fed. She said, "Let's have one more then leave."

"Yes," I replied. We finished our beers. I said, "Hold on, I will get my car to get us home." I came back, and she was on the whiskey, so I had a pint. She had more whiskey; I had a pint.

It was gone 8:00 p.m. and dark before I finally got her out the bar. I was driving in second gear with four dogs on the backseat. She asked me to pull over, and the next thing I knew, she pulled my seat lever. I was laid out with the dogs licking my face and her spoiling me. She finished and said, "Right that that's out of the way," and told me to continue on. We got to the house. She made a sloppy dog meal as I put them in their shed. We shared a tender embrace as the dogs munched their late-night dinner. I left her to take a slow drive home. I enjoyed taking her and the dogs training at the racetrack. My favourite was very fast but had a big problem. He wanted to fight when the training race was done, which is no good, and he was put down. It was not too long before Annette went back to the bar, the dogs went to a proper training centre, and I carried on with life.

There was a lovely lady that worked in a small store, and we liked each other. On a weekend, she would have lunch sometimes in the bar. We always smiled at each other across the bars that separated us. One day, I was in the shop and got a box of chocolates. At the register, she asked who the lucky lady is. I paid, picked them up, and said, "They are for you, Sally." Her face was a picture as I left saying, "I hope you enjoy them." A couple of weeks later, I saw her again. I had a few beers on board. It was Christmas; she was on her knees stocking the shelves. I bent down and kissed her soft rosy lips. She was receptive, and I left it at that. Several weeks passed before we finally decided on meeting. We went somewhere away from others that knew us. Sally talked about her life, as I did mine. We began melting into each other. She wound up lying across the seating with her head in my lap. A comfort zone was being enjoyed. Several times, I felt like I was breaking my neck to get down to her lips. Her head so close to my groin gave me a wanton desire to press it into me. We were enjoying ourselves. Body languages were beginning to tell a story of what the future was going to be. After several meetings, Sally was comfortable to introduce me to her child. She had a teenage daughter who liked me. After a couple of months, a weekend night, we would sleep together.

With her child asleep, we crept to her room; in the dark, we undressed. It was her first time for a long time. Sally thought her body was unattractive after a child. She had little confidence in herself. My hands had caressed and studied her body whenever I could. I had no idea what I was to encounter. We began to cuddle, and our hands began exploring. Everything was so kind and soothing as I glided my experienced fingers to her sensual zones. Her body responses and the sensual moments took over. After about two minutes, I sprang up to put the light on. She asked, "What's wrong?"

And I said, "Nothing, I must see this body." I threw the sheets back, and it was magnificent. Every curve was where it should be. All so very often, her body was covered in clothes. That masked the pure form of her torso. A lovely bone structure held soft and inviting flesh together. I was overcome with desire and devoured her body for what seemed an eternity. She was in ecstasy, and I was in heaven. The next morning, her daughter was looking at me, which made me think she had been listening to our adult encounter. Time progressed, and we continued having a good time together. Her daughter caught us one day when we were enjoying each other at the kitchen sink. She looked like she was thinking, *You're lucky, Mum,* rather than looking in disgust. It reminded me of a time at home when I had my girlfriend over. When Albert had finished work and got home, he and Mother would sit at the kitchen table to eat and not move until everything was finished. One night, I beckoned my girl over and sat her on me in front of the fire and TV. Certain we were safe, the nosey lady rose from the table and came into the front room. For the first time ever, she was so quiet with her movement. No grunts getting her body to stand up as we were enjoying ourselves, she walked in. She knew what I was doing and, for the first time ever, kept her mouth shut. If she had said something, Albert might have gone mad. Next day, when he was outside, she told me straight never to be doing anything like that again in her house. "Sure, Mother, anything you say" was my reply!

My creative mind and desire to make things happen was hampered because Sally's divorce was not complete. I could do nothing to change things in the garden or house. I found it hard to sit and do nothing. That was the beginning to the end. After several months of being together, a new challenge came to me. I was offered some work away from the area, which I took. The move would do two things: reignite my fire to stick around or drive the final nail in the coffin. The job would be for at least a month or more. I was going to Germany to operate some excavating and dozing equipment. Again, another adventure was to be mine. I had no idea what the man I was going to work for would be like. After arriving, I soon discovered the man was like a tyrant. Always moaning. Getting mud on his equipment was a no-no. Always wanting more than was possible. We had a couple of minor run-ins but managed to hold off on the blows. I used his nice large flat that sat on a lake. Water-skiers would be enjoying their pleasure. After a month, he was still jumping down my throat. One morning, he took me over the edge. I got him by the collar of his shirt and drew him to my face. I told him he was the biggest asshole I had ever worked for and wanted what was owed me. He worked out the hours, and I left his sorry ass there with trucks waiting to be loaded. I left, heading for the ferry port in Hamburg. I began wondering what my next move would be. Sally and I had just about split. I knew of no motorway projects. I decided to get back to my hometown. It was time to stand up and be counted.

CHAPTER 35

I HAD DONE ENOUGH of hiding from friends back home because of my failing. I decided, no more going around the long way to see my kids. Take the bull by the horns. That's when I drove through the town for the first time after such a long time. I was proud of myself. I saw my children, then I went into a bar. So many mates were greeting me. I asked myself the question, *What was I so worried about?* If one of them wanted to fight me, I was quite able to stand up for myself. I had gotten every one of my twenty-seven workers jobs with the respective company they were working for, so why would they want to beat me up? It was easy to work out. I beat myself up. I had forgotten that I had fought alongside these good men. I had forgotten we endeavoured to lay asphalt and made many roads together. I had forgotten that I had shared many good times with their mothers and fathers, being treated like one of theirs. I made my life hard for nothing, but I did what I felt I had to do.

While away from home, I had survived because of my talents. Several talents, like painting and wallpapering, kept me going in a man's house. He had an extension put on. He offered me the work when I was a barman. This was the pub where I walked in one day, and the landlord said, "I thought you were getting your nuts cut today." I said, I did, and started doing a pathetic impersonation of an Irish jig. What a mistake to make because the anaesthetic was still working. I felt like a spring chicken, but over the next few days, I felt like crap. I was black and blue for several days, but when I recovered, oh my, freedom! I made a good job of the kids bedrooms, which led to the stairs, the kitchen, front room, and study being painted and wall papered. He then asked if I could build a garage. I, of course, could not but would find the right man, and I would labour for him. I got that done, then I built paved footpaths and drive before winding up, putting new fencing in. He once took me to a big-time football club where he had a private box. Drinking champagne and being spoilt made a nice change and a great reward.

I saw a mate who offered me a place to stay in his house. Chris was down on his luck, as his wife had left him. He, like I, was carrying a heavy burden; although mine had eased, his was fresh and new. We had known each other for a long time. Again, I was lucky to have an offer because, the lady in the Mediterranean sea he fancied, and I spoilt his night. He was a happy-go-lucky man, and sharing a house would be easy for us. There was a day he was at his lowest ebb. He felt there was nothing worth living for, and I was concerned. He mentioned that he would waste his life away, and that would be for the best. He went out to drink and forget again; I was to follow later. He walked down the road as I began ripping his house apart. Finally, I found a shotgun and some ammunition. I needed to think about how I could let him know he had the gun and would feel at peace. I checked it; it was empty. I put it back and took all the cartridges. Later that night, we came home, and drinks were making him feel more confident about wasting himself. I had done my pleading bit, so I left him to it and went to my room. I heard him in the closet finding his gun. He began shouting out about the cartridges. I left my room and confronted him. It was at least an hour of explaining, no woman is worth such a sacrifice and he should go to bed. That he did, and the next morning, after several hours of talking, I was so pleased to see a new man emerging from his previous self. Months passed, and a simple opportunity arose that would give me a small place of my own.

Joseph, who was with me when I saw Monica for the first time, had a flat above a shop. He was happy to let me rent. This was not far from a party place where a spare room was being used by me and a lady friend. There was no furniture in the room, and we were on the floor. Another couple came in, and they too began to enjoy themselves. Then another pair came in and another. It was like an orgy but not an orgy. Everyone enjoyed their partner and never shared. I was living not far from my old house. The door to the nearest pub was only eighteen paces from the front door. I would, when going back to the flat, leave by the back door to see if I was drunk or not.

My eldest needed somewhere to live; she got the flat above me. It was nice to be able to cook for her and catch up with her life. I had missed so much of her growing up; at last I could play dad. It also allowed me to play dad with my other two children. I had so much to make up for, but time would never let me. The children would go up to Mother's. She would send them to the shops or tell them to walk the dogs, again expecting something to get done and she could sit in her chair. She always appeared to use and not give. While a little pocket money was one thing, it was the love that there was so little of. They kept saying about going to their grandmother's. I again began being friendly to her for the sake of the children. It had been a long time since I discovered things about Dad. After so long, nothing had changed. House just the same. Wallpaper just the same. Same chair of wisdom looking out the same window. Again, I was back on the roads working paving machines that had changed so much. Days gone by, it would take almost an hour to put one twelve-inch box on to make it wider; and now, just flick a switch, and the hydraulic ram pushes the side out. So much hard work had disappeared from the road laying; life was a lot easier.

As I had always got on with my ex-wife, one day, I asked if I could get the three children together at her place for some professional photos. No problem for her, and the date was set. My eldest girl came down from her home, and we were dressed for the occasion, but not my boy. He was not keen on the idea and stayed in his tracksuit (I guess he was like his dad and playing the rebel). The photographer came, and the photos were taken. When finished, they would be framed and presented by a proud father who had missed so much but loved his own the same as any other. I had extra photos done for the two mothers. I wrapped one for an upcoming event. It was Christmas Day, and I went with my gift, showing my pride. My three children looked so lovely in the photo. I was so proud. I walked in with the Merry Christmas greeting we all give to mothers and presented my gift.

What happened next tore me to pieces. I could have fallen into a hole and not hurt so much. She opened the gift, looked at a nicely framed photo of my children, then she said with her smirky, trying-to-sound-funny tone, "Is this it? I was expecting money." I lost it. My brain blew into a thousand pieces as those words reverberated around my head. I went at her with the most vicious tongue I could find. I verbally ripped her apart then, when I was done, left, vowing never to return again. How could this person pull me down yet again when all I tried was to be a son? Why did I get such a reaction when I had paid so many bills, wallpapered so many rooms, built a garden footpath of concrete, and endeavoured to be a decent son? It all became apparent. She had no respect for me. Was not and hardly ever was bothered about me. Wanted everything all for her and leave me downtrodden. She chose to again put another dagger in me. I threw one, which I am sure never bothered her that much. I believe she imagined I would go back, but she had no idea about the man I am. I could take no more of this selfish woman and turned my back. I never wanted to see her again after such an insult. Her action also cost her sister Bess any chance of us continuing our relationship. I once saw this lady looking at me from my mother's bedroom window as I passed. I chose to continue and leave her with the image of me in a car.

It was not long after that I had a chance to go on an asphalting tour to Scotland, Northern Ireland, and back to England. I jumped at it. 1'st place was Edinburgh University. Another majestic building that was founded in 1583, perhaps one of the best universities and ranked sixth in Europe. Naturalist Charles Darwin was a graduate here, as was a former prime minister. The university is also associated with no less than fifteen Nobel Prize winners. We were to surface new tennis courts with porous asphalt. As this was summer break, we could stay in the campus grounds, and a taxi to a pub was a must. The first one we hit, there were seven of us. It must have looked like another English invasion. We explained what we were doing, and by evening's end, we had some new mates. The next night, we went back, and as before, drinking beer and playing pool or darts were the thing. I took a shine to one lady, and she did me. Many times there was a brushing of two bodies in a packed bar. I was tempted until I looked at her man. He had a mean streak and dealt with drugs, which were never on my plate. It wasn't for any of the men I was working with either. We got the job done, then we were on a plane to Northern Ireland. We had a hired van and were given the tools we needed by the hiring company and headed to the next destination.

The University of Ulster was founded in 1968, and again porous tennis courts were to be laid. We stayed in new rooms that were vacated by people far more intelligent than me. That was never a problem because we are all unique in our own ways. We all have a talent; we just need to find the right niche in life. I never had a good education, but I learnt from men that knew their trade. It was learnt the hard way. There is nothing easy about pushing a wheelbarrow hundreds of feet or so; when the right equipment was being invented, you appreciated them. Mechanical wheelbarrows and little tractors to load them. So easy. Technology was making us soft. Younger people today have so much that can be done with fingertips; they forget or don't know how to use elbow grease. We started the job. In the evening, I went out on my own. I have done that many times when working away from home, just to get a break from the boys. We were in County Londonderry where the people were hurting each other so much, the then prime minister sent thousands of troops over to try and calm the atrocity. I went into a bar. This huge man was sitting near the door. As I walked in, he looked at me with a mean face and said, "I know everyone in this area. Who the hell are you?"

Although the problems had calmed somewhat, I was nervous because I thought, *This is it, he is going to tear me apart.* I looked at him and stated my name.

He looked at me, smiled, and said with a beautiful Irish accent, "With a name like that, you're welcome anytime." My pants never felt wet, and I felt good. He was big enough to take my head off my shoulders. We shared a beer and, over the next few weeks, became good drinking buddies. His mate was a chemist, and when another batch of elicit whiskey was ready, he would test it. This huge man was really a gentle giant. He was teaching his daughter how to make it, and his best customers were the police. The area I was in is known as the Triangle; this is derived from the three towns, Coleraine, Port Stewart, and Portrush, and they are on the Causeway Coast. This is one of the most scenic stretches of European coastline, an outstanding area of beauty. On the Giant's Causeway stands the oldest whiskey distillery in the world (Old Bushmills) and championship golf courses. I also went to Enniskillen in County Fermanagh. I wanted to go and see where an awful event happened on November 8, 1987. Just before a Remembrance Day ceremony, a bomb planted by the Provisional Irish Republican Army blew up so many people attending the service. Eleven were killed and sixty-three injured. Another was badly hurt and died while still in a coma on December 28 (my birthday), 2000. I stood at the war memorial. I gave those poor people some of my time with my head bowed. Although I was born in England, I have an Irish heritage, which I am proud of. I'm happy that the troubles have diminished to a somewhat thing of the past.

As we were one day from completing the job, I went for a last night beer with my newfound friend. He and his mate gave me a bottle of their illicit homemade whiskey and told me to treat it with respect. I was not a whiskey or short drinker but took it as a memento. We moved on down to Portrush where a road was to be resurfaced then we would be on our way home. We stayed in a bed-and-breakfast that had a view to die for, looking out over a lake with a small island and boats moored. Up the road was the Royal Portrush Golf Club; this is where the 1951 British Open was played and is credited to be the only golf course to host the event outside the UK mainland. I was in the town where a US Open winner was born, and a winner of the British Open Championship is living there. We went into a bar, and everyone was friendly and enjoying their time together. They, like in so many other pubs, went quiet until the word went around who and what we were doing. One night, in the doorway, there was a large silhouette reflecting through the door glass. No one took any notice except for us. What was it? We had never seen anything like it. After being there briefly, it moved, and I went to see. It was soldier along with two others and two policemen that were patrolling the semi dark street. Not far away was a checkpoint, which we would pass as we surfaced the road. Things like that brought home to us just how tense and bad it must have been.

We had some fun in one of the events held each year. We entered us as a tug-of-war team. We did all right, but with little experience, getting close to being the winners was a distant thought when a well-trained team blew us away. What I liked about being in this lovely land was the niceness of the people. Sit in a bar, and one man or woman starts to play an instrument, then another and another, and you are in for a good night. After all the troubles the Irish people had, it was behind them. Many were enjoying a quiet life with good interactions amongst all. I, for one, did try the Guinness and got drunk on it once, and that was it, never touched the drink again. I will always remember sitting in a bar, and the barman began pouring twenty pints, filling the glasses to a point, then going back to the first, and began topping them up. Just as the last one was done, the local factory workers came in, and their beer was ready. That needs to be done to have a good beer ready for a working man.

I got back home. A couple of weeks would be waited before another motorway job would begin. I had an idea. I was going to take a break somewhere I had never been. I looked around the travel agents and decided on Malta. I booked the flight with no hotel. I wanted to sort that out when I got to a place that I thought was nice. The idea was, start the adventure and follow my instincts. I was sitting in a town centre pub. Marti asked why I looked so happy. I explained my crazy plan, then he went and booked the same flight.

Next morning, we were on our way to Malta, a small island in the Mediterranean Sea. It covers only 122 square miles and is 176 miles south of Sicily. We landed and caught a bus to the new town, as it's known. The buses were like mobile churches with crosses hanging and little God and Jesus mementos. We were going into history big time. The little island is one of the most densely populated countries in the world, which means with a population of an estimated 452,515 people, they have only 7,516 feet each. By comparison, England, with 50,346 square miles and 53,013,000 people, have 140,000 feet each. We found a hotel in a busy little town not far from the bright lights area. We were given a room to share with a small balcony; it was good enough for a week. We got out exploring, and there were some beauties to be seen. Lovely smiles and tanned skin made them so inviting. We had some food then took a bus to go a little further and see what's what. We came to a heavy tourist area. As we walked from one bar to another, three men were beating someone up. Marti looked at me, and in we charged. I had done some street fighting. Marti was a bouncer and ten years younger. It would be a breeze. Marti knocked one over a car bonnet. I stood over a hurt man and lashed out, connecting on a chin. Marti put another down, and after a few more punches, it was all over. They were English; they understood when we said, "Get the hell away from him." The guy was a bouncer for a club. The boss was so happy we saved his man that free beer flowed and more food was eaten.

The next day, we walked around a lovely marine waiting for bars to open. As we were walking and talking, I had gone forty feet or more. I turned to

see where Marti was. He was on one knee, saying, "We must find a crapper."
I said, sure, and looked around while he had caught up with me doing a
stiff-legged walk. Further along the road, there was his heaven—a toilet on
the other side of heavy traffic and behind a safety barrier. He was gone like a
rocket, waving his hands and dodging traffic then springing over the barrier.
The toilet attendant never stood a chance as he barrelled past him to grab a
cubicle. I stopped laughing and waited in glorious sun. Bikini-topped girls
were catching my eye. He came out with a long face and a thumb, indicating
he had failed. I was laughing my ass off as he had that "keep the legs apart
because I have a sticky bottom" walk. I couldn't help myself from giving
him some stick and grinning so much. We got back to the room; we had
a game plan. I ran the bath, and in he got. Jeans, socks, T-shirt. I left the
room. When he finally got back with me, he was saying he wanted to keep
his favourite pair of jeans. We decided to enjoy the rest of the day and worry
about that tomorrow. Next morning, after they had baked in the sun on the
balcony all day, he said we need to find the dry cleaners. We found one, and
he left the shop pretty quick while I was too embarrassed to even go in there.

The next few days, we went sightseeing around this wonderful island.
It has had a succession of powers like the Phoenicians, Greeks, Romans,
Arabs, Normans, Aragonese, Habsburg Spain, Knights of St. John, French,
and the British who have all ruled the island. This little island finally gained
independence from the English in 1964 and became a republic in 1974. The
historical monuments are a sight to behold. The nine world heritage sites beg
you to learn about its past and let you marvel at the megalithic temples.

We chased a couple of girls, and we're doing all right. Eventually, one
realizes; we were led on and got suckered into buying a few drinks, but it
was fun. One bar held a karaoke night, and although I enjoy them, it's not
very often I will get up and sing. There is a song that I have dedicated to
my father, "The Living Years"; it says everything for me. I know it word for
word, and for the first time, this was the night to perform it. My turn came,
and I sang from my heart. I blasted it out so crisp and in perfect timing. The
place went mad and wanted more, but I was done, no more for me. The next
day, so many people were asking if I would sing it the following night when
again karaoke was on. No, that was it, just one go. We continued to enjoy our
time on the island until it was time to leave. The morning of our flight home
began with a trip to the cleaners. The guy handed over his jeans and said,
"We also cleaned the sticky socks we found in the legs." I lost it and fell out
the door, laughing my head off. My mate's expression was beautiful when the
man said that. He was all paid up, and with the bus in sight, it was time for
the airport and home.

CHAPTER 36

WE GOT BACK HOME, and I was offered work surfacing a part of the new motorway linking London and Birmingham. We were to be staying in a hotel. With my bottle of illicit whiskey in hand, I decided to give it to a man who was good at drinking. He was known to drink at least one bottle of sherry a day, so this would be the right person. I told him the story of how I had acquired it; I used the phrase I was told: "treat it with respect." He was all smiles and went off to his room. Later that night, he came down to the bar and was looking less than normal, his eyes a little glazed and not the best-spoken English. I asked, "How did the whiskey taste?"

And he said, "Great, I finished the bottle."

"What!" I exclaimed. He said it again and had washed it down with a little sherry. He looked somewhat ill as he got his pint. Without taking a sip, down he went into a heap of nothing. When we went to bed, we left him there. He finally made it up to his room in the early hours. It was reminiscent of a rather large friend who was so drunk in a pub back home that the landlord left him on the floor all night. When a friend and I went in for an early-morning beer, he was still there. That morning, the landlord came from the toilets and was blowing an empty toilet roll like a trumpeter blowing his own trumpet. I enquired, "Had a good s—t?" My mate fell over the guy on the floor as he burst into laughter, which of course got me going. A laughter-filled Saturday was on the cards.

A Saturday night, the hotel landlord decided on a late one, and several locals stayed on. One lady was rather nice. We began to talk to each other about all sorts of things. After we had been talking for some time, I enquired about her job. Well, blow me down—she was a stripper. My whole being was well intrigued. As the others left, it was agreed a private dance would be held for me and the landlord. We paid up, and the music played. As I had never been to a strip joint, I was going to enjoy this. I assumed I would not touch her. Only my private dancers allowed me that treat. The music played. Her clothes were coming off slowly. It wasn't long before she was naked and snuggled between my legs with her hands on the crouch. I was as willing as any man would be as she eagerly unbuttoned my jeans. The barman might have seen this before. He was cleaning the bar and not taking much interest in the proceedings. My clothes came off, and she was putting a condom on me. I was never one for those things, but what the hell—she's willing. I entered from behind, and she was really into it. I gave all I could for her to enjoy. Not wanting to miss a moment, I whipped myself out, removed the condom, and got back in. Now I was in hog heaven, pumping her as hard as I could, then time was up. I came. She tried pulling away, but my hands were on her thighs, holding tight. She called me some rather unfair names. I didn't care. As things transpired, I explained I had the chop, and she was happy enough. The evening wrapped up shortly after. I asked about seeing her again. Politely, she said, "You never know," and with that, left me standing alone and hanging on a thread. As it was, I was never to see her again.

We did our job and had some fun with the local ladies, then it was time to go back home. I was working in London for another firm when a stranger approached me and asked if I would give him some time for a chat. We went for a cup of tea, and he made an offer: would I get some guys together and lead a gang of men in Denmark. I asked what the deal was, and he told me that lodging and good money would be paid. I thought about it, and why not. It was February 1993 and only two days after being at Alan's graveside. I got some guys together who would fly out later. I packed up my flat to save an expense. With little more than a bag of clothes, another adventure was to begin. I got a train to London, then another that took me to the ferry terminal. We met at Harwich to take the ferry bound for Esbjerg, Denmark. He was a strange guy and, from what I could make out, a well-off gypsy. He had a truck and some asphalt equipment, a four-wheel drive car, and large caravan; a wife with three kids. The ferry was ready to board. He spent a lot of time talking to me. He knew he had a good guy because I was recommended, and he had watched me working. We landed in Esbjerg. I was to drive his Land Cruiser with the caravan on the back. After so long, there was another ferry to take across the Great Belt Sea. Demark had many islands, and to get to the capital, Copenhagen, we would travel over Fyn. Another ferry would take us to Korsor in Sjaelland. This ride was again another adventure, but with a big difference. He knew what he was doing and where to go, and I knew nothing. We arrived at the chosen campsite. I was showed a small wooden chalet, and he began to set up his camper with the help of his family. We overlooked a fjord, and across the water, you could see the city centre. Denmark is a Scandinavian sovereign state in northern Europe, south of Sweden and Norway. Its language has three more letters in it than the English alphabet. They speak more with their throat than their tongue, and it's a hard one to learn. He started showing me how he operated for business. He hit the doors of people he had already sold asphalt to maybe the year before. He was knocked back several times before a little success and perseverance won him more work. It was then that a couple of extra hands were needed. He flew them into Copenhagen. The boys were to stay in the chalet I had, and as it was enough for four with a little kitchen, we would manage.

We started work, and the money was cash. We had plenty to go and see the city. We began drinking in a few bars, and one became a favourite for me. I enjoyed the working people, and they did their best to speak English (their second language); some were good and some not so, but nothing that a chink of a bottle or smile would not sort out. One day, a rather tipsy lady came in and got talking to us. I gave her a beer. The barmaid was keeping a close eye on me. Lorda was an attractive woman, with a good figure and warm smile. The tipsy lady took a shine to me. She sat on my lap on a bar stool. My hands were holding her waist, and merriment was all around. The music was going, and I asked if she wanted to do a dance for us boys. She slid off me and proceeded to move her hands across and around her body. I used a term that we asphalt men use in these situations: "fancy getting your tits out for the boys"—that was it; she went topless. All the men in the bar were cheering. Lorda just kept looking at me. The dancing went on, and more clothes came off until she was naked. She finished and sat on my lap at the bar. It was a wild half hour before everything calmed down and time was being called.

It was also here that I made friends with a lot of people. After a couple of weeks, one asked me to explain the meaning of a song "He Ain't Heavy, He's My Brother." I explained that no matter what, I will always be your shoulder to help you and carry you through rough times. He looked, smiled, and with his hand on my shoulder, asked if I would carry him. I could say no more than "You bet I will."

More asphalt work was a head of us, then the boss's son turned up with some men. They had machinery and tools. Competition was on as they went looking for work. Times were hard, and no work was being offered. We and money were down to nothing. The boss never liked to give anything if it wasn't worked for. We had to eat, and giving us money for food would chew him up. He decided to go to Bornholm. This is a small Danish island below Sweden in the Baltic Sea. This island is unlike most of Denmark, as it has dramatic rock formations that slope down to deciduous forests, which were badly damaged by storms in the 1950s. The locals are so proud of their nationality and heritage. They live on an island that is about the same square miles as Malta; only 41,300 inhabitants, thus giving 153,000 square feet per person. We landed in the capital, Ronne, and headed to the small hotel we were booked in.

We began exploring this lovely town steeped in history and ruled mostly by Denmark. Sweden and the Lubeck also ruled for short periods of time, but the brave Vikings were to win it back. We went to several farms trying to get work, but the boss's efforts bared little fruit. We saw the Hammershus castle ruin at the northwest tip. This is the largest medieval fortress in Northern Europe, built in the thirteenth century and long believed it was a private residence for the archbishop of Lund. New evidence suggests it was a royal residence for Valdemar II of Denmark and a base for the Danish Crusades. With little luck, we went back to Ronne and enjoyed good people and some beers. Next day, off we went heading more into the heart of the island and came across a water park. We went for a look around to kill some time then back to hitting doors. The boss was getting frustrated because of little work. He decided we would be heading home to England.

He was rather drunk and thought he would beat up on me because of his shortcomings. We had a couple of run-ins, but this night, it could have come to blows. I was hired as an experienced man, and asphalting was second nature. He had a small paving machine, which he tried to tell me worked differently than any other built in the world. "What poppycock," I told him, as he was laying out some string. He was expecting the floating back end to follow it. He would not accept that levels and the screws work hand in hand to lay the material. Roads transition from cross falls and cambers. Without applying levels, you would achieve nothing. He could not accept that I knew what to do. With that in mind and fed up with the whole scenario, I looked at him and said, "Go f—k yourself," and went to the hotel.

I had a little trick up my sleeve. I called a lady that had given me her phone number. I rang to say that what I thought would happen. "No problem," she said. "I will put the key under the mat for you." (This lady I will always be indebted to.) I knew where she lived because we had enjoyed a few nights of passion a little time before.

I left without any goodbye or handshaking. Enough was enough of this control freak. He even had a bare knuckle fight with his son because of family disagreements. No longer was he going to tramp me anywhere without giving me any money. I got on the ferry for the mainland then headed for a train in Copenhagen. It was a nice walk through Nyhavn. This is a seventeenth-century waterfront, canal, and entertainment area, colourful buildings, and every building in its quarter-mile length is a pub and restaurant. Tourists and locals flock to eat and hear musicians play their music. On the water are historical wooden ships, which can be seen better when you take the canal tour. It's amazing to think that from the Danish-Swedish war of 1658-1660, King Christian V had it dug by prisoners, and it took three years. (It was a notorious area of prostitution and sailors when it was the main harbour two hundred years before.) For eighteen years, it was home to Hans Christian Anderson.

I got to her apartment. Sure enough, there was a key under the mat. I had a bag of clothes, and that was it. Some money but work would have to come my way fast. Birket came home with her lovely smile and warm way of being. Not long after she arrived a meal was served—simple food, which is my liking. The next day, I stayed at home; and when her day was done, we went out for a beer. I met a guy who knew me because he drank in the same bar where I had the naked lady on my lap. I asked him about finding some work, and he said, "Let's see what we can do." I met him again; luck was on my side. I was to travel with him the following morning to the factory where he worked. This was a recycling factory. The Danes are big-time recycle people. Every bottle, plastic, or glass has a deposit on it. Cans also have a deposit, and they can be taken into a store and money returned. This place received bottles that would be sorted, cleaned, and shipped back to the European country they came from. Almost any type came through the system, and what could be saved was saved. Almost every restaurant would have pallets and pallarama, folding sides that would fix on top of each other as it became fuller. Drivers collected the pallets when full. Thousands of bottles came in every day by pallet and thousands more by container. I hit it off with the boss's son, and the job was mine. Next morning, I started looking and learning. At nine, I had to go to the office to get the paperwork done. I went in, and oh my! This beautiful Danish lady with breasts designed for my hands beckoned me to her desk. A smile that warmed the cockles of my heart seduced me. She showed me where to sign, and as I leaned over the table, I had big-time hots and wanted to strip the table of papers and take her.

After everything was done, it was time to get on with the job. At lunchtimes, Karin would come into the canteen for coffee and a chat. I just looked her up and down slowly. I desired this hot lady, and I think she got to know it pretty quick. After several months, we had become better acquainted. We were happy in each other's company. It was the same with other employees. I made many more new friends, and overtime was almost every weekend, which I was so happy to do. This meant I could get a scooter (I called it Black Beauty) and have more freedom to get there as needed. I am good at looking "outside the bun." After being there for about three years or so, I put an idea to the boss. He liked it and told me to order what materials I would need. He then gave me one week to change the system. Niels would be my helper. We were already good friends, and I had held his newborn baby. Several times after work, I would go to his house, or we would go to the bar. I enjoyed his way of being and his humour. He was cutting some steel with an angle grinder and began shouting, "Help me, help me." I was welding under the new pallet opener when I heard him; I was running to him in a second. I thought he may be getting electrocuted or something, but no. He had caught his jeans on fire from the sparks while standing behind the grinder cutting steel. He was patting his groin area, and I began laughing my head off. His face was a picture and told him he was on his own and walked away. We got the job done, and the boss was very pleased with the effort. Two days after completing the job, a life-threatening event happened. I was checking out the pallet opener and placed my soda drink down. About four minutes later, I picked it up and took a drink. A wasp had entered the can, and I swallowed it. It stung me inside of my throat. I went down on the floor in agony as workmates came to my aid. The ambulance ride seemed to take for hours yet was only ten minutes. I was on a drip and my throat wrapped in ice. After a several hours of care, I was relieved to know I would be OK. I enjoyed working overtime, which allowed me my lifestyle. That meant weekend and evening food was supplied. This is something Danish companies do as a way of saying thank-you for your help. Birket and I had some good times, but sometimes, too much was getting drank, and silly things would happen. Falling off bikes was a good one. I swear if I had a motor one, I would be dead. One evening, I woke up in an ambulance with the left side of my face left on the asphalt cycle path. I was drunk and had a stupid notion. If I went fast enough, I could get through two posts, which obviously never worked. I was asked if I wanted to go to the hospital, but I said I would be OK. When they left, I went back to the bar and challenged others to get their face more messed up than mine as laughter was all around. We had a lovers' spat, and I said we would be better apart. That's what we did. We parted on a good note, which meant now and then, if we felt horny, we could share a night. Best thing. The world was again my oyster.

When I first came to Denmark, I thought a lot of fighting was to be had. But no, they fall off their bikes. That explained all the messed-up faces when I first got there. I messed up a couple of faces. I had to knock a couple of guys down that were being jerks. The women liked me and the music I would play. That would get a little dance party going with the ladies, but some guys thought they owned them. They soon discovered the ten-second rule. I hit one guy down in a bar, and his mate looked at me and said in pretty good English, "You are a guest in this country, and we don't do that."

"No," I said, "What do you do?"

"We argue for ten minutes and take a beer."

I looked him in the eye and replied, "Well, you've just seen my version." I will not give idiots the time.

My friend Thomas had offered me his sofa to sleep on. I took it when Birket and I went our separate ways. One evening, I was barhopping in the city. It was closing time in Lorda's bar. She was looking at me, and I asked, "Would you like me to stop here?"

"Yes," she replied. My loins were going daft. I was as fired as ever I could be. The last person left. We had a beer together, talking to each other across a table. It wasn't long before our hands were going all over each other and passion was high. The next day was the same at closing time; sex was wild and ours for the taking. My friend who let me have his sofa wanted to move in to his girlfriend's. The small one-bedroom flat could be mine. I was in hog heaven! I had a good job, great friends, and a horny lady, what more? We got closer together, but if she wanted to go off somewhere, she did. I would be wondering if I meant anything to her.

"What the hell was going on?" I enquired.

I would to be told, "I do what I want to do." I got to thinking that this relationship was not going to work out but maintained the relationship for sex until we finally gave up the ghost. Time was passing, and my Danish was getting better. I could converse with a lot of people that never spoke good English. That meant I won more hearts and friends. I was never going to be ignorant to a foreign country or language. Danes, like in other countries, appreciate you trying. I never imagined I would be learning such a hard one.

This was also around the time I got the nickname "the hedge man." I would leave bars and go maybe one hundred meters or so and fall off. A lot of times, there was a hedge for me. From one bar, several mates would come out and bet a beer on how far I would get before going over. One Saturday morning, I went to get my shopping for the week and enjoy my garden. I always cooked all my meals on a Sunday morning and froze them. I just had to microwave it at night. This particular Saturday morning, I cycled over to the store. I was distracted by several lovely people having a morning beer in the bar next door. There was me and about eight ladies having a laugh and playing music. Several bottles were tipped up towards my nose. More friends had arrived, and a party was on for all to enjoy. After three hours or more, I decided I must get to the store and go home, so I left to get my shopping. With cans of food, milk, and frozen meat, I filled my backpack that weighed about thirty-five pounds. As I passed the bar heading home, I was beckoned back in and, in I went. Another two hours passed. I was three sheets to the wind and ready to get back to my garden. I went up some steps and attempted to mount my bike. Finally, I was in place, and pedal power took over. I was drunk but good enough to get myself home. I went about fifty meters, and the chain fell off. I continued to pedal franticly until I was slow enough to fall to one side, letting my left leg save me from the asphalt. I managed to keep the bike upright and leant over the crossbar to try and put the chain back on when my loaded backpack shifted forward onto the back of my head, which caused me to get lower to the ground. With my hands holding the pedal and chain, my nose went into the asphalt as my feet slid backwards, and there I was pinned almost upside down for a second or two. When I finally regained my composure, I could see so many friends laughing at me. That's when I decided on another beer and a taxi home.

CHAPTER 37

I WENT HUNTING FOR ladies in a few dance places. A few treats were enjoyed. I was asked by one to fulfill a dream. She wanted bondage. simply tie her hands and feet to the bed and do whatever I wanted. As this was something I had practised before I was at ease with the request. Thomas said I would have to move from his flat because the district authority had discovered I was living there. Another friend Hemming said he had a spare room, and up the road I moved. I was taking some stuff up to the second-floor flat when I saw the lady from the above flat. She said hello and welcome. There was this hot chick, dark-brown eyes, luscious lips, and a cute backside standing halfway up the next flight. She looked to be teasing me. Bit by bit, I got all my personal stuff in and went up to hit her door. I had wine and beer in my hand and said, "If you are going to blast out the same words of a song to learn it, let me help you." That was it, another lover was mine. She was fun, but her pet wasn't. I was not happy with her young four-foot boa constrictor snake, which, on the first night, I was unaware of. Weirdest feeling ever when you are looking after your lady's needs and that thing slid up the crack of my ass! That freaked me out, I must say. That ended my night of passion, and I was never comfortable until she got rid of it. We did well and had some good times not living together, as she would come down or me go up. She had a chance of a better flat across town and on a lower level, and she moved. We did all right and lasted a few more months before I wanted to be on my own again. It was about two weeks after we parted when she came into my local pub, and wow—she was done up to the nines and looked hotter the hell, but I had to decline any offer that was laid in front of me. I was happy on my own. Other lady projects were in hand, and I would have no time for her.

I had decided to see if I could buy a summer house; this is where you can enjoy the summer then move back to your apartment for the cold winter. A friend had one for sale, which was rundown. It would take a lot of work to make it special. This would be a great challenge, and I could use my talents to make it something. I was accepted as a new home owner, and as it was still cold, there was little I could do outside. I spent time taking the ceiling down. The aged wood I used to go around the lower half of my lounge and paint above it. I also had a chance to change my job. I was going to go back on the heavy equipment in a quarry. It was hard to say goodbye to the recycling factory and a good family business. It was here, after hearing our favourite princess had died, that I lost it. A song that was dedicated to her on the radio made me cry. The foreman allowed me to go somewhere quiet and shed my tears. The day I heard of her death, I was expecting to go to Copenhagen for an English newspaper. It's there that I would sit in Tivoli and listen to the musicians play classical music while I browsed through my Sunday newspaper. This was always my little treat and solo time. The Tivoli Gardens are a fun place for everyone. It is the second oldest in the world after Dyrehavsbakken, which is opened every year by thousands of motorbikes. They travel across Denmark picking up other bikers as they pass the motorway service stations. Standing on a bridge seeing so many passing under you and others joining at the back is a sight to be seen. Many times, I went across the street and into a nice hotel lounge for a beer. Most times, the piano player would be playing and singing in the corner. One such Sunday, I approached him and asked if he knew any wurzel songs. He came from the west of England too and knew some. He was a little tipsy as I was, and the songs came out. I sat with him, and for the next forty-five minutes or so, we let rip. It was so much fun singing with this stranger. Bewildered people who had no idea what we were singing looked on. Several weeks later, I went back, and I discovered he had been fired because of that afternoon!

It was about three months after leaving the family business when the secretary called to say an invitation was extended to me. It was the boss's thirty years as chief, and the business was fifty years old. A sailing trip for the weekend to Oslo Norway, was planned. As a thank-you for all my efforts, he was hoping I would come. How could I refuse such generosity from this well-respected man? I met present staff and their partners at the factory, and we boarded a bus en route to Copenhagen harbour. It was so nice to see a happy couple again. They, after only knowing me for three years, asked me to be their best man. They married close to where we all worked. I was proud to stand next to a man that thought so much of me. Also in the crowd was another workmate that ensured my name was spelt as it is. He named his newborn son after me, stating, "If he grows up anything like you, he will be a hard worker and a good man." I was blown away when he made his intentions clear. What a tribute from someone that respected me that much, and what a feel good feeling.

We met a large ferry ship and began the trip to Oslo. We glided past the *The Little Mermaid*. She has been a tourist attraction since 1913 and is based on a same name fairy tale by Hans Christian Anderson. This unimposing statue has been damaged and defaced many times since the midsixties. Four times she has been decapitated by idiots, even knocked off its base with explosives and later found in the harbour's water. She has been found dressed in a Muslim dress, scarf, and draped in a Burqa as a statement against Turkey joining the European Union. In 2006, the International Women's Day, she was found with green paint dumped on her and a dildo stuck in her hand. She is more at peace now that the authorities have moved her. She is further out in the harbour where stupid people can't get at her. We enjoyed good food and a few beers as we sailed up the fjord towards Oslo. It's Norway's capital and most populous city. Again, another adventure that I would enjoy with so many good people. The piano was being played by a well-dressed man who never sang that much. After a few good beers, I was approached by the boss's wife to have a go after she had done a little turn. We got some songs going. Then I started with my favourite wurzel songs. We were having so much fun, as the piano player was able to follow me, and everyone wondering what the hell I was singing.

The first evening on the boat, Karin was left alone. Her husband had drunk a little too much and went to his cabin. We enjoyed some laughter and dancing, then she wanted to leave and get to her man. We agreed I would walk her to her room. As we approached the door, I knew this was going to be it. This would be the last chance I would be able to thank her. One afternoon, I talked about all the confusion in my head. I needed to express how grateful I was to have her in my world. I regarded her as a very special person. I have four other "special" ladies. We have shared an evening of passion just to be one for a night. I so wanted this lady be the fifth. But no, she was faithful, and I had to be an English gentleman at this juncture in my life. We hugged for the last time, and with a small gentle kiss on the cheek, she slipped away. Karin disappeared behind the cabin door. I stood there. I again felt alone and abandoned. With my head hanging, I walked towards the back of the boat. It was sailing further away from the land I loved. I leant on the safety rail, watching the swell being created by the huge engines that turn the propellers. I wished that she was here with me. I had thoughts of us enjoying a simple fling as we headed for the harbour, and I harboured in hers. She was supposed to be lying on a table and both of us enjoying each other. A moment of life that would never be forgotten. Alas, it was never to be. It was time to close the thought and head back into the fun for as long as the night would last.

We arrived in the port. Cloudy skies draped all across this aged city that was founded by King Harald III around 1048. In1070, it was elevated to a bishopric. That is an area historically most common within the Holy Roman Empire where a bishop held the secular authority.

As we ventured out into the city, I again, like so many other times, went off on my own, and couples went their way. I would see them in various places, but like Spain, I loved to look for little local bars and taverns where, in my mind, the real people are. This does not mean rich people are not; it means I am with the working class and feel more at ease. I was a little hung over from the party we had enjoyed the night before. Nevertheless, a sense of satisfaction for this travel reward I had been offered had me smiling whichever way I went. The trip home was enjoyed by all with more dancing and onboard entertainment. After getting back to the factory, it was last goodbyes, shaking hands and thank-yous before leaving. I probably would never to see these lovely people again.

I began working more on the outside of my house. I cleared and revamped everything outside. I took two trees down but left one standing because of a nest with newborn chicks screaming for food. I had no problem with the tree standing, and after they had left the nest, later that year, a storm rolled through. The high winds sent the tree smashing into the back of the house. It was heartbreaking to come home and see it lying on the back of the roof. It looked worse than it was, and with the help of some good neighbours, we soon had the tree cut up and stacked. Everywhere I went, new friends were coming into my life. I socialized in many bars in the city. At times, I was able to show my new workmate around. He lived not far from the quarry. His friend, a local farmer, asked if I wanted to do the chicken roundup. Everything was set, and with many others, the lights would be turned off in the chicken shed. There were so many it was never hard to grab one and then another until your hands were full. After two hours, we were running out of chickens. The last of seven thousand was hard to get. With the lights back on, we would dive in the straw until the mission was accomplished. They were ready for the slaughterhouse. Again, being treated to a meal and getting some cash went a long way to help my socializing problem.

I enjoyed heading down to the city. It was all right riding down on cycle paths. There are traffic lights for cyclists to get you across the roads safely. This was another thing I liked about Denmark; it's for the people. Everything is set up for them to get around safely. The buses and trains are so on time. There is every chance you will not be late. The buses would lower down, enabling old people or mothers with prams easier access. This was the first time I had seen mothers able to put a safety harness around the pram and a seat belt for her. How thoughtful was that. They pay the highest taxes in the world and don't mind because they respect the elders that have looked after their country. When they are working, it's their turn to look after it.

I once thought I was having a heart attack and went to the hospital. Within minutes, I was checked in, lying on a bed with monitoring sensors all over me. I had several palpitations and thought the end was near. I was concerned because I still had lots to do. I was not ready to die. I saw my funeral and me going up in a puff of smoke. I saw my friends scattering my ashes from the boat that takes tourists around the fjord. I saw many people shedding a tear and many enjoying a beer and celebrating my life. Then without warning, I saw the doctor. He came in after a twenty-four-hour observation and said he knew what the problem was. As I lay in my bed, open-heart surgery went through my mind. Would I need a new one? Would one be available? He sat in the window, and I said, "As this could be life threatening, I would like the information in English."

"No problem," as he went straight into a well-spoken analysis. It boiled down to the fact that I was drinking too much, and the wall of my stomach was breaking down.

I looked and said, "That's great," as a nurse began to remove everything. I was so happy to get out, I went straight to my favourite bar to celebrate. This is the bar where, when I could read and speak Danish, I got the national newspaper. After a couple of seconds, I fell about laughing. *Speed* in Danish is "fart," and in most cars, you have the cruise control, but in Demark, it's your "fart control." The headline read, "Another royal in the exclusive fart club." She was the third. I just fell about because I never knew there was a "fart" club in any royal family. She was driving too fast and got caught. A few weeks later, a friend had a long face. He came into the bar with a piece of paper. I asked why he looked so sad. He presented the paper to me, saying in Danish, "The police have a photo off me farting at 82 kph, and it will cost me Dkr200." Again, I fell about the place as this simple word simplified my world. My English friend Nicolas came over many times to talk about events in his life. He liked the word. On one occasion, I took him out to where an electronic radar sign states your speed. They read "your fart." He got a photo of me farting at 62 kph. We went to the bar grinning like two young lads that had just shared a funny joke.

Several weeks later, I was to go for a "cycle" ride—that's how my doctor put it. It's like the Tour de France. I had to ride a bike. The test would last fifteen minutes and get harder as the time passed. I began, and it got harder and harder. The two doctors who strapped everything on me never knew who was doing the cycling. I kept going, and finally I completed the course with sweat pouring from me. They said hardly anyone finishes such a test unless they are proper cycling people. I was proud as I staggered from the room for a shower and twelve-hour sleep. This was also a statement to me that says, "If you want it, if you want to achieve, you must work to achieve it," and that's what personal pride is about. The tax system in Denmark meant as we paid into it, we all would be looked after no matter where you came from. As everyone was looked after, I never saw a beggar until one day in Copenhagen. He was sitting at a tourist attraction and was not even Danish. I confronted him. I said that he had a place to live and money from the state, and "he was insulting the Danish people." He looked at me and said nothing because he knew I was right. He was ripping off the tourists that flock to Copenhagen. It really gets me when you find someone like that. Those that really need help can get nothing because of all those cheating. Denmark boasts one of the largest music festivals in Europe. A fantastic time is shared by more than sixty thousand fans and up to twenty-one thousand volunteers. I, with many friends, spent many festival times together. My favourite was the twenty-fifth anniversary. It was started in 1971 by two students and went from there. It was in the year 2000 that a huge tragic accident occurred when a crowd surge resulted in nine deaths, and a huge shock wave reverberated around the entire shores of Denmark. I shared some time with friends who were so shocked, they were crying in the bars.

With hard work, the inside of the house had a new bedroom, lounge, kitchen, and dining room. I also built a greenhouse and a special small putting lawn for "clock golf." I learnt this from Mr. and Mrs. Smith. Twelve numbers set around a hole. The most putts to complete would buy the next round of beers. Simple fun while having a grill with friends. I also put a tall flagpole up next to it. I would fly the Danish flag, and below would be a small English one. I got that and a small electric lawn mower with a roller on a trip to England with my good friend Niels from the recycle factory.

I took Niels to my hometown. After walking through and around the town centre, he looked at me and said, "So where is the town centre!" I could do nothing but laugh at his innocence. A kind of embarrassment lurked within me as I explained that was it; we have just gone around it. The bustling people history was all but gone, although many fond memories popped up at every turn. Seeing an old face was a wonderful feeling as they explained everyone headed for the big stores. Those were built on the outskirts of town that I walked when they were fields. He loved the oldness of the town, but after three days, he wanted out. The quaintness of the town finally got to him, and he was bored. Before we flew back to Denmark, I showed him around London, then with my mower to put roller lines across the hallowed lawn, I left England. To enable me to get so much material to the garden, I purchased an old ex-mail van. I put a collapsible box in the back, and every day, half a ton of whatever I needed would come home with me. I would also go over to a neighbour's garden. Together we were known as the terrible twins. We would drink together and always be laughing.

At night, Molles would talk in his sleep. Kirsten would complain it's always English. He had no footpath around his house and no patio because they could not afford it. I conceived a plan. At work, we would crush the small garden blocks. They were rejects from the company that produced them. Every day I would sort through what was delivered for crushing. Each day, I would arrive with the best of the blocks, stockpile them, and get to my house to continue my jobs. Finally, I had transported enough to their house. I began the task of making a small wall, followed by a footpath around the house and patio. In the patio, with red bricks, I did as requested (I built a heart for the lady); she loved it. It was talking point for the many friends they had. With the wall constructed, I was able to arrange a very unique birthday present. On Kirsten's birthday, a large lorry turned up with twelve tons of cleaned soil. The driver went to her door and said, "I have a present for you." He tipped it up, and she was speechless. Later on, some friends turned up with a bobcat, and we started to create a new lawn. With my asphalt experience, I levelled the soil until complete. I brought the grass seed and sowed. It wasn't long before a whole new garden and house were being enjoyed by many.

It was also here that my very good friend from England enjoyed a "smoke"; I was not into the stuff, but Dawn enjoyed one. A friend brought it over. Foolishly, I joined her smoking it. One word was said, and it got me laughing, and I mean laughing. I was uncontrollable for at least ten minutes. My stomach hurt for days. She was a beautiful lady and friend for thirty years. We had shared some tender evenings together but never had a relationship. We were shoulders for each other. We cared for us, and that made the relationship so special. (I think people like this are rare. Complete trust about personal things, and it stays with the person.) She thought it was fun when we got on a train. Within forty minutes, we were in Sweden enjoying a Sunday beer. To welcome her, Danish friends came over to my house; and although it was raining, we had an evening of good food, drink, and some guitar playing in the blue room, as I called it.

The house saw some goings-on in the new bedroom. I never thought about having a regular girlfriend, as I loved enjoying different women. Sometimes I would be sleeping with an old girlfriend, and that was all I needed. An ongoing relationship would have been a distraction from my goal of completing a special house and garden. The house had a name, the Love Shack; I carved the sign four feet long and eight inches wide out of wood.

Painted in white, it stood out from the black background it was screwed to. I also made a footstep to enter the house. I carved the same name in the red concrete that matched the house colour. I would fire up the special grill I had built. Friends would bring their own food to cook. I loved the grill, and the first thing I cooked on it was bubble and squeak; this is an English thing from yesteryear. Any potato and vegetables would be mixed together and fried along with eggs, bacon, and sausage. This was a Monday night treat because in those days, it would take hours to do the weekly wash. There was no time to prepare anything fancy. Parties were so easy, and it never cost me anything to throw one. With a fridge that held 180 bottles of beer, we would never go dry. The beer system was that people come over and give you the cost of the bottle you paid. That way, all you did was exchange the thirty-bottle case for another. It was important to refill the most important appliance in any garden house. With about three hundred houses on the outskirts of town, this was a special community. These areas had committees. Every year, they would go to every garden and adjudge which was best. It was never my intention to win such a thing, but I did. My goal was to create something special for myself and hopefully my young children. I hoped they would come over and I could play dad at least once a year. They never did come, although the offer was there for my lovely ex-wife too. I thought of the house as a holiday home. Not a competition winner. At the presentation, I had my camera and gave it to Molles with the instructions "take plenty of photos because this is a first"; he took loads. When I took it to the camera shop, they said, "Sorry, there's no film in it." How stupid of me. I was the first Englishman to win the best-garden prize. Others gave me photos of my moment. They gave me memories to look at later in life.

That moment with no film reminded me when I was up the Eiffel Tower in France. The view from up the top is awesome, and again, there was no film in the camera. I used to go over on the Seacat as a foot passenger every night while working and lodging down in the south east of England. For one pound, I would travel to Calais and get my duty-free cigarettes and a bottle of whiskey to sell in a pub back home. I only charged what I paid, but it meant the pub could make a little more profit. One of the strongest beers was for sale. I would drink two pints on the way over, purchase one for the turnaround and two more coming home. Drinking five pints of that stuff in just over two hours was crazy. When we arrived back in England, I was a little tipsy. It was a cheap night out. Standing at the back of this Catamaran boat with 1,100 people and 400 cars on board was a thrill. The powerful engines kicked it up to thirty-seven knots as it sped away from land. This is when I thought about another adventure. I would go and see Paris for a weekend. I landed at Calais on a Friday afternoon and found a hotel. Next morning, I was going on the train to Paris, find a hotel, then be a tourist. On my night in Calais, I was spoken to by two English teachers. They could see I was enjoying some jukebox music. They asked me to go with them, and I did. We got to a bar, and it was jamming night. Trumpets, flutes, guitars, and a violin. That was the best jam session I had ever experienced. When I left, I was lost. How did I get there? What was the name of the hotel? I had left the local bar and walked with these two young ladies. I never watched where I was going because I thought, with luck, we would all get in bed together.

I eventually found the place where my head was to rest. The next morning, it was "Paris, here I come" running around in my head. I bought a ticket and went to the platform, saying to myself, "Yahoo. I have this sorted." A train came, and I got on. There was something written on paper and hanging on the door window. It was French, and I had no idea what it was. (After about twenty minutes of seeing other trains coming and going, I was wondering when we would get going.) Then bump and off we went. I was sitting down and felt pleased with myself. After five minutes, we stopped and stayed stopped. Curious, I got up. I noticed I was the only one on the train. I walked from carriage to carriage seeing no one. Finally, I saw there was no engine, and I was in a shunting yard. I jumped off and walked back to the station. I went to the ticket office and blasted the ticket man with every expletive I knew. I finally got to Paris. After booking into a hotel, I went exploring in the beautiful city. Later that night, I was back in my hotel vicinity. I found a bar where an English merchant sailor stood. He spoke very good French and was talking to an unfriendly Frenchman. He was dissing England in the war, and I stuck my opinion in which stirred the pot even more. The poor man was translating English for me, and French for the other. I stayed in the bar for a few hours or so. I went off to bed, then first thing in the morning, I would be heading back to Dover, which was perfect because the pubs opened as I got there.

My house was almost complete inside and out. I was able to relax a little more and share a beer with friends. I met Ayla. She spoke good English and was rather attractive. We got talking, shared some beers, and kissed good night. She had a son whom I met. He was troublesome. He hung on to her apron strings. We wound up sleeping together. As we progressed, I found she did nothing, just watched TV all day. We got more attached. I encouraged her to go find a job, and she did. The only problem was, we were hardly ever alone. Her son was always around, and at times, I got fed up with it. One day, I was drinking in my favourite bar with a friend. We got on about marriage, and she popped into the conversation. As things transpired, my friend turned the whole thing around into a bet. He bet that I would never marry the woman, so I proposed, and we got married. Friends came and gave us a nice reception after we had married. We got back to the pub we met in. Food and drink were to be enjoyed. At the garden house, we would be out or inside enjoying friends. Her son would turn up, and the evening was changed. Some people would make their excuses and leave. They couldn't be doing with this interfering person who totally controlled his mother.

The bar where we met, I was to hold my fiftieth birthday. One of my mates Jorgen had done many things for me, but on this occasion, he really topped the lot. He was such a good guy. We had shared many, many good times. We had spent my forty-ninth birthday in a snowstorm on a golf course because we had arranged such a thing. We got to the small nine-hole course, and no one was in sight. After donning our rain suits, we got on the first tee. By the seventh, we were freezing cold with a blizzard all around us. We were huddled under our umbrellas smoking a cigarette, and he said, "You really are a strange man wanting to do this."

I looked and smiled at this very likable mate of mine and said, "You asked what I would like to do three weeks ago." We are doing it, but I think we need to get to a bar. We headed to our favourite bar for a lot of beers. This was what we did. We would drink together and enjoy our time. For my fiftieth, I spent two days making all the food, which was an English hot pot, quiche, and proper Queens sandwiches with the crust cut off the bread. Something happened with my two big pots of English hotpots. They had to be wasted, but undeterred, I went up to a local Chinese restaurant. I ordered a huge amount of rice and curries plus all sorts of other meals, which went down well. As the party progressed, he stopped all the music and made an announcement. He told me to watch the TV. Everyone watched. He began showing a video with him going to the airport. He told me he was working the day before and that's why we could not get together. As the video rolled, my eldest daughter was at the airport meeting him. A tap on my shoulder began me to turn, and there she was, my eldest girl, saying, "Happy birthday, Dad." I was gob smacked by such an event. I hugged her as she did me. Little tears of pride etched down my cheeks. Later I took her around the entire pub, introducing her to the lovely people that had turned up. It transpired that fifteen of my dear friends there had put their hard-earned cash together to fly all of my children in. With the other two not being quite old enough, the extra cash they had I was presented with a lovely digital camera. The following day, as I reflected on the event, I was amazed—193 people had turned up. As for my close mates, what they did, I was lost for words. Comprehending what these good people had done for me when I had only known them a few years was amazing. They considered me one of them, and I could not have been prouder.

Her son was a pain. It's not that I or others didn't like him; he just would not let his mother alone. It must have been hard for him to see her doing different things and leaving him behind. One day, we had a bit of a spat, and I went to the house alone just to get away from them. He may have known or may not, but he was pulling me down. It was like a tug-of-war. Which way will Mum go today? All for me. All for him, and she was getting frustrated too. I was at the house having a drink in the lounge when a friend came over. She had been with friends in another garden and saw my bike. That is a pointer for anyone. You got to know who was where by their bikes. One rule in the garden was, if the gate is shut, stay away. On the other hand, if it's open, you're welcome, come on in. This she did, and we talked about the situation and other things. She brought a tender subject up. As it was close to her heart, she began crying. I wrapped my arms around her, and within ten minutes, we were at it. There was no stopping and no going back. We shared a wild night, and she left the next morning. I went to the bar. My wife came up. We went back to the house. We stayed the night. She had no idea she was sleeping where her husband had another woman there twenty-four hours before. One time, it was far more complicated because she sent her son over with a message. My bed partner-to-be was sitting on the couch. He was good at trying to win his way in. But I refused him.

CHAPTER 38

I DECIDED TO FIND a way that we could have more time together. I put my house on the market, and it went for a lot more than I had paid for it. It was a wrench, but I had many friends in the area, and I knew I would always be welcome. The elderly couple across from me was sad that I would be leaving. We had such good times. You are allowed to fly the Danish flag from sunrise until sunset. He would be out at first light flying his, and I would be next. One morning, I got early and flew mine first. Next morning, his was up earlier than mine. Next morning, I would try to be first, and so on. One morning, we were at it at the same time. Two grown men, twenty-five years apart, at 4:30 a.m., laughing across the hedges that separated us, then sitting in the morning sun having a beer. The summer days are long over there, and on the longest day, the sun goes down after ten thirty. I watched it for several days, and when I put the brick floor down for my swing sofa, that's what I would be facing. With music coming from a speaker in the roof of the house and a beer and my two cats, it was a lovely way to end a day.

At the quarry, I saw this little kitten come out from under the old changing room's side panel. It looked hungry and abandoned by its mother. I spent days sitting beside the hole eating lunch and talking to it. He became braver and braver, eating ham or any meat I put down beside my leg. He got the timing good. He would sit next to the hole, waiting for me every day. I decided to take him home. In my loaded van, he lay in the windscreen getting warm by the sun. We got home. He was a little fighter, but he was with me. I lay on the sofa with no music and held him on my chest. Stroking and talking to him until he finally gave in and began purring, there and then a friendship was born. It wasn't long before one day I stopped at a shop. When I got back in my loaded van, I could hear faint cries. I looked between the boulders in the box in the back, and there he was—another kitten. When

I got him home, I introduced the obvious brothers, which did not go down well. I was under the bed with my arse stuck out and saying, "Be kind to each other." Unknown to me, my neighbour had come in and thought I had gone bonkers until I explained the cat situation. He was the one that I was sitting in his garden, enjoying a beer and grill when he said, "It's time to take your flag down." If the flag was still up at sunset, then anyone could claim it, and it would cost you a case of beers to get it back. I jumped up to run to my house. As I went through his gate, Molles and Dennis were coming out of mine, laughing their heads off. I called them everything I could as they disappeared up the path that led to their garden. Next day, I gave the case beer, and I got my beloved flag back.

I purchased a nice caravan, and we would get away on weekends, leaving her son behind. He wasn't incapable of not looking after himself. We picked a campsite that was only a forty-minute drive and rested on a fjord where I would go and fish. My small van would not pull the caravan, so I purchased a larger one. It was also good for the little garden business that was beginning to develop. I had a happy helper, and we did a lot together, which was also an education for him. With no work and no small bikes to fix, he was able to go and find some small garden jobs and make his own money, but there was a problem. He never got everything right, and I spent a lot of hours helping him correct his wrongs. Several other friends had caravans, and the weekends were fun. It was good to be away from the son. We had a stroke of luck. We were given the chance of our own small one-bedroom apartment. I would spend many nights painting and decorating this lovely little flat. It was to be my first real home after nine years of being in Denmark. When I say my first real home, I mean I could take something from nothing and create it.

I was not far from a pub that I was in when my friend that got me my first job was there with a broken wrist. We were sharing a beer with many other locals when a three-hundred-pound man decided to have a go at him. Like Pete was, with one hand, he was ready for the fight. Pete was my mate. I pushed him into a corner and said, "Just stay there, my friend, this one's on me." I turned and grabbed the man by his lapels. Before he knew it, I was throwing him across a table big enough for ten to sit around. Glasses and bottles were swept to the side as his head crashed after the rest of his body. I looked down on this pathetic creature, and every temptation was there to beat him to pieces. I tapped him on the check a couple of times and said, "Best you go home to your mother," and backed off. He gathered his composure and left while others were looking at me in amazement. They told me I had lifted him off the floor before putting him across the table. I never had any recollection of that. I enjoyed the idea that I had looked after someone that not only got me a job but also had opened the door to his lovely family whom I grew to care about very much.

Although we were living on our own, her son kept coming over to the flat every day and sometimes at night. There was never any peace at home, which put pressure on us. We had cracks that were beginning to get bigger. One night, I came home after working a long day; another was ahead of me. I got in, and Ayla was very augmentative and was gunning for a fight. I made my dinner as she continued to wind me up. I said, "Shut up, I am not in the mood to fight with you." She got angrier and locked herself in the bathroom. I was asking for her to come out so I could clean my teeth and go to bed. She was shouting and would not come out. Again, I repeated myself. Next thing I knew, the door was getting knocked. I opened it, and there stood a police officer and policewoman. They said there was a report that I was beating and abusing my wife. She had called them, claiming I was doing her harm. They had raced to the door. I said all I want to do is clean my teeth and go to bed. They agreed because they had listened through the letter box. They knew she was not getting hit. Also to back myself up, I showed the policewoman an empty bottle of wine in the kitchen and the large whiskey that was on the coffee table. They said she could be arrested for wasting police time. I said, "Please leave it at this." They did and left. Then like a cowboy with a gun in his hand, I put my finger in her cheek and said, "Now pack your bags and get the hell out of here." The following day, I came home, and all her things were gone. I was as happy as you could get. Divorce would not take long, and I was going to be free of constant knocks at the door and disturbance in the bars.

In the quarry, I could make things happen if people wanted materials. In another garden house area is where it was described as a little miracle that was performed for a sweet lady, a good friend, and she had waited five years to have a rockery done in her garden by her husband. With others, we got a plan together and handpicked boulders from the quarry where I worked. We loaded them on pallets and took them to her garden. With the effort of seven men in a morning, we had created the miracle. An ecstatic lady invited us all to come over the following Saturday for a grill and some beers. We arrived and were fed and watered. As I went up the garden path, I had a good wobble on. Finally, I got to my bike, which was leaning on their hedge. (Unknown to me, she had followed. The next day, she explained what I had done.) I was talking to my bike, asking it to be kind and keep me upright. I unlocked it and threw my leg over the saddle as my foot came down to the pedal the other lifted, and over I went. The hedge man was alive, but this time I never moved more than six inches. I went through their hedge, which left a large hole. The following day, I had no idea I had done such a thing. At another friend's garden house, I enjoyed playing with their cat, which looked mine. One of mine was killed by a car on the main road, which was about fifty feet away. The other decided he wanted to get back into the wild. One day, in my garden, he was looking at me in a strange way and went through the hedge. He never came back, although on several occasions, he was seen under it. Up the road was a school, and I saw him near a building. I stopped my van and approached him. While calling his name, he stopped and looked at me. I moved closer and closer. He never moved until he had had enough and turned to walk away.

I guess at times he missed me. I worked long days and sometimes seven days a week. Mostly it would be at the harvest time that I would finish at the quarry and drive across lovely countryside to the corn sheds. I would start work at 4:00 p.m. and work until the last tractor or lorry came in with its load. This could be up to 10:00 p.m. Again, this was a good company that supplied me with an evening meal. They fed me on weekends too, saving me loads of money. I would push the corn up into the roof of the sheds with a loader with a twenty-three-foot long plough at the front. The idea was to get corn as high as possible until it would be transported to a harbour and shipped wherever. I would spend weekend after weekend earning money. On Sundays, we always had a good cooked meat dish and a glass of wine before returning to work until dusk. I was offered another job in a quarry, which really appealed to me. Same materials for sale and crushing operation, but all I would be doing is running my loader and not doing the dust control with a tractor and tank and other tasks I did in my last job. I started, made my mark, and was well liked by everyone. This was also where one day out of the blue, a van came over the quarry top and plummeted to the floor some forty feet down. I radioed the office then went over to see what I could do. There was nothing I could do as he lay in the twisted wreckage, screaming for help. When he was eventually freed and lucky to be alive, it boiled down to one thing: he was travelling down the motorway and lost control while on the phone. He went up over a large safety berm and landed upside down in front of me.

I had just finished lunch one day. My eldest girl called me to break the news that Mother had died. She knew I was not interested but thought she would call anyway. I understood where she was coming from, because after all, she was her grandmother. We finished our conversation. As I returned to my machine, a thought went through my mind: "one down, one to go." How my life had transpired from being a caring son and nephew when young, and now, a cold and callous person for these two women that broke my heart. Did they deserve such treatment from this caring guy? Am I a Jekyll-and-Hyde person? Love on the left hand and disown with the right. I think like any normal human. If my path is crossed, then the party is over. It's when hate comes in that it is so nasty. Wanting someone dead really means the worst for any relationship. I decided to get rid of the caravan and thought I would spend more time golfing if I was not working. A Saturday morning, I was waiting with others on the second tee when, from the first tee, a golfer shouted "fore." We were forty feet to the left of his target. As I ducked with my hands about to cover my head, his ball hit me. As the hole was short, it was safe to assume he had hit it high in the air, and as we were sixty feet below his tee box, the ball fell about 250 feet and hit me plum in the middle of my head. My friend enquired about the dull thud he heard. I was still bent over and holding my knees as he lifted my cap away. A little thick blood was oozing out, and a lady in front us who was also waiting checked the wound out. She explained that her job was in an emergency room and, after pouring water over my head, told me I should go home. I stood up and looked her in the eye as I said, "Ma'am, I am strong, and there are seventeen holes to play." As we played, every now and then, she would check the wound as I begged for the kiss of life. I asked with a big smile but was refused every time by her. It hurt most when we returned to the bar. As I tried to remove my cap, it was stuck to my head. Everything was fine as we all enjoyed finishing another day off with a dance and beer. The next day, it all kicked in. I lost everything that was clear. I could see nothing and went to the emergency room. After being checked out, I was to go to my doctor the next morning; and when I did, I was sent straight to the specialist for tests.

After several hours of tests, she informed me to take several weeks off to relax and recuperate. I asked what I should do. Fishing, golfing, and walking suggestions were thrown my way. I did just that, and as it is a social system, I was getting 95 percent of my pay. It was like being in hog heaven having time off and chilling out. Boredom was setting in, so I went back to work after only three weeks. I should never have done that because the vibrations of running over the rock roads and terrain in my machine were too much. I spent the first week going slow. Not much longer after that, I was back at full speed and enjoying life to the full.

One evening, in 2005, while sitting in my little flat, I decided to see if I could find a schoolmate who, with his parents, had moved to Australia when we were twelve years old. I got onto my hometown newspaper website, which had a section Where in the World. It was for people like me to connect with others that had settled somewhere in the world. This led me onto a worldwide fan club of an American musician. As I loved music, I was intrigued. I also was distracted from the very point that I was trying to achieve. I saw these little balloon icons spread over the world. In the middle of the USA, I clicked on one. "Well, I'll be blowed," I said to myself as this rather attractive face popped up. Within two minutes, I had written a small e-mail to Diane. I stated, "I had no idea about the musician but thought you have a nice face." A day later, I had a reply, and I again wrote. I began to like her face with an unusual hairstyle and artificial colour. We talked about my job experience. I was a heavy-equipment operator. She was an accountant. This continued for several weeks, then she sent her phone number. I called, and we talked about a lot of things and carried on writing. It appeared we had so much in common about fathers. Mine had died in America, and hers basically disowning her, claiming he put up the money for a lawyer to put her in prison. My father, by leaving me, had sent me to prison. He was trapped within me, and I could not let him out. She explained more as we became more familiar. I said it was a problem that she had been to prison for stealing from her company. I did not care. How could it bother me? She had not done such a thing to me. We got closer by seeing each other on the webcam, and I was fascinated. One thing was very odd. She lived with her ex-husband and was on his computer. Her father had screwed her life, and she was down on her luck. This good Christian man let her stay in the basement of his condo. This made me feel like there was a good man in the USA. As our "relationship" grew, I spoke with him a couple of times through the webcam and also spoke with their daughter. She was a cute young lady, and through all this, we all were feeling comfortable with the situation. After several months of us doing everything on the webcam, I had to get the real thing. I wanted what I saw.

CHAPTER 39

I HAD ALWAYS WORKED hard and saved some overtime money and the cash from other small jobs I did. I got enough together to pay for Diane to come to Denmark and meet me. I want her to see my world. Her friends thought she was crazy to come so far to meet a stranger and possible danger. Sure, fly someone six thousand miles at my expense so I could kill her. How stupid is that! Excitement grew as the day arrived for her to take the plane to me. I, like so many of my friends, was excited to see this mystery woman in the flesh and share a beer. I went to the airport and waited with a stomach that was so twisted, I could not eat or drink until she was there. The flight board showed the plane had landed. I was even tenser, then as the doors opened, I looked for this lady. Finally, out she came dressed in a pink tracksuit that the Pink Panther would have been proud of. We embraced and headed for the train.

We decided to have a beer, and I was impressed that hers went down quicker than mine. A drinking partner would be good, and I thought I had found one. I did not want someone who never went to a bar or only one night a month when she wanted to go out. The world is to be enjoyed, and that means getting out in it with good people. I got her home, and sex was on the agenda. We huffed and puffed for a quickie, and then off to the bar we went. So many friends were waiting, and a party was to be had with music and lots of chinking of beer bottles. She had no job back home and had no money. There was no way I could have the seven weeks off that she would be in Denmark. I went to work, and she read her Bible and prayed, which didn't bother me. I never had to put up with it while I was at home. It was fun going out to get food and trying to explain the way Danes do things. Like one night we stayed in, and next morning, there were beer bottles in the waste container. She explained that this did not matter where she came from.

She seemed to beat up on her home country. We are a big throwaway nation and didn't really care. I explained the Danish way that we save and recycle almost everything. A deposit is paid on every bottle, whether plastic or glass; we get money back.

After a few weeks, I came home. I think I fell into a trap. I really liked the lady, and although the discussion about her moving to Denmark had arisen, it would be her daughter that would be the problem. I walked in. She was crying, claiming she missed her girl. I understood it would be so hard to try and settle. Her heart would be breaking every day missing her girl. I sat and thought about the situation and made up my mind. I said, "I have done many things here. I will move to America and start again." Her face lit up, and my jeans came off. Next day, she was telling her girl and ex-husband what the plan was. I told her that she will have to tell my friends, and when she did, some tears were shed. Exclamations like "You cannot leave us," "We are friends," and "You must stay" were said; I explained the situation. After a couple of days, things had settled down. Everywhere I went, it seemed everyone in the city knew I was going to leave.

While I was at work, she spent time finding out from government agents what needed to be done. I never knew much about it, but my sponsor would be her ex. Why would he bother to sponsor a stranger? Why would he want to cover any living expenses if I never found work? Why would he do such a thing for his ex-wife? If this was as explained (a good Christian man), then wow, maybe I should go to church. For me, there is no need. I have a good heart and care about people, and if asked, I would do the same for someone I cared about. What's the point of being nasty unless that person is someone who gave in on you at birth? I was given an opportunity by Jorgen. He said, why not leave the quarry company for another interesting challenge? I decided I would, and the owner was in shock. When he was told I was leaving, he came down into the quarry. That was a rarity and asked what was going on. I explained to him about a life-changing event. He would need to find someone else as a replacement. He understood but was sorry that I would be leaving. Any overtime I had done would normally be taken off so I could enjoy long weekends and get paid for it. The office staff was shocked with all I had amassed. He paid it as overtime. That was a first the pay clerk told me. What a compliment. There was a better one. The new operator was not as fast as me. He purchased another loader and hired another operator to do the work I did. Again, I was proud of what I had achieved for yet another company.

My new job I felt would be cool until I left for America. I was to work with Jorgen helping set up exhibition stands. I worked in the storeroom and learnt a lot. He was with me and several other friends at a Danish festival. We stood in the pouring rain and mud waiting for one particular group to play. After a few songs, the lead singer said "We are going to play a song we rarely play live." They started my song for dad, "The Living Years," which I had written to the group, explaining what the song meant to me and that I had waited twenty years to see them. What emotions went through me! As a memory, I am extremely grateful for that moment. (Thanks, guys.) I think it's fascinating how things get made and put together for exhibitions. A bonus would be to get my driving license to be changed and with no test; it came back enabling me to drive a truck. I was flabbergasted. That was a mistake, but I knew how to drive them. It allowed me to drive the lorry where exhibitions were held. I was travelling across this beautiful land and enjoying the latter part of my almost twelve years. Driving across the huge bridge that was being built when I arrived was such a feeling. We were to do one in Hamburg, Germany. We erected a small but pretty stand, and when the show was over, I was to take it down. I took Diane and, with a van, headed there. It was fun seeing so much with my woman. I knew she would, in time, show me so much of her country. I had been there several times but never to the Midwest where she lived. It would be another challenge to get myself established again. Like always, I had no fear about this. I knew many things that would be helpful to various companies. With so many various skills, never getting work was not a thought that went through my mind. Paperwork and documentation were in full swing. With everything settled, I would one day be USA-bound. Diane's time was up, and I took her back to the airport, both of us knowing that one day, she would be back. With permission on Danish territory, we would marry.

I also flew back to Oslo to break down an exhibition. I went to Sweden several times and many more all over Denmark. Many times it was like I was on a farewell tour. Seeing and enjoying a culture I had come to so enjoy. I was with others in Fyn constructing a large exhibit. Like many times, we went out on my own for a beer. I was in a bar when a half-drunk idiot from a group of four came over and started giving me a hard time. I weighed up the situation. I knew I was going to be in trouble. They were baying for blood, and it was going to be mine. I put my beer down and headed for the door. They began to follow. As they were younger, running was not an option. I got through the double door. As it opened outwards, when the first came through, I squat his head between them. He went down, and another started to come over him. Easy picking was his chin, but his foot was heading for my crown jewels. I lost balance for just a second, and one was on me. I used all the strength I had, but that was not enough. I got some hard kicks and punches before everything was done and people had dragged them off. With a bloodied face and hurting body, I rose and thanked the strangers for their help then walked back to the bar to finish my beer. A nice barmaid began cleaning my face up. She cared for me. I felt lucky but thought better of it, as I had a woman. Next day, I was the butt of jokes with my workmates. They asked many times where I was and they would come back with me. I refused to tell them because it was over. It was done, and I wanted no more.

Several moths had passed. Again, I paid for everything, and Diane had returned. With permission, we married in the same registry office as before. One surprise was my lifelong friend Nicolas who had hit me in the old rugby field. I had lost him for maybe thirty years or more. It was by chance that on a trip home, I bumped into his ex-sister-in-law who gave me her phone number. I was saddened to hear he and Annette had parted and he had moved out of town. This man and his wife, I was best man for and godfather to their first daughter. It was maybe a year or more that I finally decided to give her a call. I was in the new kitchen in my garden house with a beer in hand. I was looking forward to hear something about my hometown. She asked if I had heard anything from home. I said no, and then shock and horror came across me. The next ten minutes were the worse time I could ever imagine. His lovely baby daughter who, one Saturday evening, vomited on me. I was dressed in a white shirt and blue velvet suit ready to dance the night away, was murdered by her husband. I was stunned, in a state of shock as she explained he had stabbed her in a frenzy thirty-seven times. It's that sort of statement that sends you into another dimension, and my heart bleed for my mate. When things were clear, the next statement blew me away too: "Did you know two of my very good mates were dead?" I was in utter chaos, walking around in circles as I tried to comprehend losing two of my best buddies. The fun times we shared ran around inside me. We finished the call, and I sat in my garden with the local radio on. With memories flying around in my head, a favourite song of ours came on, and I lost it. I cried for my friends. Again I was alone with no one to lean on or listen to me. We all loved one of the great entertainers of the day. Seeing him in a nearby town hall, Taunton town hall, and finally I saw him again in Copenhagen. It was many months later when I returned home. After seeing my children, I got two small flower arrangements and laid them on their graves. When I laid them down and said goodbye in my own way, I felt better. It was a slow ride up a long road to enable myself to begin enjoying our favourite artist again.

We came out to a lovely crowd of people and well-wishers. A friend's car with champagne and chocolate strawberries whisked us off for photos around the fjord and other nice places. Diane's trip for the marriage would be for only two weeks, then she would go back to America. No date was set for me, but one day, I would follow. I was, before meeting her, applying for my Danish passport. It was something I wanted because of my respect and love for such a wonderful nation. These lovely people had taken me under their wing. They made me a success with all their advice and help. It was a wrench to see friends that had given me hope that I could become someone. Many times I would go to the local football game. Not that I liked football; I liked the people that enjoyed it. I reflected on the time my English friend who had been there about two years longer than me. He loved the game was given some surprises. I had gone back to England and returned with some good old English goodies. I made a picnic. At half time, we sat on the hallowed turf. I opened the basket full of surprises. With no meat restriction at that time, I gave foods we were weaned on. Sausage rolls, pork pie, Queen cut sandwiches, English sweets, and chocolate were to be had. He was like a kid in a candy store. Everyone thought we were crazy.

I also recalled going to a bar. A big guy was drunk and taking cigarettes from people; they were too scared to say anything. At one point, he put his hand on my shoulder. My hand landed on his. I stated, "Move it." He looked down on me, and I stared into his eyes. He said he would take me outside and beat me. I walked to the door and said, "Come on then." I stepped down the one step and turned with horror thoughts going through me. *What the hell have I done? He will tear me to bits.* My stomach churned as he stood on the step.

The owner and two others were with him, saying, "Don't do this. We have seen him fight." Seconds passed; he had turned and walked back in. I was the happiest man ever that day. I felt proud that I had stopped him from abusing others. They would have peace while enjoying others company. I walked back into the bar where I had won the tenpin bowling competition in 1999. I was beckoned to a table by an ex-Danish SAS man. He ordered a beer and patted me on the back, saying, "That was awesome to see."

"My pleasure," I exclaimed as we enjoyed a beer. That was the last time I was ever to have any trouble anywhere in Denmark. I had hoped my right fist was retired. I was wrong.

I was slowly going about the business of goodbye. Hugs were lasting longer. Handshakes had more feeling in them. I was hurting but so excited about what lay ahead. In the back of my mind, I was going to make it. A call came from the US embassy in Copenhagen, and off I went. There were some questions. I had no criminal record or drug-related problems. It should be easier for me to get a visa. Of course, having a sponsor was a major thing. Just when I thought I was good to leave the country, the lady interviewing me said, "We may have a problem." It arose from the fight I had some thirty or more years before, the evening I was arrested and charged with drunk and disorderly and causing an affray; I could not believe it. I was getting chips for my date. It was my mate fighting with the police that got me arrested. She was on the phone to England for ten minutes. I sat in a corner thinking the worst. If only he knew what was happening after all these years. I was at least twenty-five since the last time I had seen him. Eventually, she gave me the all clear. I booked a flight bound for America then called Diane. Word flew around, and with only three days left, some serious drinking had to be done. Parties in every pub I managed to get to. I moved from my flat to allow a good friend to have mine to rent. He was to do that. It meant I would retain it should things not work out. My friend whose garden I had laid the new lawn and paths in let me stay at his flat. On my final night, Niels stayed with me. He was taking me to the airport. The morning came. Last goodbyes done, there was only one more. I had checked my e-mails just in case I had a reply from the Danish Royal Household. I had written them a long letter saying how wonderful it was to have lived in such a wonderful country. I stated that if I would have been needed, I would be one of the first to stand and be counted should a war break out. I said how great its transport system is for everyone. How proud they should be of it. What other country allows the sick to be transported to a family home and back again, and it's paid for by the taxpayer? Niels and I said our goodbyes with tears in our eyes; my best buddy and I parted. He was and is special, and maybe, just maybe, the brother I wanted, such a fun and caring guy who, when he divorced his wife, wanted to do bad things. Thankfully, he had my shoulder to lean on. I always enjoyed it when he fell in love only to be rejected after a few months. Whether he laid the love on too thick, I don't know. But his heart is in the right place. He would call me and ask, "Where in the world are you?" I knew then that another failure had happened.

I would reply, "Your dinner's in the oven, and I am drinking in this bar." He would come over. We would share a drink, and next morning, I would send him on his way.

Niels had fallen for one lady who was nice. She was going away for the weekend. He begged me to help surprise her. He spent a small fortune on timber, wanting to extend her garden shed so she could get more in. I worked like a dog all weekend, and he was my helper. We got the job done. After a massive thanks, I was gone. It was to appear he had done it. She came home and saw his masterpiece. He was waiting for a happy lady to jump all over him. What a failure things turned out to be. She said that she was not happy with the relationship and wanted him to leave. He was dumbfounded but duly packed his bags. A little later, while enjoying a beer, he called me. I nearly fell of my stool laughing when he explained. Again I was glad to help him recover from shock. Finally, I got on my knees and kissed the ground. I felt a tear ebb down my cheek as I walked toward the departure section of the airport.

CHAPTER 40

FOR THE LAST TIME, I flew up and away from my adoptive land. Was my new home going to be like this? Would I be known as the hedge man in a different country? Would I fall into hedges with no one caring and only laughing at a drunk? Would I have friends like I had here or at home? While I was apprehensive, I was not scared. I knew there was a roof over my head. A Christian man and woman were going to look after me and guide me in the right direction. The plane landed in Newark. I was led downstairs into an immigration area. I went through the formalities. I was then allowed to proceed with my new ID card to get the next flight west to St. Louis. We landed. I came out, and right in front of me was my caring, loving wife. Diane smiled in such a way that it blinded me from reality. I never took any notice of her bad side. We drove to the condo, which has three floors. The room downstairs has no windows. I had never been in such a place before. The front door opened. We went in with my suitcase and a large shoulder bag of clothes. That was it. These two things and $1,000 cash. All my belongings were back in Denmark. I had no insurances. No savings. Nothing more to show for forty years of hard work, but did I need something? I am rich in the wealth of friendships. I have shared moments that are priceless. I have a small army of people that believe in me, care for me, and want nothing more than my happiness. I had everyone I know supporting me, and if I failed, they would be there to pick me up, dust me down, and help me get going again. Money amounts mean nothing compared to that. I could get a job in an instant from where I had just come. The only person who would have a nose out of joint would be the man living in my flat.

Diane's ex-husband gave me a warm welcome. Robert was a little round with a nice friendly smile. I thought how nice he was. Their daughter was nice too. It looked like the place had not been painted for years and was rather dingy looking. I had left behind bright colours and came to semidarkness. After the greeting, we went downstairs to a room with no windows. These are what many Americans might call a playroom, but for us, it was a bedroom. It was full of stuff packed in boxes stacked to the ceiling. A TV, sofa, and bed were the only space left for us to move. This was it, home and for how long. This was going to be an uphill battle getting away from this place, but I was not scared. I dropped my bags. Diane, who was all excited, asked what I would like to do. "Let's go get a beer," I said. She looked with a frown, but as I had just arrived, she drove me to a bar. This is how I get my base set up: get out there and see what's about. Find a bar, and you start your social network. We went down to a local one, which was OK. Conversation soon fired up. A welcoming record was played for me by a nice lady. After a couple of beers, I was getting told it was time to go. "What?" I said. I had only just got going. I needed to find out more. Now I had someone else tagging along that never did much bar stuff. I felt it was going to be hard work sorting things out.

We eventually went home. Robert was sitting in the chair watching TV with his eyes shut, so we just went on downstairs. Whatever we were to do, we would be running around him. The bathroom was next to the kitchen. Just to clean your teeth, you entered his domain. He was not a nasty or short-tempered man. He was a kind and caring guy. I was looking around for jobs. One caught my eye. A heavy equipment operator was needed for a temporary project about forty miles away. Transportation was not set up that would help me get there. A car was needed. Robert paid for a car to get me going, and when I was on my feet, I could pay him back. I had gotten my driving license as soon as I arrived. I was flabbergasted to see young boys and girls getting a driving license on their sixteenth birthday. Some young boys looked like they never had shaved on their light-coloured faces. Many of these young people, when they passed, were taken by their parents to get a car. It was never like that anywhere I was. I was told it gave independence for the kids and parents. As time passed, I began to understand the concept because of the way the town was laid out, it meant the kids can come and go in a car and not a cycle or walk like we did. I had also read that some fourteen thousand young Americans die every year on the roads. I enquired if they are sent to driving schools to be taught how to drive correctly. Mainly the parents teach them. If they have bad habits, chances are the kids will pick them up. That leads to problems I know. What happens to young people when they are given everything and never worked for it? What happens to children that are never disciplined? There is no respect. Older people are paying the price for it. They have no respect for us. They want you out of the way. They try to put their bit of metal in front of yours. What's wrong with defensive driving? It is much safer. So many care about no one but themselves unless they are part of the small group that does things as a family. This world today is so different. I also think it's sad seeing people come into a bar, sit down, and get out their phones. The art of conversation has begun to die.

I joined a staffing agent's list of employees. That was the first step of going for the temporary job. I spoke with the project manager and told him I could load lorries and run a loading shovel. Roger was confused by my terminology because he called them trucks and a front-end loader. He was intrigued and asked to see me. I went home all excited about the next day's interview. We walked down to the bar for a celebratory beer. Diane didn't take long to turn a conversation around to some biblical subject. A few people thought it was somewhat weird. Many days she would sit on the bed just reading the Bible. Although I lived with it, I found it a little strange. As a European, I was aware of deep beliefs about God and that stuff. I never realized it would be that close to me. As we are all individuals, we must allow others to be what they want to be, providing they are not doing anyone any harm.

I arrived at a power plant. Roger was nice to talk with, although it was hard for both of us to understand each other. His Alabama accent and my West Country accent took some working out. He explained what he wanted. I was shown a large machine. Roger asked if I could handle it. It was smaller than some of the loaders I had operated. It would be a piece of cake to run. He asked me to follow him to a work area. I was to give a demonstration of loading a truck. I went through the motions and was given the job. It would be for about three months or so depending on any weather issues, but it was a start. I worked hard loading seven trucks all day long. A lay-down area has been constructed with the material. One day, I called Roger. I told him my wheel had fallen off. He said, "Don't worry about, just keep the trucks going." I again reiterated my statement as I looked from my cab. My right front wheel was lying on the floor. Never in my life have I seen all the bolts shear that holds it on the axle. The truck driver nearly had a heart attack. I was raising my bucket to load him. I felt something not right and let my bucket down, which smashed on the floor. If I was another five feet forward, I would have wiped the side of his truck out. That would have caused injury to the truck driver.

At home, Diane and I paid for food now and then. The rent was paid by Robert. Diane did the housework, as she had no work. That also covered our rent. The job finished, and nothing was in the pipeline. I needed to keep the momentum going and hunted for other work. Heavy equipment jobs were not really out there, but equipment operators were. I got a full-time job with a company that did irrigation work. They were all right, but the work was crap. After three days, I told them goodbye. I then got another job in irrigation, and this meant working away from home on a couple of occasions.

The equipment I was given to operate was just tractors. Another machine pulled piping underground on golf courses. Working with seasoned Mexicans that had done this for years went well. I knew some Spanish but forgot so much when my Danish took over. It was enjoyable to learn another way of work. I, like many others, take a sprinkler system as nothing but it's a lot of work. We worked at a golf course, which was a two-hour run home. We stayed in local accommodation until the job was done. I was happy being away from home just like any other time in my life. I'm sure it all goes back to Mother. Not being shown love and leaving someone behind was easy for me. The next site we were to work on was a ten-hour drive and six hundred miles from home. Baton Rouge in Louisiana was my next port of call. We would be working six days a week. Every fourth week, I would leave for home early on a Thursday morning and be back ready for work on a Monday. I was excited about seeing something else and getting paid for it. Another adventure was in store for a man that should really be settled down at the age of fifty-three. Off I went into wilderness. Not even caring about leaving Diane and Robert in the same house. It never occurred that they may still be having a relationship. To be honest, I never really cared. The Jesus talk was driving me daft, and the escape was heaven.

I was off to the American south and close to the Gulf Coast. I passed through Memphis and saw a road sign, Elvis Presley Boulevard, then tuned into a local station playing all his songs. I was someone who had grown up with his music. I enjoyed singing along until I was out of range. I got into Baton Rouge, which is the capital of the state. My rented condo would be shared with two Mexicans whom I knew from the golf course. As I began exploring, I found major industries like petrochemical, medical, and a research centre. They were not far from the ninth-largest port in terms of tonnage shipped. We were to build a baseball practice pitch. I would be working a big dozer and excavator.

I had a great foreman, and we worked together well. His knowledge was immense and respected by many in the business. I was like his sidekick, never creeping, as some would call it. I was willing to learn. That is one thing that will keep you in a job. At least it's in your favour if work ran out and then picked up again. With a lot going on, a couple of young local lads were hired to help out. When we had breaks, they would talk of the horrors they saw. They were living in New Orleans when hurricane Katrina came through. One of them saw his uncle floating in the water. He dragged him until he found help. They saw bodies and complete destruction all around them. They felt lost and helpless. The stories made me appreciate what a lucky life I have had. I never saw anything like that unless it was on TV. Much destruction around the world I had seen through the media. I never experienced it close at hand. The history surrounding us dated back to 1699 when the French established a military post. It was after French explorer Sieur d'Iberville was leading an exploration party up the Mississippi River. They found a reddish cypress pole festooned with bloody animals. That marked a boundary line between the Homa and Bayou Goula tribes. In 1719, a settlement began by Europeans has grown to have over one million spread out across the area. A man-made lake was to be made to catch all the storm water. I began digging with an excavator. As I got deeper, the soil and mud turned into what's called "Louisiana blackjack," dark silt that has no body and would hold nothing up. This I found out. I went just a bit too far down with the tracks of the machine. I got into it. I took at least ten minutes to get myself out, which was a lesson learnt. I never went near it again. I was digging, exposing the blackjack. Ghostly looking tree stumps that may have been torn off by a hurricane hundreds of years ago were being exposed. It was eerie seeing something that had not seen daylight for so long. I was expecting at some time to unearth a skeleton. That never did happen, nor did I find any artefacts from when the place was lived in by the indigenous people some eight thousand years BC.

I had found a couple of bars, and one particular was a fun place with nice barmaids that had me thinking about my past: "if only I were younger." I was not far from a football and university complex. This magnificent structure that holds 92,500 people watching their favourite sport is awesome. I would guess millions have enjoyed their football here since the team was first played in the 1893 season. How awe inspiring for any rookie to get there for the first time. This is where tailgating is at its best. At least thirty thousand people gather outside with barbecues, music, and beer flowing. I was amazed to see huge mobile campers rolling into town three days before the event. When the game is halfway through, the police turn all the roads around. There is no way in, only out. It is so well done, and a credit to all that took part. Language was a problem. Ordering food from the takeaway was not easy. I would ask for a certain item. They would reply with their cajun tongue, offering three or four different versions, which I had no idea about. It was bewildering as much for them as it was for me. Perseverance paid off, and within a week, I was getting what I asked for. I also used a small restaurant. The owner took a shine to this simplistic Englishman that always had a smile on his face. I was enjoying myself in a totally new environment, with different nationalities all being together for the common cause. The owner would come out and be standing next to me, her arm resting on the chair back and her thumb stroking as much area as it could reach. I was tempted, but no. I was a married man. I had a wife at home, so I let it happen to please her but kept a distance to please me.

CHAPTER 41

I WENT HOME WHEN allowed. One Saturday night, I could not sleep and decided to start my journey back to Baton Rouge. After four hours, I was going through Memphis, with only another six-hour drive to reach my destination. I decided to go to Graceland. A man whose music I enjoyed like so many other millions. At many dances, I shook my hips or rock and rolled with a girl. I was able to park my car outside on the road at seven thirty in the morning. I went into a photo booth. I got a picture of me on Elvis Pressley Boulevard then went back to my car and left. Maybe in history, I could be the fastest visitor ever. Who else has done such a thing? I could have enjoyed so much more. My head was set in travel mode. Very little distracts me from that. At the rented apartment, my mates would be chilling. We had worked together for some time. It was fun trying to teach them English, and them teaching me Spanish. I did speak it well enough to get around Spain. Once the Danish language took over, I forgot so much. I enjoyed working and looking around Baton Rouge. After looking at apartments, I suggested to Diane maybe if we moved down there, she could get a new start. It seemed the prison sentence hung on to her like a leper. There was work for me and work for her.

Just as we were setting it up, I got a call from the Roger. It was in October 2007. He asked if I was interested in assisting him. There was a fill project at another power plant. I jumped at it and went to meet him. I also met a VP of the company. After looking at the plans, I was good to go. I understood them and got on with it. I showed my management skills. Soon I was on my own. Roger had gone back to Alabama to look after his site. Everything was going well. In December, we were invited to the company Christmas party. I was told there that my project was going well. They were pleased with me. It was also my first meeting with the owner of the company and his wife. Several managers from other sites were there on this small and personal evening. I felt such a part of a good thing and wanted only to do my best. In my mind, having nice people to work for, nothing less should be given. In January, a surprising question: could I oversee a small processing unit also at the plant? As this was something I had worked on thirty-five or more years ago, it would be a breeze. It was then that I was promoted to site manager. I was given everything required to help with my job. I shook my head that such things could happen to me in such a short time.

Diane got a break and found a job. With two incomes, we were beginning to fly. We found a house that we could rent and moved in. Her furniture from her last house was in storage. We had hardly a thing to buy. After moving in, within two weeks, a dog and cat were with us. I got a lovely dog and called her Denmark. I had promised my friends over there that "if I ever get a dog, it will be called Denmark, then I will always have you with me." She was a diamond and loved riding in my car with me, head out the window and so happy to be with her best friend. Everyone that met her would comment on what a great dog she was. We enjoyed walking and going to a bar for a drink where she loved all the attention. The cat, Mario, was brought at the same time. I am sure neither one knew which was a dog or cat. They were the best of friends and loved each other. This made up for some of the shortcomings between the wife and me.

We were both working and saved enough money to go to meet her father. She said to many people he was well off and even used the word "billionaire" to some. She swore it was him that paid for the lawyer that put her in prison. I was expecting to meet a hard man, but, no, he was a laid-back retired man with a pleasant wife. I wondered why she kept going about him being so rich. He never showed exuberance in anything. He was simply living a good life. A nice week was enjoyed. We came back home, and I was so happy to get back to work. I realized sharing a whole week with her was too much. I began to see through her, and she was driving me bonkers. It was shortly after arriving in America when she said, "I forgot to mention that my father is a multimillionaire, and one day we will not have to work again." Her conception of being rich is a lot different from mine. We will be very well off when he dies. Why did she have to keep bringing it up? I also wondered more about my wife. What type of woman I was married to?

I went to a few different sites the company had. I saw different perspectives of management and much larger operations. This was also a way of leaving the religious stuff behind. Her church time was important. I was always happy for her to go, but when she came back, it was a nightmare. Jesus this and Jesus that. One thing I am sure of: all the time she went on about it, the more I went away from it. Not that I was really into church stuff. She made me more of a rebel about it. Soon as I was out of bed in the mornings, she would have her Bible and listen to a guy on TV talking about it. I had to listen to her hallelujah every thirty bloody seconds. Drove me nuts, and I could not wait to get to my workplace. At times, I should have looked the bank accounts a bit harder. Everything looked to be all right, but sometimes things looked out of place. Where was I again? Back in the late '70s getting a repeat performance from another cheater. I would ask a question about a payment. Diane would blow me off with some excuse. I can only blame myself for not divulging further. I got to the point of not wanting to listen to reasoning. After three years, I was getting tired of her. Her company cutbacks in the glass industry took their toll. Many others had gone; eventually, she was to be gone too. Something had to be done about getting another job. She began working in a store, which again never lasted that long. Again, I was fobbed off with some story of how she lost it. So much went in one ear and out the other. Too much bull came from her mouth. I just ignored it. "Dad's money will help us," she would say. I wanted to hear no more and would go somewhere quiet. Most times, it would be the garage where I had made a small workshop. I had a TV and radio, so I was more than OK. I would not smoke in the house. I could enjoy a cigarette there. It was also a social place when her ex would come over. Now and then, we would grill. Sometimes if he drank too much, he would stay in the spare bedroom. I am sure many thought what a strange setup, but he had helped me get where I was. I was grateful, so in doing such a thing was no problem for me.

I liked his company. Many times, Diane would bring the conversation round to the Bible. They would argue about a difference of versions. That would do my head in. On a couple of occasions, I just went to bed and left them to it. I did not want stuff like that going on around me. It was, with the morning and the evening, getting too much air time for me. Of course I would respect any prayer time. If we had a special event like Thanksgiving, I do the same at any other occasion I am with people that say a prayer before a dinner. I have learnt that to be respected, I must respect others in return. You get no respect if you ignore others. Sometimes we would go out and find a bar. We found one that was small and personable. This bar was like one in my hometown. Everyone knew everyone. We sat at the bar and introduced ourselves. Within fifteen minutes, Jesus stuff was on the menu. I turned away and put some music on. There was a table of ladies just to the left of the jukebox. I saw they were looking at me. I just smiled and said hello. There was one that caught my eye as I searched the jukebox. I noticed she would still be looking in my direction then looking away. I went back to the bar, and soon she was up next to me, requesting a drink. We said hello and exchanged names. We shared a little small talk before Maggie returned to her friends.

The following week, I went in and managed to get a stool next to her at the bar. She was married to an elder man. He would dump her in the pub and chat to his friends. This gave me ample opportunities to discover more as I surfed the outlines of her body. On a couple of occasions, I put my hand on her back as I slipped sideways past her. There was nothing more. We only shared a warm touch. We liked each other, and that's how we remained, building a social relationship with not only her but her friends also. She would say I had a great sense of humour; she did too. The more she smiled, the more I liked her. A few touch moments were stolen for each of us.

We, as husband and wife, were beginning to fall apart. I was tired of the way she was. Showing such a caring manner, but underneath, it was a charade. I got to the point where I wanted to go nowhere with her. One such time was another Christmas party. After it, I was heading back home. Gusty winds were all over the Midwest. I passed some trees and went under a bridge. I became exposed on the other side. I was hit by a very strong gust of wind. I was doing sixty-eight miles an hour. I began going from the inside lane to the outside lane. I continued into the median (this is the grassed area between two sides of a motorway); there was no crash barrier. I was going down into the lowest part and began riding up the other side. This grassed area is about thirty feet wide. It's smooth, which allows police cars to get to the opposite side and begin a chase or assist someone in distress. I was slowing but not quickly enough on the moist grass. I was fast approaching the oncoming traffic lane. Several cars and a tractor trailer were barrelling towards me. I saw my end of being. I hit the asphalt edge. I was looking straight at the truck. The driver realized what was happening. He began evasive action to try and avoid me. I saw certain death coming at me. I closed my eyes. My two left tires hit the asphalt. I can only assume that as I was still basically straight, the two wheels hit at the same time. That stopped the car from continuing going sideways to going up in the air. The car bounced back from the asphalt edge. It landed about two feet away then slid to a halt near the centre on the median. The truck passed as I sat with both hands on my steering wheel in total shock. A few minutes passed. I managed to pull myself together enough to get out and see what damage was done. I looked at the new front bumper that had just been replaced after hitting a deer the week before. The impact about shattered all the new locking clips. I looked up to the skies and wondered if he or the Blarney Stone had saved me. Did the "boot" play a part in my survival? I was sure that death was staring straight at me. I got back in and put it in four-wheel drive. Still shaking, I drove back onto the asphalt. I stopped at the nearest store and put ten bags of salt in the back. With the extra weight, I took a slow ride home. So many other cars and trucks were blown into hedges and motorway walls, it was amazing. I must have witnessed at least twenty single-car accidents over the next one hundred miles.

I decided to give up smoking and devised a game plan. I set a date five weeks ahead; the last night would be a Friday. This meant that I would have the weekend to fight any cravings. I should be through them by the time I was back at work on Monday was my plan. I began cutting one small habit as each day passed, working towards my personal D-day. The last night, I went to the bar after work. There was my special lady with several others. She never smoked. I had two beers and went home with eight cigarettes left. I sat in my workshop and smoked the last ones with a few beers. I was three parts to the wind when I had the last one. I stuck the strongest smoking patch on my arm. Many think this would make you dizzy, and, yes, I guess it would; but with my plan, how would I know? I went to bed. Any dizziness was soaked up by the beer. I was a sleep in moments. The next morning, I awoke and had my cup of coffee. As I had stopped having morning coffee with a cigarette, I was all right. At about 10:00 a.m., I wanted a cigarette but ate an apple instead. That was it; smoking for me was over. Later in the day, we went to a bar. Others were smoking, including the wife, but I was fine. Funny thing was, if anyone was going to blow smoke in my face, it would be her. I think she was hoping for a failure like she was, but, no, I have a strong mind-set, and I would win. After several months, a new energy was in me, and I was on a personal high with it. Food tasted better. I hoped to be able to help others pack it up with my story. Some tried, and a few of them failed, but I will always try to inspire others as time goes by. I began to wonder about where the money was going. We always seemed to have so little. One day, I asked for the bank statements. Her words were "Here they are, but you won't like them." I asked several questions, only to be fobbed off with "This is America. We have different bills to pay than Europeans." *To hell with her*, I said to myself. I went out for a beer. I worked hard for my company and did my best to make my site a successful project. This was recognized by my company. They gave me a year's bonus. After taxes, it was entered in my bank account. My regional manager called to ask if I had looked. I called Diane to look, and sure enough, there it was.

I was so surprised and over the moon that such a thing had happened. I had thought about getting my teeth done; this would help. Years back when I was a street fighter, a good right hook took out one of my teeth. I had a plastic one on a denture put in. After many years of wearing it and dropping it while falling off bikes, it weakened until finally it broke into three pieces. With a brain like mine, I tried superglue and other glues. Nothing worked, so I just left a gap. One thing about the gap, I could have a cigarette held in it and drink my beer at the same time. This was done much to the amusement of others I met on my travels. I was always aware of my smile. For my job, I would look more presentable to everyone I dealt with. An appointment was made. I was to have the remaining top teeth out and a denture set in. Pay half of the total cost was required. I presented my card to the dental receptionist. She swiped it and swiped it again, but to no avail. I had no idea why it would not work with money in the bank. I knew she had changed from a normal bank. She had changed us to an electronic one after our regular account was frozen. That happened to pay off fines or back money for some debt. I was never told the truth. Again, that was another thing I just let slip by. The whole project for my teeth came to a standstill, and I was left high and dry.

The following day, I received an e-mail from Diane, which read, "I don't know what happened, but we are totally shut down now . . . now we are under federal investigation . . . who knows where that will lead. I guess we better be ready for whatever they are going to find." Under that was a statement from the banking people saying the account was shut down. They were left with no choice but to terminate the account. As I read this, it made no sense. Why would a bank account be terminated when there was good money in it? Why, at the bottom, was there a last statement, saying, "We are terribly sorry about this, but we have no choice," then follow it up with a "do not reply to this e-mail address because it will not yield a response." I was so unsure and confused about the situation, but I was convinced to hold on and see.

I said, "What do we do in the meantime about money?" She said maybe her dad or ex would lend us some.

CHAPTER 42

I ASKED DIANE A few days later about any news on the money. We must wait fourteen days was all I would get. With little money, I began to notice that there was plenty of food. Her car had a tank full of gas. Things were beginning to not add up. I also never really took my personal cell phone to work. What was the point as no one really called? A Saturday morning, I wanted to call my children. I looked everywhere for it and asked her where it is. She said that she had it cut off and gave it away because I always left it around. I demanded she go get it from the church person she had given it to. It had my kids' and friends' numbers that I could not afford to lose. When she returned, I could not call my children, as it was cut off; but worse than that, all my contact numbers were gone. *What was I married to?* I said to myself. It was then at that moment I decided to take matters into my own hands.

The Monday morning, I called the FBI about the situation. He put me in touch with a Secret Service agent. I gave him what details I had. He would call me back on my work phone with any information. The two days that passed. I had decided that I would, must, got to, should have done it a long time ago—leave this two-faced person behind. I rented a lockup and began moving my tools. This must have gone unnoticed because I was never challenged at any point until it was very obvious. I got a call, and things became very clear. She had cut my card off without my knowledge. The SS guy gave me the bank owner's number, and I called him. He was so surprised at what I told him. He had no idea at that point and would call me back. I sent the e-mail I received from Diane. That was not the way the bank worked. It became clear that while I toiled to keep a roof over our heads, she made the whole thing up on our home computer. I stayed calm and continued to further my investigations. I had statements sent to me. I

226

could see where all my money was going from the day my card was cut off. Hole-in-the-wall withdrawals were rife. On most days, there were multiple transactions. Other transactions from stores were also showing up. I enquired more. Videos of her taking the money were there for me to see. One security guy checked out their surveillance videos. He called and said, "I can see this dumpy lady with weird hair that looks like your wife." I asked if they would be kept, and in simple words, "You bet, we don't like things like this," said the man. I hatched a plan. This would show her that I knew what she had done. I got my card reinstated. If there would be a small charge, it would be noticed. As soon as it showed, the last $67.37 was drawn. All my money was gone, and I had nothing.

Like Ayla in Denmark, she was taunting me to do her some damage. I was not going to forfeit everything I had worked for. I am not foolish enough to give away what respect I have from others to beat a woman that had cheated me. I had never and will never hit a lady. However, this one had me wanting to do it badly. If such a thing happened, I could lose my right to be in America. That would take away everything I was so proud of. My beloved dog had to be found a home. A caring lady took her and said, "If you ever want to see her, you are welcome." It was heartbreaking leaving her. It beat hard enough to break. The walk to my car and last glance tore me apart. I sat in my car crying my heart out. It was not supposed to be this way. Denmark was my pride. I cared so much for this four-legged darling. I would fight any animal for her should she be in trouble. She was so much fun to watch chasing birds in the backyard. She was saying to them, "This is my area, get lost." She was so kind when the neighbour had a deer born in his yard. She was leaning on the fence with a look of "Can I go play, Dad?" I had lost such a character, and all because of a two-faced thief who cared about no one but herself. This was as bad, if not worse than when I lost Sonny.

After five minutes or so, I gathered enough composure to start the thirty-mile drive home. What was my next move? Where would I go? Who do I have to help me? Basically, I was on my own. I had friends, but most I never even knew their last names apart from one. We golfed and fished together. I got the last of my things out of the garage. I would move out at the end of the month. She began packing what was hers. I had arrived in the USA with two carriers of clothes; I now had three. That was it apart from my tools. With three nights left, which would have yielded a paycheque, I came home. There was nothing to eat off or cook with. Diane had it all packed up and refused to let me try to find a knife or fork. This Christian woman was heartless. All the talk about her beliefs in fact had no compassion at all. So many times she said cold nasty things about other people including her family; I was not surprised at her cold, hard-hitting tongue cutting me up. I looked at her and went to the spare bedroom. I had been sleeping there for the last several weeks. I woke early and threw the last of the bedding in a plastic bag and walked out. I left the electronic remote that opened and closed the garage door. I never bothered to close the garage door; it was left wide open. I drove away at 4:12 a.m. into the darkness. I had nothing. No money and nowhere to go. Friends that could help me, I could count on one finger. How was I to get a roof over my head? I felt the same when Mother rejected me. I was totally torn apart inside. Again, it was another woman that had destroyed me. I so wanted someone to enter the door I had left open and do her some damage. But then again, if it did happen, they would be looking for me. I wanted to verbally tear her apart like I did with my ex-secretary. I will never forget her face when she walked around a corner with her new man. I let it rip. He threatened me but soon backed off when he realized that his head would leave his shoulders. That night, he would have gotten all that was bottled up inside me all across his face. Like then, I just walked away. My dog and cat were the best of friends; they also were torn apart. Their separation must have hurt them. My two favourite comfort zones were lost forever.

I got to my workplace and called my immediate boss to explain the situation. He was a man that shot straight from the hip. Without hesitation, he picked a very sad man up. He made a beautiful statement: "You have a company credit card, go get a hotel and some food, and we will sort the rest out later." I suddenly was lifted off the ground. A little skip in my pace was evident. With that statement, I was alive. I could again climb a mountain because of whom I worked for. I had forgotten to consider my company and its core value. It bothers about who works for them from the top to the bottom. Thoughts entered my head about getting a transfer. Maybe I could start in another state on a new project. Then I could leave all this mess behind. Whatever could be done was going to be done, but first, my job site was the most important matter. My duties needed to be at the forefront.

The same day, I looked for a flat. One was becoming available not far from my workplace. I went to see, and I met a pleasant husband and wife. I was accepted, and a deposit was required. I had nothing. I told them what had happened; they still accepted me. The mountain was being climbed again quicker than I imagined. I got paid on the Friday, and the first thing I got was a bed. The night before, I had helped the present renter move some of his belongings to a new address; and at eleven thirty at night, we finally got back to this one room to sleep. There was no bed, just a fold-up couch. I slept on the floor. The landlord agreed that if I helped to move him, that would help me get in sooner. He was gone by the Friday night, and with my bed delivered, I had made a new start again. Independence was mine. I would get stronger as each day passed. I had to discover again how I let a woman take everything from me. So much of the past came up, and, yes, I had sex with this two-faced liar. I never did with my secretary, as some had suggested. To be honest, there were a couple of times when she was sitting on my sofa. I felt like seeing if she wanted some good ole loving. It's not that she wasn't so unattractive. She never made a move. There was no way I was going to because of her man. After I discovered everything she did to ruin my business, I wished I had.

I was closer to my workplace but right out in the middle of nowhere. This little bed-sit had its own bathroom. There was a shared washing room on the other side of a locking door, then another bed-sit. Both places were on top of a four-car garage and had a beautiful view across the American countryside. One evening the drier was running at 1am. I went and turned it off. The neighbour turned it back on. I again went to turn it off. As I opened the door I saw my neighbour for the first time. I politely asked him to have a little respect for those that need to sleep. he refused. My fist came up under his chin and he fell into the wall. I turned the machine off as he threatened to call the police. I told to call his mummy after,. He never did either. On many nights, I sat there on my terrace with some music, a beer, and watched thunderstorms batter a nearby town. I enjoyed buying things to make it a home. It was easy cooking for myself. That's something I have never had a problem with. I have men standing alone in a store wondering what on earth to buy. They have spent too long being spoilt. When they are out on their own, they are lost. What size pan do I get? How does this work? What washing powder do I need? Some guys simply can't fathom out what their needs are. Me, I love it. Again, another new challenge I can run with the world. I explored my new area, and of course, there are women to be found and enjoyed.

I went to the former bank we used. I wanted to see the last six months of statements before we left them. After discussing my dilemma with the bank lady we had dealt with, she gave them to me for free. She understood my plight and was happy to help. I began to go over the statements. They showed there were two loans that were taken out without my knowledge. Her car was used as collateral against one loan. I would not have been surprised if my car was not collateral against another, but I had no proof. I looked at six months' bank statements before that, and again, so much cheating had been going on. How did I not see this stuff? How did I not see payments going to these TV churches? How did I miss payments going to clothes shops and other places? I began to wonder, was Diane making up bank statements that showed me to be solvent, when in actual fact, she was robbing Peter to pay Paul? How could she stand next to me and others and show such a caring and Christian way when all she did was rob me like the company she once worked for? Her claim then was she was going to pay it back, but she got caught. I must assume this was the same scenario, but on a smaller scale. I had plenty of evidence.

I took it to a lawyer for advice. He wanted to go for the throat and said there's a good chance we could get her put in prison again. I considered it but decided to just get rid of the two-faced bitch. As I was just getting back on my feet, she was worth no more expense. So divorce we went for. She tried hard to avoid getting the paperwork until there was nowhere to hide, and it was signed. It was then I discovered that she had never taken my name. She must have cheated the registrar in Denmark. She was to have her name and mine, but all along, it was just hers. I, like the lawyer, was amazed. He asked me if I ever saw the marriage certificate. I could not answer. He said, without my name, we were never married. That explained how she got cash loans. It was her maiden name on the car titles. He spent a lot of time looking at what I had discovered. He suggested that maybe they were scammers. I protested because of my respect for the ex-husband. Who knows? When we left his home for our rental house, he presented me with a long list of money she owed him. It was over $30,000, which he thought I should pay back because I had married her. Later on, I went to him with copied bank statements after my card was shut down. I looked him in the eye and said, "Here's where your money is," and left him to work it out for himself. So many times she had cash that he was to receive but never got it. That money was part of returning the cost of the car he purchased for me. As he was so easygoing, he never mentioned not receiving any money.

While the lawyer was doing his thing, I was doing mine. I was also getting evidence through the court system. My darling wife, Diane, had two court appearances in the month of January 2007 while I was working in Louisiana. What a woman I had as a wife. She never told me the half of what she was up to. Deceit was nothing new to her, and I was just amazed at her guile. There were more surprises to come. Weekends I enjoyed looking around at my new area. I visited a few towns that surrounded me looking for a party girl. Just like the good old days, another barmaid took a liking to me. We spoke about getting it on in the pub kitchen. That's the wild side I have enjoyed without doing anyone any harm. What's wrong with a bit of wild because as a pair, you laugh about it? I went to a bar. After bumping into a friend, I was introduced to two rather nice ladies. I picked on the wrong one. If I had picked the other, chances were we might have got something going. The one I picked was not interested. We enjoyed some banter, then after two beers, I had to go because of drinking and driving.

America observes Lent in a big way, and many Americans don't eat meat for that time. The churches and other institutions hold fish fry nights. I had never eaten at a fish fry, but one particular night, I came over to one. It was in the area that I used to live. I was hoping to see some friends at a veteran's hall I went to. Out of the blue, there she was standing right beside me. Maggie beamed that lovely smile, a warm hand on my back, asking where I had been. We were friends that enjoyed the same humour and had not seen each other for at least nine months. I told her about the churchgoing Christian wife that had emptied my bank account. I explained how Diane had left me penniless and homeless, but I was on the way back. I was enjoying life without her. She, like so many others, said she was a weird one, and we were not matched. I had drunk my two-beer limit. I headed out, saying goodbye, and received a little peck on the cheek.

The following Monday, an e-mail arrived, saying it was nice to see me again and wished me well. I replied saying the same. After several e-mails and days moved on, a more serious e-mail arrived, and I wrote a more serious one back. We were going to get into deep water, and although she was married, she was not happy, and several knew it. We agreed to meet not far from where I lived. There was a state park, and that was going to be the place for us to sit and talk. She had no idea about deception and filled her car up at a gas station twenty-five miles from home, thus beginning a paper trail. She pulled into the garage, and as she was filling, I pulled alongside and said, "Of all the gas stations in the world, you had to pull into mine." That simple quote from the film *Casablanca 1942* was received with a warm but nervous smile. We drove over to the park and walked awhile before sitting on a small bench. Overlooking a pond, we had a deep and meaningful conversation. After some time, it was decided that she should get back to town, as she would be missed. With a kiss that got me going, she drove off. Again, I was left standing alone.

Time went on, e-mails continued flying around, as were text messages and phone calls. It wasn't long before he was asking questions about a certain phone number. One night, after she had confessed, he called me. I woke to answer the phone. He was saying, "Stay away. She is my wife." I knew how I felt about her even if it was wrong. Finally, I was in the right place. I was not going to give up on this lady who had, after four meetings, became my lover. The ultimatum came. He was to go and let this younger woman by twenty-two years enjoy what was left of her life. We decided he could take whatever he wanted to his new apartment. We would cover all the costs, including the divorce. She was strong about what she wanted and had made her mind up. Whether with me or without me, she stood up for herself. She wanted the change so much. I only sped up the process and gave her the confidence. My divorce date came through, and I went to the court. Diane never bothered to turn up, and it was granted. I also got a thirty-day judgment for her to return my photos. All of my travel history recorded in a picture. The people I had met and pictures of my children. Paintings they did for Dad when young ones. All the memories were left at the rented house I had deserted.

As I came from the courtroom, there was one of the ladies I had met some time ago in the town getting her divorce too. She was the one that I never picked and was rather attractive. She had a nice smile and a slim body that my hands could enjoy. I said hello and sat beside her. She was anxious to get her divorce wrapped up and move on with her life. With her nice brown eyes, she looked at me and said, "Wait for me to get my divorce, and we will go for a beer." That temptation had me thinking, but I had my girl. The proper time had come for me to settle down.

I looked at her and said, "I don't think my lady would like that," wished her luck, and left to go back to work. Maggie and I began to live together, and although there were a couple of glitches, we were happy and meant for each other. I finally got to getting back to England to see my kids. I was proud to introduce my lovely lady. Maggie and the kids hit it off. It was so gratifying after so long to see my son. He had gone from a teenager to a fine young man who has a lovely lady pregnant with their son due in September. I loved seeing my youngest daughter happy and engaged to the love of her life. To see my eldest daughter who is a devoted mom to her daughter, my granddaughter that I am seeing for the first time since she was born. I am truly blessed and proud of all my children. After an enjoyable week, it was time to come back to America and continue with our lives. In October 2012, Maggie and I got married at our dear friends', Jon and Ann's, home on a beautiful autumn day. We were so happy to have them not only as witnesses but also as supporters of a good pair. My children were on Skype watching their dad say "I do" for the last time.

Finally

Several months before I wed Maggie, I was down in the area where I first lived. There was a car that I recognized. I followed it, and it led me back to the condo. I said hello to Robert, and we began a conversation. From the front door emerged Diane. She explained that she had the cat (Mario) back from her daughter and if I would like to see it. Curiosity overwhelmed me, and I parked. Apprehensively, I went into the same home that I was in six years before. Nothing had changed. It was just the same. I was four feet away from Diane, whom I had married and gave up my beloved Denmark for. Why, if she owed so much money to Robert, would he and she be living together again as they did when I met her? Why on earth would two divorced people be in the same house after four years of living apart went racing through my mind (maybe my lawyer was right). I could have fallen over backwards as she spoke to me. It was as if we had never been together. Not one word of remorse. Not an uttering of "sorry, I screwed up." Not a glimmer of hope of recovering one dollar, but most of all, no chance of my photos. She claimed that as I left without them, she assumed I did not want them and threw them out with the rubbish. How callous was that? What type of so-called Christian would do that? As if she had not done me enough wrong, she thought of one more effort to put a knife in my back. What a resemblance to another who did me wrong so many times.

This book has finally laid down some ghosts that have haunted me and teased my thoughts for so many years. Our second trip home, I asked my mother's sister about some facts that I hoped would finally close any episodes about my father. She denied any knowledge of him. How odd is it that she knew nothing of my father? So quickly she downplayed any knowledge, which means her answer was premeditated. How would such a loving lady allow her favourite nephew to go to Ireland without knowing who was there?

She had absolutely no intention of laying him to rest for me. I find that a very sad deed.

I also witnessed my daughter marry the man she loves. She will continue to work as a manager in the pub trade she was born into. It makes me proud to see that she has like my others, worked hard to succeed in their own way. I also saw my eldest displaying what perfect motherhood is all about? She is experienced in a job that she has great knowledge of and is passionate about others. I so loved playing granddad to her beautiful daughter.

I embraced my son and his son. I know he will endeavour to be a better man at spending time with him rather than me with my son. I created a span of nine years of missing him because I never came home. He, like me, has worked with asphalt, and he even did a spell at the same sawmill that I worked. I also went back there to shake the hands of the owner and his son's. We recollected our times and talked about the sad loss of one. For me, like so many others, it's not us that should bury our children, but so often, we do. How gut wrenching it must be for any parent to lose one of their own. We, as caring and compassionate people, must embrace them for their comfort.

Several friends mentioned my brother was in a pub. I said he can stay there. Why am I cold towards him? I don't know him, and he does not know me. We are not needed for each other as we edge closer to our dying day. There is no point trying to get together—what would it do? Nothing has to be my answer. I have no interest in a man who treated my aunt Bess the way he did. No matter what she has denied me, she cared for a man who was my stepfather. She was treated as nobody when she approached his door. Her personal things were thrown out on the floor. She was told to get lost. That's no way to treat an 83yearold lady.

Albert's death was not announced, and his passing was not mourned. I will remember him for the times we shared playing his music. Even as a young man, I was so proud. He allowed me to play a record on his beloved gramophone record player. He always said his music collection would be mine when he passed. I know he had some really good 78's in their original covers. I must assume they are gone. How lovely it would have been to play his music and drift back almost fifty years with him. I am glad I grew up with Motown and disco music. There was nothing better than getting out on the floor and enjoying whoever wanted to dance. I take time and listen to today's new music and enjoy many artists. I also drift into new country and various other areas; but the 60's, 70's and 80's will hold the favourite place in my heart.

I also went to Alan's grave. This small parish church with its graveyard across the road will always be a draw for me. As I entered the graveyard and turned toward the far left side, I could not find him. I guessed I was going crazy and he was somewhere else. Alas, two nice elderly ladies pointed under some overgrown shrubbery, claiming there were more headstones. I fought through stinging nettles. Under this "so overgrown" side of the graveyard was my friend. I was saddened that no one ever came to his aid and kept his stone free from overgrowth. How I wished I had a chainsaw. The ladies said they would try to get the parish to get the place cleaned up and send me a photo. How sweet of them, I said, as I wiped a tear away.

I also shared time with old friends and thanked them for their parents. These are the people that hugged and embraced me at a young age with no restrictions. My friend's parents kept me on the right path towards a basically honest life. I probably told more little white lies to a partner than I ever did to a boss because they are the very persons that can make or break you. I have endeavoured to be the best an employee can be. I respect what they are trying to do with their business. All every person can do is their best. With that, job satisfaction comes your way. As a human, I have tried to be the best person to anyone that has entered my world. There is nothing better than putting a smile on a face. Many times, the joke has been on me, and I laugh with them. I will endeavour until my dying day to embrace all my friends and treat it like a final farewell. Handshakes are for the future; an embrace has a past.

My children are what matters, and I will do what I can to care from a distance. They know my door is open. I will never cease to love my pride. For all I have done by missing their upbringing, I am flattered that they love and care for me like they do. I know I have failed them in many ways. But because of the way they were taught to love, they have believed in me. Having grandchildren, I again see love being shared by loving parents, and that's a wonderful thing. Finally, I have enjoyed this world and so many treats it has handed me. Everyone in my life has had a place and been cared for. Many have pushed me to one side. I have no regrets, for I am allowed to screw up as others have done in their life. I have endeavoured to do my best. A spade for a spade is a very true saying. I do not hate and never will. Events have led me to the place that I am so I should be grateful not hateful to those that took my all. I have been trampled into the dirt only for a new seed to emerge from the ground and reach for the sky. May I say a sincere thank you to everyone who made me into and kept me being the person I am and will always be.

Edwards Brothers Malloy
Thorofare, NJ USA
October 15, 2013